On Being Foreign

On Being Foreign

Culture Shock in Short Fiction

Tom J. Lewis

Robert E. Jungman

Editors

An International Anthology

Intercultural Press, Inc.
Yarmouth, Maine

For information, address Intercultural Press, P.O. Box 768,
Yarmouth, Maine 04096.

Library of Congress Catalogue Card Number 86-081109
ISBN 0-933662-62-9

Printed in the United States of America

Acknowledgements

We wish to express our gratitude to Kay Yates and Jamie Heifner for the generous help they cheerfully and patiently rendered during the lengthy process of preparing the manuscript of this book.

Grateful acknowledgement is made to the authors and publishers who granted permission to reprint the following selections:

"Bárbara" from *La palabra del mudo* by Julio Ramón Ribeyro. Copyright © 1972 by Julio Ramón Ribeyro. English translation copyright © 1986 by Dianne Douglas.

"The Captive" from *The Aleph and Other Stories 1933-1969* by Jorge Luis Borges, edited and translated by Norman Thomas di Giovanni in collaboration with the author. English translation copyright © 1968, 1969, 1970 by Emecé Editores, S.A., and Norman Thomas di Giovanni; copyright © 1970 by Jorge Luis Borges, Adolfo Bioy-Casares and Norman Thomas di Giovanni. Reprinted by permission of the publisher, E.P. Dutton, a division of New American Library.

"The Door in the Wall" from *Door in the Wall* by Oliver La Farge. Copyright © 1965 by Consuelo Baca de La Farge. Reprinted by permission of Houghton Mifflin Company.

"Everything Is Nice" from *The Collected Works of Jane Bowles*. Copyright © 1966 by Jane Bowles. Reprinted by permission of Farrar, Straus & Giroux, Inc.

"The Growing Stone" from *Exile and the Kingdom* by Albert Camus, translated by Justin O'Brien. Copyright © 1957, 1958 by Alfred A. Knopf, Inc. Reprinted by permission of the publisher.

"The Little Governess" from *The Short Stories of Katherine Mansfield* by Katherine Mansfield. Copyright © 1920 by Alfred A. Knopf, Inc. and renewed 1948 by John Middleton Murry. Reprinted by permission of Alfred A. Knopf, Inc.

Works Consulted

Adler, Peter S. "The Transitional Experience: An Alternative View of Culture Shock." *Journal of Humanistic Psychology* 14.4 (1975): 13-23.

——————. "Beyond Cultural Identity: Reflections on Cultural and Multicultural Man." *Intercultural Communication: A Reader.* Eds. Larry A. Samovar and Richard E. Porter. 3rd ed. Belmont, CA: Wadsworth Publishing Company, 1982. 389-408.

Asunción-Lande, Nobleza C. "On Re-entering One's Culture." *NAFSA Newsletter* 31 (1980): 142-43.

Austin, Clyde N. *Cross-Cultural Reentry: An Annotated Bibliography.* Abilene, TX: Abilene Christian University Press, 1983.

Bennet, Janet. "Transition Shock: Putting Culture Shock in Perspective." *International and Intercultural Communication Annual* 4 (1977): 45-52.

Bochner, Stephen, ed. *Cultures in Contact. Studies in Cross-Cultural Interaction.* New York: Pergamon Press, 1981.

Brein, Michael, and Kenneth H. David. "Intercultural Communication and the Adjustment of the Sojourner." *Psychological Bulletin* 76 (1971): 215-30.

Brislin, Richard W. *Cross-Cultural Encounters. Face-to-Face Interaction.* New York: Pergamon Press, 1981.

Casse, Pierre. *Training for the Cross-Cultural Mind. A Handbook for Crosscultural Trainers and Consultants.* 2nd ed. Washington, D.C.: SIETAR, 1981.

Clarke, Arthur C. *Rendezvous with Rama.* New York: Ballantine Books, 1973.

Cleveland, Harlan, Gerard J. Mangone, and John Clarke Adams, eds. *The Overseas Americans.* New York: McGraw-Hill Book Company, 1960.

Condon, John C., and Fathi Yousef. *An Introduction to Intercultural Communication.* Indianapolis: Bobbs-Merrill Educational Publishing, 1975.

Dyal, James A. and Ruth V. Dyal. "Acculturation, Stress and Coping: Some Implications for Research and Education." *International Journal of Intercultural Relations* 5 (1981): 301-28.

Forster, E.M. *A Passage to India.* New York: Harcourt, Brace and Company, 1952.

Gorden, Raymond L. *Initial Immersion in the Foreign Culture.* Yellow Springs, OH: Antioch College, 1968.

Gudykunst, William B. "Toward a Typology of Stranger-Host Relationships." *International Journal of Intercultural Relations* 7 (1983): 401-14.

Gullahorn, John T., and Jeanne E. Gullahorn. "An Extension of the U-Curve Hypothesis." *Journal of Social Issues* 19 (1963): 33-47.

Hall, Edward T. *Beyond Culture.* Garden City, NY: Anchor Press-Doubleday, 1976.

——————————. *The Silent Language.* Greenwich, CT: Fawcett Publications, 1959.

James, Henry. *The American.* New York: W.W. Norton & Company, 1978.

Kim, Young Yun. "Communication and Acculturation." *Intercultural Communication. A Reader.* Eds. Larry A. Samovar and Richard E. Porter. 3rd ed. Belmont, CA: Wadsworth Publishing Company, 1982. 359-68.

Kimball, Solon T. "Learning a New Culture." *Crossing Cultural Boundaries: The Anthropological Experience.* Eds. Solon T. Kimball and James B. Watson. San Francisco: Chandler, 1972. 182-92.

Klein, Marjorie H. "Adaptation to New Cultural Environments." *Overview of Intercultural Education, Training and Research.* Vol. 1: *Theory.* Ed. David S. Hoopes, George W. Renwick, and Paul B. Pedersen. Washington, D.C.: Georgetown University and SIETAR, 1977. 49-55.

Kohls, L. Robert. *Survival Kit for Overseas Living.* Yarmouth, ME: Intercultural Press, Inc., 1984.

Laye, Camara. *The Radiance of the King.* Trans. James Kirkup. New York: Collier Books, 1971.

LeGuin, Ursula. *The Left Hand of Darkness.* New York: Ace Books, 1976.

Lem, Stanislaw. *Solaris.* Trans. Joanna Kilmartin and Steve Cox. New York: Berkley Publishing Corporation, 1970.

London, Jack. *Great Short Works of Jack London.* Ed. Earle Labor. New York: Harper & Row, Publishers, 1970.

Milosz, Czeslaw. "Biblical Heirs and Modern Evils." *The Immigrant Experience. The Anguish of Becoming American.* Ed. Thomas C. Wheeler. New York: Penguin Books, 1980. 193-210.

Nash, Dennison, and Louis C. Schaw. "Personality and Adaptation in an Overseas Enclave." *Human Organization* 21 (1963): 252-63.

Oberg, Kalervo. "Culture Shock: Adjustment to New Environments." *Practical Anthropology* 7 (1960): 177-82.

Schuetz, Alfred. *Collected Papers.* 3 vols. The Hague: Martinus Nijhoff, 1967.

Simmel, George. "The Stranger." *The Sociology of George Simmel.* Trans. and intro. Kurt H. Wolff. New York: The Free Press, 1950. 402-08.

Smalley, William A. "Culture Shock, Language Shock, and the Shock of Self-Discovery." *Practical Anthropology* 10 (1963): 49-56.

Stewart, Edward C. "The Survival Stage of Intercultural Communication." *International and Intercultural Communication Annual* 4 (1977): 17-31.

Stonequist, Everett V. *The Marginal Man. A Study in Personality and Culture Conflict.* 1937. New York: Russell and Russell, 1961.

Taft, Ronald. "Coping with Unfamiliar Cultures." *Studies in Cross-Cultural Psychology.* Ed. Neil Warren. London: Academic Press, 1977. 121-53.

Tolstoy, Leo. *The Cossacks.* Trans. Rosemary Edmonds. Baltimore: Penguin Books, 1960.

Contents

Preface

MAN'S ABILITY TO ADAPT TO HIS ENVIRONMENT, however extreme—whether the depths of the ocean or the distant reaches of outer space—sets him apart from most other animals. And yet, adaptable as he is, man has nearly as much difficulty in adjusting to a human culture other than his own as he does to a different physical environment. In fact, the barriers that cultural differences pose may be more formidable than those presented by even the harshest physical environment. The assumptions we hold about sex roles in our culture, for example, can frustrate and confound an outsider to a far greater degree than any climatic or geographic feature of our country. But added to this is the fact that the way in which our culture has conditioned us to perceive and act out sex roles influences, and is influenced by, every other aspect of our culture, making of our individual and collective behavior a massive webbing of patterns that few adult outsiders can ever hope to learn and to participate in fully. So complex, extensive, and fluctuating are these patterns that only a few of us ever come to understand how they work or why they take the forms that they do.

Cultural barriers would not be important if the various groupings of people on this planet never came into contact with one another. There would be no need to communicate with people who speak a different language and who conduct their lives according to a different set of assumptions about the many aspects of existence. But it is precisely because the world is not made up of isolated groups of people that cultural barriers are so important. The fact is, as Marshall McLuhan and others have pointed out, that the enormous increase in population and the great advances in mass communication and transportation that have occurred over the past century and a half have brought about a greater intermixing of peoples and cultures than ever before. The continuation of these developments, together with the rapidly increasing economic interdependence among nations, would seem to guarantee even more widespread and increasingly frequent cultural intermixing in the future as the multiplicity of societies evolves towards the "global village" McLuhan speaks of. The prospect before us is that relatively few individuals, and even fewer of the world's cultures, will escape being touched in some way by the intercultural experience.

The intercultural experience is not a recent phenomenon in human history, but for the most part it has not attracted much attention until recently. With the rise of modern anthropology and the development of the concept of culture as a complex system of communication, scholars have finally begun to study this aspect of human existence. As a result, over the past twenty years—but especially during the last ten—a considerable body of scholarship has been produced about such phenomena as "culture shock," "transition shock," and "re-entry shock," terms which refer to various effects produced in an individual by the intercultural experience.

As these terms suggest, the experience is not always positive and enriching; in fact, it is probably more often frustrating, bewildering, and, at times, even devastating. Individuals who fail to cope with culture shock frequently find it impossible to function within the new culture to which they are being exposed. And even those who do succeed in adapting to another culture usually pass through predictable stages of difficulty and stress. Greater still are the problems that come about when large numbers of individuals become involved in an intercultural situation, such as the settlement of the North American Indians on various reservations, the American occupation of Japan, or the influx of large numbers of refugees into the U.S. from Vietnam, Cuba, and Haiti.

It is this larger kind of intercultural contact that has led to a demand for methods of ameliorating the difficulties that arise when a person finds it necessary to leave his own country behind to take up life, even if only temporarily, in an entirely different culture. Since the 1930s, when anthropologists were first enlisted by the U.S. government in an effort to train government officials to work effectively with the various Indian nations, we have learned a great deal about how to prepare persons to function within an alien linguistic and cultural milieu.

One method of preparation has been simply to read and study the experience of others. The present anthology represents a variation of this method: rather than presenting first-hand accounts of intercultural contact, the anthology provides insights into this experience through the medium of short fiction by authors from a variety of cultures. We have chosen to use short stories because, as Aristotle indicates, mimetic literature often communicates ideas more vividly, hence effectively, than do either the particulars of history or the universals of philosophy, which in this case would correspond on the one hand to personal accounts of intercultural experience and on the other to the general theories of the cultural anthropologists.

The stories have been selected according to three criteria: their aesthetic value, their pertinence to the intercultural experience, and their ability to represent a broad range of cultures. Consequently, this collection of short fiction should be able to serve not only the practical end of preparing people to cope in an intercultural situation but also the more theoretical purpose of the comparative literature student, since the anthology is both international in scope and thematically interrelated. In addition, the artistry of these stories is of such high quality and the topic so inherently interesting that the anthology should provide its readers with a high level of entertainment.

Introduction

THE EXPERIENCE OF BEING FOREIGN IS AS VARIED as the individuals who undergo it and the settings in which it occurs. It is nevertheless informed by a coherent pattern that sets it apart from other kinds of experience. That this is so is reflected in the increasing attention devoted to the experience by social scientists since 1960, when the anthropologist Kalervo Oberg coined the term "culture shock" (Oberg). In more recent years, entire book-length studies have been devoted to elucidating various aspects of the experience (Condon and Yousef; Hall; Brislin).

Long before 1960, however, the experience had been explored at length and with great insight and sensitivity in works of fiction by several authors of international prominence. Leo Tolstoy's *The Cossacks* (1862), Henry James's *The American* (1877), E. M. Forster's *A Passage to India* (1924), and Camara Laye's *The Radiance of the King* (1954) are but a few examples of what has become an increasing preoccupation with the experience of being foreign by novelists throughout the world. And in one of today's most popular literary genres—science fiction—intelligent speculation as to the nature of the experience constitutes one of the leading themes (Lem; Herbert; LeGuin; Clarke).

One of the earliest formulations by a literary figure of precisely what the experience of being foreign consists in can be found in a story by Jack London, first published in 1900 and entitled "In a Far Country" (301-17). The opening paragraph offers the following account of what a person should expect to confront when undertaking a sojourn in another culture:

> When a man journeys into a far country, he must be prepared to forget many of the things he has learned, and to acquire such customs as are inherent with existence in the new land; he must abandon the old ideals and the old gods, and oftentimes he must reverse the very codes by which his conduct has hitherto been shaped. To those who have the protean faculty of adaptability, the novelty of such change may even be a source of pleasure; but to those who happen to be hardened to the ruts in which they were created, the pressure of the altered environment is unbearable, and they chafe in body and in spirit under the new restrictions which they do not understand. This chafing is bound to act and react, producing divers evils and leading to various misfortunes. It were better for the man who cannot fit himself to the new groove to return to his own country; if he delay too long, he will surely die. (302)

By this account, and others, the experience of being foreign has the potential for working a significant transformation at the deepest level of an individual's sense of being, possibly ending in his destruction. According to Czeslaw Milosz, these forces of transformation are inherent in the experience: they can be resisted but never completely avoided. As Milosz points out,

> No matter how strong the attachment to one's native land, one cannot live away from it very long and still resist what is seen every day—cannot go on complaining of the strangeness of the new language, mores, and institutions, straining sight and sound toward one's lost country. We are nourished by our senses and whether we are aware of it or not, we work constantly at ordering our chaotic perceptions and composing them into harmonious units. Total uprootedness is contrary to our nature, and the human plant once plucked from the ground tries to send its roots into the ground onto which it is thrown. This is so because we are physical beings; the place we occupy, bounded by the surface of our skin, must be located in space, not in a "nowhere." Just as our hand reaches out and takes a pencil lying on a table, thus establishing a relationship between our body and what is outside it, our imagination extends us, establishing a sensory-visual relationship between us and a street, a town, a district, and a country. In exiles from the eastern part of Europe one often notices a desperate refusal to accept that fact. They try to preserve their homeland as an ideal space in which they move, yet since it exists only in memory, not strengthened by everyday impressions, it stiffens and is transformed into words that grow more obstinate the more their tangible contents fade away. (Milosz 197)

Social scientists and social psychologists have attempted to identify the basic pattern underlying the experience of being foreign. One of the best known of these attempts is Gullahorn and Gullahorn's W-curve.

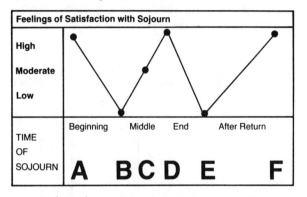

[It represents] the adjustment of the sojourner along a temporal dimension. In a very general manner, the sojourner tends to undergo a decline in adjustment shortly after entering a foreign culture, which is followed by a recovery stage with a resultant increase in adjustment; then, on returning home, the sojourner undergoes another decrease in adjustment followed by a second stage of recovery. (Brein and David 216)

A modification of the W-curve has been advocated by Robert Kohls, who proposes not one but two low points during the course of a sojourn:

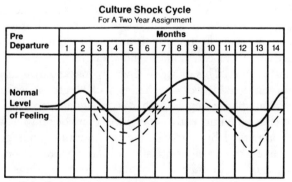

—Broken lines indicate the extreme in severity with which culture shock may attack

The interesting thing about culture shock is that there are routinely not one but *two* low points and, even more interestingly, they will accommodate themselves to the amount of time you intend to spend in the host country! That is, they will spread themselves out if you're going to stay for a longer period or contract if your initial assignment is for a shorter time. (Kohls 67)

This presupposes, of course, that the sojourner has some idea of how long he will remain in the host culture. If we accept Kohls's modifications of Gullahorn and Gullahorn's W-curve, and if we add to it a preliminary stage that takes into account the sojourner's initial contact with, and preparations for, living in the host culture, we can construct the following graph of the experience of being foreign:

The Experience of Being Foreign: A Graph of Emotional Intensity

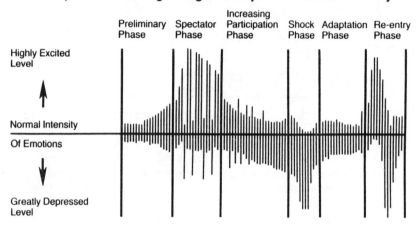

Each phase delineated by the graph is marked by a number of characteristic features, one of which is usually predominant. The first, or Preliminary Phase, includes the initial awareness of the future host culture, the decision to leave the home culture, preparations for the sojourn, farewell activities and ceremonies, and the effects of the trip from the home to host culture. This phase is generally marked by a rising sense of anticipation tempered by, or alternating with, regret at leaving.

The second phase begins with the foreigner's arrival in the new setting and ends when the early experiences there begin to pall. Arrival is usually accompanied by a rising tide of emotions, among which the foreigner is likely to career erratically. Initial impressions, which at first convey a sense of the monumentality of the experience, later tend to well inward at an increasingly unmanageable rate and to devolve at times into barely distinguishable blurs. Throughout this stage the foreigner can be characterized as a largely passive, but intensely alert, spectator. This Spectator Phase usually comes to an end when it becomes no longer feasible to maintain the passive stance toward the host culture and when the intensity of the new impressions subsides.

During the third phase, the foreigner—sometimes willingly, some-times not—finds himself taking a more active role in his new setting: he is now more a participant than a spectator. At first, this new role may produce frustration because of the difficulty of coping with even the most elementary aspects of everyday life. But once a person begins to accept the difficulties inherent in the cross-cultural situation, it becomes possible to devote attention to making sense of them, to venture forth and engage oneself, even if only tentatively, in those areas of the culture that hold forth at least a limited appeal. There comes a point in this phase when the difficulties one initially encounters may become challenges to accept rath-er than unpleasant situations to avoid. And, as the number of challenges and accomplishments accumulates, the earlier discouragement often gives way to a growing sense of self-esteem, satisfaction, and self-confidence.

On the other hand, it is in the Increasing Participation Phase that the cross-cultural experience varies the greatest from person to person. Char-acteristically it involves a clash of cultures, a conflict between one's own culture-based behaviors and values and those of the host culture. It may result in extreme resistance to adaptation and a more or less straight line descent to the nadir of culture shock. Or, for the more flexible person, it may mean a series of small maladjustments that are overcome one by one. Others experience a roller coaster of highs and lows as they surmount barriers to communication and contact only to discover abysses of value and perceptual difference.

For those who are more successful, the phase of Increasing Participa-tion constitutes an acceptance of, and tentative involvement with, the external manifestations of the host culture. But as the sojourner develops a greater ability to tolerate and cope with the external cultural patterns, little by little they become internalized, relegated to areas of the subcon-scious. Eventually the individual acquires alternative ways of behaving, feeling, and responding to others, both of which seem equally valid: one has been instilled in him by the processes of enculturation in his home-land, the other has been acquired through his recent interaction with the host culture. At some point during this process, however, there seems to occur a kind of crisis of personality, or identity, a period when the individual feels poised precariously over the abyss that seems to separate the two cultures. It is as though the sojourner's awareness of the ability to function well in the host culture has triggered an awareness of the com-pleteness of separation from the home culture. It is at this stage that all life can seem artificial and pointless. There is a deep sense of the ambiguity of one's position: on the one hand, the newly acquired cultural identity opens significantly new vistas of experience; yet on the other hand those vistas are gained through an awakening, which is both intellectual and profoundly visceral, to the insight that all experience—even the experience of one's self—is culturally determined. Hence, the sensation arises that life's deepest values are fundamentally a fabrication, an illusion, a kind of grand pretense supported by the vast majority of people.

Thus the Shock Phase strikes those who achieve some success in their first efforts at adaptation, as well as those who do not. Most people who pass through this Shock Phase of the experience of being foreign do not recognize it in precisely these terms, if, indeed, they recognize it at all. Usually a person who has been getting along in the host culture quite well for a good length of time will find himself, for no immediately identifiable reason, sunk into a lethargy or depression, indifferent both to members of the host culture and to fellow countrymen. This state can persist and develop to crisis proportions, with the foreigner manifesting a number of symptoms of severe psychological disorder. Richard Brislin has noted some of the more familiar symptoms typical of this Shock Phase:

> No one sojourner will experience all symptoms of culture shock which have been reported . . . , but almost all will experience some. There is an excessive preoccupation with personal cleanliness, manifested in worries about drinking water, food, and dirt in one's surroundings. People become irritable at very slight provocations. They overinterpret hosts' helpful suggestions as severe criticism, and they begin to feel that hosts are cheating them. Sojourners develop other negative feelings toward hosts, refusing to learn the local language and incorporating pejorative slang terms into their vocabularies. There is a sense of hopelessness with life in the host culture, and a strong desire to interact with members of one's own nationality. However, they may not interact if given the chance since they are uncomfortable with themselves and do not want fellow nationals to see them in such a state. Sojourners experience a decline in inventiveness, spontaneity, and flexibility, so much so that their work declines in quality. People feel lonely, find it difficult to communicate their feelings to others and, consequently, have a great deal of time to contemplate how unfortunate they are. (Brislin 156-57)

The Shock Phase represents a kind of existential confrontation with the abyss of meaninglessness that separates the two cultures the individual has internalized. Once the effects of facing this abyss have abated, subsequent experience usually leads to a more thorough adaptation to the culture. Adaptation is the end point of the experience of being foreign, the point at which the sense of foreignness no longer exists. In the learning of a second language, the equivalent to adaptation is not so much the achievement of native proficiency as it is surmounting the need to think through what one is going to say before saying it. Now thinking and speaking become simultaneous activities of the mind, the one being merely the internalized aspect of the other.

Among the indications that a person has reached the Adaptation Phase of the experience of being foreign are the following:

> ... one aspect of the adjustment process is an "identification" with the host country. Factors leading to identification include the development of new reference groups, a feeling of belonging, perceptions that sojourners are accepted by host-country citizens, and a sense of "shared fate" concerning current events in the host country. (Brislin 124)

The "shared fate" concept has been elaborated by other observers. It is not only a sense of being comfortable within the host culture that the assimilated foreigner develops but an awareness, from time to time at least, of being at one with it, a sense of being not only in it but of it as well. It is a phenomenon that comes close to resembling a state of mystical ecstasy and which has been explained at some length by Edward T. Hall as "congruence." He conceives of it as the relatively infrequent though not unusual resonance of a number of cultural patterns within an individual, a group, or an event which epitomizes the very essence of the culture. As he explains,

> ... congruence can be expressed as a pattern of patterns. Congruence is what all writers are trying to achieve in terms of their own style, and what everyone wants to find as he moves through life. On the highest level the human reaction to congruence is one of awe or ecstasy. Complete congruence is rare. One might say that it exists when an individual makes full use of all the potentials of a [cultural] pattern. Lincoln's Gettysburg Address is an example. Complete lack of congruence occurs when everything is so out of phase that no member of a culture could possibly conceive of himself creating such a mess.
>
> Lack of congruence in dress is always obvious and often humorous—witness the endless cartoons of natives wearing a loin cloth and a silk hat. In architecture when Culture A borrows architecture from Culture B, Culture A takes the sets [constituent parts] but not the pattern. Witness the outrageous Greek columns on any suburban mansion. (Hall 124)

Numerous examples could be cited of foreigners who have adapted so thoroughly to American culture that they have come to exemplify aspects of it. Among them are such names as Vladimir Nabokov, Henry Kissinger, Roman Polansky, Werner von Braun, and Jerzy Kosinski, to mention only a few. The phenomenon exists in other cultures as well. Joseph

Conrad, born and raised in Poland and later recognized as one of England's most important modern novelists, and the Soviet writers Fazil Iskander and Chingiz Aitmatov, born and raised in Abkhazia and Kirghizia respectively but later celebrated as masters of Russian fiction, demonstrate the widespread nature of this phenomenon.

Strictly speaking, the experience of being foreign ends with this fifth phase, Adaptation, but often there is a sequel, a further episode called the Re-entry Phase. This stage occurs when the sojourner returns to his homeland and experiences culture shock in reverse. It is a process that is all the more painful for being the least expected of all the phases described here. And, perhaps not so surprisingly, those who have succeeded in adapting best to the host culture usually have the most difficulty re-adjusting to the homeland.

While the Re-entry Phase can be regarded as a somewhat compressed version of the entire preceding five phases, usually the third phase, Increasing Participation, is somewhat modified. The returned foreigner most often goes through a period of resistance that evolves into a state of shock. Some observers, however, characterize the Re-entry Phase differently from the other five phases:

> Sojourners are excited about sharing their experiences, but none of their old friends or family members want to hear about them. As one businessman put it, others would rather talk about Uncle Charlie's roses.
>
> They realize they have changed but cannot explain how and why. Further, their friends sense a change and are likely to make trait attributions ("irritable," "mixed-up") rather than situational attributions based on the sojourner's recent experiences. Because of their disorientation and the reactions of others, returning sojourners are often rather unpleasant, feisty, and lacking in social graces. (Brislin 131).

With this description of the Re-entry Phase, the principal features of the experience of being foreign have been introduced. But the foregoing graph and description of the experience should be regarded more as an approximation than as a scientifically accurate and predictive representation of what will happen to a person who undertakes a sojourn in another culture. Just as personalities and situations differ, so is each individual's sense of his experience of being foreign likely to differ from the general pattern. For some foreigners the initial period of excitement may be missing or greatly reduced; for others the Shock Phase may be only barely noticeable or the memory of it may be suppressed; and for still others, there may be no emergence from the frustration and disappointment usually experienced at the outset of the Increasing Participation Phase. Still, despite the differences in individual instances, the pattern generally seems to hold for a majority of cases.

The stories that follow in this anthology are arranged in six groups, each group illustrating aspects of one of the six phases of the experience described above. In most instances, while one or another phase of the experience is the center of focus in a story, other phases may either be alluded to briefly or represented in a somewhat foreshortened form. And in some instances, one or two of the phases seem to interpenetrate or overlap. This is perhaps owing to the fact that the experience of being foreign, like life itself, cannot be categorized in any absolute fashion, for our sense and understanding of both is subject to a continuous process of revision and reformulation.

1. Preliminary Phase

VERY OFTEN A PERSON'S EXPERIENCE AS A FOREIGNER is shaped to a considerable extent by events at home that take place, in many instances, well before departure abroad. The three stories included in this section focus upon three different aspects of the Preliminary Phase of the experience of being foreign: deciding to leave home, preparing for life overseas, and forming stereotypes of the host culture.

The first, "Longing for America," centers upon a young Indian university student's desire to study in the United States and the difficulties he encounters in deciding whether to pursue this desire at all costs or to give it up out of love and respect for his tradition-oriented family. Hari Lal (the student in question), as we see him at the beginning of the story, would be a much different foreign student in America than will the Hari Lal that we find at the end of the story. The extent of the difference can be even better appreciated by considering his situation in the light of the other selections in this anthology illustrating the other five phases in the experience of being foreign.

The second story, "Alienation," provides an unusual example of a person who transforms himself into a foreigner long before he leaves his native culture (in this case, Peru). The fate of the main character, Roberto Lopez, is notable for the combination of ironic humor and bitter sadness that emanates from it. Roberto Lopez goes to ludicrous lengths to convert himself from a Peruvian *zambo* into an authentic replica of a North American gringo. In spite of comically desperate efforts, Roberto nevertheless fails, once he is in the U.S., to gain more than a very tenuous foothold in North American culture. What is important in Roberto's story, however, is not so much his ultimate fate, as the socio-cultural forces that trigger his desire to transform himself into someone other than the person he is in Peruvian terms and that determine, with a disturbing degree of inevitability, the direction of his transformation before he ever leaves home.

The third selection, "America," by Arthur Schnitzler, records the unusual circumstances surrounding the formation of a stereotype in the mind of an Austrian who subsequently emigrates to the country that is the object of the stereotype. The story is an exquisite demonstration of the seductive power of stereotypes in general, but in this particular case it is the irresistible lure of a stereotype of America that serves as the focal point of the larger vision. Truly powerful, and thus potentially dangerous, stereotypes derive their lure, it is insinuated, as much from the immediate circumstances of their formation as from their informational content (which all too often is inaccurate).

Schnitzler's story also illustrates vividly a heightening of sensory activity that begins shortly before departure from the home culture and reaches its high point with the sojourner's first contact with his new environment. One of the first to make extensive use of the stream of consciousness technique in writing, Schnitzler presents an in-depth view of the mind of the narrator as he walks down the gangplank to first set foot in his "new world." Sense perceptions of the narrator's immediate surroundings trigger memories of past happiness which counterpoint his somewhat bleak prospects for the future. This interplay of memory, sense perception, and expectation typify the excitement sojourners often experience as they move out of the Preliminary and into the second, or Spectator Phase.

All three stories in this section explore events that can bring a person to the threshold of the experience of being foreign. Other stories that depict aspects of the Preliminary Phase, but which have not been included, are listed at the end of this section.

David Rubin

Longing for America

BEFORE HE WENT TO BOMBAY FOUR YEARS AGO he had never left Zero Road
for more than a day at a time. The second summer after that he came
home for six weeks, but the following May, despite his promises, he
stayed on at the University to get ready for graduate work, then let
another year go by until this second difficult returning. He was aware
that during all this time Zero Road was there, nine hundred miles away
across the plains and rivers, and with an ache of affection he often
remembered his father and mother, his younger brothers, and even the
older sisters who had died. But they were vague, obscure, without geography until this moment when, after walking from the station, he stopped
dead, his eyes overwhelmed with Zero Road.

It was the morning of Divali. From the station, down Leader Road,
he had seen the streets jammed with throngs celebrating the four days of
the festival, regular mobs squeezing in around the shops to buy statues of
Lakshmi, new things for the house to honor her, lamps to light her to
their doors. If she could find your home she would bring prosperity, she
was prosperity. He had forgotten how seriously Divali was celebrated in
Allahabad, forgotten the Divalis when his father and mother performed
the rituals and threw away their few spare annas on clay lamps, mustard
oil, and foolish gifts. Lakshmi had never found them.

David Rubin's first novel, *The Greater Darkness* (1963), received the British
Writer's Club Award as "the most promising first novel published in England in
1963." *Enough of this Lovemaking*, comprised of two novellas, appeared in
1970.

Distressed, he began to grasp how far he had strayed from Zero Road, with his daily life in Bombay and his eyes and his heart set on further shores he would have thought unattainable three years before if he could even have dreamed of them. Now he felt a pang of anguish, then a hardening of his resolution until quite unexpectedly his whole mood softened and he stood in the clear, dry November sunlight drinking in the smells he had missed, almond rice with onions, pickled mangos and lemons, minty pakoras, the sweets in the Bengali stalls, sizzling twisted jalebis, frosted cake squares, all the homely smells of Zero Road blended with flowers from the garland-makers' booths, the last of one kind of jasmine, the first of another, bridal wreath, marigolds, and roses. More slowly, he began to walk again, down the road, until he saw his corner.

It was not much of a house to come back to. At least there were two rooms, one for the women and one for the men in the traditional fashion—even when the two sisters died his father had left his wife to occupy the other room by herself, for there was no one more traditional than Pundit Tivari. Two rooms and two windows perched not quite parallel to the ground over a bicycle repair shop, a Brahman restaurant, and a kind of closet, the dwelling of a disreputable Muslim tailor who pretended he was persecuted and sang love songs in the night when he was high on *bhang*. It was only a two-story building so his family had some of the roof for themselves on hot nights. There was electricity but no water apart from the tap in the street in front of the bicycle shop where tanners and Muslims and dogs and women of no caste constantly defiled it—a problem for his father and a hardship for all of them who had to walk to a temple for the water. He had forgotten the tap after all this time in a hostel in Bombay where he shared a bathroom with Christians and Muslims.

He stopped, tried to recall how he had planned his arrival, how he would tell his father that he meant to go to America though it meant defilement, how he would have prepared them with his cigarettes and his slacks and bush-shirt, which they had never seen him wear. He could not concentrate on it now, he felt the pang returning, compounded with the disquieting knowledge of his father's illness that had called him home, for it was not precisely to celebrate the holiday that he had come.

Impatiently he pushed through the crowd to his door, found himself all in a moment running up the stairs, where his feet in their Bombay shoes managed to skip the broken step and the sagging step and the step that was no longer there as deftly as when he ran barefoot. Halfway up he stopped; with his eyes just clear of the landing he could see through the open door. His father sat on a mat near the window, a book open on his lap, over his shoulders his gray Kashmir chuddar, the family's most precious article of clothing. He was not reading but staring at the floor, half asleep perhaps and dreaming as he had dreamed most of the time while they stayed poor (the poorest Brahmans, he remembered, stung with quick anger, ever known in Allahabad). Mr. Tivari had never seemed to mind being poor. Lakshmi would find them one day, he would say, perhaps she had already, for prosperity was not what the vulgar conceived it to be. He lived by teaching scriptures and the sacred epics in temples, on street corners and lately, since his illness, at home. He appeared smaller, frailer, his balding head very large on the narrow shoulders but with a certain quizzical humor in its sleepy tilt, as though he had withdrawn only temporarily from waking life to store up some new laughter against the wise world.

From the street a holy man called up for alms. Mrs. Tivari, walking swiftly with her swaying motion, came before his eyes. He had not remembered that his mother was so big, her hair so shiny, her face so silly in its speechless anger against her husband's idleness, her eyes so beautiful.

"Arrey!" she called down to the sadhu, "did we not give to you ten minutes ago?"

"Stop it," Mr. Tivari said, catching her hand to draw her back from the window. "He asks again, we must give again. Since when have we become so stingy?"

"Ha!" Mrs. Tivari exclaimed and walked into the next room.

"Wait," Mr. Tivari called down. Then he coughed hard, his shoulders shaking, and while he coughed he fumbled in his kurta pocket until he found a square silver two-anna piece. He held it up to the light, leaned over the sill and tossed it out, saying, "With blessings, but do not move in with us, someone here would make you give it back!"

The holy man gave a tinkling laugh and called up in a high voice, "I did not mean to ask of you again, Punditji, I wished only to shame the bicycle shop!"

"Ha!" Mrs. Tivari said and came out of the other room and then, glancing toward the stairs, gave a little gasping cry as her son rushed up the rest of the steps and through the door, flung himself down to kiss the ground at his father's feet and would have done the same for her had she not caught him up and embraced him.

"Hari Lal, Hari Lal!" she said, squeezing him.

"The train was late," he said just as his brothers scampered into the room. Mahesh was eleven, Triveni ten, but they seemed half their age to their brother as he gave them each the Cadbury's chocolate bars he had brought. They shrieked with delight. Mr. Tivari coughed, rolled his eyes in dismay at their barbarism, while Hari Lal sat down facing him.

"First tell me, son, why you were not home for the summer and not for Dushehra, when you had two weeks, and not for Divali last year when you had an extra day and Dushehra last year when the conflict of calendars gave you two weeks extra."

"That is no way to begin," Mrs. Tivari said. "Are you hungry, son? There is cold rice and dal. I am saving fuel for tonight."

"I am not hungry now." He looked at his father and waited in an agony of suspense.

"Have things gone well?" Mr. Tivari said more gently. "I am pleased you are in the first division. Do you like your professors? Do you respect them? How many of them are foreigners?"

"Only one," Hari Lal said. "The professor of American literature."

"He is American?"

"She is American."

"She? A woman teaching in the University?"

"There are women who teach in the University here," Hari Lal said. But he knew they were not like Barbara Ford, for whom he had the strangest feeling of love without desire, or anyway, not the ordinary desire, but a sense that she was more than herself, more than a striking face and figure and more than an image of freedom from convention (though not restraint, Dr. Ford was certainly restrained); she was America walking through the corridors of the University, conversing with her students or anyone who cared to talk to her, America in Bombay since last July and until next April. He had heard others lecture on Emerson and Fitzgerald but they had not been able to bring out the charm, the romance of the writers and the country, qualities he knew were there even before Dr. Ford so expertly made them manifest. And it was she who had encouraged him, told him how, if he did well in his examinations, there should be no difficulty in getting a fellowship for a year or perhaps longer, with the proper backing—hers, for example. She was his Lakshmi from now on.

It was not the moment to explain. He felt trapped, the silence grew intolerable until Mr. Tivari continued his questions: "And this year what did you do for Dushehra?"

"I went to Delhi."

"Hm! Almost fifty rupees up and down, unless you went on the Mail, and that is still more. I asked Mr. Shukla downstairs. And either way, it is more than it would cost to come home."

"I rode in a car with people I know. It cost nothing."

"In a car? Very good! Why did you go to Delhi?"

"To see the Ramlila at the Cricket Grounds."

"Very commendable!" Mr. Tivari said. "A religious observance converted into a spectacle with wiggling girls and people dressed up as monkeys."

"It is the same poetry of Tulsidas that you taught me."

"I do not ask you to argue. Stand up, let me look at you. You too are a spectacle. When you left with your scholarship a kurta and dhoti were good enough but now you look like a deputy collector's second clerk. And your hair is short, you have cut off your topknot."

"Be calm," Mrs. Tivari said from the next room and there was a rattling crash as a tray was knocked over in the restaurant downstairs.

"The world outside is different," Hari Lal said, sitting down again.

"The world *outside*? The world is one, inside, outside, upside down." He laughed, but gently. "You are just past eighteen and you tell me about the world."

"I have been to Bombay and Delhi and you have never left Allahabad."

"In this house we call it Prayag, we do not use Muslim names. It was Prayag three thousand years before Islam was invented, why should we use their name?"

"The world calls it Allahabad and you would know this if you had left it only once in your life."

Mr. Tivari was speechless. Mrs. Tivari came from her room.

"You must not speak to him that way," she said. "No son may speak to his father that way, and do not tell *me* about the world either, your father is right and I know what I know." She looked down at her husband over the rim of her bosom. "It is your fault, you should have greeted him properly and not tried to show he was wrong at the very beginning—remember, Prakashji is coming, so be calm!"

Mr. Tivari did not appear to have heard her. "Once," he said softly, "I went to Varanasi. Well, child, you have changed. How shall I call you now: Punditji?"

"I'm sorry, father."

"I'm glad of that. Did they teach you in Bombay to be disrespectful?"

It was going much worse than Hari Lal had anticipated. He looked toward the window as though Barbara Ford might be there to encourage him and heard his father say:

"Well, what is it they teach you there?"

"I study only English now. There are papers in Shakespeare and eighteenth century and the Romantics and contemporary . . ."

"And there is the paper in American literature," Mr. Tivari said, but more to himself. "But no philosophy! No study of truth. How can a University teach the truth anyway? The truth is one, you see it in a moment or never. It is darker than falsehood, its face is covered with a disk of gold and you cannot find your way past that with your Bombay professors. Only I can lead you past the sun glow of falsehood." He sighed, then laughed. "And you tell me I have never been out of Prayag!

What of that? Do we not have Sungam here where Ganga and Yamuna and invisible Saraswati flow together, the confluence of the holiest rivers? I have been everywhere, across the world to the court of Indra and the land of the Gandharvas."

"There are no such places, father. They are imaginary."

"How you contradict yourself! And where did you learn this?"

"In the Ramayana. I mean, in . . . a footnote."

"In a footnote?" Mr. Tivari doubled over with laughter. "That is altogether too simple! Tell me what other wisdom you have acquired."

Hari Lal stiffened with anger but he answered quietly. "I have talked to people from England and America—"

"Very good—footnotes to America—I hope that exists, at least. Have they tried to make you a Christian?"

"No. I don't know if they are Christians. To them their scriptures are poems. They recite it like poetry."

"Excellent; they are not so simple. Have you learned any of their scripture?"

"A few lines."

"Recite!"

Overcome with shyness, Hari Lal began, fighting a stammer: "The Lord is my shepherd, I shall not want."

"Hm!" Mrs. Tivari said softly and they realized that she was still standing over them. She looked at her husband as though in triumph and walked away.

"The Lord is my shepherd," Mr. Tivari repeated, then said it over in Hindi. He looked out the window. "The Lord is my teacher. Though I may want, yet I shall know the truth."

There came a call from the street.

"Is he back?" Mrs. Tivari demanded from her room.

Mr. Tivari placed his chin on the sill and looked out. "A different one," he said. "Blessings!" He threw down a coin.

"Have you forgotten it is Divali?" Mrs. Tivari demanded. "How shall we buy lamps and oil? Ours will be the only house in the Chowk without a light for Lakshmi."

Mr. Tivari began to cough. When he stopped, Hari Lal saw that he was laughing. "Hear your mother," he said. "It is a joy to see her affection for the right way. We must have lights for Lakshmi, and by good fortune I have a few annas for the purpose. I shall get them now on my way to the Fort—I am to talk there on holy Rama as son, husband, brother, and father. I like going to the Fort ghat these days for I can see the rivers come together and I think of the inevitable transformation we must all undergo to attain the true prosperity of deliverance."

"The Fort is too far for you," Mrs. Tivari said, invisible in her chamber. "You cannot walk to the Fort."

"I can, I must, I shall."

"I'll go with you," Hari Lal said. "If you wished it, I might go for you."

Mr. Tivari smiled. "Yes, I know you would go for me. You will have your chance for that soon enough. Today I want to go alone, and you must talk to your brothers, only do not exaggerate too much when you describe the splendors of that outside world you love." He folded his hands and inclined his head, elaborately ceremonious, to say, "Ram Ram." Then he stood up, drew his chuddar around his shoulders and walked slowly to the stairs.

Was there mockery in that valediction? Shamed at his suspicion, Hari Lal called his brothers, who came running into the room at once, and with a feeling of relief he began to tell them about Dr. Ford and America and the bright promise of the future. They could not, he realized, be expected to understand very precisely, but that was for the moment the least of his concerns.

Mr. Tivari was very tired when he came home. By then it was time for the evening meal and he made the ritual offering of food, sang the verses, and lit the lamp before the little statue of Vishnu in the corner and then the new clay lamps filled with mustard oil along the sills. After that they sat down to eat. Although Mrs. Tivari had prepared as much of a feast as their finances would allow, her husband scarcely touched his food. During the afternoon Hari Lal had questioned her about his health. He had been ill since the rains stopped, she said, with something like a cold that did not improve; quite often he stayed on his charpoy all day. The Ayurvedic physician had prescribed the usual herbs but they did not help. She could not say more; she was prepared for anything. She had written to Hari Lal because she had thought it might be good for his father; now (she looked at him steadily and without reproach) she was not so sure.

He thought about these things while they ate their vegetables and wheatbread. The America he longed for flickered in his consciousness, utterly preposterous, first, then utterly dark. His father spoke only once, to ask him if he had tasted meat in Bombay.

"No," Hari Lal said, wounded that his father could conceive of such a thing, and they finished their meal in silence. He was relieved when the visitors arrived until he began to suspect what their business was. Prakash was a very old and feeble man, magnificently attired in an embroidered shirt with a white flowered chuddar draped regally over his shoulders; he wore his sacred thread outside his garments like a uniform braid and in his hands, wound around with rosaries, were three books. He was apparently an astrologer and he had come, obviously, to plan a wedding. Hari Lal shivered with angry excitement and studied the other man, a fat bald-headed Brahman with bulging eyes; he was not presented, he said nothing, and as he looked around him, his features expressed a monstrous distaste for everything in the room. He was doubtless an observer for the prospective bride's family and he would certainly bargain hard.

The preliminaries were long; it was all preliminaries. Prakash, who addressed only Mr. Tivari, muttered obscure explanations, opened his books, pored over fantastical charts, chanted mantras to himself. At length he proposed a day for next September. The other cleared his throat.

"You have computed by the wrong calendar," Mr. Tivari said. "There are three, not two, calendars to consider—lunar, solar and solar-lunar."

"No, no, no, no, no!" said Prakash, grinning wickedly around toothless gums.

"What then?"

"No, no, no!" Prakash repeated with the same inexplicable grin.

"But you've scheduled my son's wedding to coincide with Janmashtami."

"Janmashtami will be in August, as it always is," the astrologer said.

"But August is not the problem, the month of Ashvin is the problem!"

Mrs. Tivari, who was sitting by the fire, laughed softly. To no one in particular she said, "I have a calendar from the newspaper with all the holidays for next year clearly indicated."

They droned on. Chilled, Hari Lal listened. It was incredible, he told himself (though he ought to have expected it, this after all is why they had dragged him home), incredible that in this day and age astrologers (and even fathers) could control one's fate, his fate.

The horoscope of a girl was set on the floor beside another, his own. There was talk of money, the stranger communicating only by nods, winks, and flickering fingers, bargaining for terms, impatience on both sides, and finally, near midnight, when the noise in the street began to subside, an agreement was reached. Prakash, silent at last, drank tea with Mr. Tivari and the stranger. Then they rose and the stranger bowed and grinned for the last time before he tottered down the stairs after the other man.

"Now, my son," Mr. Tivari said, "we must talk. We shall go on the roof."

"No," Mrs. Tivari said in her sharpest tone. "It is too cold on the roof. You can talk as well in here."

"The boys have been kept awake long enough and I have my chuddar. Come, Hari Lal."

Mrs. Tivari handed her son her shawl; embarrassed, he put it back around her and followed his father to the roof. He was aware while he left the room of her eyes and scowling brows in the glow from the embers.

"The girl is fifteen and fair," Mr. Tivari said, "of an acceptable family though not rich. If she were—enough of that. Tripathi, her father, is a scholar and a good man. Her mother was brought up in Bengal and somehow that has given her ideas about herself. The girl does not appear to have been spoiled by her. She is strong and is reported to have a good disposition and a sweet tongue. That is most important. Her name is Maya. She knows a little English, she sews well, and she has studied the sitar for two years. She writes Nagari clumsily and I hope you will help her with that. Do you have any questions?"

Hari Lal gazed around him from their dark perch. Half the lights had burned out by now. Along the square some of the buildings had chains of electric lights instead of lamps. One string of bulbs went out and there was laughter above the buzz of conversation in the Brahman restaurant. The Muslim tailor squatted on his doorstep and moaned an old song off key. Hari Lal felt cold, his tongue had gone dry. He wished he had not come home.

"How can I marry?" he managed to say. "I have a year and a half before I sit for the M. A. examinations."

"That is not so difficult. You will marry and Maya will stay with us or with her family, if she wishes, until you return. Then, when we are all together, we will try to find a place with three rooms—"

"I could not do that. What is the point of marrying now if we cannot live together for so long a time?"

"You are going on nineteen, your prospects are good, and this is the time to negotiate. You might even give up the University and stay with us from now on."

Amazed, Hari Lal stared at his father. "What would I do here?"

"What have we always done?"

"You mean, sit at the window and throw coins to beggars and dream about the court of Indra?"

"If that is how you wish to put it—why not? We have had a good life. We do not need much money to live. We have been happy."

Hari Lal thought of his mother. Mr. Tivari seemed to follow his thoughts.

"Do you think any of us would change it if we could? Your mother would be lost if she did not have me to scold and to cherish. That is more than money to her. These years she has been happier than you can imagine."

"And does that mean that I . . . and . . . Maya, this girl I've never seen, could be happy with such a life?"

"Of course. You are intelligent and you have our example."

"Father, when I marry I do not think I would live with you and mother, even if I stayed in Allahabad."

"Not live with us?"

"That is no longer the way."

"In the 'outside world'? I am beginning to see what the University has done to you. There *is* no other way, of course you would live with us. Still . . . perhaps that is not the most important thing. First is the marriage."

Hari Lal said, "I know people in Bombay who go to America to study and leave their wives and sometimes children behind. That seems to me to be a sacrifice."

"People who go to America? But you are not going to America."

"You have not asked me."

"What is there to ask? To leave India is defilement. Pundit Pandey's daughter went to London and has never come back. She is married to a Christian, she eats meat, even beef, she smokes, she drinks—"

"I would not go to America to get married. I want to go to study more—"

"You want to go?"

"—to learn. The universities here are looking for teachers of American literature and history—"

"You want to go to America? Are you not to consider our happiness?"

"Why should your happiness depend on my unhappiness?" Hari Lal asked, almost pleading.

"It does not, that is only your illusion. You still have much to learn. The first law of happiness is to accept the world as it is and things as they have to be. The circumstances of the world and the way things are have very little importance so long as you know the truth behind and above them. When you know the truth, you obey your dharma, you respect your father, accept his judgment, and life is simple, life is tranquil, and you are happy."

"You used to teach me that each one of us is alone responsible for himself."

"And our happiness then?" Mr. Tivari said with such an air of bereavement that Hari Lal felt his resolution waver. He tried to summon up the image of Dr. Ford, but she would not come and once again America flickered out. He looked at the street. Below them the tailor sang, "The whole world does nothing but fall in love. How is it that you don't know what love is?" An early poem of Firaq, who was still living in the city. How had the tailor gotten on to it? He obviously had a different scripture, a different dharma. Love: all the films were about romantic love, learned from other films, American films, and everyone who flocked to see them considered them make-believe, all the while they loved them, for that was the word, one loved that vision and longed for it where freedom was the dharma—or was it only make-believe in America too? His own father and mother were what love could be, could do. They had not met even once before their wedding. And it was true: they had been happy.

"Is she pretty?" he asked.

"Maya? What a question!" Mr. Tivari broke into his clear, happy laugh. "She has two eyes, a nose, a mouth—of course she is pretty. What girl is not at fifteen?"

"The whole world," sang the tailor, hiccuping.

"You, Hari Lal, you are the dreamer. You say I waste my time in dreams at the window, but it is you who are the dreamer. America!"

Hari Lal felt tired. ". . . fall in love," the tailor said, no longer singing. Suddenly aware that his father was shivering, Hari Lal pleaded the cold as an excuse to go to bed.

In the night he heard his father snoring over the light breathing of his brothers. He could see Mahesh's forehead and fists in the glimmer from the street light, the rest of him and Triveni beside him shadows. Not only America but even Bombay vanished in the realm of fantasy. In this house there was an odd kind of peace; with the silence, all that was preposterous faded. His father (he turned his head to note the vague outline of the charpoy in the darkest corner) was as he had to be, his mother too; they knew their place, their way, their world. It was wisdom, surely, and tempting to be wise.

But Maya: she had become real in his father's sparse description. Marriage in this way was medieval. What did Maya have to do with truth? She was more likely the disk of gold in front of it. Her name meant illusion. Though it also meant Lakshmi, prosperity. And perhaps they were the same. Poor Maya, a frightened child, probably, afraid to leave her father and mother to sleep under a stranger and find herself heavy and ungainly with a mysterious growth inside her. Or perhaps she was a prisoner, mooning over her sitar, wild to be delivered at any cost from Zero Road or wherever she lived. Or just a girl who would become a woman, a wife, a mother without any fuss, like his own mother, and scold and cherish him . . .

The temptations of wisdom increased instead of diminishing. Still,

she was only a mirage and so long as he did not really know her he would
be able to resist.

In the morning his father did not rise from his cot. "Not ill," he said.
"Tired, nothing more. Do not trouble me with questions, any of you, I
want to dream. Of Indra's court and Gandharva land." He laughed and
turned his head to the wall.

Hari Lal had given ten naya paisa to each of his brothers (God knew
what they could buy for the house with that, but it was all the change he
had). Alone with his mother in her room, he was ill at ease. Since his
Bombay transfiguration, she regarded him with a respect he could not
understand; she kept a distance. He asked her again about his father's
illness, suggesting that they call a doctor.

"We have had a doctor." she said.

"I mean a modern doctor with medicine, not herbs."

"How are we to pay a modern doctor?"

"But you can't let a few rupees stand in the way if he's seriously ill."

"Could we not? What do you suppose all of us do at such times, my
dear Hari Lal? We let it stand in the way and we grow more ill and then
we die."

"But I could get the money."

"How? Desire is not enough, and anyway, your scholarship is a
pittance, I wonder how you live on it. And then, he would never consent
to see anybody but our old physician—who is very ill, too. It may be
wrong, but he cannot be changed and he must be true to what he believes.
Be thankful we are not on the ground floor: here, at least, it is dry. What
did you say," she went on abruptly, "when he told you about Maya?"

"I . . . didn't agree to it."

"Or disagree?"

"Well, almost, it wasn't clear."

"But you will marry her, Hari Lal, you must. She is a beautiful girl
and already in love with your picture and for a poor family they have
managed a very decent dowry since she is luckily the only girl. Here she
is," she added, taking a snapshot from her sari. "Your father would never
think of this when he had all his solar-lunar calendar to calculate."

He saw an oval face, the eyes wide open and not at all shy, as he had
expected, a rather long fine nose and a small chin which hinted at stub-
bornness.

"Yes," he said. "She's pretty. That was not what concerned me."

"What is it then?" In his mother's serene patience for the first time he
suspected a sense of unshakable superiority to himself, even to his father;
her new regard for him was only toleration of his Bombay eccentricities.

"I mean, this is no way to marry in the modern world."

"What has the *modern world* to do with it?" she demanded, using his English phrase, which sounded even stranger in her homely Hindi speech. "The world changes only superficially, history makes that obvious."

He had to smile, wondering what she knew of history except legends from the epics and chronicles.

"Is there a better way?" she went on. "Do you think I have not been happy with your father? We married in this way; our betrothal was even much earlier."

"What does that have to do with us, Maya and me, I mean?"

"What doesn't it have to do with you?"

Mahesh and Triveni came in and solemnly offered their mother two tiny clay images of Lakshmi, horribly painted, too small to be more than lumps.

"Good boys," Mrs. Tivari said. "Only let your father sleep. Very good boys. I thought you would buy sweets for yourselves." She sighed. "This is the only way Lakshmi will enter this house," she said to Hari Lal.

"Son," Mr. Tivari called from the other room. Hari Lal went in and saw his father sitting by the window. He beckoned and asked him to sit beside him.

"Look into the street and tell me what you see."

"Zero Road," Hari Lal said, smiling despite himself.

"Lord Indra's court!" Mr. Tivari's answering smile was mysterious.

"The street?"

"Perhaps. I said only Lord Indra's court and you jump to conclusions. Can't I say whatever I please?" He laughed more gently than usual. "The University must be responsible for your muddled head these days. Surely I am not, nor your mother, who is the most sensible woman in the world except when perversity tempts her to oppose me. I meant only that Zero Road is all the world—can anything be more obvious? I suppose I am more attached to it than I ought to be. And you—not enough. But this is where I have taught the epics, this is . . ." He paused, put his hand on Hari Lal's. "How fortunate we have been, my dear Hari Lal. Except for when the girls died, our lives have been . . . I do not know how to say it. If only you do not disappoint us, then. . . Well, I have given you a muddled talk. If it has meant anything, remember it this afternoon when you meet Maya."

"This afternoon?" Hari Lal could not conceal his dismay. Mr. Tivari smiled, an ordinary smile this time, and said:

"You will go this afternoon to Shri Tripathi's to meet his daughter. I think it will be better if I am not there. Your mother will accompany you."

He looked out the window, wistfully, Hari Lal thought, and he wondered if his father were missing this most important occasion because he was so ill. "I have decided not to go," Mr. Tivari went on, "because I want you to feel that it is entirely your affair, since that is so important for you. I do not ask you to promise anything. You must make your own mistakes, you must find the truth for yourself. You must promise me only this."

Hari Lal waited. "Yes, father?"

"No," Mr. Tivari said, "what is the point of promises? Are you going to wear that clerk's suit? Lord, Lord!"

And Hari Lal was startled to realize that, whether suddenly or by imperceptible degrees, he had capitulated to his father, and his father knew it.

It was out of the question for them to speak. Maya stayed beside her mother all the while they walked in the largest of the Tripathi's four rooms in New Katra on the other side of the city. Shri Tripathi and his four sons were hearty and full of sympathy for Hari Lal's nervousness; he found them detestable. Mrs. Tripathi, voluminous and bulging-eyed (like her brother, the stranger who had accompanied Prakash—and both of them were there too), was endlessly inventive on the subject of the grandeurs of Burdwan Junction, the superiority of Bengali manners despite the Bengali arrogance, the decline of Allahabad, since independence, since the new cinemas opened, since . . .

Hari Lal caught a smile from Maya, very discreet but plain enough: she did not take her mother seriously. He tried to move close to her; both mothers expanded at once and he found himself still farther from her. It was infuriating. He decided that he had once and for all to show his independence. He had barely had a clear glimpse of Maya, though he could see she was even prettier than the photograph and very graceful in a terrible flower-print sari which had doubtless been magnificent thirty years before in Burdwan Junction.

"Maya," he said, and he stepped around the mothers to the side of his fiancée (for his presence there, he suddenly understood, amounted to betrothal), and when he took her hand, for only a second while they stared at one another, there was scarcely a person in the room who did not gasp, but Maya, braver than he could have hoped, returned the pressure of his fingers and did not draw away until he let her hand fall free and stepped back; Mrs. Tripathi, frowning terribly, and Mrs. Tivari, inscrutable, intervened again. He sipped his tea, sighed, saw Maya smile over her cup, and suddenly tea was over, he was walking in the street with his mother.

"You were rude," she said. "Poor Maya must have thought you a boor."

He was surprised at how much this possibility troubled him and how swiftly he refuted it—there was the warmth of her smile and her hand to reassure him. They were walking past Muir College by now and he saw a band of University students sauntering along smoking and laughing with girls in pigtails, one of them flourishing a film magazine. He was all in a moment ashamed at how easily he had surrendered to his father and mother, to Maya, how easily his longing had been supplanted by a new one. He summoned his forces for a battle, but then he looked at his mother, so impassive in her steady swaying walk, the sari bunched around her thick waist with peculiar grace, and just as suddenly he put away his hopes of freedom, let his longing go for good.

The two boys met them in the middle of the stairs, their faces frightened. There was chanting in the room. About twenty minutes before Mr. Tivari had died quietly while looking into the street, with his head propped above the sill.

In the evening the barber came to shave Hari Lal's head. He worked very fast, leaving only a strand in back for the ritual top-knot. Hari Lal was aware of humiliation in his grief, more troubling than his grief. The humiliation warned him that his surrender might be a mistake, after all. He was no longer reconciled; he felt merely trapped.

The boys had their turn next and they recovered their spirits a little for the first time since the afternoon. Hari Lal looked at their bright shiny skulls and burst into tears.

"Enough of that," Mrs. Tivari said. Her face was swollen with weeping but her voice held steady now. She had first taken it calmly but broke down when the old physician gave his opinion: Mr. Tivari's heart, exhausted by illness and work, had stopped. He spoke in a thin cracked voice that somehow provoked her fury. She had ordered him to leave, waved her arms at him, screamed, and then gone sobbing to the other room. The physician had not flinched; he sat beside the body and looked around him with a sweet and patient smile as though to say that he knew what to expect on such occasions.

"We must plan everything," Mrs. Tivari said. "I will go tomorrow afternoon to Sister's in Jaunpur with the boys. The train leaves at twenty-five minutes past four. We will take what we can carry, the rest I will leave with Maya for the two of you, and the books are yours. There is nothing more to that. Mrs. Sen at the third door down above the spice shop has been a widow for eight years; go to her and borrow a white sari, she must have many. There is nothing more to that. Stop weeping now, it is of no use. Your father will find a better lodging in the world next time, I hope, but Lord, though he was a good man he was too full of imperfection to escape the mortal world once and for all. Then you must go to bed, for it is a long journey to the rivers and the procession will start at dawn. Go to Mrs. Sen now and do not cry, for what have you to fear, what have you to mourn? Go now."

It was a surprise when he woke in the middle of the night and realized he had been sleeping comfortably. He looked at his brothers huddled together as though they were frightened. Why shouldn't they be? He was afraid too. The way, so simple to follow, was perilously easy to lose. Once he had given up his freedom he was lost at the prospect of regaining it. His affection for his father, his conflict with him, he told himself now with an echo of the anguish he had first felt when he stepped into Zero Road, his affection and his conflict had nothing to do with the darkness of truth or the splendid glow of illusion. Nothing. He blinked at the streetlight's pale glimmer, rounding on the floor. He had not yet told his mother he would give up the University—pride still rebelled at that—but of course she would have guessed it and it would be a consolation for her. The astrologer could be talked into setting the wedding date a few months earlier; if he would not, then another astrologer would have to be found. He would tell her after the funeral; she would go to Sister's anyway with the boys for a few weeks, it would be good for her, then Maya would come from her four rooms to his two, his mother would come back with the boys and take her old room, he and Maya his father's, and farewell to Bombay, he would not even think of what beside Bombay, and then nothing but verses from holy Ramayana, verses by holy Tulsidas, restive children and the books molding in the rains and crumbling to dust in May.

Then he heard his mother weeping softly in her room and he shut his eyes.

He wore a dhoti and a kurta for the first time in months; it did not feel so strange as he had expected. With three brittle old Brahmans he shouldered the bier at sunup for the three-mile walk to the burning ghats. He wanted to walk fast but the old men angrily ordered him to slow. He resented their weakness before he was touched by their devotion, for they had been his father's friends. With a mongrel crowd of acquaintances and idlers behind them, while someone chanted, they stumbled along the dusty road toward the Fort and Ewing Christian College and the funeral ghats under a cloudless dark blue sky. Because it was almost winter flowers were plentiful and cheap; the bier was smothered in red and yellow blossoms. He wondered how his mother had seen to it all, where she had gotten the money for everything, and he winced, thinking how hard she must find the walking. He turned his head to see her, caught a glimpse of Mahesh tempted just then to linger to watch some urchins playing tipcat, but he could not find his mother. Then he tripped and after that did not look back.

The trees thinned, the plain fell away to the rivers, still high from the rains, the Ganges and Jumna spilling gray-blue and green waves together, the holiest spot in India, holier even than Banaras itself. The burning ghats appeared festive. All along the wide flight of steps mourners who looked like revelers stood watching another funeral; the pyre still blazed at the bottom landing beside the river. Mr. Tivari had to wait. The other fire seemed almost finished but it flamed up again. There was nothing sad about it. Hari Lal had been to a lot of funerals: he knew that the corpse was nothing, the funeral only a consolation for the living, a distraction. The singing sounded joyous, like the conch blasts and the bells and the laughter. Mr. Tivari would have approved, it was absolutely proper. And suddenly it was his turn. The new pyre was ready; the body was placed on it, scarcely visible under the flowers. The purohit chanted holy mantras and at the right moment Hari Lal recited the verses of his Brahmanhood:

Pray that we attain the high glory of the divine sun;
May he guide us in our prayers.

Then the new verses he did not know which he had to repeat after the priest:

Ganapathi, beloved of Shiva, of Prajapati,
Bring peace to the heavens and to man
And to all the visible worlds.

It was only the beginning, it seemed intolerably long, and while he repeated the prayers he recalled unexpectedly when he had learned the Gayatri, those lines about the glory of the divine sun which he had since spoken every morning and every evening and every time he ate, even in Bombay. It was an afternoon when Zero Road was flooded and Mr. Tivari, unable to go out, had decided it was time to teach his son, and they had talked about the Gayatri while Mrs. Tivari cooked rice and dal, casting fragrant herbs in the pots, and the rain spattered on the sill and Mr. Tivari had laughed at his son's mistakes in Sanskrit. Hari Lal thought he was going to cry. The torch was put in his hand. He lit the pyre.

In the smoke of the kindling and fresh flowers he watched his father reposing on the bier, lightly, it seemed, with his winsome smile playing behind the transparent sooty swirls. The blaze took, flames leaped skyward, and Hari Lal's eyes followed them up to where they fused with the sun. He was mastered by devotion to his father, he felt a sudden joy in that devotion. When he turned he saw Maya standing on the top step far above, then his brothers with faces lost between terror and curiosity, his mother solemn, an old man laughing very gently and sweetly as he whispered to a friend. Hari Lal fancied he heard the hermits singing from across the river. The tears came to his eyes.

It was not a very elaborate pyre. It took little time to burn. Hari Lal was grateful that it did not go out, as they often did, leaving some of the corpse unconsumed. When the flames spurted up for the last time before they subsided in smoke, while the fire smoldered (for others were waiting, one could not delay), he reached in for ashes to scatter in the river to symbolize the return of the individual to the absolute, the all, the One. A noise overhead, a roar, and he faltered. He looked up to the top of the ghat. Maya was gone—had it been Maya? He was no longer sure. There was an airplane flying over, trailing a long banner with some new film title on it. The heat of the sun and the pyre burned into him. He began to sweat. A sudden spurt of unreasonable resentment coursed through him. He reached again for the ashes and with them picked up a hot coal; he gasped, flung it with the ashes into the river and fought the temptation to bring his scorched palm to his mouth. The plane buzzed more faintly in the distance, invisible in the sun's glare. The resentment vanished, he felt an unfamiliar relief.

"We must go," his mother said. "There is much to do and this is finished."

He looked at her, the tears rising again, and saw the rivers stretch into blind infinity, a golden ocean driving him in its westward tide, and he said, "I cannot marry Maya, I cannot do what I do not believe in, I cannot sacrifice myself."

She regarded him with her old serenity for some time before she spoke. "No one asks any of these things of you. You have heard your father read, 'Man is the altar, man is the sacrifice.' Come now, we must take your brothers away from here."

In the afternoon he saw her and the boys off at the station. It was crowded with holiday travelers, the windows of the train bristled with hands, waving and clinging or merely grasping for pan or fruit juice or comic books or film magazines from the vendors' carts. Mrs. Tivari smiled once at Hari Lal, then turned her head away and did not look at him again, though the boys grabbed his hands as though they would pull him through the window, even when the train had started, and then he watched with a sinking heart as it disappeared.

A half hour later, longing for the old two rooms, for his father and mother and for Maya too, he caught the Kashi Express and began the night and day of journeying that would bring him back to Bombay.

Julio Ramón Ribeyro

Alienation

DESPITE THE FACT THAT HE WAS A MULATTO named López, he longed to resemble less and less a goalie on the Alianza Lima soccer team and increasingly to take on the appearance of a blond from Philadelphia. Life had taught him that if he wanted to triumph in a colonial city it was better to skip the intermediate stages and transform himself into a gringo from the United States rather than into just a fair-skinned nobody from Lima. During the years that I knew him, he devoted all of his attention to eliminating every trace of the López and *zambo** within him and Americanizing himself before time could sentence him to an existence as a bank guard or a taxi driver. He had had to begin by killing the Peruvian in himself and extracting something from every gringo that he met. From all this plundering a new person would emerge, a fragmented being who was neither mulatto nor gringo, but rather the result of an unnatural commingling, something that the force of destiny would eventually change, unfortunately, for him, from a rosy dream into a hellish nightmare.

But let's not get ahead of ourselves. We should establish the fact that his name was Roberto, that years later he was known as Bobby, but that in the most recent official documents he is listed as Bob. At each stage in

*Ribeyro uses the term *zambo* to refer to a person who is a blend of Indian and Negro.

Julio Ramón Ribeyro (b. 1929), Peruvian, has published three novels, numerous essays, and a collection of plays since 1955. His most highly regarded literary achievement is his short stories, collected in three volumes entitled *La palabra del mudo* (1972).

his frantic ascension toward nothingness his name lost one syllable.

Everything began the afternoon when a group of us, all very fair-haired kids, were playing ball on Bolognesi Plaza. We were out of school on vacation and some of the children who lived in nearby chalets, both girls and boys, would gather on the plaza during those interminable summer afternoons. Roberto used to go there too, even though he attended a public school and lived on one of the backstreets in the district rather than in a chalet. He would go there to watch the girls play and to be recognized by some fair-faced kid who had seen him growing up on these streets and knew he was the laundry woman's son.

But really, like the rest of us, he would go there to see Queca. We were all infatuated with Queca, who, during the past couple of years, had the distinction of being chosen class queen, an honor bestowed upon her during festivities at the end of the school year. Queca didn't study with the German sisters of Saint Ursula, nor with the North Americans of Villa María, but rather with the Spanish nuns of Reparation. We didn't consider this important, or the fact that her father was a blue-collar worker who drove a bus, or that her house had only one story with geraniums instead of roses. What was important then were her rosy skin, her green eyes, her long, brown hair, the way she ran, laughed, jumped, and her incomparable legs, always bare and golden and which, in time, would become legendary.

Roberto used to come only to watch her play; really none of the boys who came from the other neighborhoods of Miraflores, or even those who later came from San Isidro and Barranco for that matter, could attract her attention. One time Peluca Rodríguez flung himself from the highest branch of a pine tree; Lucas de Tramontana arrived mounted on a shiny motorcycle that had eight headlights; Fats Gómez broke the ice cream vendor's nose for daring to whistle at us; and Armando Wolff donned fine flannel suits and even wore a bow tie. But not one of them caught Queca's eye. Queca favored no one, preferring to converse with everybody, to run, skip, laugh, and play volleyball, leaving behind at nightfall a band of adolescents overwhelmed by a sensation of intense sexual frustration that only a charitable hand underneath white sheets was able to console.

It was a fatal ball that someone tossed that afternoon and that Queca was unable to catch and that rolled toward the bench where Roberto sat, silent and observant. He had always been waiting for this moment. He leaped onto the lawn, stepped into a drainage ditch and rescued the ball, which was just about to roll under the wheels of a car. But as he returned with it, Queca, who was now facing him with outstretched hands, seemed to be adjusting her focus, observing something that she had never noticed before: a short, dark, thicklipped being with kinky hair, something that she perhaps had seen daily just as she saw park benches or pine trees. Abruptly she turned away and fled, terrified.

Roberto never forgot Queca's parting words: "I don't play with *zambos.*" These five words decided his destiny.

Every human being who suffers becomes an observer, so Roberto continued going to the plaza for several years afterwards; but his look had lost all innocence. It was no longer a mere reflection of the world, but rather an organ of vigilance—penetrating, selective, and discriminating.

Queca was growing up; her run had become modified somewhat, her skirts longer, her leaps had lost some of their imprudence and her conduct around her peers had become more distant and selective. We were all aware of these changes, but Roberto observed something more: that Queca tended to turn away from her more swarthy admirers until, after making a series of comparisons, she focused her attention only on Chalo Sander, the one boy in the group with the fairest hair, the lightest skin, and the only one who studied in a school under the direction of North American priests. By the time those alluring legs reached the peak of their development, she was speaking exclusively to Chalo Sander; the first time she walked hand in hand with him to the levee we understood that she had ceased to be one of us; there was nothing we could do but play the role of the chorus in a Greek tragedy, always present and visible, but irrecoverably separated from the gods.

Rejected and in despair, we would gather on the street corner after one of the games, where we would smoke our first cigarettes, arrogantly fondle the newly discovered fuzz on our chins and comment on the irremediable state of things. Sometimes we would go into a cantina owned by a Chinese named Manuel and have a beer. Roberto followed us around like a shadow, always scrutinizing us from the doorway, never missing a word of our conversation. Sometimes we would say to him, "Hi, *zambo,* have a drink with us," and he always said "No thanks, another time," and although he smiled and kept his distance, we knew that he shared in his own way our sense of loss.

And it was Chalo Sander, naturally, who took Queca to the graduation festivities when we finished high school. Early that evening we decided to meet in our favorite cantina where we drank a little more than usual, plotted bizarre schemes, and spoke of kidnapping, of planning a group attack of sorts. But it was all just talk. By eight o'clock that evening we were in front of the modest little house with geraniums, resigned to being witnesses of our own deprivation. Chalo arrived in his father's car, sporting an elegant white smoking jacket; he got out a few minutes later accompanied by Queca, who, with her long evening gown and high coiffure, hardly resembled our former, playful classmate. Queca, smiling and clutching in her hands a satin evening purse, never noticed us. An elusive vision, the last, because never again would things be as they had been before. All of our hopes died instantly, at that very moment which would never allow us to forget the indelible image that brought to a close a stage of our youth.

Almost everyone had deserted the plaza, some because they were getting ready to enroll at the university, others because they were migrating to other districts in search of an impossible replica of Queca. Only Roberto, who was now working as a distributor for a bakery, returned to the plaza at nightfall, a place where other boys and girls now occupied our space and imitated our games with such candor that they gave the impression that they themselves had invented them. In his solitude Roberto appeared to lead a more transient existence, but in reality his eyes were always fixed upon Queca's house. That way he was able to confirm before anyone else that Chalo Sander had been only one episode in Queca's life, a kind of rehearsal preparing her for the arrival of the original, of which Chalo had been a mere copy: Billy Mulligan, the son of a United States consulate official.

Billy was freckled, redheaded, wore flowered shirts, had enormous feet, a boisterous laugh, and the sun, instead of toasting him, made him peel; but he always came to see Queca in his own automobile rather than the one belonging to his father. Nobody knew where Queca first met him nor how he came to be there; but she began to see him more and more, until she saw only him, his tennis rackets, his sunglasses, his photographic equipment, while the outline of Chalo gradually grew more and more opaque, smaller and more distant until it finally disappeared altogether. Through the process of elimination Queca made her choice. Only Mulligan would take her to the altar and, when they were lawfully married, he would have every right to caress those thighs we had dreamed about in vain for so long.

Disillusionment generally is something that no one can tolerate; it either ends up being pushed back and forgotten, its causes evaded, or it becomes the object of ridicule and even the theme of a literary composition. It turned out that Fats Gómez went off to study in London, Peluca Rodríguez wrote a really lousy sonnet, Armando Wolff came to the conclusion that Queca was a snob, and Lucas de Tramontana deceitfully boasted that he had made love to her several times on the pier. Roberto was the only one who learned a true, valuable lesson from all this; it was Mulligan or nothing. What good was it to be blond if there were so many light-skinned braggarts who were desperate, indolent, and defeated as well. There had to be a superior state, inhabited by those who could plan their lives with confidence in this gray city and who could effortlessly reap all the best fruits the land had to offer. The problem was how, being a *zambo*, to become another Mulligan. But suffering, when it doesn't kill, sharpens ingenuity; and Roberto subjected himself to a long, thorough analysis and outlined a plan of action.

First of all he had to eliminate every trace of the *zambo* in himself. His hair didn't cause any major problem; he dyed it with peroxide and had it straightened. As for his skin, he mixed starch, rice powder, and talcum from the drugstore until he found the ideal combination; but a dyed and powdered *zambo* is still a *zambo*. He needed to know how the North American gringos dressed, talked, moved, and thought: in short, precisely who they were.

In those days we saw him marauding about during his free hours in diverse locales which seemingly had nothing in common, except for one thing: they were usually frequented by gringos. Some saw him standing in front of the country club, others at the Santa María school gates; and Lucas de Tramontana swore that he caught a glimpse of him behind a fence at the golf course, and someone else spotted him at the airport trying to carry some tourist's luggage; and then there were several who found him strolling down the halls of the North American embassy.

This phase of his plan was for him absolutely perfect. In the meantime, he was able to confirm that the gringos were distinguishable from others by the special way they dressed, which he described as sporty, comfortable, and unconventional. Because of his observations, Roberto was one of the first to discover the advantages of blue jeans, the virile cowboy look of the wide leather belt fastened by an enormous buckle, the soft comfort of white canvas shoes with rubber soles, the collegiate charm of a canvas cap with a visor, the coolness of a flowered or striped short-sleeved shirt, the variety of nylon jackets zipped up in front bearing an emblem of special significance, always influential and distinctive, and worn underneath, a white shirt also bearing an emblem of a North American university.

All of these articles of clothing were not sold in any department store but had to be brought from the United States, a place where he had no contacts. There were North American families who, prior to returning to the United States, announced in the newspaper their intention to sell everything they had. Roberto showed up on their doorstep before anyone else, acquiring in this way a wardrobe in which he invested all of his savings.

With hair that was now straightened and bleached, a pair of blue jeans and a loud shirt, Roberto was on the brink of becoming Bobby.

All of this was not without consequence. His mother said that no one would speak to him on the street, thinking he was pretentious. What was even worse, they would make jokes or whistle at him as if he were a queer. He never contributed a cent for food, but would spend hours in front of the mirror after spending all his money on clothing. His father, according to Roberto's mother, may have been a worthless scoundrel who, like the magical Fu Man Chu, absconded only a year after they met; but at least he was never ashamed to be seen with her, nor was he ashamed that he was a pilot's mate on a small boat.

Just between us, the first one to notice the change in Roberto was Peluca Rodríguez, who had requested a pair of blue jeans through a Braniff purser. When the jeans arrived he put them on and headed for the plaza to show them off, only to run into Roberto who was wearing a pair identical to his. For days he did nothing but curse the *zambo*, saying he had ruined everything, that he had probably been spying on him so as to copy him. He even noticed that he bought Lucky Strike cigarettes and that he combed his hair in such a way that a lock of it hung over his forehead.

But the worst thing concerned his job. Cahuide Morales, the owner of the bakery, was a mestizo, gruff and provincial, with a big belly, who adored roasted beef hearts and indigenous waltzes; and one who had broken his back for the last twenty years in order to stay in business. Nothing annoyed him more than for someone to pretend to be what he wasn't. Whether one was a mixed-breed or white wasn't important; what was important was the *mosca*, the *agua*, the *molido*. He knew a thousand different words for money. When he saw that his employee had bleached his hair, he allowed for another wrinkle on his forehead; and when he realized that Roberto had actually covered himself with powder, he swallowed a swear word that just about gave him indigestion; but when his employee came to work disguised as a gringo, the mixture of father, police, bully, and boss broke loose in him and he took Roberto by the scruff of the neck to the back of the store; the Morales Brothers' bakery was a serious business, and one would have to comply with regulations; he might overlook all the make-up, but if he didn't come to work in uniform like the other distributors, he was going to boot him out the door with a swift kick in the pants.

Roberto had already packaged and wrapped himself to such a degree that he couldn't afford to undo the commodity; he preferred the kick in the pants.

Those gloomy days were interminable as he looked for work. His ambition was to gain entrance into a gringo's home as a butler, gardener, chauffeur, or in some other similar capacity; but doors always closed on him. His strategy lacked something, and that was a knowledge of English. Since he didn't have funds to enroll in a language academy, he bought himself a dictionary and began copying the words in his notebook. When he reached the letter C he threw in the towel; well, this purely visual knowledge of English wasn't getting him anywhere; but, then, there was always the cinema, a school that would not only teach, but would entertain as well.

In the balconies of the new theaters he spent entire afternoons viewing westerns and detective films in the target language. The plots were irrelevant; what mattered was the way the characters spoke. He wrote down all of the words he was able to understand and repeated them until they were permanently recorded in his memory. By forcing himself to review the films, he learned complete sentences or even entire speeches. In his room in front of the mirror he was suddenly the romantic cowboy making an irresistible declaration of love to the dance-hall girl, or the ruthless gangster uttering a death sentence while riddling his adversary with bullets. Besides, the cinema nourished in him certain illusions that filled him with hope. He believed he had discovered in himself a slight resemblance to Alan Ladd, who had appeared in one of the westerns dressed in blue jeans and a red and black plaid jacket. In reality, the only thing he had in common with him was his height and the yellow lock of hair he let dangle over his forehead. Dressed the same as the actor, he saw the film ten times consecutively, always standing in the entrance way when the movie was over, waiting for people to leave and to overhear them say, "But look, how strange, that guy looks like Alan Ladd." Something that no one said, of course; well, the first time that we saw him striking that pose, we laughed in his face.

His mother told us one day that finally Roberto had found a job, not in the home of a gringo as he wanted, but perhaps something better, in the Bowling Club of Miraflores. He was serving drinks in the bar from five o'clock in the afternoon until midnight. The few times that we went there we saw him looking brilliant and diligent. He waited on the indigenous population in an unbiased, frankly impeccable manner; but with the gringos he was ingratiating and servile. As soon as one came in he was at his side, taking his order, and seconds later the customer had his hot dog and his coca-cola placed before him. He enthusiastically threw out words in English and, because he was answered in the same language, his vocabulary began increasing. Soon he possessed a good repertory of expressions with which he won over the gringos who were delighted to see a native who understood them. Since Roberto had certain problems with pronunciation, the gringos were the ones who decided to call him Bobby.

And it was with the name of Bobby López that he finally was able to

enroll in the Peruvian-North American Institute. Those who saw him
during that particular period in time say that he was the classic egghead,
one who never missed a class, or forgot his homework, or hesitated to
question the teacher about some obscure grammatical concept. Apart
from the white students who for professional reasons were taking courses
there, he met others like himself who, although from different back-
grounds and other neighborhoods and without having met previously,
nourished the same dreams and led a life similar to his. He became a good
friend of José María Cabanillas, a tailor's son from Surquillo. Cabanillas
shared the same blind admiration for gringos that he did, and years ago
he too had begun to smother the *zambo* in himself with really visible
results. Besides having the advantage of being taller and lighter-skinned
than Bobby, he resembled not Alan Ladd, who after all was a second-rate
actor admired by a small group of snobbish girls, but rather the indestructible John Wayne. The two of them formed an inseparable pair. They
finished out the year with the best grades; and Mr. Brown held them up as
examples to the rest of the students, speaking of "their sincere desire to
excel."

The two buddies must have had long, pleasant conversations together. You could always see their butts stuffed into their faded blue-jeans,
going here and there, always speaking in English to one another. But also
one must admit that the city didn't swallow them up; they disarranged
things to such an extent that neither relatives nor friends could endure
them. For that reason they rented a room in a building on Mogollón
Avenue and lived together. There they created an inviolable haven which
allowed them to establish a foreign culture within the native one and to
feel that in the middle of this murky city they were living in a California
neighborhood. Each of them contributed what he could: Bobby, his travel
posters, and José María, who was a music fan, his Frank Sinatra, Dean
Martin, and Tommy Dorsey records. What a fine pair of gringos they
made, stretched out on the sofa-bed, smoking their Lucky Strikes while
they listened to "Strangers in the Night" and viewed the bridge over the
Hudson River which was stuck to the wall. One last effort and, hop, they
would be crossing that bridge.
For us, too, it was difficult to travel to the United States. One had to
have a scholarship, or relatives already there, or lots of money. For López
and Cabanillas this was not the case. They saw no other way out but to
find an escape like other whites, thanks to the job of purser for an airline
company. Every year they would compete for the job, presenting their
credentials. They knew more English than anyone else, delighted in serving others, were self-sacrificing and tireless; but nobody knew them, they

were without recommendations, and it was obvious to the interviewers that they were dealing with powdery *zambos*. They were turned down.

They say that Bobby wept and pulled out his hair and that Cabanillas attempted suicide by jumping from a modest second floor window. Within their refuge on Mogollón Avenue they spent the darkest days of their lives; the city, which had always sheltered them, ended up being transformed into a dirty rag as if to smother them with insults and scorn. But eventually their spirit returned and new plans surfaced. Since no one wanted anything to do with them here, they would have to get out any way they could. They had no choice but to immigrate disguised as tourists.

For an entire year they worked hard and deprived themselves of everything in order to save enough for their fare and establish a common fund which would allow them to survive abroad. It so happened that the two of them were finally able to pack their bags and abandon forever that detested city in which they had suffered and to which they never wanted to return as long as they lived.

One can guess at the events that followed, and it doesn't take much imagination to complete this parable. In the neighborhood we had access to direct information: letters from Bobby to his mother, news from travelers abroad, and finally the whole story given by a witness.

Soon Bobby and José María spent in one month what they had thought would last them several months. They soon realized that all the Lópezes and Cabanillases in the entire world had convened in New York—Asians, Arabs, Aztecs, Africans, Iberians, Mayans, Chibchas, Sicilians, Carribeans, Mussulmans, Quechuas, Polynesians, Eskimos, representatives of every origin, language, race, and pigmentation—all of whom had one common goal: the desire to live as a yankee, for which they had surrendered their souls and altered their appearances. The city tolerated them for several months, complacently, while it absorbed the dollars they had saved. Then, as if through a tube, it led them toward the mechanism of expulsion.

With great difficulty, they managed to obtain a time extension on their visas, while, simultaneously, they tried to find a steady job that would enable them to remain on a par with all the Quecas of the place; and there were many, although the girls just led them on, giving them less attention than a cockroach would deserve. They ran out of clothes, Frank Sinatra's music became intolerable; and the mere thought of having to eat another hot dog, which was a luxury in Lima, nauseated them. From their cheap hotel they moved first to the Catholic shelter and then to a bench in

a public park. Soon they discovered that white substance that fell from
the sky, lightened their skin, and made them skate like idiots on the icy
sidewalks, a substance which, by its very color, was nature's deceptive
racist.

There was only one solution. Thousands of miles away, in a country
called Korea, blond North Americans were fighting against some horrible
Asians. The freedom of Western nations was in jeopardy according to the
newspapers, and statesmen confirmed it on television. But it was so
painful to send "the boys" to that place! They were dying like rats, leaving
behind pallid, grief-stricken mothers in tiny farmhouses with a room
upstairs full of old toys. Whoever went over there to Korea to fight for
one year had everything guaranteed him upon his return home: national-
ity, a job, social security, integration, medals. Everywhere there were
recruitment centers. To each volunteer the country opened its heart.

Bobby and José María enlisted so they wouldn't be deported. After
three months of training at an army base they left the country in an
enormous airplane. Life was a marvelous adventure; the trip was unforgettable. Having been born in a poor country, probably the most miserable and melancholy of all, and having known the most agitated city in
the world, with thousands of deprivations, true; but now all this was
behind them because now they were wearing a green uniform, flying over
plains, seas, and snow-capped mountains, clutching powerful weapons
and were becoming young men still filled with promise, journeying into
the realm of the unknown.

The laundress María has plenty of postcards with temples, markets,
and exotic streets, all written in a small fastidious hand. Where could
Seoul be? There are lots of ads and cabarets. Then came letters from the
front lines that he described to us after the first attack, which forced him
to take a few days off. Thanks to these documents, we were able to
reconstruct fairly well the bad things that happened to him. Progressively,
step by step, Bobby came closer to his rendezvous with destiny. It was
necessary to confront a wave of yellow-skinned soldiers who descended
from the hills like kernels of yellow corn. To combat the situation, volun-
teers were there, the unconquerable watchmen of the West.

José María was saved by a miracle and proudly showed off the stump
of his right arm when he returned to Lima months afterwards. His squad
had been sent to inspect a rice field, where supposedly the Korean advance guard was waiting to ambush them. Bobby didn't suffer, José
María said; the first blast blew his head off and it rolled into a trench, all
of its dyed hair now in the dirt. His buddy only lost an arm, but he was
there, alive, telling his story, drinking his cold beer, unpowdered now and

more a *zambo* than ever, living comfortably off what he received as compensation for having been mutilated.

By then Roberto's mother had suffered her second attack, one which erased her from the world. So, she never read the official letter informing her that Bob López had died in action and was entitled to a medal of honor and remuneration for his family. No one was able to collect it.

And Queca? Perhaps if Bob had known her story maybe his life would have been different or maybe it wouldn't; that's something no one knows. Billy Mulligan took her to his country, as was agreed, to a town in Kentucky where his father owned a business that sold canned pork. They spent several months in ecstasy in that pretty house with wide sidewalks, iron grillwork, a garden, and all the electric appliances invented by technology: a house, in short, like a hundred thousand in that country. Gradually the Irish in him, which his Puritan upbringing had suppressed for so long, began to reveal itself; at the same time, Queca's eyes grew larger and more tragic. Billy was coming home later each night; he became a devoted fan of coin swallowing machines and of car racing; his feet grew bigger and developed callouses; he discovered a malignant mole on his neck; on Saturdays he inflated himself with bourbon at the Kentucky Friends club; he had an affair with a woman employee at the firm; he wrecked the car twice; his look turned into a fixed, watery stare; and he ended up beating his wife, the pretty, unforgettable Queca, in the early hours of dawn on Sundays, while he smiled stupidly and called her a shitty half-breed.

Translated from the Spanish by Dianne Douglas.

Arthur Schnitzler

America

THE SHIP IS DOCKING; I AM SETTING MY FOOT on the new world . . .

The gray autumn morning overshadows sea and land; everything under me is still swaying; again and again I feel the unquiet rolling of the waves . . . Out of the fog rises the city . . . Next to me, with open eyes, lively, the crowd is hurrying along. Not something strange do they see, but only something new. I listen, as one or the other whispers to himself, "America"—as if he just wanted to impress on himself that he were now really here, so far away!

I am standing alone on the shore. Not about the new America am I thinking, from which I am going to have to claim the happiness that my homeland denied me—I am thinking about a different one.

I see that little room; so clearly do I see it that it seems as if I had left it yesterday instead of many years ago. On the table is the lamp with the green shade, the embroidered armchair in the corner. Copper-engravings hang on the wall; their images swim away into the shadows. Anna is next to me. She is lying at my feet, her head with its curly hair propped against my knee. I have to bend over, in order to look into her eyes.

We have stopped talking; the evening progresses, and it's quiet in the room. Outside it is beginning to rain. We hear the drops, slow and heavy, beat against the windowpane. She smiles, and I bend over to reach her

---

The Austrian writer and dramatist *Arthur Schnitzler* (1862-1931), one of the major figures of modern German literature, is especially known for his acute psychological perceptions.

mouth. I kiss her lips, her forehead, and her eyes, which she has closed. My fingers play with the fine, golden hair, which is curled behind her ear. I push it back and kiss her on this sweet, white patch of skin behind her ear. She looks up again and laughs. "Something new," she whispers, as if amazed. I hold my lips firmly pressed behind her ear. Then I say smiling, "Yes, we have discovered something new!" She bursts out laughing, and like a child she calls out happily, "America."

How funny it was then. So crazy and silly. I see her face before me, as she looked up at me with those roguish eyes and "America" echoed from her lips. How we laughed then, and how the fragrance intoxicated me, which streamed out of her hair over this America . . .

And this splendid name remained. At first we always called it out, if, of our innumerable kisses, one strayed behind the ear; then we whispered it—then we just thought it. But always it came into our consciousness.

A profusion of memories rise up in me. How once we saw a large ship pictured on an advertising billboard and, having stepped nearer, read: "From Liverpool to New York— From Bremen to New York." We burst out laughing, in the middle of the street, and she asserted quite loudly, while people were standing nearby, "Hey, we're going to travel to America today!" The people stared at her in complete amazement, especially a young man with a blond mustache, who also smiled. That annoyed me very much, and I thought, "Yes, he'd probably like to come along."

Then we were sitting once in the theatre (I no longer remember any more at which play), when someone on the stage spoke of Columbus. It was a piece in iambics, and I recall the line, "and when Columbus stepped out on the bridge." Anna pressed her arm softly against mine; I looked at her and understood her disparaging glance. Poor Columbus, as if he had discovered the true America! After the play, when we were sitting in a cafe, we spoke a great deal about the good man who had prided himself so much on his poor America. We were actually sorry for him. For a long time, I was unable to imagine him any other way than standing with a sorrowful glance on the coast of his new part of the world, oddly enough with a top-hat and a very modern overcoat, and shaking his head disappointedly. Once we drew him together on the marble surface of a coffee-house table and added some new details. She insisted that he had to be smoking a cigar; in our picture, moreover, the good explorer was carrying an umbrella, and his top-hat was crushed, naturally, by the mutineers. So Columbus became for us the humorous symbol of the history of the whole world. How crazy! How silly! . . .

And now I'm standing in the middle of a large, cold city. I'm in the false America and dreaming about my sweet, fragrant America over there. And how long ago that was! Many, many years. A pain, a madness comes over me that something has so irrevocably been lost. That I don't even know where a message from me, where a letter could reach her. That I know nothing, absolutely nothing any more about her. . .

My way takes me further along into the city, and my porter follows me. I stop a moment, close my eyes, and through a strange, deceiving game of the senses the same fragrance embraces me that wafted over me from Anna's hair when we first discovered America.

Translated from the German by Robert E. Jungman

Questions for Discussion

1. Given the fact that Hari Lal's exposure to American culture has been limited to contact with one American professor and several works of American literature, how well would he be prepared to adapt to the realities of American life?

2. Is an American exchange professor, such as the one Hari Lal became infatuated with at his university, the kind of person who would provide him with the best entrée into the realities of America and Americans? If not, what kind of person, or persons, from which walks of life, would be most representative? In general, which Americans abroad are the best representatives of life here as it might be encountered by a person from another country?

3. Given Hari Lal's personality, class origins, and sensitivity to the needs of others, how capable do you think he is of being a successful sojourner in America? Make a list of the most serious problems Hari would have as a foreign student in an American university and discuss how he would probably cope with them.

4. If Hari were to return to India with an American wife, what kind of difficulties would inevitably arise between them? Between them and Hari's family?

5. Dean Barnlund argues that one of the primary sources of difficulty in adjusting to another culture is a tendency to overlook culture differences and to persuade oneself that everyone everywhere is, at base, alike; that differences among groups of people—whether cultures, subcultures, or informal groups—are merely superficial. Which of the characters in these three stories is the one most likely to ignore cultural differences while emphasizing the universality of human experience? Do you think that Barnlund's argument has any validity?

6. America is a land of numerous subcultures and of many very different ethnic groups. How might this affect the experience of a person entering American culture for the first time? How best can one prepare

for entering such a diverse culture? Would reading literary texts produced by members of the various subcultures provide sufficient help?

7. Is Julio Ramón Ribeyro's "Alienation" a reasonably faithful account of the psychology of a person who falls in love with another culture? If people are so thoroughly the creations of their own culture, as many social scientists have argued, how is it possible for anyone to be strongly attracted to another culture?

8. Among other things, Schnitzler's "America" depicts the origin and fate (at least in part) of a cultural stereotype. Some stereotypes are more substantial than others, more durable. Is there any clue in these three stories as to how a cultural stereotype is best dealt with by the person who holds it as well as by those to whom the stereotype is applied?

9. Which American television program do you think could win a prize for being the source of the most wildly inaccurate stereotypes of American life? Which could win a prize for the most accurate? Ask a person from another country for an opinion on this matter.

10. Because Americans think of their country as a "melting pot," would they be more likely than people of other countries to be sensitive to the problems of someone leaving his native culture behind and trying to adapt to a new way of life?

List of Additional Stories

Bovey, John. "The Visa." *Desirable Aliens*. Urbana, IL: U. of Illinois Press, 1980. 114-36.

Boyle, Kay. "Kroy Wen." *Thirty Stories by Kay Boyle*. New York: Simon and Schuster, 1946. 31-6.

Clemens, Samuel Langhorn. "The Belated Russian Passport." *The Complete Stories of Mark Twain*. Ed. Charles Neider. New York: Bantam, 1957. 411-26.

Conrad, Joseph. "Karain: A Memory." *Stories and Tales of Joseph Conrad*. New York: Funk & Wagnalls, 1968. 159-97.

Dygat, Stanislaw. "El viaje." ["The Trip"] *Antologia del cuento polaco contemporáneo*. Ed. Sergio Pitol. Mexico City: Ediciones Era, 1967, 46-57.

Grin, Aleksandr. Stepanovič. "Dalëkij put'." *Rasskazy*. ["Stories"] Minsk: Nauka i texnika, 1982. 17-30.

Pardo Bazán, Emilia. "John." *Obras completas*. Vol. 1. Madrid: Aguilar, 1957. 1623-26.

————————. "Sud-Express." *Obras completas*. Vol. 1. Madrid: Aguilar, 1957. 1617-19.

Phillips, Hilda. "A Matter of Degree." *Short Story International* 6.32 (1982): 95-104.

Rodriguez, Alfonso. "La otra frontera." ["The Other Border"] *Hispanics in the United States. An Anthology of Creative Literature*. Ed. Franciso Jimenez and Gary O. Keller. Vol. 2. Ypsilanti, MI: Bilingual Review Press, 1982. 3-9.

Sneider, Vern. "A Long Way from Home." *A Long Way From Home and Other Stories*. New York: NAL Signet, 1956. 67-94.

Wright, Richard. "Big Black Good Man." *Stories in Black and White*. Ed. Eva Kissin. Philadelphia: J. B. Lippincott Company, 1970. 91-107.

Yeh, Chao-chun. "Neighbors." *Contemporary Chinese Stories*. Trans. Chi-Chen Wang. New York: Greenwood Press Publishers, 1968. 174-80.

Yezierska, Anzia. "The Miracle." *The Open Cage. An Anzia Yezierska Collection*. New York: Persia Books, 1979. 3-19.

2. Spectator Phase

The EXPERIENCE OF BEING FOREIGN USUALLY BEGINS with a sense of elation or euphoria. Even when unpleasantness is involved, one's senses are more alert to the newness of the situation than they would be to an equivalent situation in the setting of the home culture. Being more alert and excited than those around him, the newly-arrived foreigner seems either innocently awkward and inept or inherently insensitive and uncaring, depending upon the native's depth of understanding of the foreigner's situation. During this phase, mistakes in understanding the hosts are easily made, and, at first, the foreigner usually considers them only minor mistakes in what he expects to be a relatively brief and uncomplicated period of adjustment. For after all, he may reason, when a person is well-intentioned and his emotions are generally positive, any misunderstanding is bound to be only momentary. He is likely not to consider how he appears to others during this period, primarily because he is so deeply involved as a spectator of all that is going on around him that he has difficulty imagining that he himself is the spectacle.

The stories in this section depict characters who have yet to emerge from the Spectator Phase of their foreign experience. The misunderstanding that they become involved in can be characterized as exaggeratedly one-sided. That is, fairly intelligent, sensitive people find that their behavior in the host culture is being regarded as unintelligent and insensitive. The resulting situation can be either comical or thoroughly unpleasant.

Paul Bowles's story, "You Have Left Your Lotus Pods on the Bus," while being a humorous treatment of a cross-cultural encounter also explores the finer gradations of cultural misperception with great subtlety. Particularly interesting is the fact that Bowles illustrates misperceptions on both sides of the cultural gap. For example, just as the Buddhist monks fail to understand the significance of neckties worn by Westerners, so the narrator and his companion fail to understand the Thai system of having two officials on each bus. Such misperceptions occur most frequently during this second phase of the cross-cultural experience, because, as Raymond Gorden and others have pointed out, it is at this point that the sojourner's inability to understand the context of events has its first strong impact.

This same problem is treated in "Odd Tippling" by Kurt Kusenberg. Having just arrived in a new country, Kusenberg's narrator enters a restaurant to refresh himself with a glass of wine: he does not bother to inquire about the price of the wine, because he naturally assumes "that it will cost no more than in other countries or in other cities." Much to his distress, he discovers that normal economic values do not seem to apply to this transaction.

With more distressing consequences, Katherine Mansfield's "The Little Governess" explores the question of whom to trust when one is vulnerable among strangers. In doing so, it represents with considerable artistry the inner experience of the Spectator Phase of being foreign: the initial excitement and anticipation, the tendency to over-interpret, and the veering from one emotion to another. Finally, in its denouement the story demonstrates the extent to which the newly arrived foreigner's reliance upon his own cultural norms can lead him astray in a different culture.

G.S. Sharat Chandra, in "Saree of the Gods," also illustrates the two faces of cross-cultural misunderstanding: the effect of the misunderstanding on the hosts and the impact of that misunderstanding on the newly arrived foreigner. In the accident which damages the hostess's saree, neither can perceive the event from the other's cultural perspective; both evaluate it in terms of their own.

Once the sojourner acquires a greater understanding of the contexts of the new culture, the kinds of mistakes made by the characters in the stories discussed above will decrease in frequency. As the sojourner spends more time in the new culture and as the number of his interpersonal relationships with the hosts increases, he moves naturally out of the role of Spectator.

Paul Bowles

You Have Left Your Lotus Pods on the Bus

I SOON LEARNED NOT TO GO NEAR THE WINDOWS or to draw aside the double curtains in order to look at the river below. The view was wide and lively, with factories and warehouses on the far side of the Chao Phraya, and strings of barges being towed up and down through the dirty water. The new wing of the hotel had been built in the shape of an upright slab, so that the room was high and had no trees to shade it from the poisonous onslaught of the afternoon sun. The end of the day, rather than bringing respite, intensified the heat, for then the entire river was made of sunlight. With the redness of dusk everything out there became melodramatic and forbidding, and still the oven heat from outside leaked through the windows.

Brooks, teaching at Chulalongkorn University, was required as a Fulbright Fellow to attend regular classes in Thai; as an adjunct to this he arranged to spend much of his leisure time with Thais. One day he brought along with him three young men wearing the bright orange-yellow robes of Buddhist monks. They filed into the hotel room in silence and stood in a row as they were presented to me, each one responding by joining his palms together, thumbs touching his chest.

Paul Bowles has recently gained increasing recognition as one of the most important American writers of this century. His accomplishments include four novels, several collections of stories and poetry, translations from the Arabic, and collections of native North African music for the Library of Congress. His stories are available in *Collected Stories 1939-1976* (1979) and *Midnight Mass* (1981).

As we talked, Yamyong, the eldest, in his late twenties, explained that he was an ordained monk, while the other two were novices. Brooks then asked Prasert and Vichai if they would be ordained soon, but the monk answered for them.

"I do not think they are expecting to be ordained," he said quietly, looking at the floor, as if it were a sore subject all too often discussed among them. He glanced up at me and went on talking. "Your room is beautiful. We are not accustomed to such luxury." His voice was flat; he was trying to conceal his disapproval. The three conferred briefly in undertones. "My friends say they have never seen such a luxurious room," he reported, watching me closely through his steel-rimmed spectacles to see my reaction. I failed to hear.

They put down their brown paper parasols and their reticules that bulged with books and fruit. Then they got themselves into position in a row along the couch among the cushions. For a while they were busy adjusting the folds of their robes around their shoulders and legs.

"They make their own clothes," volunteered Brooks. "All the monks do."

I spoke of Ceylon; there the monks bought the robes all cut and ready to sew together. Yamyong smiled appreciatively and said: "We use the same system here."

The air-conditioning roared at one end of the room and the noise of boat motors on the river seeped through the windows at the other. I looked at the three sitting in front of me. They were very calm and self-possessed, but they seemed lacking in physical health. I was aware of the facial bones beneath their skin. Was the impression of sallowness partly due to the shaved eyebrows and hair?

Yamyong was speaking. "We appreciate the opportunity to use English. For this reason we are liking to have foreign friends. English, American; it doesn't matter. We can understand." Prasert and Vichai nodded.

Time went on, and we sat there, extending but not altering the subject of conversation. Occasionally I looked around the room. Before they had come in, it had been only a hotel room whose curtains must be kept drawn. Their presence and their comments on it had managed to invest it with a vaguely disturbing quality; I felt that they considered it a great mistake on my part to have chosen such a place in which to stay.

"Look at his tattoo," said Brooks. "Show him."

Yamyong pulled back his robe a bit from the shoulder, and I saw the two indigo lines of finely written Thai characters. "That is for good health," he said, glancing up at me. His smile seemed odd, but then, his facial expression did not complement his words at any point.

"Don't the Buddhists disapprove of tattooing?" I said.

"Some people say it is backwardness." Again he smiled. "Words for good health are said to be superstition. This was done by my abbot when I was a boy studying in the *wat*. Perhaps he did not know it was a superstition."

We were about to go with them to visit the *wat* where they lived. I pulled a tie from the closet and stood before the mirror arranging it.

"Sir," Yamyong began. "Will you please explain something? What is the significance of the necktie?"

"The significance of the necktie?" I turned to face him. "You mean, why do men wear neckties?"

"No. I know that. The purpose is to look like a gentleman."

I laughed. Yamyong was not put off. "I have noticed that some men wear the two ends equal, and some wear the wide end longer than the narrow, or the narrow longer than the wide. And the neckties themselves, they are not all the same length, are they? Some even with both ends equal reach below the waist. What are the different meanings?"

"There is no meaning," I said. "Absolutely none."

He looked to Brooks for confirmation, but Brooks was trying out his Thai on Prasert and Vichai, and so he was silent and thoughtful for a moment. "I believe you, of course," he said graciously. "But we all thought each way had a different significance attached."

As we went out of the hotel, the doorman bowed respectfully. Until now he had never given a sign that he was aware of my existence. The wearers of the yellow robe carry weight in Thailand.

A few Sundays later I agreed to go with Brooks and our friends to Ayudhaya. The idea of a Sunday outing is so repellent to me that deciding to take part in this one was to a certain extent a compulsive act. Ayudhaya lies less than fifty miles up the Chao Phraya from Bangkok. For historians and art collectors it is more than just a provincial town; it is a period and a style—having been the Thai capital for more than four centuries. Very likely it still would be, had the Burmese not laid it waste in the eighteenth century.

Brooks came early to fetch me. Downstairs in the street stood the three bhikkus with their book bags and parasols. They hailed a cab, and without any previous price arrangements (the ordinary citizen tries to fix a sum beforehand) we got in and drove for twenty minutes or a half-hour, until we got to a bus terminal on the northern outskirts of the city.

It was a nice, old-fashioned, open bus. Every part of it rattled, and the air from the rice fields blew across us as we pieced together our bits of synthetic conversation. Brooks, in high spirits, kept calling across to me: "Look! Water buffaloes!" As we went further away from Bangkok there were more of the beasts, and his cries became more frequent. Yamyong, sitting next to me, whispered: "Professor Brooks is fond of buffaloes?" I laughed and said I didn't think so.

"Then?"

I said that in America there were no buffaloes in the fields, and that was why Brooks was interested in seeing them. There were no temples in the landscape, either, I told him, and added, perhaps unwisely: "He looks at buffaloes. I look at temples." This struck Yamyong as hilarious, and he made allusions to it now and then all during the day.

The road stretched ahead, straight as a line in geometry, across the verdant, level land. Paralleling it on its eastern side was a fairly wide canal, here and there choked with patches of enormous pink lotuses. In places the flowers were gone and only the pods remained, thick green disks with the circular seeds embedded in their flesh. At the first stop the bhikkus got out. They came aboard again with mangosteens and lotus pods and insisted on giving us large numbers of each. The huge seeds popped out of the fibrous lotus cakes as though from a punchboard; they tasted almost like green almonds. "Something new for you today, I think," Yamyong said with a satisfied air.

Ayudhaya was hot, dusty, spread-out, its surrounding terrain strewn with ruins that scarcely showed through the vegetation. At some distance from the town there began a wide boulevard sparingly lined with important-looking buildings. It continued for a way and then came to an end as abrupt as its beginning. Growing up out of the scrub, and built of small russet-colored bricks, the ruined temples looked still unfinished rather than damaged by time. Repairs, done in smeared cement, veined their facades.

The bus's last stop was still two or three miles from the center of Ayudhaya. We got down into the dust, and Brooks declared: "The first thing we must do is find food. They can't eat anything solid, you know, after midday."

"Not noon exactly," Yamyong said. "Maybe one o'clock or a little later."

"Even so, that doesn't leave much time," I told him. "It's quarter to twelve now."

But the bhikkus were not hungry. None of them had visited Ayudhaya before, and so they had compiled a list of things they most wanted to see. They spoke with a man who had a station wagon parked nearby, and we set off for a ruined *stupa* that lay some miles to the southwest. It had been built atop a high mound, which we climbed with some difficulty, so that Brooks could take pictures of us standing within a fissure in the decayed outer wall. The air stank of the bats that lived inside.

When we got back to the bus stop, the subject of food arose once again, but the excursion had put the bhikkus into such a state of excitement that they could not bear to allot time for anything but looking. We went to the museum. It was quiet; there were Khmer heads and documents inscribed in Pali. The day had begun to be painful. I told myself I had known beforehand that it would.

Then we went to a temple. I was impressed, not so much by the gigantic Buddha which all but filled the interior, as by the fact that not far from the entrance a man sat on the floor playing a *ranad* (pronounced *lanat*). Although I was familiar with the sound of it from listening to recordings of Siamese music, I had never before seen the instrument. There was a graduated series of wooden blocks strung together, the whole slung like a hammock over a boat-shaped resonating stand. The tones hurried after one another like drops of water falling very fast. After the painful heat outside, everything in the temple suddenly seemed a symbol of the concept of coolness—the stone floor under my bare feet, the breeze that moved through the shadowy interior, the bamboo fortune sticks being rattled in their long box by those praying at the altar, and the succession of insubstantial, glassy sounds that came from the *ranad*. I thought: If only I could get something to eat, I wouldn't mind the heat so much.

We got into the center of Ayudhaya a little after three o'clock. It was hot and noisy; the bhikkus had no idea of where to look for a restaurant, and the prospect of asking did not appeal to them. The five of us walked aimlessly. I had come to the conclusion that neither Prasert nor Vichai understood spoken English, and I addressed myself earnestly to Yamyong. "We've got to eat." He stared at me with severity. "We are searching," he told me.

Eventually we found a Chinese restaurant on a corner of the principal street. There was a table full of boisterous Thais drinking *mekong* (categorized as whiskey, but with the taste of cheap rum) and another table occupied by an entire Chinese family. These people were doing some serious eating, their faces buried in their rice bowls. It cheered me to see them: I was faint, and had half expected to be told that there was no hot food available.

The large menu in English which was brought us must have been typed several decades ago and wiped with a damp rag once a week ever since. Under the heading SPECIALTIES were some dishes that caught my eye, and as I went through the list I began to laugh. Then I read it aloud to Brooks.

"FRIED SHARKS FINS AND BEAN SPROUT

CHICKEN CHINS STUFFED WITH SHRIMP

FRIED RICE BIRDS

SHRIMPS BALLS AND GREEN MARROW

PIGS LIGHTS WITH PICKLES

BRAKED RICE BIRD IN PORT WINE

FISH HEAD AND BEAN CURD"

Although it was natural for our friends not to join in the laughter, I felt that their silence was not merely failure to respond; it was heavy, positive.

A moment later three Pepsi-Cola bottles were brought and placed on the table. "What are you going to have?" Brooks asked Yamyong.

"Nothing, thank you," he said lightly. "This will be enough for us today."

"But this is terrible! You mean no one is going to eat *anything?*"

"You and your friend will eat your food," said Yamyong. (He might as well have said "fodder.") Then he, Prasert, and Vichai stood up, and carrying their Pepsi-Cola bottles with them, went to sit at a table on the other side of the room. Now and then Yamyong smiled sternly across at us.

"I wish they'd stop watching us," Brooks said under his breath.

"They were the ones who kept putting it off," I reminded him. But I felt guilty, and I was annoyed at finding myself placed in the position of the self-indulgent unbeliever. It was almost as bad as eating in front of Moslems during Ramadan.

We finished our meal and set out immediately, following Yamyong's decision to visit a certain temple he wanted to see. The taxi drive led us through a region of thorny scrub. Here and there, in the shade of spreading flat-topped trees, were great round pits, full of dark water and crowded with buffaloes; only their wet snouts and horns were visible. Brooks was already crying: "Buffaloes! Hundreds of them!" He asked the taxi driver to stop so that he could photograph the animals.

"You will have buffaloes at the temple," said Yamyong. He was right; there was a muddy pit filled with them only a few hundred feet from the building. Brooks went and took his pictures while the bhikkus paid their routine visit to the shrine. I wandered into a courtyard where there was a long row of stone Buddhas. It is the custom of temple-goers to plaster little squares of gold leaf into the religious statues in the *wats*. When thousands of them have been stuck onto the same surface, tiny scraps of the gold come unstuck. Then they tremble in the breeze, and the figure shimmers with a small, vibrant life of its own. I stood in the courtyard watching this quivering along the arms and torsos of the Buddhas, and I was reminded of the motion of the bô-tree's leaves. When I mentioned it to Yamyong in the taxi, I think he failed to understand, for he replied: "The bô-tree is a very great tree for Buddhists."

Brooks sat beside me on the bus going back to Bangkok. We spoke only now and then. After so many hours of resisting the heat, it was relaxing to sit and feel the relatively cool air that blew in from the rice fields. The driver of the bus was not a believer in cause and effect. He passed trucks with oncoming traffic in full view. I felt better with my eyes shut, and I might even have dozed off, had there not been in the back of the bus a man, obviously not in control, who was intent on making as much noise as possible. He began to shout, scream, and howl almost as soon as we had left Ayudhaya, and he did this consistently throughout the journey. Brooks and I laughed about it, conjecturing whether he was crazy or only drunk. The aisle was too crowded for me to be able to see him from where I sat. Occasionally I glanced at the other passengers. It was as though they were entirely unaware of the commotion behind them. As we drew closer to the city, the screams became louder and almost constant.

"God, why don't they throw him off?" Brooks was beginning to be annoyed.

"They don't even hear him," I said bitterly. People who can tolerate noise inspire me with envy and rage. Finally I leaned over and said to Yamyong: "That poor man back there! It's incredible!"

"Yes," he said over his shoulder. "He's very busy." This set me thinking what a civilized and tolerant people they were, and I marvelled at the sophistication of the word "busy" to describe what was going on in the back of the bus.

Finally we were in a taxi driving across Bangkok. I would be dropped at my hotel and Brooks would take the three bhikkus on to their *wat*. In my head I was still hearing the heartrending cries. What had the repeated word patterns meant?

I had not been able to give an acceptable answer to Yamyong in his bewilderment about the significance of the necktie, but perhaps he could satisfy my curiosity here.

"That man in the back of the bus, you know?"

Yamyong nodded. "He was working very hard, poor fellow. Sunday is a bad day."

I disregarded the nonsense. "What was he saying?"

"Oh, he was saying: 'Go into second gear,' or 'We are coming to a bridge,' or 'Be careful, people in the road.' What he saw."

Since neither Brooks nor I appeared to have understood, he went on. "All the buses must have a driver's assistant. He watches the road and tells the driver how to drive. It is hard work because he must shout loud enough for the driver to hear him."

"But why doesn't he sit up in front with the driver?"

"No, no. There must be one in front and one in the back. That way two men are responsible for the bus."

It was an unconvincing explanation for the grueling sounds we had heard, but to show him that I believed him I said: "Aha! I see."

The taxi drew up in front of the hotel and I got out. When I said good-by to Yamyong, he replied, I think with a shade of aggrievement: "Good-by. You have left your lotus pods on the bus."

Kurt Kusenberg

Odd Tippling

I ARRIVED AT THE BORDER ABOUT TEN in the morning. The customs officials examined my papers and had me count my money under their noses. Since it was considerable, I was permitted to cross without further ado. Travelers with a flimsy purse find no entry into Paturia.

For no more than an hour, I had decided, I would hike on, and then rest. I had been under way since early morning. I could have used a horse, or the carriage, but all my life I have enjoyed traveling in foreign countries on foot. Step by step I enter into them, their earth beneath the soles of my shoes. It gave me a sensual pleasure, even when I grew tired as a result; and besides, who sees more than the hiker?

One hour became two, but I still had not come to a town. The countryside was hilly with red fields. Olive trees stood out silver-green against the darker vineyards, and where someone's property ended it was edged by a low stone wall. I was just about to take a break at the side of the road somewhere when a bell sounded the noon hour. At the next turn in the road I saw the village lying there before me.

It was a good-sized place; three taverns bordered the square before the church. Trusting to luck I entered one of them, sat down in the restaurant, and asked for a glass of wine. The innkeeper placed it before me. I said a few words about the weather, about the region, and some-

Writer, art critic, and editor, *Kurt Kusenberg* (b. 1904) is sometimes described as a "Paul Klee in literature" because of his striking ability to transform our everyday world into something strange through his humor and fantasy.

thing in praise of the wine as well. But he remained silent. He looked me over, ran his hand across his mouth, and left. I heard him send out a maid to get the mayor.

The wine was good; it was a heavy one, and rose to my head. And my exhaustion, as well as the fact that I had had nothing to eat intensified its effect. I felt a great sense of well-being which, however, was not to last very long. Even before I had emptied my glass, the mayor appeared, a solid, robust man of sixty, and joined me at my table. He had not come alone. There were many men and women crowding into the restaurant and at least an equal number standing outside and peering at me through the window.

The mayor asked me if I knew what a glass of wine cost. I said no. Then he mentioned a figure so monstrous that I paled. All the money I had with me was a mere hundredth of what was being asked. I replied that the charge was extremely high. When one sits down for a glass of wine one instinctively assumes that it will cost no more than in other countries or in other cities.

The mayor's face became gloomy. What was true elsewhere, he said, was not true in his village, and what I called instinctive assumption was on the contrary something quite arbitrary. Why hadn't I inquired about the cost before I ordered the glass of wine? And now it was too late, of course. I would have to pay the full bill, or, if I were unable to, work for the innkeeper until I had made it good. That might take, the mayor added, a good five years.

I was frightened. I had come to Paturia as an idle and happy traveler, and now I was suddenly faced by long harsh forced labor. It was inconceivable. I emptied my glass and sank into gloomy brooding. The mayor didn't take his eyes off me. The men and women watched me half in sympathy and half in greed, and the innkeeper busied himself among his tables.

A man who is lost anyway doesn't give a damn whether he's hanged for a sheep or a goat. So I asked the innkeeper to bring me a second glass of wine. I intended to numb myself like a poor criminal before that final walk. The innkeeper cast an angry glance at me and shuffled away; a few spectators laughed. When the wine stood before me the mayor cleared his throat as though he were about to say something. But someone must have signaled to him, for he kept his words to himself. The people in the room and the ones outside the window glanced in turn from me to the innkeeper and whispered to themselves. I drained the glass in a single swallow and immediately demanded a third, let come what might! The wine had muddled my thinking. I was no longer quite as depressed as before, but I was nonetheless very unhappy.

The innkeeper also had a sad face when he brought me the wine. Then he sat down in the nearest chair and hung his head. The people who had been laughing at him were now laughing no more. The mayor cleared his throat. Even the second glass of wine, he explained, had appreciably lowered my bill, for two glasses of wine were much cheaper than a single one. But still the check would have been high, and my purse would probably have suffered greatly in paying it. The third glass of wine, on the other hand, had created a very different situation. I was no longer in the innkeeper's debt, but he was in mine—and by just as much as I had been in his at the beginning. Henceforth the tavern belonged to me, as well as a vineyard and a large field; in short, everything the innkeeper owned. This sounded good to my ears, at least better than what I had heard previously. I took a sip of wine; it tasted delightful.

The mayor continued: he wondered whether I could bring myself to marry the innkeeper's young daughter. It would be a good solution, for as the son-in-law of my creditor I would be sure to look out for him. And then the girl herself came to our table, a pretty, shapely creature, and sank her dark-eyed glance deep into my own eyes. I grew very confused. To exploit the situation was against my better nature, yet the girl's charm was great. I felt that everyone around me was waiting breathlessly to see what my choice would be; it did, after all, concern the fate of their own fellow citizen. My confusion increased. Although I felt the wine working on me, I ordered a fourth glass to gain some time.

The innkeeper sprang up and ran to the bar; with a smile he brought me my wine. The spectators left the restaurant, no one was standing outside the window any longer, and when I turned back to my table the girl had also vanished. Only the mayor was still sitting there. But he also rose, wished me a pleasant trip, and left. I couldn't understand it. Uncertain what would happen now, I emptied my fourth glass of wine and asked the innkeeper what my bill was. He named a figure that was nothing unusual at all; four glasses of wine cost that much anywhere. I counted out my coins onto the table in relief.

Meanwhile it had become one o'clock, just the proper time to eat lunch. But I had no desire to surrender to a new adventure, and so I stepped out into the street. As quickly as I could I strode through the village and rejoiced when it lay behind me.

Translated from the German by David B. Dickens

Katherine Mansfield

The Little Governess

OH, DEAR, HOW SHE WISHED that it wasn't night-time. She'd have much rather traveled by day, much much rather. But the lady at the Governess Bureau had said: "You had better take an evening boat and then if you get into a compartment for 'Ladies Only' in the train you will be far safer than sleeping in a foreign hotel. Don't go out of the carriage; don't walk about the corridors and *be sure* to lock the lavatory door if you go there. The train arrives at Munich at eight o'clock, and Frau Arnholdt says that the Hotel Grunewald is only one minute away. A porter can take you there. She will arrive at six the same evening so you will have a nice quiet day to rest after the journey and rub up your German. And when you want anything to eat I would advise you to pop into the nearest baker's and get a bun and some coffee. You haven't been abroad before, have you?" "No." "Well, I always tell my girls that it's better to mistrust people at first rather than trust them, and it's safer to suspect people of evil intentions rather than good ones. . . . It sounds rather hard but we've got to be women of the world, haven't we?"

It had been nice in the Ladies' Cabin. The stewardess was so kind and changed her money for her and tucked up her feet. She lay on one of the hard pink-sprigged couches and watched the other passengers, friend-

Katherine Mansfield (1888-1923), born in New Zealand and educated in England, is generally regarded as one of the principal founders of the modern short story. Her stories are available in *The Short Stories of Katherine Mansfield* (1980).

ly and natural, pinning their hats to the bolsters, taking off their boots and skirts, opening dressing-cases and arranging mysterious rustling little packages, tying their heads up in veils before lying down. *Thud, thud, thud,* went the steady screw of the steamer. The stewardess pulled a green shade over the light and sat down by the stove, her skirt turned back over her knees, a long piece of knitting on her lap. On a shelf above her head there was a water-bottle with a tight bunch of flowers stuck in it. "I like traveling very much," thought the little governess. She smiled and yielded to the warm rocking.

But when the boat stopped and she went up on deck, her dress-basket in one hand, her rug and umbrella in the other, a cold, strange wind flew under her hat. She looked up at the masts and spars of the ship black against a green glittering sky and down to the dark landing stage where strange muffled figures lounged, waiting; she moved forward with the sleepy flock, all knowing where to go to and what to do except her, and she felt afraid. Just a little—just enough to wish—oh, to wish that it was daytime and that one of those women who had smiled at her in the glass, when they both did their hair in the Ladies' Cabin, was somewhere near now. "Tickets, please. Show your tickets. Have your tickets ready." She went down the gangway balancing herself carefully on her heels. Then a man in a black leather cap came forward and touched her on the arm. "Where for, Miss?" He spoke English—he must be a guard or a stationmaster with a cap like that. She had scarcely answered when he pounced on her dress-basket. "This way," he shouted, in a rude, determined voice, and elbowing his way he strode past the people. "But I don't want a porter." What a horrible man! "I don't want a porter. I want to carry it myself." She had to run to keep up with him, and her anger, far stronger than she, ran before her and snatched the bag out of the wretch's hand. He paid no attention at all, but swung on down the long dark platform, and across a railway line. "He is a robber." She was sure he was a robber as she stepped between the silvery rails and felt the cinders crunch under her shoes. On the other side—oh, thank goodness!—there was a train with Munich written on it. The man stopped by the huge lighted carriages. "Second class?" asked the insolent voice. "Yes, a Ladies' compartment." She was quite out of breath. She opened her little purse to find something small enough to give this horrible man while he tossed her dress-basket into the rack of an empty carriage that had a ticket, *Dames Seules,* gummed on the window. She got into the train and handed him twenty centimes. "What's this?" shouted the man, glaring at the money and then at her, holding it up to his nose, sniffing at it as though he had never in his life seen, much less held, such a sum. "It's a franc. You know that, don't you? It's a franc. That's my fare!" A franc! Did he imagine that she was going to give him a franc for playing a trick like that just because she was a girl and traveling alone at night? Never, never! She squeezed her purse in her hand and simply did not see him—she looked at a view of St. Malo on the wall opposite and simply did not hear him. "Ah, no. Ah, no. Four sous. You make a mistake. Here, take it. It's a franc I want." He leapt on the step of the train and threw the money on to her lap. Trembling with terror she screwed herself tight, tight, and put out an icy hand and took the money—stowed it away in her hand. "That's all you're going to get," she said. For a minute or two she felt his sharp eyes pricking her all over, while he nodded slowly, pulling down his mouth: "Very-well. *Trés bien.*" He shrugged his shoulders and disappeared into the dark. Oh, the relief! How simply terrible that had been! As she stood up to feel if the dress-basket was firm she caught sight of herself in the mirror, quite white, with big round eyes. She untied her "motor veil" and unbuttoned her green cape. "But it's all over now," she said to the mirror face, feeling in some way that it was more frightened than she.

People began to assemble on the platform. They stood together in little groups talking; a strange light from the station lamps painted their faces almost green. A little boy in red clattered up with a huge tea wagon and leaned against it, whistling and flicking his boots with a serviette. A woman in a black alpaca apron pushed a barrow with pillows for hire. Dreamy and vacant she looked—like a woman wheeling a perambulator—up and down, up and down—with a sleeping baby inside it. Wreaths of white smoke floated up from somewhere and hung below the roof like misty vines. "How strange it all is," thought the little governess, "and the middle of the night, too." She looked out from her safe corner, frightened no longer but proud that she had not given the franc. "I can look after myself—of course I can. The great thing is not to—." Suddenly from the corridor there came stamping of feet and men's voices, high and broken with snatches of loud laughter. They were coming her way. The little governess shrank into her corner as four young men in bowler hats passed, staring through the door and window. One of them, bursting with the joke, pointed to the notice *Dames Seules* and the four bent down the better to see the one little girl in the corner. Oh dear, they were in the carriage next door. She heard them tramping about and then a sudden hush followed by a tall thin fellow with a tiny black moustache who flung her door open. "If mademoiselle cares to come in with us," he said, in French. She saw the others crowding behind, peeping under his arm and over his shoulder, and she sat very straight and still. "If mademoiselle will do us the honour," mocked the tall man. One of them could be quiet no longer; his laughter went off in a loud crack. "Mademoiselle is serious," persisted the young man, bowing and grimacing. He took off his hat with a flourish, and she was alone again.

"*En voiture. En voi-ture!*" Some one ran up and down beside the train. "I wish it wasn't night-time. I wish there was another woman in the carriage. I'm frightened of the men next door." The little governess looked out to see her porter coming back again—the same man making for her carriage with his arms full of luggage. But—but what was he doing? He put his thumb nail under the label *Dames Seules* and tore it right off and then stood aside squinting at her while an old man wrapped in a plaid cape climbed up the high step. "But this is a ladies' compartment." "Oh, no, Mademoiselle, you make a mistake. No, no, I assure you. Merci, Monsieur." "*En voi-turre!*" A shrill whistle. The porter stepped off triumphant and the train started. For a moment or two big tears brimmed her eyes and through them she saw the old man unwinding a scarf from his neck and untying the flaps of his Jaeger cap. He looked very old. Ninety at least. He had a white moustache and big gold-rimmed spectacles with little blue eyes behind them and pink wrinkled cheeks. A nice face—and charming the way he bent forward and said in halting French: "Do I disturb you, Mademoiselle? Would you rather I took all these things out of the rack and found another carriage?" What! That old man have to move all those heavy things just because she . . . "No, it's quite all right. You don't disturb me at all." "Ah, a thousand thanks." He sat down opposite her and unbuttoned the cape of his enormous coat and flung it off his shoulders.

The train seemed glad to have left the station. With a long leap it sprang into the dark. She rubbed a place in the window with her glove but she could see nothing—just a tree outspread like a black fan or a scatter of lights, or the line of a hill, solemn and huge. In the carriage next door the young men started singing "*Un, deux, trois.*" They sang the same song over and at the tops of their voices.

"I never could have dared to go to sleep if I had been alone," she decided. "I *couldn't* have put my feet up or even taken off my hat." The singing gave her a queer little tremble in her stomach and, hugging herself to stop it, with her arms crossed under her cape, she felt really glad to have the old man in the carriage with her. Careful to see that he was not looking she peeped at him through her long lashes. He sat extremely upright, the chest thrown out, the chin well in, knees pressed together, reading a German paper. That was why he spoke French so funnily. He was a German. Something in the army, she supposed—a Colonel or a General—once, of course, not now; he was too old for that now. How spic and span he looked for an old man. He wore a pearl pin stuck in his black tie and a ring with a dark red stone on his little finger; the tip of a white silk handkerchief showed in the pocket of his double-breasted jacket. Somehow, altogether, he was really nice to look at. Most old men were so horrid. She couldn't bear them doddery—or they had a disgusting cough or something. But not having a beard—that made all the difference—and then his cheeks were so pink and his moustache so very white. Down went the German paper and the old man leaned forward with the same delightful courtesy: "Do you speak German Mademoiselle?" "*Ja, ein wenig, mehr als Französisch,*" said the little governess, blushing a deep color that spread slowly over her cheeks and made her blue eyes look almost black. "Ach, so!" The old man bowed graciously. "Then perhaps you would care to look at some illustrated papers." He slipped a rubber band from a little roll of them and handed them across. "Thank you very much." She was very fond of looking at pictures, but first she would take off her hat and gloves. So she stood up, unpinned the brown straw and put it neatly in the rack beside the dress-basket, stripped off her brown kid gloves, paired them in a tight roll and put them in the crown of the hat for safety, and then sat down again, more comfortable this time, her feet crossed, the papers on her lap. How kindly the old man in the corner watched her bare little hand turning over the big white pages, watched her lips moving as she pronounced the long words to herself, rested upon her hair that fairly blazed under the light. Alas! how tragic for a little governess to possess hair that made one think of tangerines and marigolds, of apricots and tortoise-shell cats and champagne! Perhaps that was what the old man was thinking as he gazed and gazed, and that not even the dark ugly clothes could disguise her soft beauty. Perhaps the flush that licked his cheeks and lips was a flush of rage that anyone so young and tender should have to travel alone and unprotected through the night. Who knows he was not murmuring in his sentimental German fashion: "*Ja, es ist eine Tragödie!* Would to God I were the child's grandpapa!"

"Thank you very much. They were very interesting." She smiled prettily handing back the papers. "But you speak German extremely well," said the old man. "You have been in Germany before, of course?" "Oh no, this is the first time"—a little pause, then—"this is the first time that I have ever been abroad at all." "Really! I am surprised. You gave me the impression, if I may say so, that you were accustomed to traveling." "Oh, well—I have been about a good deal in England, and to Scotland, once." "So. I myself have been in England once, but I could not learn English." He raised one hand and shook his head, laughing. "No, it was too difficult for me. . . . 'Ow-do-you-do. Please vich is ze vay to Leicestaire Square.'" She laughed too. "Foreigners always say . . ." They had quite a little talk about it. "But you will like Munich," said the old man. "Munich is a wonderful city. Museums, pictures, galleries, fine buildings and shops, concerts, theatres, restaurants—all are in Munich. I have travelled all over Europe many, many times in my life, but it is always to

Munich that I return. You will enjoy yourself there." "I am not going to
stay in Munich," said the little governess, and she added shyly, "I am
going to a post as governess to a doctor's family in Augsburg." "Ah, that
was it." Augsburg he knew. Augsburg—well—was not beautiful. A solid
manufacturing town. But if Germany was new to her he hoped she would
find something interesting there too. "I am sure I shall." "But what a pity
not to see Munich before you go. You ought to take a little holiday on
your way"—he smiled —"and store up some pleasant memories." "I am
afraid I could not do that," said the little governess, shaking her head,
suddenly important and serious. "And also, if one is alone . . ." He quite
understood. He bowed, serious too. They were silent after that. The train
shattered on, baring its dark, flaming breast to the hills and to the valleys.
It was warm in the carriage. She seemed to lean against the dark rushing
and to be carried away and away. Little sounds made themselves heard;
steps in the corridor, doors opening and shutting—a murmur of voices—
whistling. . . . Then the window was pricked with long needles of
rain. . . . But it did not matter . . . it was outside . . . and she had her
umbrella . . . she pouted, sighed, opened and shut her hands once and fell
fast asleep.

"Pardon! Pardon!" The sliding back of the carriage door woke her
with a start. What had happened? Some one had come in and gone out
again. The old man sat in his corner, more upright than ever, his hands in
the pockets of his coat, frowning heavily. "Ha! ha! ha!" came from the
carriage next door. Still half asleep, she put her hands to her hair to make
sure it wasn't a dream. "Disgraceful!" muttered the old man more to
himself than to her. "Common, vulgar fellows! I am afraid they disturbed
you, gracious Fräulein, blundering in here like that." No, not really. She
was just going to wake up, and she took out her silver watch to look at the
time. Half-past four. A cold blue light filled the window panes. Now
when she rubbed a place she could see bright patches of fields, a clump of
white houses like mushrooms, a road "like a picture" with poplar trees on
either side, a thread of river. How pretty it was! How pretty and how
different! Even those pink clouds in the sky looked foreign. It was cold,
but she pretended that it was far colder and rubbed her hands together
and shivered, pulling at the collar of her coat because she was so happy.

The train began to slow down. The engine gave a long shrill whistle.
They were coming to a town. Taller houses, pink and yellow, glided by,
fast asleep behind their green eyelids, and guarded by the poplar trees that
quivered in the blue air as if on tiptoe, listening. In one house a woman
opened the shutters, flung a red and white mattress across the window
frame and stood staring at the train. A pale woman with black hair and a
white woolen shawl over her shoulders. More women appeared at the

doors and at the windows of the sleeping houses. There came a flock of sheep. The shepherd wore a blue blouse and pointed wooden shoes. Look! look what flowers—and by the railway station too! Standard roses like bridesmaids' bouquets, white geraniums, waxy pink ones that you would *never* see out of a greenhouse at home. Slower and slower. A man with a watering-can was spraying the platform. "A-a-a-ah!" Somebody came running and waving his arms. A huge fat woman waddled through the glass doors of the station with a tray of strawberries. Oh, she was thirsty! She was very thirsty! "A-a-a-ah!" The same somebody ran back again. The train stopped.

The old man pulled his coat round him and got up, smiling at her. He murmured something she didn't quite catch, but she smiled back at him as he left the carriage. While he was away the little governess looked at herself again in the glass, shook and patted herself with the precise practical care of a girl who is old enough to travel by herself and has nobody else to assure her that she is "quite all right behind." Thirsty and thirsty! The air tasted of water. She let down the window and the fat woman with the strawberries passed as if on purpose; holding up the tray to her. "*Nein, danke,*" said the little governess, looking at the big berries on their gleaming leaves. "*Wie viel?*" she asked as the fat woman moved away. "Two marks fifty, Fräulein." "Good gracious!" She came in from the window and sat down in the corner, very sobered for a minute. Half a crown! "H-o-o-o-o-o-e-e-e!" shrieked the train, gathering itself together to be off again. She hoped the old man wouldn't be left behind. Oh, it was daylight—everything was lovely if only she hadn't been so thirsty. Where was the old man—oh, here he was—she dimpled at him as though he were an old accepted friend as he closed the door and, turning, took from under his cape a basket of the strawberries. "If Fräulein would honour me by accepting these . . ." "What, for me?" But she drew back and raised her hands as though he were about to put a wild little kitten on her lap.

"Certainly, for you," said the old man. "For myself it is twenty years since I was brave enough to eat strawberries." "Oh, thank you very much. *Danke bestens,*" she stammered, "*Sie sind so sehr schön!*" "Eat them and see," said the old man looking pleased and friendly. "You won't have even one?" "No, no, no." Timidly and charmingly her hand hovered. They were so big and juicy she had to take two bites to them—the juice ran all down her fingers —and it was while she munched the berries that she first thought of the old man as a grandfather. What a perfect grandfather he would make! Just like one out of a book!

The sun came out, the pink clouds in the sky, the strawberry clouds were eaten by the blue. "Are they good?" asked the old man. "As good as they look?"

When she had eaten them she felt she had known him for years. She

told him about Frau Arnholdt and how she had got the place. Did he
know the Hotel Grunewald? Frau Arnholdt would not arrive until the
evening. He listened, listened until he knew as much about the affair as
she did, until he said—not looking at her—but smoothing the palms of his
brown suede gloves together: "I wonder if you would let me show you a
little of Munich today. Nothing much—but just perhaps a picture gallery
and the Englischer Garten. It seems such a pity that you should have to
spend the day at the hotel, and also a little uncomfortable . . . in a strange
place. *Nicht wahr?* You would be back there by the early afternoon or
whenever you wish, of course, and you would give an old man a great
deal of pleasure."

It was not until long after she had said "Yes"— because the moment
she had said it and he had thanked her he began telling her about his
travels in Turkey and attar of roses—that she wondered whether she had
done wrong. After all, she really did not know him. But he was so old and
he had been so very kind—not to mention the strawberries. . . . And she
couldn't have explained the reason why she said "No," and it was her *last*
day in a way, her last day to really enjoy herself in. "Was I wrong? Was I?"
A drop of sunlight fell into her hands and lay there, warm and quivering.
"If I might accompany you as far as the hotel," he suggested, "and call for
you again at about ten o'clock." He took out his pocket-book and handed
her a card. "Herr Regierungsrat. . . ." He had a title! Well, it was bound
to be all right! So after that the little governess gave herself up to the
excitement of being really abroad, to looking out and reading the foreign
advertisement signs, to being told about the places they came to—having
her attention and enjoyment looked after by the charming old grandfather—until they reached Munich and the Hauptbahnhof. "Porter! Porter!" He found her a porter, disposed of his own luggage in a few words,
guided her through the bewildering crowd out of the station down the
clean white steps into the white road to the hotel. He explained who she
was to the manager as though all this had been bound to happen, and
then for one moment her little hand lost itself in the big brown suede ones.
"I will call for you at ten o'clock." He was gone.

"This way, Fräulein," said a waiter, who had been dodging behind
the manager's back, all eyes and ears for the strange couple. She followed
him up two flights of stairs into a dark bedroom. He dashed down her
dress-basket and pulled up a clattering, dusty blind. Ugh! what an ugly,
cold room—what enormous furniture! Fancy spending the day in here!
"Is this the room Frau Arnholdt ordered?" asked the little governess. The
waiter had a curious way of staring as if there was something funny about
her. He pursed up his lips about to whistle, and then changed his mind.
"*Gewiss,*" he said. Well, why didn't he go? Why did he stare so? "*Gehen
Sie,*" said the little governess, with frigid English simplicity. His little eyes,

like currants, nearly popped out of his doughy cheeks. "*Gehen Sie so-fort,*" she repeated icily. At the door he turned. "And the gentleman," said he, "shall I show the gentleman upstairs when he comes?"

Over the white streets big white clouds fringed with silver—and sunshine everywhere. Fat, fat coachmen driving fat cabs; funny women with little round hats cleaning the tramway lines; people laughing and pushing against one another; trees on both sides of the streets and every-where you looked almost, immense fountains; a noise of laughing from the footpaths or the middle of the streets or the open windows. And beside her, more beautifully brushed than ever, with a rolled umbrella in one hand and yellow gloves instead of brown ones, her grandfather who had asked her to spend the day. She wanted to run, she wanted to hang on his arm, she wanted to cry every minute, "Oh, I am so frightfully happy!" He guided her across the roads, stood still while she "looked," and his kind eyes beamed on her and he said "just whatever you wish." She ate two white sausages and two little rolls of fresh bread at eleven o'clock in the morning and she drank some beer, which he told her wasn't intoxicat-ing, wasn't at all like English beer, out of a glass like a flower vase. And then they took a cab and really she must have seen thousands and thou-sands of wonderful classical pictures in about a quarter of an hour! "I shall have to think them over when I am alone." . . . But when they came out of the picture gallery it was raining. The grandfather unfurled his umbrella and held it over the little governess. They started to walk to the restaurant for lunch. She, very close beside him so that he should have some of the umbrella, too. "It goes easier," he remarked in a detached way, "if you take my arm, Fräulein. And besides it is the custom in Germany." So she took his arm and walked beside him while he pointed out the famous statues, so interested that he quite forgot to put down the umbrella even when the rain was long over.

After lunch they went to a café to hear a gipsy band, but she did not like that at all. Ugh! such horrible men were there with heads like eggs and cuts on their faces, so she turned her chair and cupped her burning cheeks in her hands and watched her old friend instead. . . . Then they went to the Englischer Garten.

"I wonder what the time is," asked the little governess. "My watch has stopped. I forgot to wind it in the train last night. We've seen such a lot of things that I feel it must be quite late." "Late!" He stopped in front of her laughing and shaking his head in a way she had begun to know. "Then you have not really enjoyed yourself. Late! Why, we have not had any ice cream yet!" "Oh, but I have enjoyed myself," she cried, distressed, "more than I can possibly say. It has been wonderful! Only Frau Arnholdt is to be at the hotel at six and I ought to be there by five." "So you shall. After the ice cream I shall put you into a cab and you can go there comfortably." She was happy again. The chocolate ice cream melted—melted in little sips a long way down. The shadows of the trees danced on the table cloths, and she sat with her back safely turned to the ornamental clock that pointed to twenty-five minutes to seven. "Really and truly," said the little governess earnestly, "this has been the happiest day of my life. I've never even imagined such a day." In spite of the ice cream her grateful baby heart glowed with love for the fairy grandfather.

So they walked out of the garden down a long alley. The day was nearly over. "You see those big buildings opposite," said the old man. "The third storey—that is where I live. I and the old housekeeper who looks after me." She was very interested. "Now just before I find a cab for you, will you come and see my little 'home' and let me give you a bottle of the attar of roses I told you about in the train? For remembrance?" She would love to. "I've never seen a bachelor's flat in my life," laughed the little governess.

The passage was quite dark. "Ah, I suppose my old woman has gone out to buy me a chicken. One moment." He opened a door and stood aside for her to pass, a little shy but curious, into a strange room. She did not know quite what to say. It wasn't pretty. In a way it was very ugly—but neat, and, she supposed, comfortable for such an old man. "Well, what do you think of it?" He knelt down and took from a cupboard a round tray with two pink glasses and a tall pink bottle. "Two little bedrooms beyond," he said gaily, "and a kitchen. It's enough, eh?" "Oh, quite enough." "And if ever you should be in Munich and care to spend a day or two—why there is always a little nest—a wing of a chicken, and a salad, and an old man delighted to be your host once more and many many times, dear little Fräulein!" He took the stopper out of the bottle and poured some wine into the two pink glasses. His hand shook and the wine spilled over the tray. It was very quiet in the room. She said: "I think I ought to go now." "But you will have a tiny glass of wine with me—just one before you go?" said the old man. "No, really no. I never drink wine. I—I have promised never to touch wine or anything like that." And though he pleaded and though she felt dreadfully rude, especially when he seemed to take it to heart so, she was quite determined. "No, *really*, please." "Well, will you just sit down on the sofa for five minutes and let me drink your health?" The little governess sat down on the edge of the red velvet couch and he sat down beside her and drank her health at a gulp. "Have you really been happy today?" asked the old man, turning round, so close beside her that she felt his knee twitching against hers. Before she could answer he held her hands. "And are you going to give me one little kiss before you go?" he asked, drawing her closer still.

It was a dream! It wasn't true! It wasn't the same old man at all. Ah, how horrible! The little governess stared at him in terror. "No, no, no!"

she stammered, struggling out of his hands. "One little kiss. A kiss. What is it? Just a kiss, dear little Fräulein. A kiss." He pushed his face forward, his lips smiling broadly; and how his little blue eyes gleamed behind the spectacles! "Never—never. How can you!" She sprang up, but he was too quick and he held her against the wall, pressed against her his hard old body and his twitching knee and, though she shook her head from side to side, distracted, kissed her on the mouth. On the mouth! Where not a soul who wasn't a near relation had ever kissed her before. . . .

She ran, ran down the street until she found a broad road with tram lines and a policeman standing in the middle like a clockwork doll. "I want to get a tram to the Hauptbahnhof," sobbed the little governess. "Fräulein?" She wrung her hands at him. "The Hauptbahnhof. There—there's one now," and while he watched very much surprised, the little girl with her hat on one side, crying without a handkerchief, sprang on to the tram—not seeing the conductor's eyebrows, nor hearing the *hoch-wohlgebildete Dame* talking her over with a scandalized friend. She rocked herself and cried out loud and said "Ah, ah!" pressing her hands to her mouth. "She has been to the dentist," shrilled a fat old woman, too stupid to be uncharitable. "*Na, sagen Sie'mal*, what toothache! The child hasn't one left in her mouth." While the tram swung and jangled through a world full of old men with twitching knees.

When the little governess reached the hall of the Hotel Grunewald the same waiter who had come into her room in the morning was standing by a table, polishing a tray of glasses. The sight of the little governess seemed to fill him out with some inexplicable important content. He was ready for her question; his answer came pat and suave. "Yes, Fräulein, the lady has been here. I told her that you have arrived and gone out again immediately with a gentleman. She asked me when you were coming back again—but of course I could not say. And then she went to the manager." He took up a glass from the table, held it up to the light, looked at it with one eye closed, and started polishing it with a corner of his apron. ". . ." "Pardon, Fräulein? Ach, no, Fräulein. The manager could tell her nothing—nothing." He shook his head and smiled at the brilliant glass. "Where is the lady now?" asked the little governess, shuddering so violently that she had to hold her handkerchief up to her mouth. "How should I know?" cried the waiter, and as he swooped past her to pounce upon a new arrival his heart beat so hard against his ribs that he nearly chuckled aloud. "That's it! that's it!" he thought. "That will show her." And as he swung the new arrival's box on to his shoulders—hoop!—as though he were a giant and the box a feather, he minced over again the little governess's words, "*Gehen Sie. Gehen Sie sofort*. Shall I! Shall I!" he shouted to himself.

G.S. Sharat Chandra

Saree of the Gods

ONE OF THE THINGS THAT PRAPULLA HAD INSISTED was to have a place waiting for them in New York where other Indian immigrants lived. She had worried a great deal over this sudden change in her life. First, there was her fear of flying over Mount Everest, a certain intrusion over Lord Shiva's territory which he did not approve of for any believing Hindu. Then the abrupt severance of a generation of relationships and life in a joint family. She had spent many a restless night. In daylight, she'd dismiss her nightmares as mere confusions of a troubled mind and set herself to conquer her problems as she faced them, like the educated and practical woman that she was. If anything happened to the transgressing jet, she would clutch her husband and child to her breasts and plummet with at least a partial sense of wholeness, to whatever ocean the wrath of the god would cast her. She would go down like those brave, legendary sea captains in the history books and movies. But moving over to the West, where you lived half the year like a monk in a cave because of the weather, was something she was unable to visualize. Besides, how was she going to manage her household without the maid-servant and her stalwart mother-in-law? To be left alone in a strange apartment all day while Shekar went to work was a recurring fear. She had heard that in New York City, even married women wore mini-skirts or leather slacks and

G. S. Sharat Chandra (b. 1935) gave up the teaching of law in 1967 in order to pursue his interest in literature. His short stories and poetry have appeared in several publications around the world.

thought nothing of being drunk or footloose, not to mention their sexual escapades in summer in parks or parked automobiles. But cousin Manjula who had returned from the States was most reassuring:

"All that is nonsense! Women there are just like women here! Only they have habits and customs quite different from ours. There are hundreds of Indian families in New York. Once you've acclimatized yourself to the country, you'll find it hard to sit and brood. You may run into families from Bangalore in the same apartment house, who knows!"

Prapulla liked the apartment house as soon as she saw some sareed women in the lobby. It was Shekar who looked distraught at the Indian faces. In the time it took for them to arrive from the airport to the apartment, he had seen many of his brown brethren on the city streets, looking strange and out of place. Now he dreaded being surrounded by his kind, ending up like them building little Indias in the obscure corners of New York. He wasn't certain what Prapulla thought about it. She was always quiet on such subjects. Back in India, she was a recluse when it came to socializing and on the few occasions they had entertained foreigners at the firm, she would seek the nearest sofa as a refuge and drop her seven yards of brocade at anchor. She left the impression of being a proper Hindu wife, shy, courteous and traditional.

En route to New York on the jumbo, Shekar had discreetly opened up the conversation about what she'd wear once they were in America. At the mention of skirts she had flared up so defiantly he had to leave the seat. For Prapulla, it was not convenience but convention that made the difference. She had always prized her sarees, especially the occasions she wore her wedding saree with its blue handspun silk and its silver border of gods. There were times she had walked into a crowded room where others were dressed differently and had relished the sudden flush of embarrassment on their faces at her exquisite choice of wear.

The first day of their new life went quite smoothly. When Shekar returned from the office, she was relieved to hear that all had gone well and he had made friends with two of his American colleagues. Shekar described them. Don Dellow was in the firm for fifteen years and was extremely pleasant and helpful. Jim Dorsen and his wife Shirley had always wanted to visit India and shared great interest in the country and its culture.

"I bought them lunch at the corner deli, you know, and you should've seen their faces when I asked for corned beef on rye!" Shekar chuckled. It was during that weekend that Shekar suggested they ought to invite the Dellows and the Dorsens for dinner so she could meet and get to know the wives. Prapulla shrugged her shoulders. It was so soon. She was still unaccustomed to walking into the sterilized supermarkets where you

shopped like a robot with a pushcart, led on to the products by where
they lay waiting like cheese in a trap, rather than having them beseech you
like the vendors and merchants in the bazaars and markets in her country.
Besides, everything had a fixed price tag. The frozen vegetables, the
canned fruits and spices, the chicken chopped into shapes that were not
its own but of the plastic, all bothered her. But Shekar had not complained about her cooking yet. He was so busy gabbing and gulping, she
wasn't even sure he knew what was on the plate. Then Shekar walked in
from the office Thursday and announced he had invited his friends for
dinner on Saturday.

"They both accepted with great delight. It's rather important I develop a strong bond with them."

Prapulla pulled out a pad and started making the shopping list.
Shekar was about to ask her what she'd wear but changed his mind.

The Dorsens arrived first. Shirley Dorsen introduced herself and
immediately took a liking to Prapulla. The Dellows, caught in traffic,
came late. Judy Dellow was a lean Spanish woman in her late twenties.
She wore a velvet dress with lace cuffs and asked for bourbon. The living
room filled with the aroma of spices. In the background, Subbalakshmi
recited on the stereo.

"What sort of music is this?" Jim asked, looking somewhat sullen.
He had just finished his drink. Shirley was on her fourth.

"Karnatak music," explained Prapulla. "Subbalakshmi is the sopra-
no of South Indian music. She sings mostly devotional songs and lyrics."

"Sounds rather strange and off key to me," said Jim nodding his head
in dismay. He sang for the church choir on Sundays.

Shekar announced dinner. He had set the wine glasses next to the
handloomed napkins like he had seen in *Good Housekeeping*. As soon as
everyone was seated, he abruptly got up. "Gee! I forgot to pour the wine!"
he despaired. When he returned, he held an opaque bottle with a long
German name.

"What kind of wine is it?" asked Jim.

"The best German riesling there is!" replied Shekar with authority.

"My, you do know your liquor!" said Shirley, impressed.

"Like a book!" quipped Prapulla.

"It's a misconception," Shekar continued hastily, "that French wines
are the best. Germans actually mastered the art of wine making long
before the French. Besides, you can't beat a German riesling to go with
Indian food."

"Excellent!" said Jim. Shekar filled the glasses apologizing again for
not having filled them beforehand. "You see, good wine has to be chilled
right," he added avoiding Prapulla's unflinching stare. They began to eat.

Shirley attacked everything, mumbling superlatives between mouthfuls. Shekar kept a benevolent eye on the plates and filled them as soon as they were empty. Prapulla sat beaming an appropriate smile. When everyone had their fill, Prapulla got up for dessert.

"Is it going to be one of the exotic Indian sweets?" Shirley asked.

"Of course," butted Shekar.

Prapulla returned from the kitchen with Pepperidge Farm turnovers. "Sorry, I had an accident with the jamoons," she said meekly.

"Don't worry dear. Turnovers do perfectly well," said Shirley, giving her an understanding look.

Shekar had placed a box of cigars on the coffee table. As they all sat, he offered it to his guests who waved it away in preference to their own crumpled packages of Salem. Don and Jim talked about a contract the firm had lost. A junior engineer from Bombay who used to work for the firm had bungled it. They asked Shekar if he knew the man. Shekar had already stiffened in the chair but he pressed for details. But they veered the conversation away from the topic to compliment him on his choice of brandy.

Prapulla entered with a tray of coffee mixed with cream and sugar, just like back home. Subbalakshmi coughed, cleared her throat and strummed the veena in prayer.

Judy raved about Prapulla's saree. Prapulla, momentarily saved from embarrassment over the coffee, began to explain the ritual importance of the wedding saree. She pulled the upper part from her shoulder and spread it on the table. The silver border with the embroidered legend of the creation of the universe, the different avatars of Lord Shiva and the demons he killed while on earthly mission gleamed under the light. Her favorite one depicted Shiva drinking the poison emitted by the sea serpent with which the universe was churned from the ocean. The craftsman had even put a knot of gold at Shiva's neck to indicate the poison the god had held in his throat. A sheer triumph of skill.

"With the exception of Shiva as the begging ascetic, the saree-maker has woven all the other avatars. This blank space on the border perhaps is the space left to challenge our imagination!" mused Prapulla. Shirley, with a snifterful of brandy leaned from her chair for a closer look. The brandy tipped. "Oh no!" screamed everyone. Judy ran into the kitchen for a towel but the alcohol hissed like a magical serpent over the saree spreading its poisonous hood. The silver corroded fast and the avatars, disfigured or mutilated, almost merged. Prapulla sat dazed, just staring at her saree. The silence was unbearable. Jim puffed on his pipe like a condemned man. Judy, after trying valiantly to wipe the brandy, bent her head over her hand. Shirley looked red, like she was either going to scream or giggle. Shekar came to the rescue:

"Don't worry. I know a way I can lift the smudges. It's nothing!"
No one believed him. Prapulla abruptly got up and excused herself.

"I guess we should better be leaving," said Don looking at his watch.
"I've to drive the babysitter home and she lives three traffic jams away!"

Shekar hurried to the closet for their coats. "I hope you enjoyed the
dinner!" he said meekly, piling up the coats over his shoulder. Prapulla
appeared at the door in a different saree. She seemed to have recollected
herself and felt bad about everyone leaving so soon. "You know, my
husband is right. I've already dipped the saree border in the lotion. It'll be
as good as new by morning," she said. They shook hands and Shirley
hugged Prapulla and rocked her. "I'll call you dear, let me know how it
comes off!" she whispered drunkenly and backed into her coat like an
animal perfectly trained.

Prapulla stood at the door with one hand on her stomach, and as the
guests disappeared down the elevator, she banged the door shut and ran
into the bedroom. She remembered the day she had shopped for the saree.
It was a week before her wedding. The entire family had gone to the silk
bazaar and spent the day looking for the perfect one. They had at last
found it in the only hand-spun saree shop in the market. The merchant
had explained that the weaver who had knitted the god into its border
had died soon after, taking his craft with him. This was his last saree, his
parting gift to some lucky bride "You modern young people may not
believe in old wives tales, but I know that he was a devotee of Shiva.
People say the Lord used to appear for him!" the merchant had said.

She sobbed into her shoulders. Where was she going to find a replacement? How was she ever going to explain the tragedy to her family?
A wedding saree, selected by the bride became her second self, the sail of
her destiny, the roof that protected her and her offspring from evil. She
rushed to Ratri's room to make sure that no mythical serpent or scorpion
had already appeared over her daughter's head.

She could hear Shekar washing the dishes in the kitchen and turning
the sinkerator that gurgled like a demon with its gulletful of leftovers. She
found the impulse to make sure that Shekar had not fallen into it. It was
not really Shirley's fault. It was the brandy that her "Americanized"
husband kept pouring into her glass. He was so imitative and flippant,
lavishing food and liquor that they could scarcely afford on people that
were yet to be called friends. He had drunk more than he should have as if
to prove that he held his liquor well enough to win points for promotion!
Who really discovered brandy? Shekar had brackishly turned the picture
of Napoleon on the bottle toward his guests, but surely it must have been
a demon who despised her or was sent to convey the god's displeasure at
her mixed company, her expatriatism.

She grew tired of her mind's hauntings. There was no way to change the events or turn back now. When Ratri grew up, she would cut the saree and make a dress for her. She'd write to her mother-in-law and send money for a special puja at the temple.

In her dream, it was her funeral. Four priests carried her on bamboo. The family walked behind. Shekar, dressed in traditional dhoti walked ahead with the clay vessel of hot coals with which he'd kindle the first spark of fire. The procession moved briskly to the crematory grounds. A pyre was built and her corpse decked with her favorite flowers was laid on top. Someone tied the border of the saree firmly to a log. The bereaved went around chanting the necessary hymns and the priests sprinkled holy water over her. Suddenly she was ablaze. She felt nothing but an intense heat around her. The flames did not seem to touch her. She pinched herself. She was not on the pyre but was standing with her family. It was her wedding saree wrapped around a giant bottle of brandy that was burning! Inside the bottle a demon danced, spitting fire. The avatars slowly uncurled from the silver border like an inflated raft and ascended the smoke. They were all in miniature, fragile in their postures and luminous. The brandy in the bottle foamed and swirled like an ocean. The demon raved in its ring of fire. Prapulla screamed. One of the uncles gently touched her on the arm and said:

"Do not be alarmed. The demon points its tongue upwards. The gods have flown to their proper heaven."

When she woke herself from the nightmare, Shekar was soundly snoring on the bedside. The sky outside hung in a spent, listless grayness. She could see a haze of light back of a skyscraper. Dawn would soon brim the horizon of her new world with neither birds nor the song of priests in the air. She sat in the dark of the living room with the saree on her lap, caressing its border absentmindedly. A brittled piece broke and fell.

Questions for Discussion

1. How would you describe the attitudes of the main characters of each of the four stories toward the difficulties arising out of their misperceptions? What kinds of attitudes would seem to enable the sojourner to overcome these difficulties?

2. In what kinds of cross-cultural situations would a sojourner be likely to experience the most serious misperceptions? Is the solitary sojourner at a greater disadvantage than the person travelling in a group?

3. The little governess is advised not to trust anyone. Is this good advice for a sojourner? If not, how can the sojourner learn who can be trusted?

4. Does the fact that the major characters in "The Little Governess" and "Saree of the Gods" are women have anything to do with the tragic outcome of their cross-cultural encounters? Will a woman inevitably have more difficulty in a cross-cultural situation? What types of problems are unique for a sojourner who is a woman?

5. Given that the stories by Bowles and Kusenberg are humorous accounts of cultural misunderstandings, what attitudes or factors might have resulted in a different, more unpleasant outcome for the main characters? Conversely, how could the situations of the two women in the stories by Mansfield and Chandra have resulted in comedy rather than personal tragedy?

6. According to Raymond Gorden, not having sufficient time to think things out before reacting is a major source of difficulty during the earliest stages of a sojourn. In which of the stories of this section is Gorden's idea best illustrated?

7. To what extent do the problems of the main character in "Saree of the Gods" derive from her desire to make her American friends aware that she comes from the upper levels of Indian society? How much does a sojourner's ability to maneuver in a new culture depend upon his socio-economic status at home? Will a tendency to insist upon maintaining a previous social status inevitably lead to serious difficulties in a new culture? Are some cultures more status conscious than others?

8. In the Spectator Phase, how valuable is previous cross-cultural experience? Do you think that this has anything to do with the fact that sojourners in the stories by Bowles and Kusenberg resolve their problems successfully as opposed to those in the stories by Mansfield and Chandra?

9. Which of the four main characters in this section do you find most credible? Why?

10. Does the first-person point of view in "You Have Left Your Lotus Pods on the Bus" and "Odd Tippling" seem to be a more effective way of illuminating problems in cross-cultural encounters than the third-person point of view used in the other two stories?

List of Additional Stories

Adams, Alice R. "A Swedish Remembrance." *Short Story International* 6.32(1982): 137-42.

――――――. "Mexican Dust." *The New Yorker* 24 Jan. 1983: 38-42.

Bovey, John. "The Garden Wall." *Desirable Aliens.* Urbana, IL: University of Illinois Press, 1980. 15-29.

Bowles, Paul. "Under the Sky." *Collected Stories 1939-1976.* Santa Barbara, CA: Black Sparrow, 1979. 77-82.

Byrne, Donn. "Hail and Farewell." *An Alley of Flashing Spears and Other Stories.* London: Sampson Low, Marston & Co., n. d. 186-93.

Fuller, Hoyt W. "The Senegalese." *American Negro Short Stories.* Ed. John Henrik Clarke. New York: Hill and Wang, 1966. 226-45.

Grin, Aleksandr Stepanovič. "Plemja Siurg." ["The Tribe of Siurg"] *Rasskazy.* ["Stories"] Minsk: Nauka i texnika, 1981. 7-17.

Helprin, Mark. "Ellis Island." *Ellis Island and Other Stories.* New York: Delta-Seymour Lawrence, 1982. 128-96.

Iskander, Fazil. "Angličanin s ženoj i rebënkom." ["An Englishman with Wife and Child"] *Derevo deststva.* ["The Tree of Childhood"] Moscow: Sovetskij pisatel, 1974. 143-172.

Jones, Richard. "Cuisine Bourgeoisie." *Winter's Tales 19.* Ed. A. D. Maclean. London: Macmillan Ltd., 1973. 69-86.

Lessing, Doris. "The Woman." *The Habit of Loving.* New York: Thomas Y. Crowell, 1957. 54-70.

Milla, José. "El chapín." ["The Chapín"] *Cuadros guatemaltecos.* ["Guatemalan Sketches"] Ed. George J. Edberg. New York: Macmillan, 1965. 15-23.

Montague, Margaret Prescott. "England to America." *First-Prize Stories 1919-1954. From the O. Henry Memorial Awards.* New York: Hanover House, 1954. 1-13.

Nuyda, Hermel A. "Pulse of the Land." *Modern Philippine Short Stories.* Albuquerque, NM: University of New Mexico Press, 1962. 219-28.

Oates, Joyce Carol. "The Translation." *Night Side. Eighteen Tales.* New York: The Vanguard Press, Inc., 1977. 110-33.

Pardo Bazán, Emilia. "En Babilonia." *Obras completas.* Vol. 1. Madrid: Aguilar, 1957. 1619-21.

——————. "Por España." *Obras completas.* Vol. 1. Madrid: Aguilar, 1957. 1661-63.

Ribeyro, Julio Ramón. "Bárbara." *La palabra del mudo.* Lima: Milla Batres, 1972. 93-99.

Roth, Henry. "The Surveyor." *The Best American Short Stories 1967.* Ed. Martha Foley and David Burnett. New York: Ballantine Books, 1967. 273-91.

Sanchez Boudy, José. "El silencio." *Hispanics in the United States. An Anthology of Creative Literature.* Ed. Francisco Jimenez and Gary Keller. Vol. 2. Ypsilanti, MI: Bilingual Review Press, 1982. 102-12.

Segal, Lore. "The First American." *The New Yorker* 30 May 1983: 36-42.

Singer, Isaac Bashevis. "The Son from America." *A Crown of Feathers.* Greenwich, CT: Fawcett Publictions, Inc., 1973. 100-07.

Sneider, Vern. "Uncle Bosko." *A Long Way from Home and Other Stories.* New York: NAL Signet, 1956. 153-191.

Traven B. "Assembly Line." *The Night Visitor and Other Stories.* New York: Hill and Wang, 1966. 73-88.

——————. "Conversion of Some Indians." *The Night Visitor and Other Stories.* New York: Hill and Wang, 1966. 183-91.

Tucker, Bob. "The Tourist Trade." *Tomorrow, the Stars.* Ed. Robert A. Heinlein. New York: Berkley Publishing Corporation, 1952. 53-63.

3. Increasing Participation Phase

☙

As one begins to participate meaningfully in the new culture, one sometimes experiences situations which tend to turn him away from the host culture: we have seen an example of this in the character of Prapulla in Chandra's "Saree of the Gods." Overcoming these negative impulses during the Spectator Phase is not easy. It requires determination and a steadfast effort of will. Moreover, the early efforts may not seem to produce the returns that one expects. At first, a person may discover not only that he is failing to understand others but that he himself is being misunderstood, or even that he is being understood but not in the way that he would like to be. The efforts to become involved may also seem unfairly one-sided: it is the foreigner who is trying to understand others, it is the foreigner who is setting aside his cultural values, it is he who is risking embarrassment and even shame by venturing into situations of which he has little understanding. In contrast, host culture natives appear to be making almost no effort to meet him half way, and they seem to risk little or nothing, for all the communicational advantages belong to them. Entering into this phase of the experience of being foreign may be next to impossible for a person whose ego-investment is unusually great, because it requires at least a temporary letting go of established concepts of selfhood and of the emotional investment in oneself that has built up over the years.

But if these obstacles can be faced and to a degree overcome, the rewards can be great. The ensuing involvement in the host culture can more than make up for initial bruises to the ego. One gains increased confidence from understanding others and from the growing sense of being able to make oneself understood. And although the terms in which one is understood are different, the increasing sense of interaction with others more than makes up for the reduced efficiency in communication that was apparent in those early efforts.

"The Growing Stone" by Albert Camus depicts the sojourner's moving from the Spectator Phase into that of Increasing Participation, discovering along the way a new means of communicating with others while experiencing the risk inherent in venturing forth into largely uncharted territory. At first only mildly sympathetic to the problems of the people he has been employed to help, the French engineer D'Arrast finds himself more and more involved in their personal lives and in the end achieves acceptance.

The second story of this section, "Everything Is Nice" by Jane Bowles, emphasizes the difficulties that can arise when the sojourner makes a determined effort to become involved with her hosts. Even one's best intentions may be called into question. The protagonist, Jeanie, is mocked by one of her Moslem acquaintances for spending "half the week with Moslem friends and half with Nazarenes." Jeanie's sincere effort to become involved with her hosts is perceived by them as too calculated. She also learns that dividing one's loyalties between two different, conflicting cultures can lead to suspicion and rejection by both.

"Robert Aghion" by Hermann Hesse, which depicts an English missionary's involvement with Indian culture, could serve as a paradigm for the first three phases of the culture shock experience. Each step is captured with striking precision, until the hero abandons his missionary goal and commits himself to learning the culture and understanding the people. Yet, in the end, he is confronted with an ambiguity so deceptively profound that it becomes clear that, despite his effort, he has only scratched the surface of understanding. This kind of ambiguity and the feelings of confusion it provokes in the sojourner is, of course, one of several symptoms of the next phase of the experience of being foreign, the Shock Phase.

Albert Camus

The Growing Stone

THE AUTOMOBILE SWUNG CLUMSILY AROUND THE CURVE in the red sand-
stone trail, now a mass of mud. The headlights suddenly picked out in the
night—first on one side of the road, then on the other—two wooden huts
with sheet-metal roofs. On the right near the second one, a tower of
coarse beams could be made out in the light fog. From the top of the
tower a metal cable, invisible at its starting-point, shone as it sloped down
into the light from the car before disappearing behind the embankment
that blocked the road. The car slowed down and stopped a few yards
from the huts.

The man who emerged from the seat to the right of the driver labored
to extricate himself from the car. As he stood up, his huge, broad frame
lurched a little. In the shadow beside the car, solidly planted on the
ground and weighed down by fatigue, he seemed to be listening to the
idling motor. Then he walked in the direction of the embankment and
entered the cone of light from the headlights. He stopped at the top of the
slope, his broad back outlined against the darkness. After a moment he
turned around. In the light from the dashboard he could see the chauffeur's black face, smiling. The man signaled and the chauffeur turned off
the motor. At once a vast cool silence fell over the trail and the forest.
Then the sound of the water could be heard.

Albert Camus (1913-1960), one of the leading figures associated with post-war
French existentialism, received the Nobel Prize for "his important literary produc-
tion, which with clear-sighted earnestness illumines the problems of the human
conscience of our time."

77

The man looked at the river below him, visible solely as a broad dark motion, flecked with occasional shimmers. A denser motionless darkness, far beyond, must be the other bank. By looking fixedly, however, one could see on that still bank a yellowish light like an oil lamp in the distance. The big man turned back toward the car and nodded. The chauffeur switched off the lights, turned them on again, then blinked them regularly. On the embankment the man appeared and disappeared, taller and more massive each time he came back to life. Suddenly, on the other bank of the river, a lantern held up by an invisible arm swung back and forth several times. At a final signal from the lookout, the chauffeur turned off his lights once and for all. The car and the man disappeared into the night. With the lights out, the river was almost visible—or at least a few of its long liquid muscles shining intermittently. On each side of the road, the dark masses of forest foliage stood out against the sky and seemed very near. The fine rain that had soaked the trail an hour earlier was still hovering in the warm air, intensifying the silence and immobility of this broad clearing in the virgin forest. In the black sky misty stars flickered.

But from the other bank rose sounds of chains and muffled plashings. Above the hut on the right of the man still waiting there, the cable stretched taut. A dull creaking began to run along it, just as there rose from the river a faint yet quite audible sound of stirred-up water. The creaking became more regular, the sound of water spread farther and then became localized, as the lantern grew larger. Now its yellowish halo could be clearly seen. The halo gradually expanded and again contracted while the lantern shone through the mist and began to light up from beneath a sort of square roof of dried palms supported by thick bamboos. This crude shelter, around which vague shadows were moving, was slowly approaching the bank. When it was about in the middle of the river, three little men, almost black, were distinctly outlined in the yellow light, naked from the waist up and wearing conical hats. They stood still with feet apart, leaning somewhat to offset the strong drift of the river pressing with all its invisible water against the side of a big crude raft that eventually emerged from the darkness. When the ferry came still closer, the man could see behind the shelter on the downstream side two tall Negroes likewise wearing nothing but broad straw hats and cotton trousers. Side by side they weighed with all their might on long poles that sank slowly into the river toward the stern while the Negroes, with the same slow motion, bent over the water as far as their balance would allow. In the bow the three mulattoes, still and silent, watched the bank approach without raising their eyes toward the man waiting for them.

The ferry suddenly bumped against something. And the lantern swaying from the shock lighted up a pier jutting into the water. The tall Negroes stood still with hands above their heads gripping the ends of the poles, which were barely stuck in the bottom, but their taut muscles rippled constantly with a motion that seemed to come from the very thrust of the water. The other ferrymen looped chains over the posts on the dock, leaped onto the boards, and lowered a sort of gangplank that covered the bow of the raft with its inclined plane.

The man returned to the car and slid in while the chauffeur stepped on the starter. The car slowly climbed the embankment, pointed its hood toward the sky, and then lowered it toward the slope. With brakes on, it rolled forward, slipped somewhat on the mud, stopped, started up again. It rolled onto the pier with a noise of bouncing planks, reached the end, where the mulattoes, still silent, were standing on either side, and plunged slowly toward the raft. The raft ducked its nose in the water as soon as the front wheels struck it and almost immediately bobbed back to receive the car's full weight. Then the chauffeur ran the vehicle to the stern, in front of the square roof where the lantern was hanging. At once the mulattoes swung the inclined plane back onto the pier and jumped simultaneously onto the ferry, pushing it off from the muddy bank. The river strained under the raft and raised it on the surface of the water, where it drifted slowly at the end of the long drawbar running along the cable overhead. The tall Negroes relaxed their effort and drew in their poles. The man and the chauffeur got out of the car and came over to stand on the edge of the raft facing up stream. No one had spoken during the maneuver, and even now each remained in his place, motionless and quiet except for one of the tall Negroes who was rolling a cigarette in coarse paper.

The man was looking at the gap through which the river sprang from the vast Brazilian forest and swept down toward them. Several hundred yards wide at that point, the muddy, silky waters of the river pressed against the side of the ferry and then, unimpeded at the two ends of the raft, sheered off and again spread out in a single powerful flood gently flowing through the dark forest toward the sea and the night. A stale smell, come from the water or the spongy sky, hung in the air. Now the slapping of the water under the ferry could be heard, and at intervals the calls of bullfrogs from the two banks or the strange cries of birds. The big man approached the small, thin chauffeur, who was leaning against one of the bamboos with his hands in the pockets of his dungarees, once blue but now covered with the same red dust that had been blowing in their faces all day long. A smile spread over his face, all wrinkled in spite of his youth. Without really seeing them, he was staring at the faint stars still swimming in the damp sky.

But the birds' cries became sharper, unfamiliar chatterings mingled with them, and almost at once the cable began to creak. The tall Negroes plunged their poles into the water and groped blindly for the bottom. The man turned around toward the shore they had just left. Now that shore was obscured by the darkness and the water, vast and savage like the continent of trees stretching beyond it for thousands of kilometers. Between the near-by ocean and this sea of vegetation, the handful of men drifting at that moment on a wild river seemed lost. When the raft bumped the new pier it was as if, having cast off all moorings, they were landing on an island in the darkness after days of frightened sailing.

Once on land, the men's voices were at last heard. The chauffeur had just paid them and, with voices that sounded strangely gay in the heavy night, they were saying farewell in Portuguese as the car started up again.

"They said sixty, the kilometers to Iguape. Three hours more and it'll be over. Socrates is happy," the chauffeur announced.

The man laughed with a warm, hearty laugh that resembled him.

"Me too, Socrates, I'm happy too. The trail is hard."

"Too heavy, Mr. D'Arrast, you too heavy," and the chauffeur laughed too as if he would never stop.

The car had taken on a little speed. It was advancing between high walls of trees and inextricable vegetation, amidst a soft, sweetish smell. Fireflies on the wing constantly crisscrossed in the darkness of the forest, and every once in a while red-eyed birds would bump against the windshield. At times a strange, savage sound would reach them from the depths of the night and the chauffeur would roll his eyes comically as he looked at his passenger.

The road kept turning and crossed little streams on bridges of wobbly boards. After an hour the fog began to thicken. A fine drizzle began to fall, dimming the car's lights. Despite the jolts, D'Arrast was half asleep. He was no longer riding in the damp forest but on the roads of the Serra that they had taken in the morning as they left São Paulo. From those dirt trails constantly rose the red dust which they could still taste, and on both sides, as far as the eye could see, it covered the sparse vegetation of the plains. The harsh sun, the pale mountains full of ravines, the starved zebus encountered along the roads, with a tired flight of ragged urubus as their only escort, the long, endless crossing of an endless desert . . . He gave a start. The car had stopped. Now they were in Japan: fragile houses on both sides of the road and, in the houses, furtive kimonos. The chauffeur was talking to a Japanese wearing soiled dungarees and a Brazilian straw hat. Then the car started up again.

"He said only forty kilometers."

"Where were we? In Tokyo?"

"No. Registro. In Brazil all the Japanese come here."

"Why?"

"Don't know. They're yellow, you know, Mr. D'Arrast."

But the forest was gradually thinning out, and the road was becoming easier, though slippery. The car was skidding on sand. The window let in a warm, damp breeze that was rather sour.

"You smell it?" the chauffeur asked, smacking his lips. "That's the good old sea. Soon, Iguape."

"If we have enough gas," D'Arrast said. And he went back to sleep peacefully.

Sitting up in bed early in the morning, D'Arrast looked in amazement at the huge room in which he had just awakened. The lower half of the big walls was newly painted brown. Higher up, they had once been painted white, and patches of yellowish paint covered them up to the ceiling. Two rows of beds faced each other. D'Arrast saw only one bed unmade at the end of his row and that bed was empty. But he heard a noise on his left and turned toward the door, where Socrates, a bottle of mineral water in each hand, stood laughing, "Happy memory!" he said. D'Arrast shook himself. Yes, the hospital in which the Mayor had lodged them the night before was named "Happy Memory." "Sure memory," Socrates continued. "They told me first build hospital, later build water. Meanwhile, happy memory, take fizz water to wash." He disappeared, laughing and singing, not at all exhausted apparently by the cataclysmic sneezes that had shaken him all night long and kept D'Arrast from closing an eye.

Now D'Arrast was completely awake. Through the iron-latticed window he could see a little red-earth courtyard soaked by the rain that was noiselessly pouring down on a clump of tall aloes. A woman passed holding a yellow scarf over her head. D'Arrast lay back in bed, then sat up at once and got out of the bed, which creaked under his weight. Socrates came in at that moment: "For you, Mr. D'Arrast. The mayor is waiting outside." But, seeing the look on D'Arrast's face, he added: "Don't worry; he never in a hurry."

After shaving with the mineral water, D'Arrast went out under the portico of the building. The Mayor—who had the proportions and, under his gold-rimmed glasses, the look of a nice little weasel—seemed lost in dull contemplation of the rain. But a charming smile transfigured him as soon as he saw D'Arrast. Holding his little body erect, he rushed up and tried to stretch his arms around the engineer. At that moment an automobile drove up in front of them on the other side of the low wall, skidded in the wet clay, and came to a stop on an angle. "The Judge!" said the Mayor. Like the Mayor, the Judge was dressed in navy blue. But he was much younger, or at least seemed so because of his elegant figure and his look of a startled adolescent. Now he was crossing the courtyard in their direction, gracefully avoiding the puddles. A few steps from D'Arrast, he was already holding out his arms and welcoming him. He was proud to greet the noble engineer who was honoring their poor village; he was delighted by the priceless service the noble engineer was going to do Iguape by building that little jetty to prevent the periodic flooding of the lower quarters of town. What a noble profession, to command the waters and dominate rivers! Ah, surely the poor people of Iguape would long remember the noble engineer's name and many years from now would still mention it in their prayers. D'Arrast, captivated by such charm and eloquence, thanked him and didn't dare wonder what possible connection a judge could have with a jetty. Besides, according to the Mayor, it was time to go to the club, where the leading citizens wanted to receive the noble engineer appropriately before going to inspect the poorer quarters. Who were the leading citizens?

"Well," the Mayor said, "myself as Mayor, Mr. Carvalho here, the Harbor Captain, and a few others less important. Besides, you won't have to pay much attention to them, for they don't speak French."

D'Arrast called Socrates and told him he would meet him when the morning was over.

"All right," Socrates said, "I'll go to the Garden of the Fountain."

"The Garden?"

"Yes, everybody knows. Have no fear, Mr. D'Arrast."

The hospital, D'Arrast noticed as he left it, was built on the edge of the forest, and the heavy foliage almost hung over the roofs. Over the whole surface of the trees was falling a sheet of fine rain which the dense forest was noiselessly absorbing like a huge sponge. The town, some hundred houses roofed with faded tiles, extended between the forest and the river, and the water's distant murmur reached the hospital. The car entered drenched streets and almost at once came out on a rather large rectangular square which showed, among numerous puddles in its red clay, the marks of tires, iron wheels, and horseshoes. All around, brightly plastered low houses closed off the square, behind which could be seen the two round towers of a blue-and-white church of colonial style. A smell of salt water coming from the estuary dominated this bare setting. In the center of the square a few wet silhouettes were wandering. Along the houses a motley crowd of gauchos, Japanese, half-breed Indians, and elegant leading citizens, whose dark suits looked exotic here, were sauntering with slow gestures. They stepped aside with dignity to make way for the car, then stopped and watched it. When the car stopped in front of one of the houses on the square, a circle of wet gauchos silently formed around it.

At the club—a sort of small bar on the second floor furnished with a bamboo counter and iron cafe tables—the leading citizens were numerous. Sugar-cane alcohol was drunk in honor of D'Arrast after the Mayor, glass in hand, had wished him welcome and all the happiness in the world. But while D'Arrast was drinking near the window, a huge lout of a fellow in riding-breeches and leggings came over and, staggering somewhat, delivered himself of a rapid and obscure speech in which the engineer recognized solely the word "passport." He hesitated and then took out the document, which the fellow seized greedily. After having thumbed through the passport, he manifested obvious displeasure. He resumed his speech, shaking the document under the nose of the engineer, who, without getting excited, merely looked at the angry man. Whereupon the Judge, with a smile, came over and asked what was the matter. For a moment the drunk scrutinized the frail creature who dared to interrupt him and then, staggering even more dangerously, shook the passport in the face of his new interlocutor. D'Arrast sat peacefully beside a cafe table and waited. The dialogue became very lively, and suddenly the Judge broke out in a deafening voice that one would never have suspected in him. Without any forewarning, the lout suddenly backed down like a child caught in the act. At a final order from the Judge, he sidled toward the door like a punished schoolboy and disappeared.

The Judge immediately came over to explain to D'Arrast, in a voice that had become harmonious again, that the uncouth individual who had just left was the Chief of Police, that he had dared to claim the passport was not in order, and that he would be punished for his outburst. Judge Carvalho then addressed himself to the leading citizens, who stood in a circle around him, and seemed to be questioning them. After a brief discussion, the Judge expressed solemn excuses to D'Arrast, asked him to agree that nothing but drunkenness could explain such forgetfulness of the sentiments of respect and gratitude that the whole town of Iguape owed him, and, finally, asked him to decide himself on the punishment to be inflicted on the wretched individual. D'Arrast said that he didn't want any punishment, that it was a trivial incident, and that he was particularly eager to go to the river. Then the Mayor spoke up to assert with much simple good-humor that a punishment was really mandatory, that the guilty man would remain incarcerated, and that they would all wait until their distinguished visitor decided on his fate. No protest could soften that smiling severity, and D'Arrast had to promise that he would think the matter over. Then they agreed to visit the poorer quarters of the town.

The river was already spreading its yellowish waters over the low, slippery banks. They had left behind them the last houses of Iguape and stood between the river and a high, steep embankment to which clung

huts made of clay and branches. In front of them, at the end of the
embankment, the forest began again abruptly, as on the other bank. But
the gap made by the water rapidly widened between the trees until reaching a vague grayish line that marked the beginning of the sea. Without
saying a word, D'Arrast walked toward the slope, where the various
flood levels had left marks that were still fresh. A muddy path climbed
toward the huts. In front of them, Negroes stood silently staring at the
newcomers. Several couples were holding hands, and on the edge of the
mound, in front of the adults, a row of black children with bulging bellies
and spindly legs were gaping with round eyes.

When he arrived in front of the huts, D'Arrast beckoned to the
Harbor Captain. He was a fat, laughing Negro wearing a white uniform.
D'Arrast asked him in Spanish if it were possible to visit a hut. The
Captain was sure it was, he even thought it a good idea, and the noble
engineer would see very interesting things. He harangued the Negroes at
length, pointing to D'Arrast and to the river. They listened without saying
a word. When the Captain had finished, no one stirred. He spoke again,
in an impatient voice. Then he called upon one of the men, who shook his
head. Whereupon the Captain said a few brief words in a tone of command. The man stepped forth from the group, faced D'Arrast, and with a
gesture showed him the way. But his look was hostile. He was an elderly
man with short, graying hair and a thin, wizened face; yet his body was
still young, with hard wiry shoulders and muscles visible through his
cotton pants and torn shirt. They went ahead, followed by the Captain
and the crowd of Negroes, and climbed a new, steeper embankment
where the huts made of clay, tin, and reeds clung to the ground with such
difficulty that they had to be strengthened at the base with heavy stones.
They met a woman going down the path, sometimes slipping in her bare
feet, who was carrying on her head an iron drum full of water. Then they
reached a small irregular square bordered by three huts. The man walked
toward one of them and pushed open a bamboo door on hinges made of
tropical liana. He stood aside without saying a word, staring at the
engineer with the same impassive look. In the hut, D'Arrast saw nothing
at first but a dying fire built right on the ground in the exact center of the
room. Then in a back corner he made out a brass bed with a bare, broken
mattress, a table in the other corner covered with earthenware dishes,
and, between the two, a sort of stand supporting a color print representing Saint George. Nothing else but a pile of rags to the right of the
entrance and, hanging from the ceiling, a few loincloths of various colors
drying over the fire. Standing still, D'Arrast breathed in the smell of
smoke and poverty that rose from the ground and choked him. Behind
him, the Captain clapped his hands. The engineer turned around and,

against the light, saw the graceful silhouette of a black girl approach and hold out something to him. He took a glass and drank the thick sugarcane alcohol. The girl held out her tray to receive the empty glass and went out with such a supple motion that D'Arrast suddenly wanted to hold her back.

But on following her out he didn't recognize her in the crowd of Negroes and leading citizens gathered around the hut. He thanked the old man, who bowed without a word. Then he left. The Captain, behind him, resumed his explanations and asked when the French company from Rio could begin work and whether or not the jetty could be built before the rainy season. D'Arrast didn't know; to tell the truth, he wasn't thinking of that. He went down toward the cool river under the fine mist. He was still listening to that great pervasive sound he had been hearing continually since his arrival, which might have been made by the rustling of either the water or the trees, he could not tell. Having reached the bank, he looked out in the distance at the vague line of the sea, the thousands of kilometers of solitary waters leading to Africa and, beyond, his native Europe.

"Captain," he asked, "what do these people we have just seen live on?"

"They work when they're needed," the Captain said. "We are poor."

"Are they the poorest?"

"They are the poorest."

The Judge, who arrived at that moment, slipping somewhat in his best shoes, said they already loved the noble engineer who was going to give them work.

"And, you know, they dance and sing every day."

Then, without transition, he asked D'Arrast if he had thought of the punishment.

"What punishment?"

"Why, our Chief of Police."

"Let him go." The Judge said that this was not possible; there had to be a punishment. D'Arrast was already walking toward Iguape.

In the little Garden of the Fountain, mysterious and pleasant under the fine rain, clusters of exotic flowers hung down along the lianas among the banana trees and pandanus. Piles of wet stones marked the intersection of paths on which a motley crowd was strolling. Half-breeds, mulattoes, a few gauchos were chatting in low voices or sauntering along the bamboo paths to the point where groves and bush became thicker and more impenetrable. There, the forest began abruptly.

D'Arrast was looking for Socrates in the crowd when Socrates suddenly bumped him from behind.

"It's holiday," he said, laughing, and clung to D'Arrast's tall shoulders to jump up and down.

"What holiday?"

"Why, you not know?" Socrates said in surprise as he faced D'Arrast. "The feast of good Jesus. Each year they all come to the grotto with a hammer."

Socrates pointed out, not a grotto, but a group that seemed to be waiting in a corner of the garden.

"You see? One day the good statue of Jesus, it came upstream from the sea. Some fishermen found it. How beautiful! How beautiful! Then they washed it here in the grotto. And now a stone grew up in the grotto. Every year it's the feast. With the hammer you break, you break off pieces for blessed happiness. And then it keeps growing and you keep breaking. It's the miracle!"

They had reached the grotto and could see its low entrance beyond the waiting men. Inside, in the darkness studded with the flickering flames of candles, a squatting figure was pounding with a hammer. The man, a thin gaucho with a long mustache, got up and came out holding in his open palm, so that all might see, a small piece of moist schist, over which he soon closed his hand carefully before going away. Another man then stooped down and entered the grotto.

D'Arrast turned around. On all sides pilgrims were waiting, without looking at him, impassive under the water dripping from the trees in thin sheets. He too was waiting in front of the grotto under the same film of water, and he didn't know for what. He had been waiting constantly, to tell the truth, for a month since he had arrived in this country. He had been waiting—in the red heat of humid days, under the little stars of night, despite the tasks to be accomplished, the jetties to be built, the roads to be cut through—as if the work he had come to do here were merely a pretext for a surprise or for an encounter he did not even imagine but which had been waiting patiently for him at the end of the world. He shook himself, walked away without anyone in the little group paying attention to him, and went toward the exit. He had to go back to the river and go to work.

But Socrates was waiting for him at the gate, lost in voluble conversation with a short, fat, strapping man whose skin was yellow rather than black. His head, completely shaved, gave even more sweep to a considerable forehead. On the other hand, his broad, smooth face was adorned with a very black beard, trimmed square.

"He's champion!" Socrates said by way of introduction. "Tomorrow he's in the procession."

The man, wearing a sailor's outfit of heavy serge, a blue-and-white jersey under the pea jacket, was examining D'Arrast attentively with his calm black eyes. At the same time he was smiling, showing all his very white teeth between his full, shiny lips.

"He speaks Spanish," Socrates said and, turning toward the stranger, added: "Tell Mr. D'Arrast." Then he danced off toward another group. The man ceased to smile and looked at D'Arrast with outright curiosity.

"You are interested, Captain?"

"I'm not a captain," D'Arrast said.

"That doesn't matter. But you're a noble. Socrates told me."

"Not I. But my grandfather was. His father too and all those before his father. Now there is no more nobility in our country."

"Ah!" the Negro said, laughing. "I understand; everybody is a noble."

"No, that's not it. There are neither noblemen nor common people."

The fellow reflected; then he made up his mind.

"No one works? No one suffers?"

"Yes, millions of men."

"Then that's the common people."

"In that way, yes, there is a common people. But the masters are policemen or merchants."

The mulatto's kindly face closed in a frown. Then he grumbled: "Humph! Buying and selling, eh! What filth! And with the police, dogs command."

Suddenly, he burst out laughing.

"You, you don't sell?"

"Hardly at all. I make bridges, roads."

"That's good. Me, I'm a ship's cook. If you wish, I'll make you our dish of black beans."

"All right."

The cook came closer to D'Arrast and took his arm.

"Listen, I like what you tell me. I'm going to tell you too. Maybe you will like."

He drew him over near the gate to a damp wooden bench beneath a clump of bamboos.

"I was at sea, off Iguape, on a small coastwise tanker that supplies the harbors along here. It caught fire on board. Not by my fault! I know my job! No, just bad luck. We were able to launch the lifeboats. During the night, the sea got rough; it capsized the boat and I went down. When I came up, I hit the boat with my head. I drifted. The night was dark, the waters are vast, and, besides, I don't swim well; I was afraid. Just then I saw a light in the distance and recognized the church of the good Jesus in Iguape. So I told the good Jesus that at his procession I would carry a

hundred-pound stone on my head if he saved me. You don't have to
believe me, but the waters became calm and my heart too. I swam slowly,
I was happy, and I reached the shore. Tomorrow I'll keep my promise."

He looked at D'Arrast in a suddenly suspicious manner.

"You're not laughing?"

"No, I'm not laughing. A man has to do what he has promised."

The fellow clapped him on the back.

"Now, come to my brother's, near the river. I'll cook you some
beans."

"No," D'Arrast said, "I have things to do. This evening, if you wish."

"Good. But tonight there's dancing and praying in the big hut. It's
the feast for Saint George." D'Arrast asked him if he danced too. The
cook's face hardened suddenly; for the first time his eyes became shifty.

"No, no, I won't dance. Tomorrow I must carry the stone. It is heavy.
I'll go this evening to celebrate the saint. And then I'll leave early."

"Does it last long?"

"All night and a little into the morning."

He looked at D'Arrast with a vaguely shameful look.

"Come to the dance. You can take me home afterward. Otherwise,
I'll stay and dance. I probably won't be able to keep from it."

"You like to dance?"

"Oh yes! I like. Besides, there are cigars, saints, women. You forget
everything and you don't obey any more."

"There are women too? All the women of the town?"

"Not of the town, but of the huts."

The ship's cook resumed his smile. "Come. The Captain I'll obey.
And you will help me keep my promise tomorrow."

D'Arrast felt slightly annoyed. What did that absurd promise mean
to him? But he looked at the handsome frank face smiling trustingly at
him, its dark skin gleaming with health and vitality.   •

"I'll come," he said. "Now I'll walk along with you a little."

Without knowing why, he had a vision at the same time of the black
girl offering him the drink of welcome.

They went out of the garden, walked along several muddy streets,
and reached the bumpy square, which looked even larger because of the
low structures surrounding it. The humidity was now dripping down the
plastered walls, although the rain had not increased. Through the spongy
expanse of the sky, the sound of the river and of the trees reached them
somewhat muted. They were walking in step, D'Arrast heavily and the
cook with elastic tread. From time to time the latter would raise his head
and smile at his companion. They went in the direction of the church,
which could be seen above the houses, reached the end of the square,

walked along other muddy streets now filled with aggressive smells of cooking. From time to time a woman, holding a plate or kitchen utensil, would peer out inquisitively from one of the doors and then disappear at once. They passed in front of the church, plunged into an old section of similar low houses, and suddenly came out on the sound of the invisible river behind the area of the huts that D'Arrast recognized.

"Good. I'll leave you. See you this evening," he said.

"Yes, in front of the church."

But the cook did not let go of D'Arrast's hand. He hesitated. Finally he made up his mind.

"And you, have you never called out, made a promise?"

"Yes, once, I believe."

"In a shipwreck?"

"If you wish." And D'Arrast pulled his hand away roughly. But as he was about to turn on his heels, he met the cook's eyes. He hesitated, and then smiled.

"I can tell you, although it was unimportant. Someone was about to die through my fault. It seems to me that I called out."

"Did you promise?"

"No. I should have liked to promise."

"Long ago?"

"Not long before coming here."

The cook seized his beard with both hands. His eyes were shining.

"You are a captain," he said. "My house is yours. Besides, you are going to help me keep my promise, and it's as if you had made it yourself. That will help you too."

D'Arrast smiled, saying: "I don't think so."

"You are proud, Captain."

"I used to be proud; now I'm alone. But just tell me: has your good Jesus always answered you?"

"Always . . . no, Captain!"

"Well, then?"

The cook burst out with a gay, childlike laugh.

"Well," he said, "he's free, isn't he?"

At the club, where D'Arrast lunched with the leading citizens, the Mayor told him he must sign the town's guest-book so that some trace would remain of the great event of his coming to Iguape. The Judge found two or three new expressions to praise, besides their guest's virtues and talents, the simplicity with which he represented among them the great country to which he had the honor to belong. D'Arrast simply said that it was indeed an honor to him and an advantage to his firm to have been awarded the allocation of this long construction job. Whereupon the

Judge expressed his admiration for such humility. "By the way," he asked, "have you thought of what should be done to the Chief of Police?" D'Arrast smiled at him and said: "Yes, I have a solution." He would consider it a personal favor and an exceptional grace if the foolish man could be forgiven in his name so that his stay here in Iguape, where he so much enjoyed knowing the beautiful town and generous inhabitants, could begin in a climate of peace and friendship. The Judge, attentive and smiling, nodded his head. For a moment he meditated on the wording as an expert, then called on those present to applaud the magnanimous traditions of the great French nation and, turning again toward D'Arrast, declared himself satisfied. "Since that's the way it is," he concluded, "we shall dine this evening with the Chief." But D'Arrast said that he was invited by friends to the ceremony of the dances in the huts. "Ah, yes!" said the Judge. "I am glad you are going. You'll see, one can't resist loving our people."

That evening, D'Arrast, the ship's cook, and his brother were seated around the ashes of a fire in the center of the hut the engineer had already visited in the morning. The brother had not seemed surprised to see him return. He spoke Spanish hardly at all and most of the time merely nodded his head. As for the cook, he had shown interest in cathedrals and then had expatiated at length on the black bean soup. Now night had almost fallen and, although D'Arrast could still see the cook and his brother, he could scarcely make out in the back of the hut the squatting figures of an old woman and of the same girl who had served him. Down below, he could hear the monotonous river.

The cook rose, saying: "It's time." They got up, but the women did not stir. The men went out alone. D'Arrast hesitated, then joined the others. Night had now fallen and the rain had stopped. The pale-black sky still seemed liquid. In its transparent dark water, stars began to light up, low on the horizon. Almost at once they flickered out, falling one by one into the river as if the last lights were trickling from the sky. The heavy air smelled of water and smoke. Near by the sound of the huge forest could be heard too, though it was motionless. Suddenly drums and singing broke out in the distance, at first muffled and then distinct, approaching closer and closer and finally stopping. Soon after, one could see a procession of black girls wearing low-waisted white dresses of coarse silk. In a tight-fitting red jacket adorned with a necklace of vari-colored teeth, a tall Negro followed them and, behind him, a disorderly crowd of men in white pajamas and musicians carrying triangles and broad, short drums. The cook said they should follow the men.

The hut, which they reached by following the river a few hundred yards beyond the last huts, was large, empty, and relatively comfortable, with plastered walls. It had a dirt floor, a roof of thatch and reeds supported by a central pole, and bare walls. On a little palm-clad altar at the end, covered with candles that scarcely lighted half the hall, there was a magnificent colored print in which Saint George, with alluring grace, was getting the better of a bewhiskered dragon. Under the altar a sort of niche decorated with rococo paper sheltered a little statue of red-painted clay representing a horned god, standing between a candle and a bowl of water. With a fierce look the god was brandishing an oversized knife made of silver paper.

The cook led D'Arrast to a corner, where they stood against the wall near the door. "This way," he whispered, "we can leave without disturbing." Indeed, the hut was packed tight with men and women. Already the heat was rising. The musicians took their places on both sides of the little altar. The men and women dancers separated into two concentric circles with the men inside. In the very center the black leader in the red jacket took his stand. D'Arrast leaned against the wall, folding his arms.

But the leader, elbowing his way through the circle of dancers, came toward them and, in a solemn way, said a few words to the cook. "Unfold your arms, Captain," the cook said. "You are hugging yourself and keeping the saint's spirit from descending." Obediently D'Arrast let his arms fall to his sides. Still leaning against the wall, with his long, heavy limbs and his big face already shiny with sweat, D'Arrast himself looked like some bestial and kindly god. The tall Negro looked at them and, satisfied, went back to his place. At once, in a resounding voice, he intoned the opening notes of a song that all picked up in chorus, accompanied by the drums. Then the circles began to turn in opposite directions in a sort of heavy, insistent dance rather like stamping, slightly emphasized by the double line of swaying hips.

The heat had increased. Yet the pauses gradually diminished, the stops became less frequent, and the dance speeded up. Without any slowing of the others' rhythm, without ceasing to dance himself, the tall Negro again elbowed his way through the circles to go toward the altar. He came back with a glass of water and a lighted candle that he stuck in the ground in the center of the hut. He poured the water around the candle in two concentric circles and, again erect, turned maddened eyes toward the roof. His whole body taut and still, he was waiting. "Saint George is coming. Look! Look!" whispered the cook, whose eyes were popping.

Indeed, some dancers now showed signs of being in a trance, but a rigid trance with hands on hips, step stiff, eyes staring and vacant. Others quickened their rhythm, bent convulsively backward, and began to utter inarticulate cries. The cries gradually rose higher, and when they fused in a collective shriek, the leader, with eyes still raised, uttered a long, barely phrased outcry at the top of his lungs. In it the same words kept recurring. "You see," said the cook, "he says he is the god's field of battle." Struck by the change in his voice, D'Arrast looked at the cook, who, leaning forward with fists clenched and eyes staring, was mimicking the others' measured stamping without moving from his place. Then he noticed that he himself, though without moving his feet, had for some little time been dancing with his whole weight.

But all at once the drums began to beat violently and suddenly the big devil in red broke loose. His eyes flashing, his four limbs whirling around him, he hopped with bent knee on one leg after the other, speeding up his rhythm until it seemed that he must eventually fly to pieces. But abruptly he stopped on the verge of one leap to stare at those around him with a proud and terrible look while the drums thundered on. Immediately a dancer sprang from a dark corner, knelt down, and held out a short saber to the man possessed of the spirit. The tall Negro took the saber without ceasing to look around him and then whirled it above his head. At that moment D'Arrast noticed the cook dancing among the others. The engineer had not seen him leave his side.

In the reddish, uncertain light a stifling dust rose from the ground, making the air even thicker and sticking to one's skin. D'Arrast felt gradually overcome by fatigue and breathed with ever greater difficulty. He did not even see how the dancers had got hold of the huge cigars they were now smoking while still dancing; their strange smell filled the hut and rather made his head swim. He merely saw the cook passing near him, still dancing and puffing on a cigar. "Don't smoke," he said. The cook grunted without losing the beat, staring at the central pole with the expression of a boxer about to collapse, his spine constantly twitching in a long shudder. Beside him a heavy Negress, rolling her animal face from side to side, kept barking. But the young Negresses especially went into the most frightful trance, their feet glued to the floor and their bodies shaken from feet to head by convulsive motions that became more violent upon reaching the shoulders. Their heads would wag backward and forward, literally separated from a decapitated body. At the same time all began to howl incessantly with a long collective and toneless howl, apparently not pausing to breathe or to introduce modulations—as if the bodies were tightly knotted, muscles and nerves, in a single exhausting outburst, at last giving voice in each of them to a creature that had until then been absolutely silent. And, still howling, the women began to fall one by one. The black leader knelt by each one and quickly and convulsively pressed her temples with his huge, black-muscled hand. Then they would get up, staggering, return to the dance, and resume their howls, at first feebly and then louder and faster, before falling again, and getting up again, and beginning over again, and for a long time more, until the general howl decreased, changed, and degenerated into a sort of coarse barking which shook them with gasps. D'Arrast, exhausted, his muscles taut from his long dance as he stood still, choked by his own silence, felt himself stagger. The heat, the dust, the smoke of the cigars, the smell of bodies now made the air almost unbreathable. He looked for the cook, who had disappeared. D'Arrast let himself slide down along the wall and squatted, holding back his nausea.

When he opened his eyes, the air was still as stifling but the noise had stopped. The drums alone were beating out a figured bass, and groups in every corner of the hut, covered with whitish cloths, were marking time by stamping. But in the center of the room, from which the glass and candle had now been removed, a group of black girls in a semi-hypnotic state were dancing slowly, always on the point of letting the beat get ahead of them. Their eyes closed and yet standing erect, they were swaying lightly on their toes, almost in the same spot. Two of them, fat ones, had their faces covered with a curtain of raffia. They surrounded another girl, tall, thin, and wearing a fancy costume. D'Arrast suddenly recognized her as the daughter of his host. In a green dress and a huntress's hat of blue gauze turned up in front and adorned with plumes, she held in her hand a green-and-yellow bow with an arrow on the tip of which was spitted a multicolored bird. On her slim body her pretty head swayed slowly, tipped backward a little, and her sleeping face reflected an innocent melancholy. At the pauses in the music she staggered as if only half awake. Yet the intensified beat of the drums provided her with a sort of invisible support around which to entwine her languid arabesques until, stopping again together with the music, tottering on the edge of equilibrium, she uttered a strange bird cry, shrill and yet melodious.

D'Arrast, bewitched by the slow dance, was watching the black Diana when the cook suddenly loomed up before him, his smooth face now distorted. The kindness had disappeared from his eyes, revealing nothing but a sort of unsuspected avidity. Coldly, as if speaking to a stranger, he said: "It's late, Captain. They are going to dance all night long, but they don't want you to stay now." With head heavy, D'Arrast got up and followed the cook, who went along the wall toward the door. On the threshold the cook stood aside, holding the bamboo door, and D'Arrast went out. He turned back and looked at the cook, who had not moved. "Come. In a little while you'll have to carry the stone."

"I'm staying," the cook said with a set expression.

"And your promise?"

Without replying, the cook gradually pushed against the door that D'Arrast was holding open with one hand. They remained this way for a second until D'Arrast gave in, shrugging his shoulders. He went away.

The night was full of fresh aromatic scents. Above the forest the few stars in the austral sky, blurred by an invisible haze, were shining dimly. The humid air was heavy. Yet it seemed delightfully cool on coming out of the hut. D'Arrast climbed the slippery slope, staggering like a drunken man in the potholes. The forest, near by, rumbled slightly. The sound of the river increased. The whole continent was emerging from the night, and loathing overcame D'Arrast. It seemed to him that he would have liked to spew forth this whole country, the melancholy of its vast expanses, the glaucous light of its forests, and the nocturnal lapping of its big deserted rivers. This land was too vast, blood and seasons mingled here, and time liquefied. Life here was flush with the soil, and, to identify with it, one had to lie down and sleep for years on the muddy or dried-up ground itself. Yonder, in Europe, there was shame and wrath. Here, exile or solitude, among these listless and convulsive madmen who danced to die. But through the humid night, heavy with vegetable scents, the wounded bird's outlandish cry, uttered by the beautiful sleeping girl, still reached his ears.

When D'Arrast, his head in the vise of a crushing migraine, had awakened after a bad sleep, a humid heat was weighing upon the town and the still forest. He was waiting now under the hospital portico, looking at his watch, which had stopped, uncertain of the time, surprised by the broad daylight and the silence of the town. The almost clear blue sky hung low over the first dull roofs. Yellowish urubus, transfixed by heat, were sleeping on the house across from the hospital. One of them suddenly fluttered, opened his beak, ostensibly got ready to fly away, flapped his dusty wings twice against his body, rose a few inches above the roof, fell back, and went to sleep almost at once.

The engineer went down toward the town. The main square was empty, like the streets through which he had just walked. In the distance, and on both sides of the river, a low mist hung over the forest. The heat fell vertically, and D'Arrast looked for a shady spot. At that moment, under the overhang on one of the houses, he saw a little man gesturing to him. As he came closer, he recognized Socrates.

"Well, Mr. D'Arrast, you like the ceremony?"

D'Arrast said that it was too hot in the hut and that he preferred the sky and the night air.

"Yes," Socrates said, "in your country there's only the Mass. No one dances." He rubbed his hands, jumped on one foot, whirled about, laughed uproariously. "Not possible, they're not possible." Then he looked at D'Arrast inquisitively. "And you, are you going to Mass?"

"No."

"Then, where are you going?"

"Nowhere. I don't know."

Socrates laughed again. "Not possible! A noble without a church, without anything!"

D'Arrast laughed likewise. "Yes, you see, I never found my place. So I left."

"Stay with us, Mr. D'Arrast, I love you."

"I'd like to, Socrates, but I don't know how to dance." Their laughter echoed in the silence of the empty town.

"Ah," Socrates said, "I forget. The Mayor wants to see you. He is lunching at the club." And without warning he started off in the direction of the hospital.

"Where are you going?" D'Arrast shouted.

Socrates imitated a snore. "Sleep. Soon the procession." And, half running, he resumed his snores.

The Mayor simply wanted to give D'Arrast a place of honor to see the procession. He explained it to the engineer while sharing with him a dish of meat and rice such as would miraculously cure a paralytic. First they would take their places on a balcony of the Judge's house, opposite the church, to see the procession come out. Then they would go to the town hall in the main street leading to the church, which the penitents would take on their way back. The Judge and the Chief of Police would accompany D'Arrast, the Mayor being obliged to take part in the ceremony. The Chief of Police was in fact in the clubroom and kept paying court to D'Arrast with an indefatigable smile, lavishing upon him incomprehensible but obviously well-meaning speeches. When D'Arrast left, the Chief of Police hastened to make a way for him, holding all doors open before him.

Under the burning sun, in the still empty town, the two men walked toward the Judge's house. Their steps were the only sound heard in the silence. But all of a sudden a firecracker exploded in a neighboring street and flushed on every roof the heavy, awkward flocks of bald-necked urubus. Almost at once dozens of firecrackers went off in all directions, doors opened, and people began to emerge from the houses and fill the narrow streets.

The Judge told D'Arrast how proud he was to receive him in his unworthy house and led him up a handsome baroque staircase painted chalky blue. On the landing, as D'Arrast passed, doors opened and children's dark heads popped out and disappeared at once with smothered laughter. The main room, beautiful in architecture, contained nothing but rattan furniture and large cages filled with squawking birds. The balcony on which the Judge and D'Arrast settled overlooked the little square in front of the church. The crowd was now beginning to fill it, strangely silent, motionless under the heat that came down from the sky in almost visible waves. Only the children ran around the square, stopping abruptly to light firecrackers, and sharp reports followed one another in rapid succession. Seen from the balcony, the church with its plaster walls, its dozen blue steps, its blue-and-gold towers, looked smaller.

Suddenly the organ burst forth within the church. The crowd, turned toward the portico, drew over to the sides of the square. The men took off their hats and the women knelt down. The distant organ played at length something like marches. Then an odd sound of wings came from the forest. A tiny airplane with transparent wings and frail fuselage, out of place in this ageless world, came in sight over the trees, swooped a little above the square, and, with the clacking of a big rattle, passed over the heads raised toward it. Then the plane turned and disappeared in the direction of the estuary.

But in the shadow of the church a vague bustle again attracted attention. The organ had stopped, replaced now by brasses and drums, invisible under the portico. Black-surpliced penitents came out of the church one by one, formed groups outside the doors, and began to descend the steps. Behind them came white penitents bearing red-and-blue banners, then a little group of boys dressed up as angels, sodalities of Children of Mary with little black and serious faces. Finally, on a multicolored shrine borne by leading citizens sweating in their dark suits, came the effigy of the good Jesus himself, a reed in his hand and his head crowned with thorns, bleeding and tottering above the crowd that lined the steps.

When the shrine reached the bottom of the steps, there was a pause during which the penitents tried to line up in a semblance of order. Then it was that D'Arrast saw the ship's cook. Bare from the waist up, he had just come out under the portico carrying on his bearded head an enormous rectangular block set on a cork mat. With steady tread he came down the church steps, the stone perfectly balanced in the arch formed by his short, muscular arms. As soon as he fell in behind the shrine, the procession moved. From the portico burst the musicians, wearing bright-colored coats and blowing into beribboned brasses. To the beat of a quick march, the penitents hastened their step and reached one of the streets opening off the square. When the shrine had disappeared behind them, nothing could be seen but the cook and the last of the musicians. Behind them, the crowd got in motion amidst exploding firecrackers, while the plane, with a great rattle of its engine, flew back over the groups trailing behind. D'Arrast was looking exclusively at the cook, who was disappearing into the street now and whose shoulders he suddenly thought he saw sag. But at that distance he couldn't see well.

Through the empty streets, between closed shops and bolted doors, the Judge, the Chief of Police, and D'Arrast reached the town hall. As they got away from the band and the firecrackers, silence again enveloped the town and already a few urubus returned to the places on the roofs that they seemed to have occupied for all time. The town hall stood in a long, narrow street leading from one of the outlying sections to the church square. For the moment, the street was empty. From the balcony could be seen, as far as the eye could reach, nothing but a pavement full of potholes, in which the recent rain had left puddles. The sun, now slightly lower, was still nibbling at the windowless facades of the houses across the street.

They waited a long time, so long that D'Arrast, from staring at the reverberation of the sun on the opposite wall, felt his fatigue and dizziness returning. The empty street with its deserted houses attracted and repelled him at one and the same time. Once again he wanted to get away from this country; at the same time he thought of that huge stone; he would have liked that trial to be over. He was about to suggest going down to find out something when the church bells began to peal forth loudly. Simultaneously, from the other end of the street on their left, a clamor burst out and a seething crowd appeared. From a distance the people could be seen swarming around the shrine, pilgrims and penitents mingled, and they were advancing, amidst firecrackers and shouts of joy, along the narrow street. In a few seconds they filled it to the edges, advancing toward the town hall in an indescribable disorder—ages, races, and costumes fused in a motley mass full of gaping eyes and yelling mouths. From the crowd emerged an army of tapers like lances with flames fading into the burning sunlight. But when they were close and the crowd was so thick under the balcony that it seemed to rise up along the walls, D'Arrast saw that the ship's cook was not there.

Quick as lightning, without excusing himself, he left the balcony and the room, dashed down the staircase, and stood in the street under the deafening sound of the bells and firecrackers. There he had to struggle against the crowd of merrymakers, the taper-bearers, the shocked penitents. But, bucking the human tide with all his weight, he cut a path in such an impetuous way that he staggered and almost fell when he was eventually free, beyond the crowd, at the end of the street. Leaning against the burning-hot wall, he waited until he had caught his breath. Then he resumed his way. At that moment a group of men emerged into the street. The ones in front were walking backward, and D'Arrast saw that they surrounded the cook.

He was obviously dead tired. He would stop, then, bent under the huge stone, run a little with the hasty step of stevedores and coolies—the rapid, flat-footed trot of drudgery. Gathered about him, penitents in surplices soiled with dust and candle-drippings encouraged him when he stopped. On his left his brother was walking or running in silence. It seemed to D'Arrast that they took an interminable time to cover the space separating them from him. Having almost reached him, the cook stopped again and glanced around with dull eyes. When he saw D'Arrast—yet without appearing to recognize him—he stood still, turned toward him. An oily, dirty sweat covered his face, which had gone gray; his beard was full of threads of saliva; and a brown, dry froth glued his lips together. He tried to smile. But, motionless under his load, his whole body was trembling except for the shoulders, where the muscles were obviously caught in a sort of cramp. The brother, who had recognized D'Arrast, said to him simply: "He already fell." And Socrates, popping up from nowhere, whispered in his ear: "Dance too much, Mr. D'Arrast, all night long. He's tired."

The cook advanced again with his jerky trot, not like a man who wants to progress but as if he were fleeing the crushing load, as if he hoped to lighten it through motion. Without knowing how, D'Arrast found himself at his right. He laid his hand lightly on the cook's back and walked beside him with hasty, heavy steps. At the other end of the street the shrine had disappeared, and the crowd, which probably now filled the square, did not seem to advance any more. For several seconds, the cook, between his brother and D'Arrast, made progress. Soon a mere space of some twenty yards separated him from the group gathered in front of the town hall to see him pass. Again, however, he stopped. D'Arrast's hand became heavier. "Come on, cook, just a little more," he said. The man trembled; the saliva began to trickle from his mouth again, while the sweat literally spurted from all over his body. He tried to breathe deeply and stopped short. He started off again, took three steps, and tottered. And suddenly the stone slipped onto his shoulder, gashing it, and then forward onto the ground, while the cook, losing his balance, toppled over on his side. Those who were preceding him and urging him on jumped back with loud shouts. One of them seized the cork mat while the other took hold of the stone to load it on him again.

Leaning over him, D'Arrast with his bare hand wiped the blood and dust from the shoulder, while the little man, his face against the ground, panted. He heard nothing and did not stir. His mouth opened avidly as if each breath were his last. D'Arrast grasped him around the waist and raised him up as easily as if he had been a child. Holding him upright in a tight clasp with his full height leaning over him, D'Arrast spoke into his face as if to breathe his own strength into him. After a moment, the cook, bloody and caked with earth, detached himself with a haggard expression on his face. He staggered toward the stone, which the others were raising a little. But he stopped, looked at the stone with a vacant stare, and shook his head. Then he let his arms fall at his sides and turned toward D'Arrast. Huge tears flowed silently down his ravaged face. He wanted to speak, he was speaking, but his mouth hardly formed the syllables. "I promised," he was saying. And then: "Oh, Captain! Oh, Captain!" and the tears drowned his voice. His brother suddenly appeared behind him, threw his arms around him, and the cook, weeping, collapsed against him, defeated, with his head thrown back.

D'Arrast looked at him, not knowing what to say. He turned toward the crowd in the distance, now shouting again. Suddenly he tore the cork mat from the hands holding it and walked toward the stone. He gestured to the others to hold it up and then he loaded it almost effortlessly. His head pressed down under the weight of the stone, his shoulders hunched, and breathing rather hard, he looked down at his feet as he listened to the cook's sobs. Then with vigorous tread he started off on his own, without flagging covered the space separating him from the crowd at the end of the street, and energetically forced his way through the first rows, which stood aside as he approached. In the hubbub of bells and firecrackers he entered the square between two solid masses of onlookers, suddenly silent and gaping at him in amazement. He advanced with the same impetuous pace, and the crowd opened a path for him to the church. Despite the weight which was beginning to crush his head and neck, he saw the church and the shrine, which seemed to be waiting for him at the door. He had already gone beyond the center of the square in that direction when brutally, without knowing why, he veered off to the left and turned away from the church, forcing the pilgrims to face him. Behind him, he heard someone running. In front of him mouths opened on all sides. He didn't understand what they were shouting, although he seemed to recognize the one Portuguese word that was being constantly hurled at him. Suddenly Socrates appeared before him, rolling startled eyes, speaking incoherently and pointing out the way to the church behind him. "To the church! To the church!" was what Socrates and the crowd were shouting at him. Yet D'Arrast continued in the direction in which he was launched. And Socrates stood aside, his arms raised in the air comically, while the crowd gradually fell silent. When D'Arrast entered the first street, which he had already taken with the cook and therefore knew it led to the river section, the square had become but a confused murmur behind him.

The stone weighted painfully on his head now and he needed all the strength of his long arms to lighten it. His shoulders were already stiffening when he reached the first streets on the slippery slope. He stopped and listened. He was alone. He settled the stone firmly on its cork base and went down with a cautious but still steady tread toward the huts. When he reached them, his breath was beginning to fail, his arms were trembling under the stone. He hastened his pace, finally reached the little square where the cook's hut stood, ran to it, kicked the door open, and brusquely hurled the stone onto the still glowing fire in the center of the room. And there, straightening up until he was suddenly enormous, drinking in with desperate gulps the familiar smell of poverty and ashes, he felt rising within him a surge of obscure and panting joy that he was powerless to name.

When the inhabitants of the hut arrived, they found D'Arrast standing with his shoulders against the back wall and eyes closed. In the center of the room, in the place of the hearth, the stone was half buried in ashes and earth. They stood in the doorway without advancing and looked at D'Arrast in silence as if questioning him. But he didn't speak. Whereupon the brother led the cook up to the stone, where he dropped on the ground. The brother sat down too, beckoning to the others. The old woman joined him, then the girl of the night before, but no one looked at D'Arrast. They were squatting in a silent circle around the stone. No sound but the murmur of the river reached them through the heavy air. Standing in the darkness, D'Arrast listened without seeing anything, and the sound of the waters filled him with a tumultuous happiness. With eyes closed, he joyfully acclaimed his own strength; he acclaimed, once again, a fresh beginning in life. At that moment, a firecracker went off that seemed very close. The brother moved a little away from the cook and, half turning toward D'Arrast but without looking at him, pointed to the empty place and said: "Sit down with us."

Translated from the French by Justin O'Brien

Jane Bowles

Everything Is Nice

THE HIGHEST STREET IN THE BLUE MOSLEM TOWN skirted the edge of a cliff. She walked over to the thick protecting wall and looked down. The tide was out, and the flat dirty rocks below were swarming with skinny boys. A Moslem woman came up to the blue wall and stood next to her, grazing her hip with the basket she was carrying. She pretended not to notice her, and kept her eyes fixed on a white dog that had just slipped down the side of a rock and plunged into a crater of sea water. The sound of its bark was earsplitting. Then the woman jabbed the basket firmly into her ribs, and she looked up.

"That one is a porcupine," said the woman, pointing a henna-stained finger into the basket.

This was true. A large dead porcupine lay there, with a pair of new yellow socks folded on top of it.

She looked again at the woman. She was dressed in a haik, and the white cloth covering the lower half of her face was loose, about to fall down.

"I am Zodelia," she announced in a high voice. "And you are Bet-soul's friend." The loose cloth slipped below her chin and hung there like a bib. She did not pull it up.

Jane Bowles (1917-1973), although she published only one novel (*Two Serious Ladies*), one play (*In the Summer House*) and ten short stories, has received high praise for her craft from such authors as John Ashberry, Truman Capote, and Tennessee Williams. All of her work is available in *My Sister's Hand in Mine* (1977).

"You sit in her house and you sleep in her house and you eat in her house," the woman went on, and she nodded in agreement. "Your name is Jeanie and you live in a hotel with other Nazarenes. How much does the hotel cost you?"

A loaf of bread shaped like a disc flopped on to the ground from inside the folds of the woman's haik, and she did not have to answer her question. With some difficulty the woman picked the loaf up and stuffed it in between the quills of the porcupine and the basket handle. Then she set the basket down on the top of the blue wall and turned to her with bright eyes.

"I am the people in the hotel," she said. "Watch me."

She was pleased because she knew that the woman who called herself Zodelia was about to present her with a little skit. It would be delightful to watch, since all the people of the town spoke and gesticulated as though they had studied at the *Comédie Française.*

"The people in the hotel," Zodelia announced, formally beginning her skit. "I am the people in the hotel."

"'Good-bye, Jeanie, good-bye. Where are you going?'

"'I am going to a Moslem house to visit my Moslem friends, Betsoul and her family. I will sit in a Moslem room and eat Moslem food and sleep on a Moslem bed.'

"'Jeanie, Jeanie, when will you come back to us in the hotel and sleep in your own room?'

"'I will come back to you in three days. I will come back and sit in a Nazarene room and eat Nazarene food and sleep on a Nazarene bed. I will spend half the week with Moslem friends and half with Nazarenes.'"

The woman's voice had a triumphant ring as she finished her sentence; then, without announcing the end of the sketch, she walked over to the wall and put one arm around her basket.

Down below, just at the edge of the cliff's shadow, a Moslem woman was seated on a rock, washing her legs in one of the holes filled with sea water. Her haik was piled on her lap and she was huddled over it, examining her feet.

"She is looking at the ocean," said Zodelia.

She was not looking at the ocean; with her head down and the mass of cloth in her lap she could not possibly have seen it; she would have had to straighten up and turn around.

"She is *not* looking at the ocean," she said.

"She is looking at the ocean," Zodelia repeated, as if she had not spoken.

She decided to change the subject. "Why do you have a porcupine with you?" she asked her, although she knew that some of the Moslems, particularly the country people, enjoyed eating them.

"It is a present for my aunt. Do you like it?"

"Yes," she said. "I like porcupines. I like big porcupines and little ones, too."

Zodelia seemed bewildered, and then bored, and she decided she had somehow ruined the conversation by mentioning small porcupines.

"Where is your mother?" Zodelia said at length.

"My mother is in her country in her own house," she said automatically; she had answered the question a hundred times.

"Why don't you write her a letter and tell her to come here? You can take her on a promenade and show her the ocean. After that she can go back to her own country and sit in her house." She picked up her basket and adjusted the strip of cloth over her mouth. "Would you like to go to a wedding?" she asked her.

She said she would love to go to a wedding, and they started off down the crooked blue street, heading into the wind. As they passed a small shop Zodelia stopped. "Stand here," she said. "I want to buy something."

After studying the display for a minute or two Zodelia poked her and pointed to some cakes inside a square box with glass sides. "Nice?" she asked her. "Or not nice?"

The cakes were dusty and coated with a thin, ugly-colored icing. They were called *Galletas Ortiz*.

"They are very nice," she replied, and bought her a dozen of them. Zodelia thanked her briefly and they walked on. Presently they turned off the street into a narrow alley and started downhill. Soon Zodelia stopped at a door on the right, and lifted the heavy brass knocker in the form of a fist.

"The wedding is here?" she said to her.

Zodelia shook her head and looked grave. "There is no wedding here," she said.

A child opened the door and quickly hid behind it, covering her face. She followed Zodelia across the black and white tile floor of the closed patio. The walls were washed in blue, and a cold light shone through the broken panes of glass far above their heads. There was a door on each side of the patio. Outside one of them, barring the threshold, was a row of pointed slippers. Zodelia stepped out of her own shoes and set them down near the others.

She stood behind Zodelia and began to take off her own shoes. It took her a long time because there was a knot in one of her laces. When she was ready, Zodelia took her hand and pulled her along with her into a dimly lit room, where she led her over to a mattress which lay against the wall.

"Sit," she told her, and she obeyed. Then, without further comment she walked off, heading for the far end of the room. Because her eyes had not grown used to the dimness, she had the impression of a figure disappearing down a long corridor. Then she began to see the brass bars of a bed, glowing weakly in the darkness.

Only a few feet away, in the middle of the carpet, sat an old lady in a dress made of green and purple curtain fabric. Through the many rents in the material she could see the printed cotton dress and the tan sweater underneath. Across the room several women sat along another mattress, and further along the mattress three babies were sleeping in a row each one close against the wall with its head resting on a fancy cushion.

"Is it nice here?" It was Zodelia, who had returned without her haik. Her black crepe European dress hung unbelted down to her ankles, almost grazing her bare feet. The hem was lopsided. "It is nice here?" she asked again, crouching on her haunches in front of her and pointing at the old woman. "That one is Tetum," she said. The old lady plunged both hands into a bowl of raw chopped meat and began shaping the stuff into little balls.

"Tetum," echoed the ladies on the mattress.

"This Nazarene," said Zodelia, gesturing in her direction, "spends half her time in a Moslem house with Moslem friends and the other half in a Nazarene hotel with other Nazarenes."

"That's nice," said the women opposite. "Half with Moslem friends and half with Nazarenes."

The old lady looked very stern. She noticed that her bony cheeks were tatooed with tiny blue crosses.

"Why?" asked the old lady abruptly in a deep voice. "*Why* does she spend half her time with Moslem friends and half with Nazarenes?" She fixed her eye on Zodelia, never ceasing to shape the meat with her swift fingers. Now she saw that her knuckles were also tattooed with blue crosses.

Zodelia stared back at her stupidly. "I don't know why," she said, shrugging one fat shoulder. It was clear that the picture she had been painting for them had suddenly lost all its charm for her.

"Is she crazy?" the old lady asked.

"No," Zodelia answered listlessly. "She is not crazy." There were shrieks of laughter from the mattress.

The old lady fastened her sharp eyes on the visitor, and she saw that they were heavily outlined in black. "Where is your husband?" she demanded.

"He's traveling in the desert."

"Selling things," Zodelia put in. This was the popular explanation for her husband's trips; she did not try to contradict it.

"Where is your mother?" the old lady asked.

"My mother is in our country in her own house."

"Why don't you go and sit with your mother in her own house?" she scolded. "The hotel costs a lot of money."

"In the city where I was born," she began, "there are many, many automobiles and many, many trucks."

The women on the mattress were smiling pleasantly. "Is that true?" remarked the one in the center in a tone of polite interest.

"I hate trucks," she told the woman with feeling.

The old lady lifted the bowl of meat off her lap and set it down on the carpet. "Trucks are nice," she said severely.

"That's true," the women agreed, after only a moment's hesitation. "Trucks are very nice."

"Do *you* like trucks?" she asked Zodelia, thinking that because of their relatively greater intimacy she might perhaps agree with her.

"Yes," she said. "They are nice. Trucks are very nice." She seemed lost in meditation, but only for an instant. "Everything is nice," she announced, with a look of triumph.

"It's the truth," the women said from their mattress. "Everything is nice."

They all looked happy, but the old lady was still frowning. "Aicha!" she yelled, twisting her neck so that her voice could be heard in the patio. "Bring the tea!"

Several little girls came into the room carrying the tea things and a low round table.

"Pass the cakes to the Nazarene," she told the smallest child, who was carrying a cut-glass dish piled with cakes. She saw that they were the ones she had bought for Zodelia: she did not want any of them. She wanted to go home.

"Eat!" the women called out from their mattress. "Eat the cakes."

The child pushed the glass dish forward.

"The dinner at the hotel is ready," she said, standing up.

"Drink tea," said the old woman scornfully. "Later you will sit with the other Nazarenes and eat their food."

"The Nazarenes will be angry if I'm late." She realized that she was lying stupidly, but she could not stop. "They will hit me!" She tried to look wild and frightened.

"Drink tea. They will not hit you," the old woman told her. "Sit down and drink tea."

The child was still offering her the glass dish as she backed away toward the door. Outside she sat down on the black and white tiles to lace her shoes. Only Zodelia followed her into the patio.

"Come back," the others were calling. "Come back into the room."

Then she noticed the porcupine basket standing nearby against the wall. "Is that old lady in the room your aunt? Is she the one you were bringing the porcupine to?" she asked her.

"No. She is not my aunt."

"Where is your aunt?"

"My aunt is in her own house."

"When will you take the porcupine to her?" She wanted to keep talking, so that Zodelia would be distracted and forget to fuss about her departure.

"The porcupine sits here," she said firmly. "In my own house."

She decided not to ask her again about the wedding.

When they reached the door Zodelia opened it just enough to let her through. "Good-bye," she said behind her. "I shall see you tomorrow, if Allah wills it."

"When?"

"Four o'clock." It was obvious that she had chosen the first figure that had come into her head. Before closing the door she reached out and pressed two of the dry Spanish cakes into her hand. "Eat them," she said graciously. "Eat them at the hotel with the other Nazarenes."

She started up the steep alley, headed once again for the walk along the cliff. The houses on either side of her were so close that she could smell the dampness of the walls and feel it on her cheeks like a thicker air.

When she reached the place where she had met Zodelia she went over to the wall and leaned on it. Although the sun had sunk behind the houses, the sky was still luminous and the blue of the wall had deepened. She rubbed her fingers along it: the wash was fresh and a little of the powdery stuff came off. And she remembered how once she had reached out to touch the face of a clown because it had awakened some longing. It had happened at a little circus, but not when she was a child.

Hermann Hesse

Robert Aghion

IN THE COURSE OF THE EIGHTEENTH CENTURY a new type of Christianity and Christian endeavor grew up in England, expanding rather quickly from a negligible root into a large exotic tree. Today it is known to all as the Evangelical Mission to the Heathen.

On the surface there would seem to have been ample reason and justification for the missionary activity of the English Protestants. Since the glorious age of discovery, lands had been explored and conquered in every part of the earth. Scientific interest in the configuration of remote islands and mountain ranges as well as the heroism of navigators and adventurers had given way to a modern spirit, a new sort of interest in exotic regions, no longer hinging on adventurous exploits and experiences, strange animals and romantic palm forests, but on pepper and sugar, silks and furs, rice and sago, in short on the commodities with which traders make money. This commercial activity had often been pursued blindly and ruthlessly; certain rules having currency in Christian Europe had been forgotten and infringed upon. Terrified natives had been hunted like wild animals in America, Africa, and India; enlightened Christian Europeans had conducted themselves like foxes in a chicken coop, and one need not be oversqueamish to conclude that their behavior was monstrous, more like that of crude, swinish bandits than of Chris-

---

The German writer *Hermann Hesse* (1877-1962), winner of the Nobel Prize for Literature in 1946, is best known for his novels *Siddharta, Demian, Steppenwolf*, and *Das Glasperlenspiel* (English trans. *Magister Ludi*).

tians. Reactions of shame and indignation in their home countries led among other things to the missionary movement, springing from a laudable desire that the heathen peoples of the earth might receive something better and nobler from Europe than gunpowder and brandy.

In the latter half of the century it was not uncommon for high-minded private citizens to take an active interest in this missionary idea and to provide the wherewithal for its implementation. At that time, however, there were no regular missionary societies and organizations such as flourish today; each benefactor individually tried, so far as his resources permitted, to further the cause in his own way, and a man who in those days went to remote parts as a missionary did not, as he would now, cross the seas like a well-addressed piece of mail to embark on prearranged and well-organized activities, but, with little more than his trust in God to prepare himself for his task, flung himself headlong into a dubious adventure.

In the 1790s a London merchant, whose brother had grown wealthy in India and there died childless, decided to provide a sizable sum of money for the dissemination of the Gospel in that country. A member of the powerful East India Company and several clergymen were taken on as advisers and a plan was drawn up. As a first step three or four young men were to be provided with adequate equipment and travel money and sent out as missionaries.

The announcement of this undertaking quickly attracted any number of adventurous souls, unsuccessful actors and discharged barbers' apprentices felt that this journey was just what they needed, and the pious committee had the greatest difficulty in carrying on their search for worthy candidates over the heads of these undesirable applicants. Working through private channels, they addressed themselves chiefly to young theologians, but the English clergymen of the day were not at all weary of their homeland or eager for strenuous, not to say dangerous, undertakings; the search dragged out, and the donor began to be impatient.

At length the news of his intentions and difficulties reached a village parsonage in Lancashire, where it so happened that Robert Aghion, the parson's young nephew, was performing the duties of a curate in return for his board and lodging. Aghion was the son of a sea captain and of a pious, hardworking Scotswoman; he had hardly known his father, who had died when he was very young, and his uncle, who thought well of his talents, had sent him to school and systematically prepared him for the ministry, in which he had made as much progress as could be expected of a candidate with good credentials but no private fortune. In the meantime he assisted his uncle and benefactor, during whose lifetime he could not hope for a parish of his own. And since the parson was still hale and hearty, the nephew's prospects were none too brilliant. As a poor young fellow with little hope of coming into a living before his middle years, he was not regarded as a desirable match, not at least by respectable girls, and he had never met any others.

Thanks to his deeply pious mother, he was animated by a simple Christian faith which he rejoiced in proclaiming from the pulpit. But his mind found its greatest pleasure in the observation of nature, for which he possessed a keen eye. A modest, unspoiled young man with capable eyes and hands, he found satisfaction in seeing and knowing, collecting and investigating the things of nature that came his way. As a boy he had grown flowers and studied botany, for a time he had taken a lively interest in stones and fossils, and recently, especially since he had been living in the country, he had developed a particular love for the colorful insect world. Most of all, he loved the butterflies; their dramatic transformation from the caterpillar and chrysalis state delighted him time and time again, while their colors and designs gave him the pure pleasure of which less gifted men are capable only in early childhood.

Such was the young theologian who was first to perk up his ears at the news of the mission. In his innermost soul it aroused a longing that pointed like a compass needle to India. His mother had died a few years before; he was not engaged, nor had he given any young girl his secret promise. He wrote to London, received an encouraging reply and travel money, and set out at once with a small chest of books and a bundle of clothes, regretting only that he could not take his herbariums, fossils, and butterfly cases with him.

Arrived in the somber, noisy city, the candidate went to the pious merchant's tall, solemn house and entered with beating heart. In the gloomy corridor an enormous wall map of the eastern hemisphere and then in the first room a large tiger skin spoke to him of the country he longed for. Bewildered and uneasy, he followed the distinguished-looking servant to the room where the master of the house was waiting. He was received by a tall, grave, close-shaven old gentleman with sharp steely-blue eyes and a look of severity, who, however, took a liking to the timid young candidate after the first few words, bade him be seated, and continued the interview with an air of trusting benevolence. When it was completed the merchant asked for and received the applicant's credentials, and rang for the servant, who silently led the young theologian to a guest room, where a moment later a second servant appeared with tea, wine, ham, bread and butter. Then Aghion was left alone with his collation. After stilling his hunger and thirst, he made himself comfortable in a blue-velvet armchair, pondered his situation, and looked idly about the room. After a short time he discovered two more messengers from the remote tropical country, a stuffed red-brown monkey in a corner beside the fireplace, and above it, fastened to the blue-silk hangings, the tanned skin of an enormous snake, whose eyeless head hung down blind and limp. These were things he appreciated and which he hastened to examine close at hand and to feel. Though the thought of the living boa, which he tried to substantiate by bending the glistening silvery skin into a tube, was somewhat horrifying and repugnant to him, the sight nevertheless fired his curiosity about the mysterious far country. He was determined to let himself be frightened neither by snakes nor by monkeys, and thought with delight of the fabulous flowers, trees, birds, and butterflies there must be in those blessed climes.

By then it was coming on evening, and a silent servant brought in a lighted lamp. Outside the tall window it was foggy dusk. The silence of the distinguished house, the faint surge of the big city in the distance, the solitude of the tall, cool room in which he felt like a prisoner, the lack of anything to do, and the eerie uncertainty of his situation combined with the gathering darkness of the autumn night to subdue the young man's eager expectations. After two hours, which he spent listening and waiting in the armchair, he gave up all hope for the present day. Suddenly grown tired, he lay down on the excellent bed and soon fell asleep.

In the middle of the night, as it seemed to him, he was awakened by a servant, who announced that the young gentleman was expected for dinner and should please make haste. Barely awake, Aghion crawled into his clothes. Staggering and wild-eyed, he followed the servant through rooms and corridors and down a flight of stairs to the large dining room, where in the glare of the chandeliers the lady of the house, clad in velvet and sparkling with jewels, examined him through a lorgnette and the master introduced him to two clergymen, who during the meal subjected their young brother to a sharp examination, endeavoring in particular to satisfy themselves as to the genuineness of his Christian faith. The sleepy apostle had difficulty in understanding all the questions, not to say answering them; but his timidity became him, and the gentlemen, who had become accustomed to candidates of a very different stamp, were well disposed toward him. After dinner maps were spread out in the next room, and Aghion was shown a yellow spot, indicating the town where he was to proclaim the word of God.

The following day he was taken to see the venerable gentleman who was the merchant's chief ecclesiastical adviser. The old man was instantly won by Robert's candor. He was not long in fathoming his cast of mind and, perceiving little religious militancy, began to feel sorry for him. He proceeded to expatiate on the perils of the ocean voyage and the hardships of life in the tropics, for it struck him as absurd that a young man should sacrifice and destroy himself in India when he seemed to have no special gifts or inclinations to prepare him for such a mission. Then he laid his hand on the candidate's shoulder, looked into his eyes with earnest kindness, and said: "What you say is all very well and I feel sure you are telling the truth; but I still fail to understand exactly what draws you to India. Be frank with me, my friend, and tell me without reservation: is it some worldly interest, or is it solely a heartfelt desire to carry our beloved Gospel to the poor heathen?" At this Robert Aghion blushed like a thief caught in the act. He cast down his eyes and said nothing for a time; then he admitted freely that though his pious intentions were quite sincere, it would never have occurred to him to apply for a post in India or to become a missionary altogether had he not been tempted by a longing for the rare plants and animals of that country, and in particular the butterflies. The old man saw that the youth had yielded up his ultimate secret and had nothing more to confess. He nodded and said with a friendly smile: "Well, that's a sin that you yourself will have to attend to. You shall go to India, my dear boy!" And growing grave again, he laid both hands on his head and solemnly blessed him in the words of the Bible.

Three weeks later the young missionary, well provided with chests and trunks, embarked as a passenger on a fine sailing vessel. He saw his native land sink into the gray sea, and in the very first week, before they had even sighted Spain, learned to know the moods and perils of the ocean. In those days it was not possible for a traveler to India to reach his goal as green and untired as today, when we board a comfortable steamer in Europe, avoid the circuit of Africa by passing through the Suez Canal, and reach our destination lethargic and befuddled by too much sleeping and eating. In those days sailing ships had to fight their way for months around the vastness of Africa, imperiled by storms and becalmed for days at a time. The passenger learned to bear heat and cold, to endure hunger and sleepless nights. A man who had such a journey behind him had long ceased to be an untried neophyte; he had learned to stand on his own feet more or less. And so it was with our missionary. The voyage from England to India took him 156 days, and the young man who landed in Bombay was a lean and weather-beaten mariner.

His enthusiasm and curiosity were still with him, though they had grown more serene. Whenever he had gone ashore in the course of his voyage, he had looked about him with the eyes of a naturalist; he had contemplated every tropical island with eagerness and awe. His courage and eagerness were undiminished as he set foot on the soil of India and made his way into the radiantly beautiful city.

He set out immediately to find the address he had been given; the house lay beneath tall coconut palms in a quiet suburban street. As he went in, his eyes grazed the small front garden, and though he had more important things to do and to look at just then, he found time to notice a bush with dark leaves and yellow flowers, around which a swarm of white butterflies were flitting merrily. With this image still in his slightly dazzled eyes, he climbed a few flat steps, crossed the wide, shady veranda, and passed through the house door, which was open. A white-clad Hindu servant with bare brown legs came running over the cool red-tile floor and made a deep bow. He said a few words of Hindustani in a nasal singsong, but soon noticed that the stranger did not understand him, and led him with supple bows and serpentine gestures of obeisance and invitation to a doorless doorway, covered with a loosely hanging bast mat. The mat was drawn aside from within, and out stepped a large, gaunt, domineering-looking man wearing a white tropical suit and straw sandals. In an incomprehensible Indian tongue he shot a few words of abuse at the servant, who made himself very small and slipped away. Then he turned to Aghion and bade him in English to come in.

The missionary tried to apologize for his unannounced arrival and to justify the unfortunate servant, who had done no wrong. But the other replied with a gesture of impatience: "You'll soon learn how to deal with the rascals. Come in. I've been expecting you."

"You must be Mr. Bradley," said the new arrival courteously, though he felt chilled and intimidated at this first step into the exotic household and at the sight of his future mentor.

"Yes, I'm Bradley, and you're Aghion, I presume. Well, don't stand there, come in! Have you had your lunch?"

With the curt, haughty manner of an experienced overseer and business agent, the big raw-boned man with brown hairy hands took charge of his guest. He ordered him a meal of mutton, rice, and fiery curry, assigned him a room, showed him through the house, took his letters and instructions, answered his first eager questions, and supplied him with the most indispensable rules of life in India. The house resounded with his cold, irascible commands and vituperations as he set the four Hindu servants in motion. He sent for an Indian tailor and commanded him to supply Aghion immediately with a dozen appropriate garments. Grateful and somewhat abashed, Aghion took all this as it came, though he would have preferred a quieter, more peaceful introduction to India; he would have liked to spend a little time making himself at home and unburdening himself of his impressions and of the emotions of his journey in a friendly conversation. Six months at sea had taught him to adapt himself to any situation. Nevertheless, when late in the afternoon Mr. Bradley went to town on business, the young missionary gave a happy sigh of relief and decided to go out by himself and quietly pay his respects to the land of India.

Solemnly he left his airy room, which had neither door nor window but only large openings in every wall, and went outside. He was wearing a broad-brimmed hat with a long sun veil and holding a stout walking stick. At the first step into the garden he drew a deep breath and looked around him; with eager senses he drank in the air and the fragrances, lights and colors of the strange, legendary country, to whose conquest he was expected to make a modest contribution, and to which he was quite ready to abandon himself.

What he now saw and felt was very much to his liking and seemed to confirm his dreams and intimations a thousand times over. In the violent sunlight he saw tall dense bushes studded with large blossoms that struck him by the intensity of their color; he saw the smooth slender trunks of coconut trees culminating, at an amazing height, in the still, round crowns; behind the house there was a fan palm, stiffly holding out its astonishingly regular giant wheel of man-sized leaves. At the edge of the path his naturalist's eye perceived a little creature which he approached cautiously. It was a green chameleon with a small triangular head and malignant little eyes. As he bent down over it, he felt as happy as a small boy.

Strange music awakened him from his devout immersion. From the whispering stillness of the deep green wilderness of tree and garden there burst the rhythmic sound of trumpets and drums and piercingly high-pitched woodwinds. He listened in surprise, and since he could see nothing, started in the direction of the sound, curious to discover the nature and source of this festive and barbaric music. He left the garden, whose gate was wide open, and followed the grassy road through a friendly landscape of gardens, palm groves, and smiling light-green rice fields, until, rounding the corner of a garden, he found himself in a villagelike alley bordered by Indian huts. The little houses were built of clay, or merely of bamboo poles, and roofed with dry palm leaves. In every doorway brown Hindu families were standing or squatting. He looked around him with curiosity; this was his first glimpse of the village life of these strange brown-skinned people; their beautiful, childlike eyes were full of unconscious, unrelieved sadness, and from the very first he loved them. He saw lovely women with quiet, doelike eyes peering through masses of long deep-black plaited hair; they wore silver ornaments on their noses and on their wrists and ankles, and had rings on their toes. The children were naked except for silver or horn amulets hanging from their necks by thin strings of bast.

The wild music was still playing; it was now very near, and at the next street corner he found what he was looking for—a weird, fantastically shaped, frighteningly tall building with an enormous gate at the center. Looking up in amazement, he saw that the whole enormous facade, up to its fine, distant tip, was composed of stone figures representing fabulous animals, men, gods, and devils, a tangled forest of torsos, limbs, and heads. The terrifying stone colossus was a Hindu temple; as it lay gleaming in the level rays of the evening sun, it told the astonished newcomer very clearly that these half-naked people with their animal-like gentleness were not the creatures of a primitive paradise, but had possessed ideas and gods, arts and religions for several thousand years.

The music fell silent, and from the temple emerged a throng of pious Indians in white and colored garments, led by a small group of grave Brahmans clearly set apart from the rest, the haughty bearers of an erudition and dignity that had frozen into set forms thousands of years before. They strode past the white man as nobles might stride past a common journeyman, and neither they nor the humble figures following them looked as if they had the slightest inclination to let a newly arrived foreigner instruct them in things divine or human.

When the crowd had dispersed and the street had grown quieter, Robert Aghion approached the temple and began with perplexed curiosity to study the figures of the façade, but soon gave up in dejection and terror, for the grotesque allegorical language of these sculptures confused and frightened him no less than the few shamelessly lewd scenes which he found naively depicted amid the swarm of gods.

As he turned away and looked about him for the way home, the temple and the street suddenly darkened; a brief, quivering play of colors crossed the sky, and quickly night fell. Though the young missionary had long been familiar with this eerily sudden darkening, it sent a slight shudder through him. With the deepening dusk thousands of insects set up a strident singing and chirping in every tree and bush round about, and in the distance he heard the strange wild sound of an animal crying out with rage or fear. Having luckily found the right way, Aghion hurried homeward. It was only a short distance, but by the time he arrived the whole countryside was shrouded in deep night and the high black sky was studded with stars.

Deep in thought he reached the house and made his way to the first lighted room. Mr. Bradley was waiting for him. "Ah," he said. "So there you are. You oughtn't to go out so late in the evening. It's dangerous. Which reminds me, can you handle a gun?"

"A gun? No. I've never learned to."

"Then you must learn soon . . . Where have you been?"

Full of enthusiasm, Aghion told him what he had seen and inquired eagerly to what religion this temple belonged, what sort of gods or idols were worshiped there, what all the carvings and the strange music meant, whether the proud men in white garments were priests, and what gods they served. But here he experienced his first disappointment. His mentor was not the least bit interested in such things. No one, he said, could make head nor tail of these idolatries, they were nothing but a hideous, obscene muddle; the Brahmans were lazy, good-for-nothing exploiters, the Indians in general were a swinish lot of beggars and scoundrels, and if a self-respecting Englishman knew what was good for him he would have nothing to do with them.

"But," said Aghion uncertainly, "isn't it my mission to show these misguided people the right way? If I'm to do that, mustn't I get acquainted with them and love them and know all about them—"

"You'll soon know more about them than you want to. Of course you must learn Hindustani and later on perhaps a few more of these beastly nigger languages. But when it comes to love, you won't get very far."

"But the people seemed inoffensive enough."

"Think so? Well, you'll see. I don't know what you're planning to do with the Hindus, and I can't judge. Our job is to bring this godless rabble a smattering of civilization and some conception of decency; I doubt if we ever get any further than that."

"But our morality, sir, or what you call decency, is the morality of Christ."

"You mean love? Well, just tell a Hindu you love him. Today he'll beg from you and tomorrow he'll steal your shirt out of your bedroom."

"Possibly."

"Definitely, my dear sir. The people you'll be dealing with here are irresponsible children; they still have no conception of honesty and right. They have nothing in common with our innocent English schoolchildren. No, they're a nation of sneaky brown brats, who are never happier than when they've committed some abomination. Mark my words!"

Sadly Aghion realized that further questioning would be useless; he resolved for the present to work hard, to do as he was told, and to learn as much as he could. But regardless of whether the stern Bradley was right or wrong, the mere sight of the prodigious temple and of the haughty, unapproachable Brahmans convinced Aghion that his work and mission in this country would be far more difficult than he had first thought.

Next morning the chests containing his belongings arrived. Carefully he unpacked, piling shirts on shirts and books on books. Some of the objects made him thoughtful: a small black-framed engraving—the glass had been broken in transit—representing Mr. Defoe, the author of *Robin-*

son Crusoe; his mother's old prayer book, familiar to him since his earliest childhood; and encouraging tokens of the future: a map of India given to him by his uncle and two butterfly nets which he himself had had made in London. One of these he set aside for use during the next few days.

By evening his belongings had been sorted and stowed away; he had hung the engraving over his bed, and the whole room was in shipshape order. Following Bradley's advice, he had set the legs of his table and bedstead in little earthenware bowls and filled the bowls with water as a protection against ants. Mr. Bradley had been out on business all day, and it seemed very strange to the young man to be lured to meals by a sign from the servant and to be waited on by this brown-skinned man with whom he could not exchange a single word.

Next morning Aghion set to work. Bradley introduced him to Vyardenya, the handsome dark-eyed young man who was to teach him Hindustani. The smiling young Indian spoke quite well and had the best of manners; but he shrank back in fright when the unsuspecting Englishman held out his hand to him, and indeed avoided all bodily contact with the white man, which would have defiled him, since he was a member of a high caste. He was even unwilling to sit on a chair that had been used by a foreigner and each day brought with him, neatly rolled under his arm, his own pretty bast mat, which he spread out on the tile floor and sat on cross-legged and nobly erect. His student, with whose zeal he had every reason to be pleased, resolved to acquire this art, and during his lessons sat beside him on a similar mat, though every bone in his body ached until he had got used to it. Patiently and industriously, he learned word by word, beginning with the common formulas of greeting, which the teacher smilingly repeated over and over again. Each day Aghion flung himself with renewed courage into his struggle with the Indian palatals and gutturals, which at first sounded to him like inarticulate gurgling but which he gradually learned to distinguish and imitate.

Interesting as the Hindustani language was and quickly as the morning hours passed with the courteous teacher, the afternoons and especially the evenings were long enough to make the ambitious young missionary aware of the solitude in which he was living. His host, whose relationship with him was ill-defined and whose manner toward him was half that of a patron and half that of a superior officer, was seldom at home; he usually came back from town at about noon, sometimes on foot and sometimes on horseback, and presided over the noonday meal, to which he occasionally invited an English clerk. Then he lay down on the veranda for two or three hours to smoke and to sleep. Toward evening he would go back to his office or warehouse for another few hours. From time to time he went off for several days to buy produce, which was no great blow to Aghion, who, try as he might, was unable to make friends with the gruff, taciturn businessman. Moreover, Bradley often conducted himself in a way that the missionary could not approve of, as for example when he would spend the evening drinking a mixture of water, rum, and lime juice with the clerk until they were both quite tipsy; at first he had invited the young clergyman to join them, but the answer had always been a gentle refusal.

Under these circumstances Aghion's daily life was not exactly amusing. In the long dreary afternoons when the wooden house was besieged by the searing heat, he had gone into the kitchen and tried to practice his first feeble knowledge of the language on the servants. The Moslem cook maintained a haughty silence and did not even seem to see Aghion, but the water carrier and the houseboy, who had nothing to do but squat idly on their mats chewing betel nuts, had no objection to amusing themselves over the young sahib's desperate efforts to make himself understood.

But one day Bradley appeared in the kitchen door just as the two rascals were slapping their lean thighs with pleasure at the missionary's mistakes. For a moment Bradley looked on tight-lipped, then quick as a flash he boxed the houseboy's ears, gave the water carrier a kick, and without a word pulled the terrified Aghion into the living room. "How often," he said angrily, "do I have to tell you to keep away from the servants? You're spoiling them, with the best of intentions, of course. Besides it simply won't do for an Englishman to play the clown in front of those brown scoundrels." And he left the room before Aghion could reply.

The only break in the missionary's solitude was on Sunday, when he went to church regularly; once he even delivered the sermon in place of the none too industrious English parson. But though at home he had preached lovingly to the farm people and weavers, here, in a congregation of rich businessmen, tired sickly ladies, and gay young clerks, he felt out of place, uninspired.

Often when he thought of his situation he felt depressed and sorry for himself, but there was one consolation that never failed him: his nature studies. He would sling his specimen box over his shoulder and take his butterfly net, which he had provided with a long, thin bamboo pole. He delighted in the very things that most Englishmen complained of most bitterly, the blazing hot sun and the Indian climate in general, for he had kept himself fresh in body and soul. To the naturalist this country was an immeasurable treasure trove; at every step unknown trees, flowers, birds, and insects caught his attention, and he resolved that in time he would learn to know them all by name. By then the strange lizards and scorpions, the great centipedes and other monsters seldom frightened him, and since he had intrepidly killed a fat snake in the bathroom with a wooden bucket, he felt that he had little to fear from even the most forbidding of animals.

When for the first time he swung his net at a magnificent large butterfly, when he saw he had captured it and carefully took hold of the radiant proud creature, whose broad wings glittered like alabaster beneath a vaporous downy film of color, his heart beat with an impetuous joy that he had not experienced since he had captured his first swallow's nest as a boy. He cheerfully accepted the hardships of the jungle; he did not lose heart when he sank into hidden mud holes, when he was mocked by howling troops of monkeys, or attacked by enraged swarms of ants. Only once was he really afraid—when with the sound of a storm or an earthquake a herd of elephants came rumbling through the dense woods, and he cowered, trembling and praying, behind a great rubber tree. In his airy bedroom he got used to the furious chattering of the monkeys that woke him up in the morning and to the howling of the jackals at night. His eyes shone bright and alert in his sun-tanned face, which had grown leaner and more manly.

He also explored the city, and especially the peaceful gardenlike villages round about, and the more he saw of the Hindus the better he liked them. The one thing that distressed him was that the women of the lower castes tended to go about naked from the waist up. Though it was often a lovely sight, the missionary found it very hard to get used to seeing women's bare throats, arms, and breasts on the street.

Apart from this stumbling block nothing gave him so much food for thought as the enigma of these people's spiritual life. Wherever he looked, he saw religion. Assuredly one would not see so much piety in London on the highest Church holiday as here on every weekday; on every hand there were temples and sacred images, prayer and sacrifices, processions and ceremonies, penitents and priests. But how could anyone find his way in this tangle of faiths? There were Brahmans and Moslems, fire worshipers and Buddhists, devotees of Shiva and of Krishna; there were turbans and smooth-shaved heads, worshipers of snakes and worshipers of holy tortoises. What god did all these misguided souls serve? What sort of god was he, and which of all these many cults was the oldest, holiest, and purest? No one knew, and especially to the Indians themselves it was a matter of total indifference; if a man was not satisfied with the faith of his fathers, he took up another, or went out as a penitent to find, if not to found, another religion. Food was offered up in little bowls to gods and spirits whose names no one knew, and all these hundreds of religions, temples, and priesthoods lived cheerfully side by side; never did it occur to the adherents of one faith to hate or kill those of another, as was customary in the Christian countries of Europe. Much of what he found was lovely and charming, the playing of flutes, for example, or the flower offerings, and on many pious faces there was a peace and a serene light that one would have sought in vain on English faces. Another thing that struck him as beautiful and holy was the commandment, strictly observed by the Hindus, not to kill any living thing, and sometimes he felt ashamed and in need of self-justification when he had mercilessly killed a beautiful butterfly or beetle and mounted it on a pin. Yet among these same peoples, who looked upon the lowliest worm as God's creature and therefore sacred, and who showed the most fervent devotion in their prayers and temple services, theft and falsehood, perjury and breach of trust were everyday matters that aroused no indignation or even surprise in any one. The more the well-intentioned apostle pondered, the more these people struck him as an impenetrable riddle, defying all logic and theory. Despite Bradley's prohibition he had resumed his conversations with the houseboy. At one moment they had seemed the best of friends, but an hour later the boy had stolen one of his shirts. When earnestly and lovingly called to account, the servant first protested his innocence but soon smilingly confessed and brought back the shirt. There was a small hole in it, he explained, so he had felt sure that the sahib would not want to wear it.

On another occasion the water carrier filled him with astonishment. This man received board and wages for providing the kitchen and bathroom with water from the nearest cistern. He performed his daily task in the morning and in the evening; the rest of the day he sat in the kitchen or in the servants' hut, chewing betel or a stick of sugarcane. Once when the other servant had gone out, Aghion, whose trousers were covered with grass seed after one of his walks, asked the water carrier to brush them. The man only laughed and thrust his hands behind his back. The missionary became angry and ordered him to do as he was told. At that he complied, but grumbling and in tears; when he had finished he looked very unhappy and sat there muttering and expostulating for a whole hour. With great difficulty Aghion threaded his way through a series of misunderstandings and finally discovered that he had gravely offended the man by ordering him to do work incompatible with his position.

All these little experiences gradually condensed into an invisible wall that separated the missionary from his surroundings and left him more and more painfully alone. In his desperation he flung himself all the more eagerly into his language lessons and made good progress in the fervent hope of gaining access to this strange people. More and more often he ventured to speak to natives in the street; he went to the tailor's, the clothier's, the shoemaker's without an interpreter. Now and then he

succeeded in striking up a conversation by such stratagems as complimenting a craftsman on his work or a mother on her baby; and often,
through the words and glances of these heathen and in particular through
their good, childlike laughter, their soul spoke to him so clearly and
fraternally that for moments at a time all barriers vanished and he lost his
feeling of strangeness.

After a while he gained the impression that most children and simple
country people were accessible to him and that what came between him
and the city people was the distrust and depravity they had acquired from
contact with European sailors and businessmen. He began to venture
farther and farther into the country, often on horseback, taking with him
copper coins and sometimes lumps of sugar for the children. Deep in the
hills he would hitch his horse to a palm tree, enter a peasant's mud hut,
and ask for a drink of water or coconut milk. Almost always a friendly
conversation ensued; men, women, and children would join in, and he
was not at all displeased when they laughed merrily in their candid
amazement at his still imperfect knowledge of the language.

He made no attempt to speak of God. Not only did it seem to him
that there was no hurry; he also discovered that it was a thorny, well-nigh
impossible undertaking, for he simply could find no words in Hindustani
for the most common Christian concepts. Moreover, he felt that he would
have no right to set himself up as these people's teacher and bid them
make important changes in their way of life until he knew all about this
way of life and could live and speak with the Hindus on a more or less
equal footing.

This enlarged the sphere of his studies. He learned all he could about
the life and work of the natives; he asked them about trees and fruits,
domestic animals and implements and made a point of learning their
names; little by little he fathomed the secrets of wet and dry rice culture,
of cotton growing and the preparation of bast; he watched builders,
potters, and straw plaiters at work, and took a special interest in wool
weaving, a craft with which he was familiar at home. He looked on as the
fat, rose-red water buffaloes drew plows through muddy rice paddies, he
watched domesticated elephants at work, and saw tame monkeys bring
coconuts down from the trees for their master.

On one of his excursions, which took him to a peaceful valley between high green hills, he was surprised by a sudden downpour and
sought shelter in the first hut he could reach. In the small room with its
mud-covered bamboo walls he found a little family, which greeted him
with awe-struck amazement. The mother had dyed her gray hair a flaming red with henna, and as she turned to the stranger with the most
hospitable of smiles she showed him a mouth full of equally red teeth,

revealing her weakness for betel nuts. Her husband was a tall, grave-faced man whose long hair was still black. He rose from the ground, assumed a royally erect posture, exchanged greetings with the guest, and offered him a freshly opened coconut. The Englishman took a swallow of the sweetish milk. A little boy who had fled into the corner behind the stone fireplace peered out at him from under his glistening black hair with frightened, curious eyes; he was naked except for a glittering brass amulet on his dark chest. Several large bunches of bananas had been hung up over the door to ripen; what light there was in the hut came from the open doorway, but there was no sign of poverty, only an extreme simplicity and a pleasant order and cleanliness.

A quiet homelike feeling, rising from remote childhood memories—the kind of feeling that tends to come over a wanderer at the sight of a contented household and that he had never experienced in Mr. Bradley's bungalow—descended on the missionary. It almost seemed to him that in this house he had not only found refuge from the rain, but that, having been lost in the dark labyrinths of life, he had at last found the light and joy of an authentic, natural, self-sufficient way of life. The rain drummed furiously on the reed roof and in the doorway formed a sheet as thick and smooth as a glass wall.

The old people chatted with their unusual guest and when at length they politely asked the natural question—what had he come to this country for?—he felt uncomfortable and changed the subject. Once again it struck the modest young man as monstrously presumptuous that he should have come here as the envoy of a faraway nation to take away these people's faith and impose another upon them. He had always thought his misgivings would evaporate once he learned the language; but today it became clear to him beyond the shadow of a doubt that this had been a delusion and that the better he understood these brown people the less right and inclination he would feel to tell them how to live.

The rain abated and the water, turbid with red clay, drained from the sloping path; sunbeams forced their way between the glistening wet palm trunks and were reflected with dazzling brightness on the great shiny leaves of the pisang trees. The missionary thanked his hosts and was preparing to leave when a shadow fell across the floor and the room darkened. Quickly he turned around and saw a figure, a girl or young woman, step soundlessly through the doorway. Startled at the unexpected sight, she fled behind the fireplace, where the little boy was hiding.

"Bid the gentleman good day," her father called out to her. Shyly she took two steps forward, crossed her hands before her breasts, and bowed several times. Raindrops shimmered in her thick deep-black hair; embarrassed, the Englishman set his hand gently on her head and pronounced a greeting. He felt the soft, living hair in his fingers. A reddish-brown cloth was knotted below her breasts, otherwise she wore nothing except for a coral necklace and on one ankle a heavy gold bangle. Thus she stood in her beauty before the astonished stranger; the sun shone softly on her hair and on her smooth brown shoulders, and her teeth sparkled in her young mouth. Robert Aghion was enchanted at the sight: he tried to look deep into her gentle, quiet eyes, but then quickly he grew flustered; the moist fragrance of her hair and the sight of her bare shoulders and breasts confused him, and he cast down his eyes. He reached into his pocket, took out a pair of steel scissors which he used for his nails and beard and also for cutting plants, and gave them to the lovely girl, well aware that he was making her a sumptuous gift. Surprised and pleased, she took them shyly while her parents poured forth thanks. When he left the hut after bidding the family goodbye, she followed him outside, took his left hand, and kissed it. The warm tender touch to her flowerlike lips sent his blood coursing, he would have liked to kiss her on the mouth. Instead he took both her hands in his right hand, looked into her eyes, and asked: "How old are you?"

"I don't know," she said.

"What's your name then?"

"Naissa."

"Goodbye, Naissa, and don't forget me."

"Naissa will not forget the gentleman."

Deep in thought, he set out for home. He arrived after dark. Only as he entered his room did it come to him that he had not brought home a single butterfly or beetle, a single leaf or flower. His lodgings, the gloomy bachelor's house with its idle servants and the cold morose Mr. Bradley, had never seemed so alien and dismal as in that evening hour when he sat at the wobbly table, trying to read the Bible by his little oil lamp.

That night, when he finally fell asleep despite the turmoil of his thoughts and the buzzing of the mosquitoes, the missionary was beset by strange dreams.

He was walking through a darkening palm grove. Yellow flecks of sunlight were playing over the red-brown ground. Parrots were crying out overhead; high, high up in the trees monkeys were performing intrepid gymnastic feats; little birds glittered like jewels, insects of every kind proclaimed their joy of life in sounds, colors, and movements. As he walked amid this splendor, the missionary was filled with happiness and gratitude; he called out to one of the simian acrobats, and lo and behold, the agile creature climbed obediently down to the ground and stood before Aghion like a servant, making gestures of devotion. Aghion realized that all the creatures in his enchanted place were his to command. He summoned the birds and butterflies, and they came in great glittering swarms; he waved and beat time with his hands, nodded his head, gave orders by clicking his tongue and looking this way and that, and all the glorious creatures arranged themselves in the golden air into hovering rounds and processions; they piped and hummed, chirped and trilled in delicate chorus, pursued and caught one another, described solemn circles and droll spirals in the air. It was a magnificent ballet and concert, a paradise regained; yet the dreamer's joy in this harmonious magical world, which obeyed him and belonged to him, was tinged with pain. Deep within his happiness there lurked a faint forboding, a suspicion that all this was undeserved and must pass away, for how can a pious missionary feel otherwise in the presence of sensuous pleasure?

Nor did his foreboding deceive him. Even as he was reveling in the sight of a monkey quadrille and stroking a great blue velvet butterfly, which had settled trustingly on his left hand and was letting itself be caressed like a dove, shadows of fear and desolation came fluttering through the magic grove to darken the dreamer's soul. A bird cried out in sudden terror, a fitful wind roared through the treetops, the joyful warm sunlight grew dim and pale. Soon all the birds darted off, the lovely great butterflies, defenseless in their terror, were carried away by the wind, and raindrops splashed angrily on the foliage. Faint thunder rumbled across the sky and died away in the distance.

And then Mr. Bradley appeared. The last bright bird had vanished. As gigantic and somber as the ghost of the slain king, Bradley spat contemptuously and poured forth a stream of angry, scornful, insulting words: Aghion was a lazy scoundrel; his patron in London was paying him to convert the heathen, and instead he loafed and roamed about the country looking for bugs. Bowed with contrition, Aghion was forced to admit that Bradley was right, that he had neglected his duties.

Thereupon, the great rich patron from England, Aghion's employer, and several English clergymen appeared; along with Bradley, they harried and drove the missionary through thicket and brier, until they came to a bristling street in the suburbs of Bombay, and there lay the towering, grotesque Hindu temple. A motley crowd poured in and out, naked coolies and proud white-clad Brahmans. But across from the temple the dreamer saw a Christian church, and above the door there was an immense stone carving of God, hovering in the clouds with a flowing beard and grave fatherly eyes.

The harried missionary climbed the steps of the church, held out his arms to the Hindus, and began to preach. In a loud voice he called upon them to look and compare, to observe how different the true God was from their wretched grimacing idols with all their countless arms and

elephant trunks. He pointed a finger at the tangled figures on the façade
of the Indian temple, and then with a gesture of invitation at the divine
image on his church. But terror seized him when, following his own
gesture, he looked up; for God had changed, he had acquired three heads
and six arms, and in place of his rather idiotic and ineffectual solemnity,
his faces had taken on the knowing smile that is often seen on the images
of the Indian gods. Faltering, the preacher looked about him for Bradley,
his patron, and the clergymen, but they had all vanished; he was alone
and helpless on the church steps, and now God too forsook him, for he
was waving his six arms in the direction of the temple and smiling at the
Hindu gods with divine serenity.

Utterly forsaken and disgraced, Aghion stood on the church steps.
He closed his eyes and held himself erect; all hope was gone; he waited
with the calm of despair for the heathen to stone him. But after a few
anguished moments, he felt himself thrust aside by a strong but gentle
hand, and when he opened his eyes, he saw the great stone God striding
down the steps with dignity, while across the way the divine figures
descended in swarms from their places on the façade of the temple. After
greeting them one and all, God entered the Hindu temple, where with a
kindly gesture he received the homage of the white-clad Brahmans.
Meanwhile the heathen gods with their trunks, ringlets, and slit eyes went
into the church, where they found everything to their liking. Many of the
devout folk followed them, and in the end gods and people were moving
in pious procession from church to temple and from temple to church;
gong and organ mingled fraternally, and dark, silent Indians offered up
lotus blossoms on sober English-Christian altars.

In the midst of the festive crowd the dreamer saw the lovely Naissa
with her smooth, glistening black hair and her childlike eyes. Surrounded
by a throng of the faithful, she came from the temple, mounted the steps
of the church, and stood before the missionary. She looked gravely and
lovingly into his eyes, nodded to him, and held out a lotus blossom. In a
surge of delight he bent down over her clear quiet face, kissed her on the
lips, and enfolded her in his arms.

Before he had time to hear what Naissa might have to say about that,
Aghion woke from his dream and found himself stretched out on his bed
in deep darkness, exhausted and terrified. A painful confusion of all his
feelings and impulses tormented him to the point of despair. His dream
had laid bare his own self, his weakness and faintheartedness, his lack of
faith in his mission, his love for the brown heathen girl, his un-Christian
hatred of Bradley, and his guilty conscience toward his English patron.

For a time he lay forlornly in the darkness, overwrought and on the
verge of tears. He tried to pray but couldn't; he tried to think of Naissa as

a demon and of his love as a sin, but that too was impossible. At length, following a half-conscious impulse, still immersed in the shadows and terrors of his dream, he arose and went to Bradley's room, driven as much by an instinctive need for a human presence as by a pious wish to repent of his revulsion for this man, to speak frankly with him and make a friend of him.

He crept silently across the dark veranda on thin bast soles. The bamboo door to Bradley's room reached only halfway up the frame, and Aghion saw that the room was dimly lighted. Like many Europeans in India Bradley was in the habit of leaving a small oil lamp lighted all night. Cautiously Aghion pushed the flimsy door and went in.

The wick smoldered in an earthenware bowl on the floor, casting great dim shadows on the bare walls. A brown moth whirred around the flame. The mosquito net had been carefully drawn around the large bed. The missionary picked up the lamp, approached the bed, and opened the netting by a hand's breadth. He was just about to call the speaker by name when to his consternation he saw that Bradley was not alone. He was lying on his back in a thin silk nightdress, and his face with its jutting chin looked no softer or friendlier than by day. And beside him lay a second figure, a woman with long black hair. She was lying on her side, her face turned toward the missionary, and he recognized her; she was the big strapping girl who called for the washing each week.

Without stopping to close the netting, Aghion fled to his room. He tried to get back to sleep, but in vain; the day's experience, his dream, and finally the sight of the naked, sleeping woman had thoroughly roused him. His revulsion for Bradley had grown so strong that he dreaded the moment when he would have to see him and speak to him at breakfast. But what tormented him most was the question: was it his duty to reprimand Bradley for his conduct and try to reform him? Aghion's whole nature said no, but it seemed incumbent on him as a clergyman to overcome his cowardice and call the sinner to account. He lit his lamp and, plagued by the buzzing gnats, read the New Testament for several hours, but found no certainty or consolation. He was close to cursing all India, or at least his curiosity and spirit of adventure that had led him into this blind alley. Never had the future looked so dark and never had he felt so little cut out for an apostle and martyr.

His eyes were hollow and his features drawn when he went to breakfast. He stirred his fragrant tea morosely, broke off a banana and toyed with the peel until Mr. Bradley appeared. The master of the house muttered his usual "good morning," and set the houseboy and the water carrier in motion with loud commands. Slowly and circumspectly he picked the most perfect banana from the bunch and ate it quickly and haughtily, while the servant led his horse into the sunny yard.

"There's a matter I should like to discuss with you," said the mission-ary when Bradley was on the point of leaving. Bradley looked up suspi-ciously.

"I haven't much time. Does it have to be just now?"

"Yes, I believe so. I consider it my duty to tell you that I know of your illicit relations with a Hindu woman. You can imagine how painful it is for me—."

Bradley jumped up and burst into an angry laugh. "Painful!" he cried. "Aghion, you're a bigger fool than I thought. Obviously I don't give a damn what you think of me, but for you to nose around my house and spy on me is contemptible. I won't have it. I'll give you until Sunday. By then you'll kindly find yourself new lodgings. I won't keep you here a day longer."

Aghion had expected a sharp reply, but not this. Nevertheless, he was not to be intimidated.

"I shall be glad," he said with composure, "to relieve you of my burdensome presence. Good morning, Mr. Bradley!"

He walked out and Bradley looked after him, half-dismayed and half-amused. Then he stroked his stiff mustache, puckered up his mouth, whistled for his dog, and went down the wooden stairs to the yard, where his horse was waiting.

The brief, stormy exchange had come as a relief to both men; it cleared the air. Aghion, to be sure, found himself suddenly faced with problems which only a short while before had been pleasantly remote. But the more he pondered, the more clearly he saw that, though his quarrel with Bradley had been incidental, it had now become necessary for him to do something about the confusion of his affairs, and the thought cheered him. Life in this house, the empty hours, his unfilled desires, the want of an outlet for his energies, had become a torment which his simple, straightforward nature could not have borne much longer in any case.

It was still early in the morning, and a corner of the garden, his favorite spot, was still shady and cool. The branches of the untended bushes hung down over a small masonry pool which had originally been built for bathing but after long neglect had now become the home of a tribe of yellow turtles. He moved his bamboo reclining chair beside it, lay down, and watched the silent creatures swimming lazily about in the tepid green water, peering about them with their shrewd little eyes. In the yard nearby the stable boy was squatting idly in his corner, singing. The monotonous nasal song sounded like ripples ebbing away in the balmy air. Before he knew it, Aghion was overcome with weariness after his agitated, sleepless night; he closed his eyes, his arms dropped, and he fell asleep.

Awakened by the sting of a gnat, he saw to his shame that he had slept away most of the morning. But he felt refreshed and began at once to put his thoughts and desires in order, and calmly to unravel the tangled skein of his life. And now he knew, beyond any possible doubt, what had been paralyzing him and giving him anguished dreams: that though his coming to India had been a good and wise decision he lacked the inner vocation and drive to be a missionary. He was modest enough to regard this as a defeat and as a distressing shortcoming; but he saw no ground for despair. Quite to the contrary, now that he had made up his mind to find more suitable work, he was truly able to look upon India, with its immeasurable riches, as a promising haven and home. Unfortunate as it might be that all these natives had given themselves to false gods, it was not up to him to alter the fact. It was up to him to conquer this country for himself, to glean what was best in it for himself and others by bringing his practiced eye, his knowledge, and his youthful energy to bear, and by willingly accepting what hard work should present itself.

That very afternoon, after a brief interview, he was engaged by a Mr. Sturrock, a resident of Bombay, as secretary and overseer of a nearby coffee plantation. Aghion wrote a letter to his former patron, explaining his decision and undertaking to repay the money he had received, and Sturrock promised to forward it to London. When the new overseer returned home, he found Bradley alone at the dinner table, in his shirt sleeves. Before even sitting down, Aghion told him what he had done that day.

With his mouth full, Bradley nodded, poured a little whiskey into his drinking water, and said almost amiably: "Sit down and help yourself; the fish is cold. You could almost call us colleagues now. Well, I wish you luck. It's easier to raise coffee than to convert Hindus, no doubt about that, and for all I know it's just as useful. I wouldn't have given you credit for so much sense, Aghion."

The plantation that was to be his new home was two days' journey inland. Aghion was to set out in two days with a group of coolies, which left him only a day in which to attend to his affairs. Aghion asked leave to take a horse the following morning, and though surprised, Bradley asked no questions. After he had bidden the servant take away the lamp with its thousands of whirring insects, the two men sat facing each other in the warm balmy evening and felt closer to one another than they had in all their many months of forced cohabitation.

"Tell me something," Aghion began after a long silence. "Did you ever really believe in my plans to become a missionary?"

"Of course," said Bradley calmly. "I could see you were serious about it."

"But you must have seen how unfit I was for the work. Why didn't you tell me?"

"I had no instructions to do that. I don't like people meddling in my business, and I don't poke my nose into theirs. Besides, I've seen people do the craziest things here in India and succeed. Converting the heathen was your affair, not mine. And now you've seen your mistake all by yourself. In time you'll see others."

"For instance?"

"For instance, about that lecture you gave me this morning."

"Oh, the girl."

"Yes. You were a clergyman; but you'll have to admit that a normal man can't live and work and keep his health for years without having a woman now and then. Good God, there's nothing to blush about. Look: a white man in India, who hasn't brought a wife over with him from England, hasn't got much choice. There are no English girls. The ones that are born here are sent back to England when they're little. We can only choose between sailors' whores and Hindu women, and I prefer the Hindu women. What's so bad about that?"

"On that score we don't agree, Mr. Bradley. I stand with the Bible and our Church, which declare all relations with women out of wedlock to be evil and wrong."

"But if we can't get anything else?"

"Why not? If a man really loves a girl, he should marry her."

"A Hindu girl?"

"Why not?"

"Aghion, you're more broad-minded than I am. I'd sooner bite off my finger than marry a colored woman. And you'll feel the same way about it later on."

"Oh, no, I hope not. As long as we've got this far, I may as well tell you: I love a Hindu girl and I intend to make her my wife."

Bradley's face grew grave. "Don't do it," he said almost imploringly.

"But I will!" cried Aghion with enthusiasm. "We'll become engaged, and then I'll teach her and guide her until she can be baptized; and then we'll be married in the English church."

"What's her name?" Bradley asked thoughtfully.

"Naissa."

"And her father's?"

"I don't know."

"Well, it will take some time before she's ready for baptism; in the meanwhile think it over. Of course an Englishman can fall in love with an

Indian girl, a lot of them are pretty enough. And they're said to be faithful and to make good wives. But I still can't help regarding them as animals, more like playful antelopes or pretty does than human beings."

"Isn't that a prejudice? All men are brothers, and the Indians are an old and noble people."

"You know more about that than I do, Aghion. But for my part, I have a good deal of respect for prejudices."

He stood up, said good night, and went to his bedroom, where the night before he had slept with the pretty laundry woman. "Animals," he had said, and as Aghion thought about it now, his heart rebelled.

Early next morning, before Bradley was up, Aghion sent for his horse and rode off. The monkeys were still screaming their morning concert in the treetops. The sun was still low in the sky as he neared the hut where he had met the pretty Naissa. He tied up his mount and approached on foot. The little boy was sitting naked on the threshold, playing with a young goat and laughing as it butted him in the chest.

Just as the visitor was turning off the path, a girl, whom he recognized immediately as Naissa, came from inside the hut and stepped over the little boy. Carrying a tall earthenware pitcher in her right hand, she passed Aghion without seeming to notice him, and he delightedly followed her. He quickly caught up with her and called out a greeting. She answered in a soft voice, raised her head, and looked at him calmly out of her lovely golden-brown eyes, giving no sign of recognition. When he took her hand, she withdrew as though frightened, and hurried on her way. He followed her to the brick basin fed by a meager spring, whose water came trickling over old, moss-covered stones; he tried to help her fill the pitcher and lift it up, but she silently resisted, and the look on her face was cold and unfriendly. Surprised and disappointed at so much coyness, he reached into his pocket for the gift he had brought her, and all in all he felt rather hurt when she immediately dropped her reserve and reached for it. The gift was a small enameled box with flowers prettily painted on it and a mirror on the inside of the round lid. He showed her how to open it and put it into her hand.

"For me?" she asked, with great childlike eyes.

"For you," he said, and while she played with the box, he stroked her velvet-soft arm and her long black hair.

She thanked him and with an uncertain gesture picked up the pitcher. He tried to say something tender and loving, which apparently she only half understood. As he stood beside her, groping helplessly for words, he was suddenly struck by the enormity of the gulf between them. He reflected sadly on how little they had in common and how very, very long it would be before she could ever be his bride and companion, before she could understand his language, know him for what he was, and share his thoughts.

Meanwhile she had started slowly back to the hut, and he walked beside her. The little boy was engaged in a breathless game of tag with the goat; his black-brown back shimmered like metal in the sun, and his rice-bloated belly made his legs look scrawny. For a brief moment the Englishman was appalled when it came to him that if he married Naissa this child of nature would be his brother-in-law. To divert his mind from such thoughts, he looked at the girl again, at her entrancingly fine face with its great eyes and cool childlike lips. And he could not help wondering whether he would succeed in obtaining a first kiss from those lips that very day.

He was shaken out his tender reverie by a figure which suddenly emerged from the hut and stood like a ghost before his incredulous eyes. The form that appeared in the door frame, crossed the threshold, and stood before him was a second Naissa, a mirror image of the first. The mirror image smiled at him and greeted him, reached in her loincloth, and produced an object which she triumphantly raised over her head. It glistened in the sun and in a moment he recognized it. It was the little pair of scissors he had given Naissa, and the girl to whom he had just given the little box, into whose lovely eyes he had gazed and whose arm he had caressed, was not Naissa, but her sister. As the two girls stood side by side, still barely distinguishable, the lover felt infinitely cheated and lost. Two fawns could not have looked more alike, and if in that moment he had been left free to choose one of them and take her away with him and keep her forever, he would not have known which one he loved. He soon saw, to be sure, that the real Naissa was the older of the two, and somewhat smaller than her sister; but his love, which he had been so sure of only a few minutes past, had broken into two halves, just like his image of the girl, which had doubled so unexpectedly and eerily before his eyes.

Bradley learned nothing of this incident and asked no questions when Aghion returned home at noon and silently sat down at the table. Next morning Aghion's coolies came for his chests and sacks. When Aghion thanked Bradley for everything and held out his hand, Bradley shook it heartily and said: "Pleasant journey, my boy. A time will come when you will be sick of those sweet Hindu mugs and long for an honest, leathery face. When that happens, come and see me; we still disagree about a good many things, but then we'll see eye to eye."

Translated from the German by Ralph Mannheim

Questions for Discussion

1. In "The Growing Stone," how do D'Arrast's attitudes toward the small, rural Brazilian community differ at the end of the story from those which he holds at the beginning? What factors are responsible for his change?

2. In *The Myth of Sisyphus,* Camus argues that, in an "absurd" world, man is responsible for providing the meaning of his own life. This meaning generally comes about through a consciously made, personal "commitment" involving other human beings. To what extent, then, does D'Arrast represent Camus' concept of "engaged" man?

3. If a proper "commitment" necessarily involves other people, would not a successful adaptation require a similar feeling of responsibility for others? Can a person whose sole concerns are for himself ever make a successful adaptation to another culture?

4. In Jane Bowles's story, the leading character decides to spend half her time with Christian friends and half with Moslem friends. How successful would you expect this type of attitude to be in the long run? How would her Moslem friends be likely to perceive this division of time?

5. Is everything really nice in "Everything Is Nice"? If not, what is wrong? What might Jeanie do to better convey her desire to make friends with the Moslem women? Why did Jane Bowles select "Everything Is Nice" for the title of her story?

6. What is the significance of Jeanie's remembering the paint on a clown's face as she ponders the blue paint she has rubbed off a wall at the end of "Everything Is Nice"? Where else in the story does the color blue appear? What does the color seem to stand for?

7. What are Robert Aghion's reasons for wanting to go to India at the beginning of Hesse's story? Is his desire to be a missionary a "commitment" in Camus' sense of the word?

8. What causes Robert Aghion to abandon his initial purpose? Does his ceasing to be a missionary mean that Robert Aghion is an "uncommitted" man?

9. The protagonists in "The Growing Stone" and "Robert Aghion" both find themselves in cultures that have a strong belief in "fate" as the primary force controlling men's lives. Does this notion of fate present unique problems for a European or American, who usually believes that he has some control over his own destiny? In what kinds of situations might these contrasting beliefs pose the greatest difficulties?

10. What effect on the sojourners' adaptation would the presence of an accompanying spouse and family have? What about the effect of friends?

List of Additional Stories

Arévalo Martínez, Rafael. "Por cuatrocientos dólares (Un guatemalteco en Alaska)." ["For Four Hundred Dollars (A Guatemalan in Alaska)"] *El hombre que parceía caballo*. ["The Man Who Looked Like a Horse"] Guatemala City: Biblioteca Letras Centroamericanas, 1975. 51-79.

Baykurt, Fakir. "Monica." *Short Story International* 7.40 (1983): 79-87.

Bovey, John. "The Furies." *Desirable Aliens*. Urbana, IL: University of Illinois, 1980. 100-13.

_____. "The Garden Wall." *Desirable Aliens*. Urbana, IL: University of Illinois, 1980. 15-29.

Bowles, Jane. "A Guatemalan Idyll." *The Collected Works of Jane Bowles*. New York: Farrar, Straus, & Giroux, 1966. 321-58.

Bowles, Paul. "Tea on the Mountain." *Collected Stories 1939-1976*. Santa Barbara, CA: Black Sparrow Press, 1979. 15-26.

Boyle, Kay. "Fife." *The Smoking Mountain. Stories of Postwar Germany*. New York: McGraw-Hill, 1951. 89-100.

Bradbury, Ray. "Interval in Sunlight." *The Stories of Ray Bradbury*. New York: Alfred A. Knopf, 1980. 832-51.

Cheever, John. "Bella Lingua." *The Short Stories of John Cheever*. New York: Alfred A. Knopf, 1978. 302-18.

Chekhov, Anton Pavlovich. "Doč' Al'biona." ["Daughter of Albion"] *Polnoe sobranie sočinenij i pisem v tridcati tomax. Sočinenija*. ["Complete Collected Works and Letters in Thirty Volumes. Works"] Vol. 2. Moscow: Nauka, 1975. 195-98.

_____. "Patriot svoego otečestva." [A Patriot of the Fatherland"] ["Complete Collected Works and Letters in Thirty Volumes. Works"] *Polnoe sobranie sočinenij i pisem v tridcati tomax. Sočinenija*. Vol. 2. Moscow: Nauka, 1975. 66-67.

Dean, Geoffrey. "Strangers' Country." *Short Story International* 6.35 (1982): 9-21.

Farrell, James T. "A Dream of Love." *French Girls Are Vicious and Other Stories*. New York: The Vanguard Press, 1955. 61-79.

_____. "French Girls Are Vicious." *French Girls Are Vicious and Other Stories*. New York: The Vanguard Press, 1955. 15-43.

_____. "I Want to Meet a French Girl." *French Girls Are Vicious and Other Stories*. New York: The Vanguard Press, 1955. 91-100.

Gordimer, Nadine. "One Whole Year, and Even More." *Not for Publication, and Other Stories*. New York: Viking, 1965. 93-116.

Green, Graham. "A Chance for Mr. Lever." *Collected Stories*. New York: Viking Press, 1973. 490-509.

Haylock, John. "Fan Mail." *Short Story International* 8.45 (1984): 20-37.

_____. "Romance Trip." *Short Story International* 5.27 (1981): 21-41.

Jhabvala, Ruth Prawer. "In Love with a Beautiful Girl." *A Stronger Climate*. London: John Murray, 1968. 11-32.

_____. "A Star and Two Girls." *An Experience of India*. New York: W. W. Norton and Company, 1972. 46-79.

_____. "The Young Couple." *A Stronger Climate*. London: John Murray, 1968. 49-66.

La Farge, Oliver. "The Ancient Strength." *The Door in Wall*. Cambridge, MA: Houghton, Mifflin, 1965. 105-32.

Mansfield, Katherine. "Bains Turcs." *The Short Stories of Katherine Mansfield*. New York: Alfred A. Knopf, 1980. 159-63.

_____. "Germans at Meat." *The Short Stories of Katherine Mansfield*. New York: Alfred A. Knopf, 1980. 37-40.

_____. "A Truthful Adventure." *The Short Stories of Katherine Mansfield*. New York: Alfred A. Knopf, 1980. 18-24.

Matos, Autun Gustav. "The Neighbor." *A World of Great Stories*. Ed. Hiram Haydn and John Cournos. New York: Crown Publishers, 1947. 711-17.

Nosaka, Akiyuki. "American Hijiki." *Contemporary Japanese Literature*. Ed. Howard Hibbett. New York: Alfred A. Knopf, 1977. 435-68.

Sagan, Françoise. "The Sun Also Sets." *Short Story International* 5.27 (1981): 43-46.

Solouxin, Vladimir. "Obed za granicej." ["Dinner Abroad"] *Olepinskie prudy*. ["Olepinsky ponds"] Moscow: Sovremennik, 1973. 146-51.

Spingarn, Lawrence. "The Ritual Bath." *Short Story International* 4.21 (1980): 151-58.

Theroux, Paul. "The Greenest Island." *World's End and Other Stories*. New York: Washington Square Press, 1980. 172-217.

Updike, John. "Avec La Bébé-Sitter." *The Music School*. New York: Alfred A. Knopf, 1980. 66-75.

4. Shock Phase

CULTURE SHOCK IS POPULARLY UNDERSTOOD as the stunning impact that cultural differences have upon an individual. Often people will extend the term to any situation in which they are surprised to find themselves being misinterpreted and are unable to make themselves understood, regardless of whether or not cultural differences are a factor. Technically, however, culture shock applies to a fairly limited set of symptoms, a number of which are referred to in the general introduction. These include an inexplicable depression, withdrawal inward and isolation from others, somatic disorders that are difficult to locate and identify precisely, irritability, uncharacteristically eccentric and compulsive behavior, and unpredictable outbursts of aggression, among others.

Contrary to most popular views, shock does not occur upon immediate contact with a different culture. Rather it sets in much later, usually after a person has become involved with the host culture to a considerable extent and over a relatively long period of time. Moreover, the person who suffers from it may not be aware of what is happening to him until well after it has become apparent to others.

The stories that follow in this section provide a view of culture shock as it is understood in the technical sense, i.e. as only one phase of the more complex experience of being foreign. The story that opens this section, "Pastor Dowe at Tacaté" by Paul Bowles, presents a closely detailed account of the internalization of a second culture. The more external the forms of the Indian culture that Pastor Dowe agrees to adopt as outward signs of the ideas he wishes to convey, the more those outward forms compete with and displace the Pastor's innermost ideas, beliefs, and values. So thoroughly does Pastor Dowe adapt his own beliefs to the Indian forms of expression that his own become lost to him and he to them. Ironically, the end of the story finds him suddenly awakened to and frightened by the extent of the change that is upon him.

The destructive psychological effects of severe culture shock are also quite evident in "The Blue Hotel" by Stephen Crane, where the Swede alternates between manic and depressive states of behavior, between arrogant self-assertion and paranoiac fears of being killed. Although he has already spent a considerable amount of time in America and has supposedly adapted to American culture, his preconceptions of the American West and of the readiness of cowboys to resort to violence at the least provocation have a deep psychological impact; these preconceptions, as it turns out, do in fact bring about his death, almost as a self-fulfilling prophecy.

As we see in this story, latent psychological abnormalities tend to come to the fore when the individual is driven back on himself and feels unable to rely on outside help. As a result, he may, for the first time in his life, be forced to confront his existential situation. If this confrontation is successful, the sojourner will emerge stronger and more confident in his future dealings with both himself and his adopted culture.

If not, the sojourner may end up as Kayerts and Carlier in Joseph Conrad's "An Outpost of Progress." Left to themselves in the middle of Africa to manage a trading outpost, the two men deteriorate psychologically and morally after a long period of separation from the culture which spawned them. Conrad's story illustrates the truth in Jack London's warning to those who would travel to a far country: "It were better for the man who cannot fit himself to the new groove to return to his own country: If he delay too long he will surely die."

Paul Bowles

Pastor Dowe at Tacaté

PASTOR DOWE DELIVERED HIS FIRST SERMON in Tacaté on a bright Sunday morning shortly after the beginning of the rainy season. Almost a hundred Indians attended, and some of them had come all the way from Balaché in the valley. They sat quietly on the ground while he spoke to them for an hour or so in their own tongue. Not even the children became restive; there was the most complete silence as long as he kept speaking. But he could see that their attention was born of respect rather than of interest. Being a conscientious man he was troubled to discover this.

When he had finished the sermon, the notes for which were headed "Meaning of Jesus," they slowly got to their feet and began wandering away, quite obviously thinking of other things. Pastor Dowe was puzzled. He had been assured by Dr. Ramos of the University that his mastery of the dialect was sufficient to enable his prospective parishioners to follow his sermons, and he had had no difficulty conversing with the Indians who had accompanied him up from San Gerónimo. He stood sadly on the small thatch-covered platform in the clearing before his house and watched the men and women walking slowly away in different directions. He had the sensation of having communicated absolutely nothing to them.

All at once he felt he must keep the people here a little longer, and he called out to them to stop. Politely they turned their faces toward the pavilion where he stood, and remained looking at him, without moving. Several of the smaller children were already playing a game, and were darting about silently in the background. The pastor glanced at his wrist watch and spoke to Nicolás, who had been pointed out to him as one of the most intelligent and influential men in the village, asking him to come up and stand beside him.

Once Nicolás was next to him, he decided to test him with a few questions. "Nicolás," he said in his dry, small voice, "what did I tell you today?"

Nicolás coughed and looked over the heads of the assembly to where an enormous sow was rooting in the mud under a mango tree. Then he said: "Don Jesucristo."

"Yes," agreed Pastor Dowe encouragingly. "*Bai*, and Don Jesucristo what?"

"A good man," answered Nicolás with indifference.

"Yes, yes, but what more?" Pastor Dowe was impatient; his voice rose in pitch.

Nicolás was silent. Finally he said, "Now I go," and stepped carefully down from the platform. The others again began to gather up their belongings and move off. For a moment Pastor Dowe was furious. Then he took his notebook and his Bible and went into the house.

At lunch Mateo, who waited on table, and whom he had brought with him from Ocosingo, stood leaning against the wall smiling.

"Señor," he said, "Nicolás says they will not come again to hear you without music."

"Music!" cried Pastor Dowe, setting his fork on the table. "Ridiculous! What music? We have no music."

"He says the father at Yalactín used to sing."

"Ridiculous!" said the pastor again. "In the first place I can't sing, and in any case it's unheard of! *Inaudito!*"

"*Si, verdad?*" agreed Mateo.

The pastor's tiny bedroom was breathlessly hot, even at night. However, it was the only room in the little house with a window on the outside; he could shut the door onto the noisy patio where by day the servants invariably gathered for their work and their conversations. He lay under the closed canopy of his mosquito net, listening to the barking of the dogs in the village below. He was thinking about Nicolás. Apparently Nicolás had chosen for himself the role of envoy from the village to the mission. The pastor's thin lips moved. "A troublemaker," he whispered to himself. "I'll speak with him tomorrow."

Early the next morning he stood outside Nicolás's hut. Each house in Tacaté had its own small temple: a few tree trunks holding up some thatch to shelter the offerings of fruit and cooked food. The pastor took care not to go near the one that stood near by; he already felt enough like a pariah, and Dr. Ramos had warned him against meddling of that sort.

He called out.

A little girl about seven years old appeared in the doorway of the house. She looked at him wildly for a moment with huge round eyes before she squealed and disappeared back into the darkness. The pastor waited and called again. Presently a man came around the hut from the back and told him that Nicolás would return. The pastor sat down on a stump. Soon the little girl stood again in the doorway; this time she smiled coyly. The pastor looked at her severely. It seemed to him she was too old to run about naked. He turned his head away and examined the thick red petals of a banana blossom hanging nearby. When he looked back she had come out and was standing near him, still smiling. He got up and walked toward the road, his head down, as if deep in thought. Nicolás entered through the gate at the moment, and the pastor, colliding with him, apologized.

"Good," grunted Nicolás. "What?"

His visitor was not sure how he ought to begin. He decided to be pleasant.

"I am a good man," he smiled.

"Yes," said Nicolás. "Don Jesucristo is a good man."

"No, no, no!" cried Pastor Dowe.

Nicolás looked politely confused, but said nothing.

Feeling that his command of the dialect was not equal to this sort of situation, the pastor wisely decided to begin again. "Hachakyum made the world. Is that true?"

Nicolás nodded in agreement, and squatted down at the pastor's feet, looking up at him, his eyes narrowed against the sun.

"Hachakyum made the sky," the pastor began to point, "the mountains, the trees, those people there. Is that true?"

Again Nicolás assented.

"Hachakyum is good. Hachakyum made you. True?" Pastor Dowe sat down again on the stump.

Nicolás spoke finally, "All that you say is true."

The pastor permitted himself a pleased smile and went on. "Hachakyum made everything and everyone because He is mighty and good."

Nicolás frowned. "No!" he cried. "That is not true! Hachakyum did not make everyone. He did not make you. He did not make guns or Don Jesucristo. Many things He did not make!"

The pastor shut his eyes a moment, seeking strength. "Good," he said at last in a patient voice. "Who made the other things? Who made me? Please tell me."

Nicolás did not hesitate. "Metzabok."

"But who is Metzabok?" cried the pastor, letting an outraged note show in his voice. The word for God he had always known only as Hachakyum.

"Metzabok makes all the things that do not belong here," said Nicolás.

The pastor rose, took out his handkerchief and wiped his forehead. "You hate me," he said, looking down at the Indian. The word was too strong, but he did not know how to say it any other way.

Nicolás stood up quickly and touched the pastor's arm with his hand.

"No. That is not true. You are a good man. Everyone likes you."

Pastor Dowe backed away in spite of himself. The touch of the brown hand was vaguely distasteful to him. He looked beseechingly into the Indian's face and said, "But Hachakyum did not make me?"

"No."

There was a long pause.

"Will you come next time to my house and hear me speak?"

Nicolás looked uncomfortable.

"Everyone has work to do," he said.

"Mateo says you want music," began the pastor.

Nicolás shrugged. "To me it is not important. But the others will come if you have music. Yes, that is true. They like music."

"But *what* music?" cried the pastor in desperation.

"They say you have a *bitrola*."

The pastor looked away, thinking: "There is no way to keep anything from these people." Along with all his other household goods and the things left behind by his wife when she died, he had brought a little portable phonograph. It was somewhere in the storeroom piled with the empty valises and cold-weather garments.

"Tell them I will play the *bitrola*," he said, going through the gate.

The little girl ran after him and stood watching him as he walked up the road.

On his way through the village the pastor was troubled by the reflection that he was wholly alone in this distant place, alone in his struggle to bring the truth to its people. He consoled himself by recalling that it is only in each man's own consciousness that the isolation exists; objectively man is always a part of something.

When he arrived home he sent Mateo to the storeroom to look for the portable phonograph. After a time the boy brought it out, dusted it and stood by while the pastor opened the case. The crank was inside. He took it out and wound the spring. There were a few records in the compartment at the top. The first he examined were "Let's Do It," "Crazy Rhythm," and "Strike up the Band," none of which Pastor Dowe considered proper accompaniments to his sermons. He looked further. There was a recording of Al Jolson singing "Sonny Boy" and a cracked copy of "She's Funny That Way." As he looked at the labels he remembered how the music on each disc had sounded. Unfortunately Mrs. Dowe had disliked hymn music; she had called it "mournful."

"So here we are," he sighed, "without music."

Mateo was astonished. "It does not play?"

"I can't play them this music for dancing, Mateo."

"Cómo no, señor! They will like it very much!"

"No, Mateo!" said the pastor forcefully, and he put on "Crazy Rhythm" to illustrate his point. As the thin metallic tones issued from the instrument, Mateo's expression changed to one of admiration bordering on beatitude. "Qué bonito!" he said reverently. Pastor Dowe lifted the tone arm and the hopping rhythmical pattern ceased.

"It cannot be done," he said with finality, closing the lid.

Nevertheless on Saturday he remembered that he had promised Nicolás there would be music at the service, and he decided to tell Mateo to carry the phonograph out to the pavilion in order to have it there in case the demand for it should prove to be pressing. This was a wise precaution, because the next morning when the villagers arrived they were talking of nothing but the music they were to hear.

His topic was "The Strength of Faith," and he had got about ten minutes into the sermon when Nicolás, who was squatting directly in front of him, quietly stood up and raised his hand. Pastor Dowe frowned and stopped talking.

Nicolás spoke: "Now music, then talk. Then music, then talk. Then music." He turned around and faced the others. "That is a good way." There were murmurs of assent, and everyone leaned a bit farther forward on his haunches to catch whatever musical sounds might issue from the pavilion.

The pastor sighed and lifted the machine onto the table, knocking off the Bible that lay at the edge. "Of course," he said to himself with a faint bitterness. The first record he came to was "Crazy Rhythm." As it started to play, an infant nearby, who had been singsonging a series of meaningless sounds, ceased making its parrotlike noises, remaining silent and transfixed as it stared at the platform. Everyone sat absolutely quiet until the piece was over. Then there was a hubbub of approbation. "Now more talk," said Nicolás, looking very pleased.

The pastor continued. He spoke a little haltingly now, because the music had broken his train of thought, and even by looking at his notes he could not be sure just how far he had got before the interruption. As he continued, he looked down at the people sitting nearest him. Beside

Nicolás he noticed the little girl who had watched him from the doorway, and he was gratified to see that she was wearing a small garment which managed to cover her. She was staring at him with an expression he interpreted as one of fascinated admiration.

Presently, when he felt that his audience was about to grow restive (even though he had to admit that they never would have shown it outwardly) he put on "Sonny Boy." From the reaction it was not difficult to guess that this selection was finding less favor with its listeners. The general expression of tense anticipation at the beginning of the record soon relaxed into one of routine enjoyment of a less intense degree. When the piece was finished, Nicolás got to his feet again and raised his hand solemnly, saying: "Good. But the other music is more beautiful."

The pastor made a short summation, and, after playing "Crazy Rhythm" again, he announced that the service was over.

In this way "Crazy Rhythm" became an integral part of Pastor Dowe's weekly service. After a few months the old record was so badly worn that he determined to play it only once at each gathering. His flock submitted to this show of economy with bad grace. They complained, using Nicolás as emissary.

"But the music is old. There will be no more if I use it all," the pastor explained.

Nicolás smiled unbelievingly. "You say that. But you do not want us to have it."

The following day, as the pastor sat reading in the patio's shade, Mateo again announced Nicolás, who had entered through the kitchen and, it appeared, had been conversing with the servants there. By now the pastor had learned fairly well how to read the expressions on Nicolás's face; the one he saw there now told him that new exactions were at hand.

Nicolás looked respectful. "Señor," he said, "we like you because you have given us music when we asked you for it. Now we are all good friends. We want you to give us salt."

"Salt?" exclaimed Pastor Dowe, incredulous. "What for?"

Nicolás laughed good-naturedly, making it clear that he thought the pastor was joking with him. Then he made a gesture of licking. "To eat," he said.

"Ah, yes," murmured the pastor, recalling that among the Indians rock salt is a scarce luxury.

"But we have no salt," he said quickly.

"Oh, yes, señor. There." Nicolás indicated the kitchen.

The pastor stood up. He was determined to put an end to this haggling, which he considered a demoralizing element in his official relationship with the village. Signaling for Nicolás to follow, he walked into the kitchen, calling as he entered, "Quintina, show me our salt."

Several of the servants, including Mateo, were standing in the room. It was Mateo who opened a low cupboard and disclosed a great stack of grayish cakes piled on the floor. The pastor was astonished. "So many kilos of salt!" he exclaimed. "*Cómo se hace?*"

Mateo calmly told him it had been brought with them all the way from Ocosingo. "For us," he added, looking about at the others.

Pastor Dowe seized upon this, hoping it was meant as a hint and could be recognized as one. "Of course," he said to Nicolás. "This is for my house."

Nicolás looked unimpressed. "You have enough for everyone in the village," he remarked. "In two Sundays you can get more from Ocosingo. Everyone will be very happy all the time that way. Everyone will come each time you speak. You give them salt and make music."

Pastor Dowe felt himself beginning to tremble a little. He knew he was excited and so he was careful to make his voice sound natural.

"I will decide, Nicolás," he said. "Good-bye."

It was clear that Nicolás in no way regarded these words as a dismissal. He answered, "Good-bye," and leaned back against the wall calling, "Marta!" The little girl, of whose presence in the room the pastor now became conscious, moved out from the shadows of a corner. She held what appeared to him to be a large doll, and was being very solicitous of it. As the pastor stepped out into the bright patio, the picture struck him as false, and he turned around and looked back into the kitchen, frowning. He remained in the doorway in an attitude of suspended action for a moment, staring at little Marta. The doll, held lovingly in the child's arms, and swaddled in a much-used rag, was making spasmodic movements.

The pastor's ill-humor was with him; probably he would have shown it no matter what the circumstances. "What is it?" he demanded indignantly. As if in answer the bundle squirmed again, throwing off part of the rag that covered it, and the pastor saw what looked to him like a comic-strip caricature of Red Riding Hood's wolf peering out from under the grandmother's nightcap. Again Pastor Dowe cried, "What is it?"

Nicolás turned from his conversation, amused, and told Marta to hold it up and uncover it so the señor could see it. This she did, pulling away the wrapping and exposing to view a lively young alligator which, since it was being held more or less on its back, was objecting in a routine fashion to the treatment by rhythmically paddling the air with its little back feet. Its rather long face seemed, however, to be smiling.

"Good heavens!" cried the pastor in English. The spectacle struck him as strangely scandalous. There was a hidden obscenity in the sight of the mildly agitated little reptile with its head wrapped in a rag, but Marta was still holding it out toward him for his inspection. He touched the smooth scales of its belly with his fingers, and withdrew his hand, saying, "Its jaws should be bound. It will bite her."

Mateo laughed. "She is too quick," and then said it in dialect to Nicolás, who agreed, and also laughed. The pastor patted Marta on the head as she returned the animal to her bosom and resumed cradling it tenderly.

Nicolás's eyes were on him. "You like Marta?" he asked seriously.

The pastor was thinking about the salt. "Yes, yes," he said with the false enthusiasm of the preoccupied man. He went to his bedroom and shut the door. Lying on the narrow bed in the afternoon was the same as lying on it at night: there was the same sound of dogs barking in the village. Today there was also the sound of wind going past the window. Even the canopy of mosquito netting swayed a little from time to time as the air came into the room. The pastor was trying to decide whether or not to give in to Nicolás. When he got very sleepy, he thought: "After all, what principle am I upholding in keeping it from them? They want music. They want salt. They will learn to want God." This thought proved relaxing to him, and he fell asleep to the sound of the dogs barking and the wind shrilling past the window.

During the night the clouds rolled down off the mountains into the valley, and when dawn came they remained there, impaled on the high trees. The few birds that made themselves heard sounded as though they were singing beneath the ceiling of a great room. The wet air was thick with wood smoke, but there was no noise from the village; a wall of cloud lay between it and the mission house.

From his bed, instead of the wind passing the window, the pastor heard the slow drops of water falling upon the bushes from the eaves. He lay still awhile, lulled by the subdued chatter of the servant's voices in the kitchen. Then he went to the window and looked out into the grayness. Even the nearest trees were invisible; there was a heavy odor of earth. He dressed, shivering as the damp garments touched his skin. On the table lay a newspaper:

BARCELONA BOMBARDEADO POR
DOSCIENTOS AVIONES

As he shaved, trying to work up a lather with the tepid water Quintina had brought him, full of charcoal ashes, it occurred to him that he would like to escape from the people of Tacaté and the smothering feeling they gave him of being lost in antiquity. It would be good to be free from that infinite sadness even for a few hours.

He ate a larger breakfast than usual and went outside to the sheltered platform, where he sat down in the dampness and began to read the seventy-eighth Psalm, which he had thought of using as the basis of a sermon. As he read he looked out at the emptiness in front of him. Where he knew the mango tree stood he could see only the white void, as if the land dropped away at the platform's edge for a thousand feet or more.

"He clave the rocks in the wilderness, and gave them drink as out of the great depths." From the house came the sound of Quintina's giggling. "Mateo is probably chasing her around the patio," thought the pastor; wisely he had long since given up expecting any Indian to behave as he considered an adult should. Every few seconds on the other side of the pavilion a turkey made its hysterical gobbling sound. The pastor spread his Bible out on the table, put his hands to his ears, and continued to read: "He caused an east wind to blow in the heaven: and by His power He brought in the south wind."

"Passages like that would sound utterly pagan in the dialect," he caught himself thinking. He unstopped his ears and reflected: "But to their ears everything must have a pagan sound. Everything I say is transformed on the way to them into something else." This was a manner of thinking that Pastor Dowe had always taken pains to avoid. He fixed his eyes on the text with determination, and read on. The giggling in the house was louder; he could hear Mateo too now. "He sent divers sorts of flies among them;. . . and frogs, which destroyed them." The door into the patio was opened and the pastor heard Mateo coughing as he stood looking out. "He certainly has tuberculosis," said the pastor to himself, as the Indian spat repeatedly. He shut his Bible and took off his glasses, feeling about on the table for their case. Not encountering it, he rose, and taking a step forward, crushed it under his heel. Compassionately, he stooped down and picked it up. The hinges were snapped and the metal sides under their artificial leather covering were bent out of shape. Mateo could have hammered it back into a semblance of its form, but Pastor Dowe preferred to think: "All things have their death." He had had the case eleven years. Briefly he summed up its life: the sunny afternoon when he had bought it on the little side street in downtown Havana; the busy years in the hills of southern Brazil; the time in Chile when he had dropped the case, with a pair of dark glasses in it, out the bus window, and everyone in the bus had got out and helped him look for it; the depressing year in Chicago when for some reason he had left it in a bureau drawer most of the time and had carried his glasses loose in his coat pocket. He remembered some of the newspaper clippings he had kept in the case, and many of the little slips of paper with ideas jotted down on them. He looked tenderly down at it, thinking: "And so this is the place and time, and these are the circumstances of its death." For some reason he was happy to have witnessed this death; it was comforting to know exactly how the case had finished its existence. He still looked at it with sadness for a moment. Then he flung it out into the white air as if the precipice were really there. With his Bible under his arm he strode to the door and brushed past Mateo without saying a word. But as he walked into his room it seemed to him that Mateo had looked at him in a strange fashion, as if he knew something and were waiting to see when the pastor would find out, too.

Back in his suffocating little room the pastor felt an even more imperious need to be alone for a time. He changed his shoes, took his cane and went out into the fog. In this weather there was only one path practicable, and that led downward through the village. He stepped ahead over the stones with great caution, for although he could discern the ground at his feet and the spot where he put the tip of his cane each time, beyond that on all sides was mere whiteness. Walking along thus, he reflected, was like trying to read a text with only one letter visible at a time. The wood smoke was sharp in the still air.

For perhaps half an hour Pastor Dowe continued this way, carefully putting one foot before the other. The emptiness around him, the lack of all visual detail, rather than activating his thought, served to dull his perceptions. His progress over the stones was laborious but strangely relaxing. One of the few ideas that came into his head as he moved along was that it would be pleasant to pass through the village without anyone's noticing him, and it seemed to him that it might be managed; even at ten feet he would be invisible. He could walk between the huts and hear the babies crying, and when he came out at the other end no one would know he had been there. He was not sure where he would go then.

The way became suddenly rougher as the path went into a zigzagging descent along the steep side of a ravine. He had reached the bottom before he raised his head once. "Ah," he said, standing still. The fog was now above him, a great gray quilt of cloud. He saw the giant trees that stood around him and heard them dripping slowly in a solemn, uneven chorus onto the wild coca leaves beneath.

"There is no place such as this on the way to the village," thought the pastor. He was mildly annoyed, but more astonished, to find himself standing by these trees that looked like elephants and were larger than any other trees he had seen in the region. Automatically he turned around in the path and started back up the slope. Beside the overpowering sadness of the landscape, now that it was visible to him, the fog up there was a comfort and a protection. He paused for a moment to stare back at the fat, spiny tree trunks and the welter of vegetation beyond. A small sound behind him made him turn his head.

Two Indians were trotting down the path toward him. As they came up they stopped and looked at him with such expectancy on their dark little faces that Pastor Dowe thought they were going to speak. Instead the one ahead made a grunting sound and motioned to the other to follow. There was no way of effecting a detour around the pastor, so they brushed violently against him as they went by. Without once looking back they hurried on downward and disappeared among the green coca leaves.

This unlikely behavior on the part of the two natives vaguely intrigued him; on an impulse he determined to find an explanation for it. He started after them.

Soon he had gone beyond the spot where he had turned back a moment ago. He was in the forest; the plant odor was almost unbearable—a smell of living and dead vegetation in a world where slow growth and slow death are simultaneous and inseparable. He stopped once and listened for footsteps. Apparently the Indians had run on ahead of him; nevertheless he continued on his way. Since the path was fairly wide and well broken in, it was only now and then that he came into contact with a hanging tendril or a projecting branch.

The posturing trees and vines gave the impression of having been arrested in furious motion, and presented a monotonous succession of tortured *tableaux vivants*. It was as if, for the moment while he watched, the desperate battle for air had been suspended and would be resumed only when he turned away his head. As he looked, he decided that it was precisely this unconfirmable quality of surreptitiousness which made the place so disquieting. Now and then, high above his head, a blood-colored butterfly would float silently through the gloom from one tree trunk to another. They were all alike; it seemed to him that it must be always the same insect. Several times he passed the white grillwork of great spider webs flung between the plants like gates painted on the dark wall behind. But all the webs looked uninhabited. The large, leisurely drops of water still continued to fall from above; even if it had been raining hard, the earth could not have been wetter.

The pastor was astigmatic, and since he was beginning to be dizzy from watching so many details, he kept his eyes looking straight ahead as he walked, deviating his gaze only when he had to avoid the plant life that had grown across the path. The floor of the forest continued flat. Suddenly he became aware that the air around him was reverberating with faint sounds. He stood still, and recognized the casual gurgle a deep stream makes from time to time as it moves past its banks. Almost immediately ahead of him was the water, black and wide, and considering its proximity, incredibly quiet in its swift flowing. A few paces before him a great dead tree, covered with orange fungus, lay across the path. The pastor's glance followed the trunk to the left; at the small end, facing him, sat the two Indians. They were looking at him with interest, and he knew they had been waiting for him. He walked over to them, greeted them. They replied solemnly, never taking their shining eyes from his face.

As if they had rehearsed it, they both rose at the same instant and walked to the water's edge, where they stood looking down. Then one of them glanced back at the pastor and said simply, "Come." As he made his way around the log he saw that they were standing by a long bamboo raft which was beached on the muddy bank. They lifted it and dropped one end into the stream.

"Where are you going?" asked the pastor. For reply they lifted their short brown arms in unison and waved them slowly in the direction of downstream. Again the one who had spoken before said, "Come." The pastor, his curiosity aroused, looked suspiciously at the delicate raft, and back at the two men. At the same time he felt that it would be pleasanter to be riding with them than to go back through the forest. Impatiently he again demanded, "Where are you going? Tacaté?"

"Tacaté," echoed the one who up to this point had not spoken.

"Is it strong?" queried the pastor, stooping to push lightly on a piece of bamboo. This was merely a formality; he had perfect faith in the Indians' ability to master the materials of the jungle.

"Strong," said the first. "Come."

The pastor glanced back into the wet forest, climbed onto the raft, and sat doubled up on its bottom in the stern. The two quickly jumped aboard and pushed the frail craft from the bank with a pole.

Then began a journey which almost at once Pastor Dowe regretted having undertaken. Even as the three of them shot swiftly ahead, around the first bend in the stream, he wished he had stayed behind and could be at this moment on his way up the side of the ravine. And as they sped on down the silent waterway he continued to reproach himself for having come along without knowing why. At each successive bend in the tunnel-like course, he felt farther from the world, or did he mean farther from God? A region like this seemed outside God's jurisdiction. When he had reached that idea he shut his eyes. It was an absurdity, manifestly impossible—in any case, inadmissible—yet it had occurred to him and was remaining with him in his mind. "God is always with me," he said to himself silently, but the formula had no effect. He opened his eyes quickly and looked at the two men. They were facing him, but he had the impression of being invisible to them; they could see only the quickly dissipated ripples left behind on the surface of the water, and the irregular arched ceiling of vegetation under which they had passed.

The pastor took his cane from where it was lying hidden, and gesticulated with it as he asked, "Where are we going?" Once again they both pointed vaguely into the air, over their shoulders, as if the question were of no interest, and the expression on their faces never changed. Loath to let even another tree go past, the pastor mechanically immersed his cane in the water as though he would stop the constant forward thrusting of the raft; he withdrew it immediately and laid it dripping across the bottom.

Even that much contact with the dark stream was unpleasant to him. He tried to tell himself that there was no reason for his sudden spiritual collapse, but at the same time it seemed to him that he could feel the innermost fibers of his consciousness in the process of relaxing. The journey downstream was a monstrous letting go, and he fought against it with all his power. "Forgive me, O God, I am leaving You behind. Forgive me for leaving You behind." His nails pressed into his palms as he prayed.

And so he sat in agonized silence while they slid ahead through the forest and out into a wide lagoon where the gray sky was once more visible. Here the raft went much more slowly, and the Indians propelled it gently with their hands toward the shore where the water was shallow. Then one of them poled it along with the bamboo stick. The pastor did not notice the great beds of water hyacinth they passed through, or the silken sound they made as they rubbed against the raft. Out here under the low-hanging clouds there was occasionally a bird cry or a sudden rustle in the high grass by the water's edge. Still the pastor remained sunk within himself, feeling, rather than thinking: "Now it is done. I have passed over into the other land." And he remained so deeply preoccupied with this emotional certainty that he was not aware of it when they approached a high escarpment rising sheer from the lagoon, nor of when they drew up onto the sand of a small cove at one side of the cliff. When he looked up the two Indians were standing on the sand, and one of them was saying, "Come." They did not help him get ashore; he did this with some difficulty, although he was conscious of none.

As soon as he was on land they led him along the foot of the cliff that curved away from the water. Following a tortuous track beaten through the undergrowth they came out all at once at the very foot of the wall of rock.

There were two caves—a small one opening to the left, and a wider, higher one to the right. They halted outside the smaller. "Go in," they said to the pastor. It was not very light inside, and he could see very little. The two remained at the entrance. "Your god lives here," said one. "Speak with him."

The pastor was on his knees. "O Father, hear my voice. Let my voice come through to you. I ask it in Jesus' name. . . ." The Indian was calling to him, "Speak in our tongue." The pastor made an effort, and began a halting supplication in the dialect. There were grunts of satisfaction out-side. The concentration demanded in order to translate his thoughts into the still unfamiliar language served to clear his mind somewhat. And the comforting parallel between this prayer and those he offered for his congregation helped to restore his calm. As he continued to speak, always with fewer hesitations, he felt a great rush of strength going through him. Confidently he raised his head and went on praying, his eyes on the wall in front of him. At the same moment he heard the cry: "Metzabok hears you now. Say more to him."

The pastor's lips stopped moving, and his eyes saw for the first time the red hand painted on the rock before him, and the charcoal, the ashes, the flower petals and the wooden spoons strewn about. But he had no sensation of horror; that was over. The important thing now was that he felt strong and happy. His spiritual condition was a physical fact. Having prayed to Metzabok was also a fact, of course, but his deploring of it was in purely mental terms. Without formulating the thought, he decided that forgiveness would be forthcoming when he asked God for it.

To satisfy the watchers outside the cave he added a few formal phrases to his prayer, rose, and stepped out into the daylight. For the first time he noticed a certain animation in the features of the two little men. One said, "Metzabok is very happy." The other said, "Wait." Whereupon they both hurried over to the larger of the two apertures and disappeared inside. The pastor sat on a rock, resting his chin on the hand that held the head of his cane. He was still suffused with the strange triumphant sensation of having returned to himself.

He heard them muttering for a quarter of an hour or so inside the cave. Presently they came out, still looking very serious. Moved by curios-ity, the pastor risked a question. He indicated the larger cave with a finger and said, "Hachakyum lives there?" Together they assented. He wanted to go further and ask if Hachakyum approved of his having spoken with Metzabok, but he felt the question would be imprudent; besides, he was certain the answer would be in the affirmative.

They arrived back in the village at nightfall, after having walked all the way. The Indians' gait had been far too swift for Pastor Dowe, and they had stopped only once to eat some sapotes they had found under the trees. He asked to be taken to the house of Nicolás. It was raining lightly when they reached the hut. The pastor sat down in the doorway beneath the overhanging eaves of cane. He felt utterly exhausted; it had been one of the most tiring days of his life, and he was not home yet.

His two companions ran off when Nicolás appeared. Evidently he already knew of the visit to the cave. It seemed to the pastor that he had never seen his face so full of expression or so pleasant. "*Utz, utz,*" said Nicolás. "Good, good. You must eat and sleep."

After a meal of fruit and maize cakes, the pastor felt better. The hut was filled with wood smoke from the fire in the corner. He lay back in a low hammock which little Marta, casually pulling on a string from time to time, kept in gentle motion. He was overcome with a desire to sleep, but his host seemed to be in a communicative mood, and he wanted to profit by it. As he was about to speak, Nicolás approached, carrying a rusty tin biscuit box. Squatting beside the hammock he said in a low voice: "I will show you my things." The pastor was delighted; this bespoke a high degree of friendliness. Nicolás opened the box and took out some sample-size squares of printed cloth, an old vial of quinine tablets, a torn strip of newspaper, and four copper coins. He gave the pastor time to examine each carefully. At the bottom of the box were a good many orange and blue feathers which Nicolás did not bother to take out. The pastor realized that he was seeing the treasures of the household, that these items were rare objects of art. He looked at each thing with great seriousness handing it back with a verbal expression of admiration. Finally he said: "Thank you," and fell back into the hammock. Nicolás returned the box to the women sitting in the corner. When he came back over to the pastor he said: "Now we sleep."

"Nicolás," asked the pastor, "is Metzabok bad?"

"*Bai*, señor. Sometimes very bad. Like a small child. When he does not get what he wants right away, he makes fires, fever, wars. He can be very good, too, when he is happy. You should speak with him every day. Then you will know him."

"But you never speak with him."

"*Bai*, we do. Many do, when they are sick or unhappy. They ask him to take away the trouble. I never speak with him," Nicolás looked pleased, "because Hachakyum is my good friend and I do not need Metzabok. Besides, Metzabok's home is far—three hours' walk. I can speak with Hachakyum here." The pastor knew he meant the little altar outside. He nodded and fell asleep.

The village in the early morning was a chaos of shrill sounds: dogs, parrots and cockatoos, babies, turkeys. The pastor lay still in his hammock awhile listening, before he was officially wakened by Nicolás. "We must go now, señor," he said. "Everyone is waiting for you."

The pastor sat up, a little bit alarmed. "Where?" he cried.

"You speak and make music today."

"Yes, yes." He had quite forgotten it was Sunday.

The pastor was silent, walking beside Nicolás up the road to the mission. The weather had changed, and the early sun was very bright. "I have been fortified by my experience," he was thinking. His head was clear; he felt amazingly healthy. The unaccustomed sensation of vigor gave him a strange nostalgia for the days of his youth. "I must always have felt like this then. I remember it," he thought.

At the mission there was a great crowd—many more people than he had ever seen attend a sermon at Tacaté. They were chatting quietly, but when he and Nicolás appeared there was an immediate hush. Mateo was standing in the pavilion waiting for him, with the phonograph open. With a pang the pastor realized he had not prepared a sermon for his flock. He went into the house for a moment, and returned to seat himself at the table in the pavilion, where he picked up his Bible. He had left his few notes in the book, so that it opened to the seventy-eighth Psalm. "I shall read them that," he decided. He turned to Mateo. "Play the *disco*," he said. Mateo put on "Crazy Rhythm." The pastor quickly made a few pencil alterations in the text of the psalm, substituting the names of minor local deities, like Usukun and Sibanaa for such names as Jacob and Ephraim, and local place names for Israel and Egypt. And he wrote the word Hachakyum each time the word God or the Lord appeared. He had not finished when the record stopped. "Play it again," he commanded. The audience was delighted, even though the sound was abominably scratchy. When the music was over for the second time, he stood and began to paraphrase the psalm in a clear voice. "The children of Sibanaa, carrying bows to shoot, ran into the forest to hide when the enemy came. They did not keep their promises to Hachakyum, and they would not live as He told them to live." The audience was electrified. As he spoke, he looked down and saw the child Marta staring up at him. She had let go of her baby alligator, and it was crawling with a surprising speed toward the table where he sat. Quintina, Mateo, and the two maids were piling up the bars of salt on the ground to one side. They kept returning to the kitchen for more. He realized that what he was saying doubtless made no sense in terms of his listeners' religion, but it was a story of the unleashing of divine displeasure upon an unholy people, and they were enjoying it vastly. The alligator, trailing its rags, had crawled to within a few inches of the pastor's feet, where it remained quiet, content to be out of Marta's arms.

Presently, while he was still speaking, Mateo began to hand out the salt, and soon they all were running their tongues rhythmically over the large rough cakes, but continuing to pay strict attention to his words. When he was about to finish, he motioned to Mateo to be ready to start the record again the minute he finished; on the last word he lowered his arm as a signal, and "Crazy Rhythm" sounded once more. The alligator began to crawl hastily toward the far end of the pavilion. Pastor Dowe bent down and picked it up. As he stepped forward to hand it to Mateo, Nicolás rose from the ground, and taking Marta by the hand, walked over into the pavilion with her.

"Señor," he said, "Marta will live with you. I give her to you."

"What do you mean?" cried the pastor in a voice which cracked a little. The alligator squirmed in his hand.

"She is your wife. She will live here."

Pastor Dowe's eyes grew very wide. He was unable to say anything for a moment. He shook his hands in the air and finally he said: "No" several times.

Nicolás' face grew unpleasant. "You do not like Marta?"

"Very much. She is beautiful." The pastor sat down slowly on his chair. "But she is a little child."

Nicolás frowned with impatience. "She is already large."

"No, Nicolás. No. No."

Nicolás pushed his daughter forward and stepped back several paces, leaving her there by the table. "It is done," he said sternly. "She is your wife. I have given her to you."

Pastor Dowe looked out over the assembly and saw the unspoken approval in all the faces. "Crazy Rhythm" ceased to play. There was silence. Under the mango tree he saw a woman toying with a small, shiny object. Suddenly he recognized his glasses case; the woman was stripping the leatheroid fabric from it. The bare aluminum with its dents flashed in the sun. For some reason even in the middle of this situation he found himself thinking: "So I was wrong. It is not dead. She will keep it, the way Nicolás has kept the quinine tablets."

He looked down at Marta. The child was staring at him quite without expression. Like a cat, he reflected.

Again he began to protest. "Nicolás," he cried, his voice very high, "this is impossible!" He felt a hand grip his arm, and turned to receive a warning glance from Mateo.

Nicolás had already advanced toward the pavilion, his face like a thundercloud. As he seemed about to speak, the pastor interrupted him quickly. He had decided to temporize. "She may stay at the mission today," he said weakly.

"She is your wife," said Nicolás with great feeling. "You cannot send her away. You must keep her."

"*Diga que sí*," Mateo was whispering. "Say yes, señor."

"Yes," the pastor heard himself saying. "Yes. Good." He got up and walked slowly into the house, holding the alligator with one hand and pushing Marta in front of him with the other. Mateo followed and closed the door after them.

"Take her into the kitchen, Mateo," said the pastor dully, handing the little reptile to Marta. As Mateo went across the patio leading the child by the hand, he called after him. "Leave her with Quintina and come to my room."

He sat down on the edge of his bed, staring ahead of him with unseeing eyes. At each moment his predicament seemed to him more terrible. With relief he heard Mateo knock. The people outdoors were slowly leaving. It cost him an effort to call out, "*Adelante.*" When Mateo had come in, the pastor said, "Close the door."

"Mateo, did you know they were going to do this? That they were going to bring that child here?"

"*Sí, señor.*"

"You knew it! But why didn't you say anything? Why didn't you tell me?"

Mateo shrugged his shoulders, looking at the floor. "I didn't know it would matter to you," he said. "Anyway, it would have been useless."

"Useless? Why? You could have stopped Nicolás," said the pastor, although he did not believe it himself.

Mateo laughed shortly. "You think so?"

"Mateo, you must help me. We must oblige Nicolás to take her back."

Mateo shook his head. "It can't be done. These people are very severe. They never change their laws."

"Perhaps a letter to the administrator at Ocosingo . . ."

"No, señor. That would make still more trouble. You are not a Catholic." Mateo shifted on his feet and suddenly smiled thinly. "Why not let her stay? She doesn't eat much. She can work in the kitchen. In two years she will be very pretty."

The pastor jumped, and made such a wide and vehement gesture with his hands that the mosquito netting, looped above his head, fell down about his face. Mateo helped him disentangle himself. The air smelled of dust from the netting.

"You don't understand anything!" shouted Pastor Dowe, beside himself. "I can't talk to you! I don't want to talk to you! Go out and leave me alone." Mateo obediently left the room.

Pounding his left palm with his right wrist, over and over again, the pastor stood in his window before the landscape that shone in the strong sun. A few women were still eating under the mango tree; the rest had gone back down the hill.

He lay on his bed throughout the long afternoon. When twilight came he had made his decision. Locking his door, he proceeded to pack what personal effects he could into his smallest suitcase. His Bible and notebooks went on top with his toothbrush and atabrine tablets. When Quintina came to announce supper he asked to have it brought to his bed, taking care to slip the packed valise into the closet before he unlocked the door for her to enter. He waited until the talking had ceased all over the house, until he knew everyone was asleep. With the small bag not too heavy in one hand he tiptoed into the patio, out through the door into the fragrant night, across the open space in front of the pavilion, under the mango tree and down the path leading to Tacaté. Then he began to walk fast, because he wanted to get through the village before the moon rose.

There was a chorus of dogs barking as he entered the village street. He began to run, straight through to the other end. And he kept running even then, until he had reached the point where the path, wider here, dipped beneath the hill and curved into the forest. His heart was beating rapidly from the exertion. To rest, and to try to be fairly certain he was not being followed, he sat down on his little valise in the center of the path. There he remained a long time, thinking of nothing, while the night went on and the moon came up. He heard only the light wind among the leaves and vines. Overhead a few bats reeled soundlessly back and forth. At last he took a deep breath, got up, and went on.

Stephen Crane

The Blue Hotel

THE PALACE HOTEL AT FORT ROMPER WAS PAINTED a light blue, a shade
that is on the legs of a kind of heron, causing the bird to declare its
position against any background. The Palace Hotel, then, was always
screaming and howling in a way that made the dazzling winter landscape
of Nebraska seem only a gray swampish hush. It stood alone on the
prairie, and when the snow was falling the town two hundred yards away
was not visible. But when the traveller alighted at the railway station he
was obliged to pass the Palace Hotel before he could come upon the
company of low clapboard houses which composed Fort Romper, and it
was not to be thought that any traveller could pass the Palace Hotel
without looking at it. Pat Scully, the proprietor, had proved himself a
master of strategy when he chose his paints. It is true that on clear days,
when the transcontinental express, long lines of swaying Pullmans, swept
through Fort Romper, passengers were overcome at the sight, and the cult
that knows the brown-reds and the subdivisions of the dark greens of the
East expressed shame, pity, horror, in a laugh. But to the citizens of this
prairie town and to the people who would naturally stop there, Pat Scully
had performed a feat. With this opulence and splendor, these creeds,
classes, egotisms, that streamed through Romper on the rails day after
day, they had no color in common.

As if the display delights of such a blue hotel were not sufficiently

---

The American Naturalist writer *Stephen Crane* (1871-1900) is well-known for his
poems, his short stories, and his famous novel *The Red Badge of Courage*.

enticing, it was Scully's habit to go every morning and evening to meet the leisurely trains that stopped at Romper and work his seductions upon any man that he might see wavering, gripsack in hand.

One morning, when a snow-crusted engine dragged its long string of freight cars and its one passenger coach to the station, Scully performed the marvel of catching three men. One was a shaky and quick-eyed Swede, with a great shining cheap valise; one was a tall bronzed cowboy, who was on his way to a ranch near the Dakota line; one was a little silent man from the East, who didn't look it, and didn't announce it. Scully practically made them prisoners. He was so nimble and merry and kindly that each probably felt it would be the height of brutality to try to escape. They trudged off over the creaking board sidewalks in the wake of the eager little Irishman. He wore a heavy fur cap squeezed tightly down on his head. It caused his two red ears to stick out stiffly, as if they were made of tin.

At last, Scully, elaborately, with boisterous hospitality, conducted them through the portals of the blue hotel. The room which they entered was small. It seemed to be merely a proper temple for an enormous stove, which, in the center, was humming with godlike violence. At various points on its surface the iron had become luminous and glowed yellow from the heat. Beside the stove Scully's son Johnnie was playing High-Five with an old farmer who had whiskers both gray and sandy. They were quarrelling. Frequently the old farmer turned his face toward a box of sawdust—colored brown from tobacco juice—that was behind the stove, and spat with an air of great impatience and irritation. With a loud flourish of words Scully destroyed the game of cards, and bustled his son upstairs with part of the baggage of the new guests. He himself conducted them to three basins of the coldest water in the world. The cowboy and the Easterner burnished themselves fiery red with this water, until it seemed to be some kind of metal polish. The Swede, however, merely dipped his fingers gingerly and with trepidation. It was notable that throughout this series of small ceremonies the three travellers were made to feel that Scully was very benevolent. He was conferring great favors upon them. He handed the towel from one to another with an air of philanthropic impulse.

Afterward they went to the first room, and sitting about the stove, listened to Scully's officious clamor at his daughters, who were preparing the midday meal. They reflected in the silence of experienced men who tread carefully amid new people. Nevertheless, the old farmer, stationary, invincible in his chair near the warmest part of the stove, turned his face from the sawdust box frequently and addressed a glowing commonplace to the strangers. Usually he was answered in short but adequate sentences by either the cowboy or the Easterner. The Swede said nothing. He seemed to be occupied in making furtive estimates of each man in the room. One might have thought that he had the sense of silly suspicion which comes to guilt. He resembled a badly frightened man.

Later, at dinner, he spoke a little, addressing his conversation entirely to Scully. He volunteered that he had come from New York, where for ten years he had worked as a tailor. These facts seemed to strike Scully as fascinating, and afterward he volunteered that he had lived at Romper for fourteen years. The Swede asked about the crops and the price of labor. He seemed barely to listen to Scully's extended replies. His eyes continued to rove from man to man.

Finally, with a laugh and a wink, he said that some of these Western communities were very dangerous; and after his statement he straightened his legs under the table, tilted his head, and laughed again, loudly. It was plain that the demonstration had no meaning to the others. They looked at him wondering and in silence.

II

As the men trooped heavily back into the front room, the two little windows presented views of a turmoiling sea of snow. The huge arms of the wind were making attempts—mighty, circular, futile—to embrace the flakes as they sped. A gate-post like a still man with a blanched face stood aghast amid this profligate fury. In a hearty voice Scully announced the presence of a blizzard. The guests of the blue hotel, lighting their pipes, assented with grunts of lazy masculine contentment. No island of the sea could be exempt in the degree of this little room with its humming stove. Johnnie, son of Scully, in a tone which defined his opinion of his ability as a card-player, challenged the old farmer of both gray and sandy whiskers to a game of High-Five. The farmer agreed with a contemptuous and bitter scoff. They sat close to the stove, and squared their knees under a wide board. The cowboy and the Easterner watched the game with interest. The Swede remained near the window, aloof, but with a countenance that showed signs of an inexplicable excitement.

The play of Johnnie and the gray-beard was suddenly ended by another quarrel. The old man arose while casting a look of heated scorn at his adversary. He slowly buttoned his coat, and then stalked with fabulous dignity from the room. In the discreet silence of all the other men the Swede laughed. His laughter rang somehow childish. Men by this time had begun to look at him askance, as if they wished to inquire what ailed him.

A new game was formed jocosely. The cowboy volunteered to become the partner of Johnnie, and they all then turned to ask the Swede to throw in his lot with the little Easterner. He asked some questions about the game, and, learning that it wore many names, and that he had played it when it was under an alias, he accepted the invitation. He strode toward the men nervously, as if he expected to be assaulted. Finally, seated, he gazed from face to face and laughed shrilly. This laugh was so strange that the Easterner looked up quickly, the cowboy sat intent and with his mouth open, and Johnnie paused, holding the cards with still fingers.

Afterward there was a short silence. Then Johnnie said, "Well, let's get at it. Come on now!" They pulled their chairs forward until their knees were bunched under the board. They began to play, and their interest in the game caused the others to forget the manner of the Swede.

The cowboy was a board-whacker. Each time that he held superior cards he changed them, one by one, with exceeding force, down upon the improvised table, and took the tricks with a glowing air of prowess and pride that sent thrills of indignation into the hearts of his opponents. A game with a board-whacker in it is sure to become intense. The countenances of the Easterner and the Swede were miserable whenever the cowboy thundered down his aces and kings, while Johnnie, his eyes gleaming with joy, chuckled and chuckled.

Because of the absorbing play none considered the strange ways of the Swede. They paid strict heed to the game. Finally, during a lull caused by a new deal, the Swede suddenly addressed Johnnie: "I suppose there have been a good many men killed in this room." The jaws of the others dropped and they looked at him.

"What in hell are you talking about?" said Johnnie.

The Swede laughed again his blatant laugh, full of a kind of false courage and defiance. "Oh, you know what I mean all right," he answered.

"I'm a liar if I do!" Johnnie protested. The card was halted, and the men stared at the Swede. Johnnie evidently felt that as the son of the proprietor he should make a direct inquiry. "Now, what might you be drivin' at, mister?" He asked. The Swede winked at him. It was a wink full of cunning. His fingers shook on the edge of the board. "Oh, maybe you think I have been to nowheres. Maybe you think I'm a tenderfoot?"

"I don't know nothin' about you," answered Johnnie. "and I don't give a damn where you've been. All I got to say is that I don't know what you're driving at. There ain't never been nobody killed in this room."

The cowboy, who had been steadily gazing at the Swede, then spoke: "What's wrong with you, mister?"

Apparently it seemed to the Swede that he was formidably menaced.

He shivered and turned white near the corners of his mouth. He sent an appealing glance in the direction of the little Easterner. During these moments he did not forget to wear his air of advanced pot-valor. "They say they don't know what I mean," he remarked mockingly to the Easterner.

The latter answered after prolonged and cautious reflection. "I don't understand you," he said, impassively.

The Swede made a movement then which announced that he thought he had encountered treachery from the only quarter where he had expected sympathy, if not help. "Oh, I see you are all against me. I see—"

The cowboy was in a state of deep stupefaction. "Say," he cried, as he tumbled the deck violently down upon the board, "say, what are you gittin' at, hey?"

The Swede sprang up with the celerity of a man escaping from a snake on the floor. "I don't want to fight!" he shouted. "I don't want to fight!"

The cowboy stretched his long legs indolently and deliberately. His hands were in his pockets. He spat into the sawdust-box. "Well, who the hell thought you did?" he inquired.

The Swede backed rapidly toward the corner of the room. His hands were out protectingly in front of his chest, but he was making an obvious struggle to control his fright. "Gentlemen," he quavered, "I suppose I am going to be killed before I can leave this house! I suppose I am going to be killed before I can leave this house!" In his eyes was the dying-swan look. Through the windows could be seen the snow turning blue in the shadow of dusk. The wind tore at the house, and some loose thing beat regularly against the clapboards like a spirit tapping.

A door opened, and Scully himself entered. He paused in surprise as he noted the tragic attitude of the Swede. Then he said, "What's the matter here?"

The Swede answered him swiftly and eagerly: "These men are going to kill me."

"Kill you!" ejaculated Scully. "Kill you! What are you talkin'?"

The Swede made the gesture of a martyr.

Scully wheeled sternly upon his son. "What is this, Johnnie?"

The lad had grown sullen. "Damned if I know," he answered. "I can't make no sense to it." He began to shuffle the cards, fluttering them together with an angry snap. "He says a good many men have been killed in this room, or something like that. And he says he's goin' to be killed here too. I don't know what ails him. He's crazy, I shouldn't wonder."

Scully then looked for explanation to the cowboy, but the cowboy simply shrugged his shoulders.

"Kill you?" said Scully again to the Swede. "Kill you? Man, you're off your nut."

"Oh, I know," burst out the Swede. "I know what will happen. Yes, I'm crazy—yes. Yes, of course, I'm crazy—yes. But I know one thing—" There was a sort of sweat of misery and terror upon his face. "I know I won't get out of here alive."

The cowboy drew a deep breath, as if his mind was passing into the last stages of dissolution. "Well, I'm doggoned," he whispered to himself.

Scully wheeled suddenly and faced his son. "You've been troublin' this man!"

Johnnie's voice was loud with its burden of grievance, "Why, good Gawd, I ain't done nothin' to 'im."

The Swede broke in. "Gentlemen, do not disturb yourselves. I will leave this house. I will go away, because" —he accused them dramatically with his glance—"because I do not want to be killed."

Scully was furious with his son. "Will you tell me what is the matter, you young divil? What's the matter, anyhow? Speak out!"

"Blame it!" cried Johnnie in despair, "don't I tell you I don't know? He—he says we want to kill him, and that's all I know. I can't tell what ails him."

The Swede continued to repeat: "Never mind, Mr. Scully; never mind. I will leave this house. I will go away, because I do not wish to be killed. Yes, of course, I am crazy—yes. But I know one thing! I will go away. I will leave this house. Never mind, Mr. Scully: never mind. I will go away."

"You will not go 'way," said Scully. "You will not go 'way until I hear the reason of this business. If anybody has troubled you I will take care of him. This is my house. You are under my roof, and I will not allow any peaceable man to be troubled here." He cast a terrible eye upon Johnnie, the cowboy, and the Easterner.

"Never mind, Mr. Scully; never mind. I will go away. I do not wish to be killed." The Swede moved toward the door which opened upon the stairs. It was evidently his intention to go at once for his baggage.

"No, no," shouted Scully peremptorily; but the white-faced man slid by him and disappeared. "Now," said Scully severely, "what does this mane?"

Johnnie ánd the cowboy cried together: "Why, we didn't do nothin' to 'im!"

Scully's eyes were cold. "No," he said, "you didn't?"

Johnnie swore a deep oath. "Why, this is the wildest loon I ever see. We didn't do nothin' at all. We were just sittin' here playin' cards, and he—"

The father suddenly spoke to the Easterner. "Mr. Blanc," he asked, "what has these boys been doin'?"

The Easterner reflected again. "I didn't see anything wrong at all," he said at last, slowly.

Scully began to howl. "But what does it mane?" He stared ferociously at his son. "I have a mind to lather you for this, my boy."

Johnnie was frantic. "Well, what have I done?" he bawled at his father.

III

"I think you are tongue-tied," said Scully finally to his son, the cowboy, and the Easterner; and at the end of this scornful sentence he left the room.

Upstairs the Swede was swiftly fastening the straps of his great valise. Once his back happened to be half turned toward the door, and, hearing a noise there, he wheeled and sprang up, uttering a loud cry. Scully's wrinkled visage showed grimly in the light of the small lamp he carried. This yellow effulgence, streaming upward, colored only his prominent features, and left his eyes, for instance, in mysterious shadow. He resembled a murderer.

"Man! man!" he exclaimed, "have you gone daffy?"

"Oh, no! Oh, no!" rejoined the other. "There are people in this world who know pretty nearly as much as you do—understand?"

For a moment they stood gazing at each other. Upon the Swede's deathly pale cheeks were two spots brightly crimson and sharply edged, as if they had been carefully painted. Scully placed the light on the table and sat himself on the edge of the bed. He spoke ruminatively. "By cracky, I never heard of such a thing in my life. It's a complete muddle. I can't, for the soul of me, think how you ever got this idea into your head." Presently he lifted his eyes and asked: "And did you sure think they were going to kill you?"

The Swede scanned the old man as he if wished to see into his mind. "I did," he said at last. He obviously suspected that this answer might precipitate an outbreak. As he pulled on a strap his whole arm shook, the elbow wavering like a bit of paper.

Scully banged his hand impressively on the footboard of the bed. "Why, man, we're goin' to have a line of ilictric street-cars in this town next spring."

"'A line of electric street-cars,'" repeated the Swede stupidly.

"And," said Scully, "there's a new railroad goin' to be built down from Broken Arm to here. Not to mention the four churches and the smashin' big brick schoolhouse. Then there's the big factory, too. Why, in two years Romper'll be a met-tro-*pol*-is."

Having finished the preparation of his baggage, the Swede straightened himself. "Mr. Scully," he said, with sudden hardihood, "how much do I owe you?"

"You don't owe me anythin'," said the old man, angrily.

"Yes, I do," retorted the Swede. He took seventy-five cents from his pocket and tendered it to Scully; but the latter snapped his fingers in disdainful refusal. However, it happened that they both stood gazing in a strange fashion at three silver pieces on the Swede's open palm.

"I'll not take your money," said Scully at last. "Not after what's been goin' on here." Then a plan seemed to strike him. "Here," he cried, picking up his lamp and moving toward the door. "Here! Come with me a minute."

"No," said the Swede, in overwhelming alarm.

"Yes," urged the old man. "Come on! I want you to come and see a picter—just across the hall—in my room."

The Swede must have concluded that his hour was come. His jaw dropped and his teeth showed like a dead man's. He ultimately followed Scully across the corridor, but he had the step of one hung in chains.

Scully flashed the light high on the wall of his own chamber. There was revealed a ridiculous photograph of a little girl. She was leaning against a balustrade of gorgeous decoration, and the formidable bang to her hair was prominent. The figure was as graceful as an upright sled-stake, and, withal, it was of the hue of lead. "There," said Scully, tenderly, "that's the picter of my little girl that died. Her name was Carrie. She had the purtiest hair you ever saw! I was that fond of her, she—"

Turning then, he saw that the Swede was not comtemplating the picture at all, but, instead, was keeping keen watch on the gloom in the rear.

"Look, man!" cried Scully, heartily. "That's the picter of my little gal that died. Her name was Carrie. And then here's the picter of my oldest boy. Michael. He's a lawyer in Lincoln, an' doin' well. I gave that boy a grand eddication, and I'm glad for it now. He's a fine boy. Look at 'im now. Ain't he bold as blazes, him there in Lincoln, an honored an' respicted gintleman! An honored and respected gintleman," concluded Scully with a flourish. And, so saying, he smote the Swede jovially on the back.

The Swede faintly smiled.

"Now," said the old man, "there's only one more thing." He dropped suddenly to the floor and thrust his head beneath the bed. The Swede could hear his muffled voice. "I'd keep it under me piller if it wasn't for that boy Johnnie. Then there's the old woman—Where is it now? I never put it twice in the same place. Ah, now come out with you!"

Presently he backed clumsily from under the bed, dragging with him an old coat rolled into a bundle. "I've fetched him," he muttered. Kneeling on the floor, he unrolled the coat and extracted from its heart a large yellow-brown whiskey bottle.

His first manoeuver was to hold the bottle up to the light. Reassured, apparently, that nobody had been tampering with it, he thrust it with a generous movement toward the Swede.

The weak-kneed Swede was about to eagerly clutch this element of strength, but he suddenly jerked his hand away and cast a look of horror upon Scully.

"Drink," said the old man affectionately. He had risen to his feet, and now stood facing the Swede.

There was a silence. Then again Scully said: "Drink!"

The Swede laughed wildly. He grabbed the bottle, put it to his mouth; and as his lips curled absurdly around the opening and his throat worked, he kept his glance, burning with hatred, upon the old man's face.

IV

After the departure of Scully the three men, with the cardboard still upon their knees, preserved for a long time an astounded silence. Then Johnnie said: "That's the doddangedest Swede I ever see."

"He ain't no Swede," said the cowboy, scornfully.

"Well, what is he then?" cried Johnnie. "What is he then?"

"It's my opinion," replied the cowboy deliberately, "he's some kind of a Dutchman." It was a venerable custom of the country to entitle as Swedes all light-haired men who spoke with a heavy tongue. In consequence the idea of the cowboy was not without its daring. "Yes, sir," he repeated. "It's my opinion this feller is some kind of a Dutchman."

"Well, he says he's a Swede, anyhow," muttered Johnnie, sulkily. He turned to the Easterner: "What do you think, Mr. Blanc?"

"Oh, I don't know," replied the Easterner.

"Well, what do you think makes him act that way?" asked the cowboy.

"Why, he's frightened." The Easterner knocked his pipe against a rim of the stove. "He's clear frightened out of his boots."

"What at?" cried the others again.

"Oh, I don't know, but it seems to me this man has been reading dime novels, and he thinks he's right out in the middle of it—the shootin' and stabbin' and all."

"But," said the cowboy, deeply scandalized, "this ain't Wyoming, ner none of them places. This is Nebrasker."

"Yes," added Johnnie, "an' why don't he wait till he gits out West?"

The travelled Easterner laughed. "It isn't different there even—not in these days. But he thinks he's right in the middle of hell."

Johnnie and the cowboy mused long.

"It's awful funny," remarked Johnnie at last.

"Yes," said the cowboy. "This is a queer game. I hope we don't git snowed in, because then we'd have to stand this here man bein' around with us all the time. That wouldn't be no good."

"I wish pop would throw him out," said Johnnie.

Presently they heard a loud stamping on the stairs, accompanied by ringing jokes in the voice of old Scully, and laughter, evidently from the Swede. The men around the stove stared vacantly at each other. "Gosh!" said the cowboy. The door flew open, and old Scully, flushed and anecdotal, came into the room. He was jabbering at the Swede, who followed him, laughing bravely. It was the entry of two roisterers from a banquet hall.

"Come now," said Scully sharply to the three seated men, "move up and give us a chance at the stove." The cowboy and the Easterner obediently sidled their chairs to make room for the newcomers. Johnnie, however, simply arranged himself in a more indolent attitude, and then remained motionless.

"Come! Git over, there," said Scully.

"Plenty of room on the other side of the stove," said Johnnie.

"Do you think we want to sit in the draught?" roared the father.

But the Swede here interposed with a grandeur of confidence. "No, no. Let the boy sit where he likes," he cried in a bullying voice to the father.

"All right! All right!" said Scully, deferentially. The cowboy and the Easterner exchanged glances of wonder.

The five chairs were formed in a crescent about one side of the stove. The Swede began to talk; he talked arrogantly, profanely, angrily. Johnnie, the cowboy, and the Easterner maintained a morose silence, while old Scully appeared to be receptive and eager, breaking in constantly with sympathetic ejaculations.

Finally the Swede announced that he was thirsty. He moved in his chair, and said that he would go for a drink of water.

"I'll git it for you," cried Scully at once.

"No," said the Swede, contemptuously. "I'll get it for myself." He arose and stalked with the air of an owner off into the executive parts of the hotel.

As soon as the Swede was out of hearing Scully sprang to his feet and whispered intensely to the others: "Upstairs he thought I was tryin' to poison 'im."

"Say," said Johnnie, "this makes me sick. Why don't you throw 'im out in the snow?"

"Why, he's all right now," declared Scully. "It was only that he was from the East, and he thought this was a tough place. That's all. He's all right now."

The cowboy looked with admiration upon the Easterner. "You were straight," he said. "You were on to that there Dutchman."

"Well," said Johnnie to his father, "he may be all right now, but I don't see it. Other time he was scared, but now he's too fresh."

Scully's speech was always a combination of Irish brogue and idiom, Western twang and idiom, and scraps of curiously formal diction taken from the story-books and newspapers. He now hurled a strange mass of language at the head of his son. "What do I keep? What do I keep? What do I keep?" he demanded, in a voice of thunder. He slapped his knee impressively, to indicate that he himself was going to make reply, and that all should heed. "I keep a hotel," he shouted. "A hotel, do you mind? A guest under my roof has sacred privileges. He is to be intimidated by none. Not one word shall he hear that would prejudice him in favor of goin' away. I'll not have it. There's no place in this here town where they can say they never took in a guest of mine because he was afraid to stay here." He wheeled suddenly upon the cowboy and the Easterner. "Am I right?"

"Yes, Mr. Scully," said the cowboy, "I think you're right."

"Yes, Mr. Scully," said the Easterner, "I think you're right."

V

At six-o'clock supper, the Swede fizzed like a fire-wheel. He sometimes seemed on the point of bursting into riotous song, and in all his madness he was encouraged by old Scully. The Easterner was encased in research; the cowboy sat in wide-mouthed amazement, forgetting to eat, while Johnnie wrathily demolished great plates of food. The daughters of the house, when they were obliged to replenish the biscuits, approached as warily as Indians, and, having succeeded in their purpose, fled with ill-concealed trepidation. The Swede domineered the whole feast, and he gave it the appearance of a cruel bacchanal. He seemed to have grown suddenly taller; he gazed, brutally disdainful, into every face. His voice rang through the room. Once when he jabbed out harpoon-fashion with his fork to pinion a biscuit, the weapon nearly impaled the hand of the

Easterner, which had been stretched quietly out for the same biscuit.

After supper, as the men filed toward the other room, the Swede smote Scully ruthlessly on the shoulder. "Well, old boy, that was a good, square meal." Johnnie looked hopefully at his father; he knew that shoulder was tender from an old fall; and, indeed, it appeared for a moment as if Scully was going to flame out over the matter, but in the end he smiled a sickly smile and remained silent. The others understood from his manner that he was admitting his responsibility for the Swede's new view-point.

Johnnie, however, addressed his parent in an aside. "Why don't you license somebody to kick you downstairs?" Scully scowled darkly by way of reply.

When they were gathered about the stove, the Swede insisted on another game of High-Five. Scully gently deprecated the plan at first, but the Swede turned a wolfish glare upon him. The old man subsided, and the Swede canvassed the others. In his tone there was always a great threat. The cowboy and the Easterner both remarked indifferently that they would play. Scully said that he would presently have to go meet the 6:58 train, and so the Swede turned menacingly upon Johnnie. For a moment their glances crossed like blades, and then Johnnie smiled and said, "Yes, I'll play."

They formed a square, with the little board on their knees. The Easterner and the Swede were again partners. As the play went on, it was noticeable that the cowboy was not board-whacking as usual. Meanwhile, Scully, near the lamp, had put on his spectacles and, with an appearance curiously like an old priest, was reading a newspaper. In time he went out to meet the 6:58 train, and, despite his precautions, a gust of polar wind whirled into the room as he opened the door. Besides scattering the cards, it chilled the players to the marrow. The Swede cursed frightfully. When Scully returned, his entrance disturbed a cosy and friendly scene. The Swede again cursed. But presently they were once more intent, their heads bent forward and their hands moving swiftly. The Swede had adopted the fashion of board-whacking.

Scully took up his paper and for a long time remained immersed in matters which were extraordinarily remote from him. The lamp burned badly, and once he stopped to adjust the wick. The newspaper, as he turned from page to page, rustled with a slow and comfortable sound. Then suddenly he heard three terrible words: "You are cheatin'!"

Such scenes often prove that there can be little of dramatic import in environment. Any room can present a tragic front; any room can be comic. This little den was now hideous as a torture-chamber. The new faces of the men themselves had changed it upon the instant. The Swede held a huge fist in front of Johnnie's face, while the latter looked steadily over it into the blazing orbs of his accuser. The Easterner had grown pallid; the cowboy's jaw had dropped in that expression of bovine amazement which was one of his important mannerisms. After the three words, the first sound in the room was made by Scully's paper as it floated forgotten to his feet. His spectacles had also fallen from his nose, but by a clutch he had saved them in air. His hand, grasping the spectacles, now remained poised awkwardly and near his shoulder. He stared at the card players.

Probably the silence was while a second elapsed. Then, if the floor had been suddenly twitched out from under the men they could not have moved quicker. The five had projected themselves headlong toward a common point. It happened that Johnnie, in rising to hurl himself upon the Swede, had stumbled slightly because of his curiously instinctive care for the cards and the board. The loss of the moment allowed time for the arrival of Scully, and also allowed the cowboy time to give the Swede a great push which sent him staggering back. The men found tongue together, and hoarse shouts of rage, appeal, or fear burst from every throat. The cowboy pushed and jostled feverishly at the Swede, and the Easterner and Scully clung wildly to Johnnie; but through the smoky air, above the swaying bodies of the peace-compellers, the eyes of the two warriors ever sought each other in glances of challenge that were at once hot and steely.

Of course the board had been overturned, and now the whole company of cards was scattered over the floor, where the boots of the men trampled the fat and painted kings and queens as they gazed with their silly eyes at the war that was waging above them.

Scully's voice was dominating the yells. "Stop now! Stop, I say! Stop, now—"

Johnnie, as he struggled to burst through the rank formed by Scully and the Easterner, was crying, "Well, he says I cheated! He says I cheated! I won't allow no man to say I cheated! If he says I cheated, he's a—!"

The cowboy was telling the Swede, "Quit, now! Quit, d'ye hear—"

The screams of the Swede never ceased: "He did cheat! I saw him! I saw him—"

As for the Easterner, he was importuning in a voice that was not heeded: "Wait a moment, can't you? Oh, wait a moment. What's the good of a fight over a game of cards? Wait a moment—"

In this tumult no complete sentences were clear. "Cheat"—"Quit"— "He says"—these fragments pierced the uproar and rang out sharply. It was remarkable that, whereas Scully undoubtedly made the most noise, he was the least heard of any of the riotous band.

Then suddenly there was a great cessation. It was as if each man had paused for breath; and although the room was still lighted with the anger of men, it could be seen that there was no danger of immediate conflict, and at once Johnnie, shouldering his way forward, almost succeeded in confronting the Swede. "What did you say I cheated for? What did you say I cheated for? I don't cheat, and I won't let no man say I do!"

The Swede said, "I saw you! I saw you!"

"Well," cried Johnnie, "I'll fight any man what says I cheat!"

"No, you won't," said the cowboy. "Not here."

"Ah, be still, can't you?" said Scully, coming between them.

The quiet was sufficient to allow the Easterner's voice to be heard. He was repeating. "Oh, wait a moment, can't you? What's the good of a fight over a game of cards? Wait a moment!"

Johnnie, his red face appearing above his father's shoulder, hailed the Swede again. "Did you say I cheated?"

The Swede showed his teeth. "Yes."

"Then," said Johnnie, "we must fight."

"Yes, fight," roared the Swede. He was like a demoniac. "Yes, fight! I'll show you what kind of a man I am! I'll show you who you want to fight! Maybe you think I can't fight! Maybe you think I can't! I'll show you, you skin, you card-sharp! Yes, you cheated! You cheated! You cheated!"

"Well, let's go at it, then, mister," said Johnnie, coolly.

The cowboy's brow was beaded with sweat from his efforts in intercepting all sorts of raids. He turned in despair to Scully. "What are you goin' to do now?"

A change had come over the Celtic visage of the old man. He now seemed all eagerness; his eyes glowed.

"We'll let them fight," he answered, stalwartly. "I can't put up with it any longer. I've stood this damned Swede till I'm sick. We'll let them fight."

VI

The men prepared to go out-of-doors. The Easterner was so nervous that he had great difficulty in getting his arms into the sleeves of his new leather coat. As the cowboy drew his fur cap down over his ears his hands trembled. In fact, Johnnie and old Scully were the only ones who displayed no agitation. These preliminaries were conducted without words.

Scully threw open the door. "Well, come on," he said. Instantly a terrific wind caused the flame of the lamp to struggle at its wick, while a puff of black smoke sprang from the chimney-top. The stove was in mid-current of the blast, and its voice swelled to equal the roar of the storm. Some of the scarred and bedabbled cards were caught up from the floor and dashed helplessly against the farther wall. The men lowered their heads and plunged into the tempest as into a sea.

No snow was falling, but great whirls and clouds of flakes, swept up from the ground by the frantic winds, were streaming southward with the speed of bullets. The covered land was blue with the sheen of an unearthly satin, and there was no other hue save where, at the low, black railway station—which seemed incredibly distant—one light gleamed like a tiny jewel. As the men floundered into a thigh-deep drift, it was known that the Swede was bawling out something. Scully went to him, put a hand on his shoulder, and projected an ear. "What's that you say?" he shouted.

"I say," bawled the Swede again, "I won't stand much show against this gang. I know you'll all pitch on me."

Scully smote him reproachfully on the arm. "Tut, man!" he yelled. The wind tore the words from Scully's lips and scattered them far alee.

"You are all a gang of—" boomed the Swede, but the storm also seized the remainder of this sentence.

Immediately turning their backs upon the wind, the men had swung around a corner to the shelter side of the hotel. It was the function of the little house to preserve here, amid this great devastation of snow, an irregular V-shape of heavily encrusted grass, which crackled beneath the feet. One could imagine the great drifts piled against the windward side. When the party reached the comparative peace of this spot it was found that the Swede was still bellowing.

"Oh, I know what kind of a thing this is! I know you'll all pitch on me. I can't lick you all!"

Scully turned upon him panther-fashion. "You'll not have to whip all of us. You'll have to whip my son Johnnie. An' the man what troubles you durin' that time will have me to dale with."

The arrangements were swiftly made. The two men faced each other, obedient to the harsh commands of Scully, whose face, in the subtly luminous gloom, could be seen set in the austere impersonal lines that are pictured on the countenances of the Roman veterans. The Easterner's teeth were chattering, and he was hopping up and down like a mechanical toy. The cowboy stood rocklike.

The contestants had not stripped off any clothing. Each was in his ordinary attire. Their fists were up, and they eyed each other in a calm that had the elements of leonine cruelty in it.

During this pause, the Easterner's mind, like a film, took lasting impressions of three men—the iron-nerved master of the ceremony; the Swede, pale, motionless, terrible; and Johnnie, serene yet ferocious, brutish yet heroic. The entire prelude had in it a tragedy greater than the tragedy of action, and this aspect was accentuated by the long, mellow cry of the blizzard, as it sped the tumbling and wailing flakes into the black abyss of the south.

"Now!" said Scully.

The two combatants leaped forward and crashed together like bullocks. There was heard the cushioned sound of blows, and of a curse squeezing out from between the tight teeth of one.

As for the spectators, the Easterner's pent-up breath exploded from him with a pop of relief, absolute relief from the tension of the preliminaries. The cowboy bounded into the air with a yowl. Scully was immovable as from supreme amazement and fear of the fury of the fight which he himself had permitted and arranged.

For a time the encounter in the darkness was such a perplexity of flying arms that it presented no more detail than would a swiftly revolving wheel. Occasionally a face, as if illuminated by a flash of light, would shine out, ghastly and marked with pink spots. A moment later, the men might have been known as shadows, if it were not for the involuntary utterance of oaths that came from them in whispers.

Suddenly a holocaust of warlike desire caught the cowboy, and he bolted forward with the speed of a bronco. "Go it, Johnnie! Go it! Kill him! Kill Him!"

Scully confronted him, "Kape back." he said; and by his glance the cowboy could tell that this man was Johnnie's father.

To the Easterner there was a monotony of unchangeable fighting that was an abomination. This confused mingling was eternal to his sense, which was concentrated in a longing for the end, the priceless end. Once the fighters lurched near him, and as he scrambled hastily backward he heard them breathe like men on the rack.

"Kill him, Johnnie! Kill him! Kill him! Kill him!" The cowboy's face was contorted like one of those agony masks in museums.

"Keep still," said Scully, icily.

Then there was a sudden loud grunt, incomplete, cut short, and Johnnie's body swung away from the Swede and fell with sickening heaviness to the grass. The cowboy was barely in time to prevent the mad Swede from flinging himself upon his prone adversary. "No, you don't," said the cowboy, interposing an arm. "Wait a second."

Scully was at his son's side. "Johnnie! Johnnie, me boy!" His voice had a quality of melancholy tenderness. "Johnnie! Can you go on with it?" He looked anxiously down into the bloody, pulpy face of his son.

There was a moment of silence, and then Johnnie answered in his ordinary voice, "Yes, I—it—yes."

Assisted by his father he struggled to his feet. "Wait a bit now till you git your wind," said the old man.

A few paces away the cowboy was lecturing the Swede. "No, you don't! Wait a second!"

The Easterner was plucking at Scully's sleeve. "Oh, this is enough," he pleaded. "This is enough! Let it go as it stands. This is enough!"

"Bill," said Scully, "git out of the road." The cowboy stepped aside. "Now." The combatants were actuated by a new caution as they advanced toward collision. They glared at each other, and then the Swede aimed a lightning blow that carried with it his entire weight. Johnnie was evidently half stupid from weakness, but he miraculously dodged, and his fist sent the overbalanced Swede sprawling.

The cowboy, Scully, and the Easterner burst into a cheer that was like a chorus of triumphant soldiery, but before its conclusion the Swede had scuffled agilely to his feet and come in berserk abandon at his foe. There was another perplexity of flying arms, and Johnnie's body again swung away and fell, even as a bundle might fall from a roof. The Swede instantly staggered to a little wind-waved tree and leaned upon it, breathing like an engine, while his savage and flame-lit eyes roamed from face to face as the men bent over Johnnie. There was a splendor of isolation in his situation at this time which the Easterner felt once when, lifting his eyes from the man on the ground, he beheld that mysterious and lonely figure, waiting.

"Are you any good yet, Johnnie?" asked Scully in a broken voice.

The son gasped and opened his eyes languidly. After a moment he answered, "No—I ain't—any good—any—more." Then, from shame and bodily ill, he began to weep, the tears furrowing down through the bloodstains on his face. "He was too—too—too heavy for me."

Scully straightened and addressed the waiting figure. "Stranger," he said, evenly, "it's all up with our side." Then his voice changed into that vibrant huskiness which is commonly the tone of the most simple and deadly announcements. "Johnnie is whipped."

Without replying, the victor moved off on the route to the front door of the hotel.

The cowboy was formulating new and unspellable blasphemies. The Easterner was startled to find that they were out in a wind that seemed to come direct from the shadowed arctic floes. He heard again the wail of the snow as it was flung to its grave in the south. He knew now that all this time the cold had been sinking into him deeper and deeper, and he wondered that he had not perished. He felt indifferent to the condition of the vanquished man.

"Johnnie, can you walk?" asked Scully.

"Did I hurt—hurt him any?" asked the son.

"Can you walk, boy? Can you walk?"

Johnnie's voice was suddenly strong. There was a robust impatience in it. "I asked you whether I hurt him any!"

"Yes, yes, Johnnie," answered the cowboy, consolingly; "he's hurt a good deal."

They raised him from the ground, and as soon as he was on his feet he went tottering off, rebuffing all attempts at assistance. When the party rounded the corner they were fairly blinded by the pelting of the snow. It burned their faces like fire. The cowboy carried Johnnie through the drift to the door. As they entered, some cards again rose from the floor and beat against the wall.

The Easterner rushed to the stove. He was so profoundly chilled that he almost dared to embrace the glowing iron. The Swede was not in the room. Johnnie sank into a chair and, folding his arms on his knees, buried his face in them. Scully, warming one foot and then the other at a rim of the stove, muttered to himself with Celtic mournfulness. The cowboy had removed his fur cap, and with a dazed and rueful air he was running one hand through his tousled locks. From overhead they could hear the creaking of boards, as the Swede tramped here and there in his room.

The sad quiet was broken by the sudden flinging open of a door that led toward the kitchen. It was instantly followed by an inrush of women. They precipitated themselves upon Johnnie amid a chorus of lamentation. Before they carried their prey off to the kitchen, there to be bathed and harangued with that mixture of sympathy and abuse which is a feat of their sex, the mother straightened herself and fixed old Scully with an eye of stern reproach. "Shame be upon you, Patrick Scully!" she cried. "Your own son, too. Shame be upon you!"

"There, now! Be quiet, now!" said the old man, weakly.

"Shame be upon you, Patrick Scully!" The girls, rallying to this slogan, sniffled disdainfully in the direction of those trembling accomplices, the cowboy and the Easterner. Presently they bore Johnnie away, and left the three men to dismal reflection.

VII

"I'd like to fight this here Dutchman myself," said the cowboy, breaking a long silence.

Scully wagged his head sadly. "No, that wouldn't do. It wouldn't be right. It wouldn't be right."

"Well, why wouldn't it?" argued the cowboy. "I don't see no harm in it."

"No," answered Scully, with mournful heroism. "It wouldn't be right. It was Johnnie's fight, and now we mustn't whip the man just because he whipped Johnnie."

"Yes, that's true enough," said the cowboy; "but—he better not get fresh with me, because I couldn't stand no more of it."

"You'll not say a word to him," commanded Scully, and even then they heard the tread of the Swede on the stairs. His entrance was made theatric. He swept the door back with a bang and swaggered to the middle of the room. No one looked at him. "Well," he cried, insolently, at Scully, "I s'pose you'll tell me now how much I owe you?"

The old man remained stolid. "You don't owe me nothin'."

The cowboy addressed the Swede. "Stranger, I don't see how you come to be so gay around here."

Old Scully was instantly alert. "Stop!" he shouted, holding his hand forth, fingers upward. "Bill, you shut up!"

The cowboy spat carelessly into the sawdust-box. "I didn't say a word, did I?" he asked.

"Mr. Scully," called the Swede, "how much did I owe you?" It was seen that he was attired for departure, and that he had his valise in his hand.

"You don't owe me nothin'," repeated Scully in the same imperturbable way.

"Huh!" said the Swede. "I guess you're right. I guess if it was any way at all, you'd owe me somethin'. That's what I guess." He turned to the cowboy. "'Kill him! Kill him! Kill him!'" he mimicked, and then guffawed victoriously. "'Kill him!'" He was convulsed with ironical humor.

But he might have been jeering the dead. The three men were immovable and silent, staring with glassy eyes at the stove.

The Swede opened the door and passed into the storm, one derisive glance backward at the still group.

As soon as the door was closed, Scully and the cowboy leaped to their feet and began to curse. They trampled to and fro, waving their arms and smashing into the air with their fists. "Oh, but that was a hard minute!" wailed Scully. "That was a hard minute! Him there leerin' and scoffin'! One bang at his nose was worth forty dollars to me that minute! How did you stand it, Bill?"

"How did I stand it?" cried the cowboy in a quivering voice. "How did I stand it? Oh!"

The old man burst into sudden brogue. "I'd like to take that Swade," he wailed, "and hould 'im down on a shtone flure and bate 'im to a jelly wid a shtick!"

The cowboy groaned in sympathy. "I'd like to git him by the neck and ha-amer him"—he brought his hand down on the chair with a noise like a pistol-shot—"hammer that there Dutchman until he couldn't tell himself from a dead coyote!"

"I'd bate 'im until he—"

"I'd show *him* some things—"

And then together they raised a yearning, fanatic cry— "Oh-o-oh! If we only could—"

"Yes!"

"Yes!"

"And then I'd—"

"O-o-oh!"

VIII

The Swede, tightly gripping his valise, tacked across the face of the storm as if he carried sails. He was following a line of little naked, gasping trees which, he knew, must mark the way of the road. His face, fresh from the pounding of Johnnie's fists, felt more pleasure than pain in the wind and the driving snow. A number of square shapes loomed upon him finally, and he knew them as the houses of the main body of the town. He found a street and made travel along it, leaning heavy upon the wind whenever, at a corner, a terrific blast caught him.

He might have been in a deserted village. We picture the world as thick with conquering and elate humanity, but here, with the bugles of the tempest pealing, it was hard to imagine a peopled earth. One viewed the existence of man then as a marvel, and conceded a glamor of wonder to these lice which were caused to cling to a whirling, fire-smitten, ice-locked, disease-stricken, space-lost bulb. The conceit of man was explained by this storm to be the very engine of life. One was a coxcomb not to die in it. However, the Swede found a saloon.

In front of it an indomitable red light was burning, and the snow-flakes were made blood-color as they flew through the circumscribed territory of the lamp's shining. The Swede pushed open the door of the saloon and entered. A sanded expanse was before him, and at the end of it four men sat about a table drinking. Down one side of the room extended a radiant bar, and its guardian was leaning upon his elbows listening to the talk of the men at the table. The Swede dropped his valise upon the floor and, smiling fraternally upon the barkeeper, said, "Gimme some whiskey, will you?" The man placed a bottle, a whiskey glass, and a glass of ice-thick water upon the bar. The Swede poured himself an abnormal portion of whiskey and drank it in three gulps. "Pretty bad night," remarked the bartender, indifferently. He was making the pretension of blindness which is usually a distinction of his class; but it could have been seen that he was furtively studying the half-erased bloodstains on the face of the Swede. "Bad night," he said again.

"Oh, it's good enough for me," replied the Swede, hardily, as he poured himself some more whiskey. The barkeeper took his coin and maneuvered it through its reception by the highly nickelled cash-machine. A bell rang; a card labelled "20 cts." had appeared.

"No," continued the Swede, "this isn't too bad weather. It's good enough for me."

"So?" murmured the barkeeper, languidly.

The copious drams made the Swede's eyes swim, and he breathed a trifle heavier. "Yes, I like this weather. I like it. It suits me." It was apparently his design to impart a deep significance to these words.

"So?" murmured the bartender again. He turned to gaze dreamily at the scroll-like birds and bird-like scrolls which had been drawn with soap upon the mirrors in back of the bar.

"Well, I guess I'll take another drink," said the Swede, presently. "Have something?"

"No, thanks; I'm not drinkin'," answered the bartender. Afterward he asked, "How did you hurt your face?"

The Swede immediately began to boast loudly. "Why, in a fight. I thumped the soul out of a man down here at Scully's hotel."

The interest of the four men at the table was at last aroused.

"Who was it?" said one.

"Johnnie Scully," blustered the Swede. "Son of the man what runs it. He will be pretty near dead for some weeks, I can tell you. I made a nice thing of him, I did. He couldn't get up. They carried him in the house. Have a drink?"

Instantly the men in some subtle way encased themselves in research. "No, thanks," said one. The group was of curious formation. Two were prominent local business men; one was the district attorney; and one was a professional gambler of the kind known as "square." But a scrutiny of the group would not have enabled an observer to pick the gambler from the men of more reputable pursuits. He was, in fact, a man so delicate in manner, when among people of fair class, and so judicious in his choice of victims, that in the strictly masculine part of the town's life he had come to be explicitly trusted and admired. People called him a thoroughbred. The fear and contempt with which his craft was regarded were undoubtedly the reason why his quiet dignity shone conspicuous above the quiet dignity of men who might be merely hatters, billiard-markers, or grocery clerks. Beyond an occasional unwary traveller who came by rail, this gambler was supposed to prey solely upon reckless and senile farmers, who, when flush with good crops, drove into town in all the pride and confidence of an absolutely invulnerable stupidity. Hearing at times in circuitous fashion of the despoilment of such a farmer, the important men of Romper invariably laughed in contempt of the victim, and if they thought of the wolf at all, it was with a kind of pride at the knowledge that he would never dare think of attacking their wisdom and courage. Besides, it was popular that this gambler had a real wife and two real children in a neat cottage in a suburb, where he led an exemplary home life; and when any one even suggested a discrepancy in his character, the crowd immediately vociferated descriptions of this virtuous family circle. Then men who led exemplary home lives, and men who did not lead exemplary home lives, all subsided in a bunch, remarking that there was nothing more to be said.

However, when a restriction was placed upon him—as, for instance, when a strong clique of members of the new Pollywog Club refused to permit him, even as a spectator, to appear in the rooms of the organization—the candor and gentleness with which he accepted the judgment disarmed many of his foes and made his friends more desperately partisan. He invariably distinguished between himself and a respectable Romper man so quickly and frankly that his manner actually appeared to be continual broadcast compliment.

And one must not forget to declare the fundamental fact of his entire position in Romper. It is irrefutable that in all affairs outside his business, in all matters that occur eternally and commonly between man and man, this thieving card-player was so generous, so just, so moral, that, in a contest, he could have put to flight the consciences of nine tenths of the citizens of Romper.

And so it happened that he was seated in this saloon with the two prominent local merchants and the district attorney.

The Swede continued to drink raw whiskey, meanwhile babbling at the barkeeper and trying to induce him to indulge in potations. "Come on. Have a drink. Come on. What—no? Well, have a little one, then. By gawd, I've whipped a man tonight, and I want to celebrate. I whipped him good, too. Gentlemen," the Swede cried to the men at the table, "have a drink?"

"Ssh!" said the barkeeper.

The group at the table, although furtively attentive, had been pretending to be deep in talk, but now a man lifted his eyes toward the Swede and said, shortly, "Thanks. We don't want any more."

At this reply the Swede ruffled out his chest like a rooster. "Well," he exploded, "it seems I can't get anybody to drink with me in this town. Seems so, don't it? Well!"

"Ssh!" said the barkeeper.

"Say," snarled the Swede, "don't you try to shut me up. I won't have it. I'm a gentleman, and I want people to drink with me. An I want 'em to drink with me now. Now—do you understand?" He rapped the bar with his knuckles.

Years of experience had calloused the bartender. He merely grew sulky. "I hear you," he answered.

"Well," cried the Swede, "listen hard then. See those men over there? Well, they're going to drink with me, and don't you forget it. Now you watch."

"Hi!" yelled the barkeeper, "this won't do!"

"Why won't it?" demanded the Swede. He stalked over to the table, and by chance laid his hand upon the shoulder of the gambler. "How about this?" he asked wrathfully. "I asked you to drink with me."

The gambler simply twisted his head and spoke over his shoulder. "My friend, I don't know you."

"Oh, hell!" answered the Swede, "come and have a drink."

"Now, my boy," advised the gambler, kindly, "take your hand off my shoulder and go 'way and mind your own business." He was a little, slim man, and it seemed strange to hear him use this tone of heroic patronage to the burly Swede. The other men at the table said nothing.

"What! You won't drink with me, you little dude? I'll make you, then! I'll make you!" The Swede had grasped the gambler frenziedly at the throat, and was dragging him from his chair. The other men sprang up. The barkeeper dashed around the corner of his bar. There was a great tumult, and then was seen a long blade in the hand of the gambler. It shot forward, and a human body, this citadel of virtue, wisdom, power, was pierced as easily as if it had been a melon. The Swede fell with a cry of supreme astonishment.

The prominent merchants and the district attorney must have at once tumbled out of the place backward. The bartender found himself hanging limply to the arm of a chair and gazing into the eyes of a murderer.

"Henry," said the latter, as he wiped his knife on one of the towels that hung beneath the bar rail, "you tell 'em where to find me. I'll be home, waiting for 'em." Then he vanished. A moment afterward the barkeeper was in the street dinning through the storm for help and, moreover, companionship.

The corpse of the Swede, alone in the saloon, had its eye fixed upon a dreadful legend that dwelt atop of the cash-machine: "This registers the amount of your purchase."

IX

Months later, the cowboy was frying pork over the stove of a little ranch near the Dakota line, when there was a quick thud of hoofs outside, and presently the Easterner entered with the letters and the papers.

"Well," said the Easterner at once, "the chap that killed the Swede has got three years? Wasn't much, was it?"

"He has? Three years?" The cowboy poised his pan of pork while he ruminated upon the news. "Three years. That ain't much."

"No. It was a light sentence," replied the Easterner as he unbuckled his spurs. "Seems there was a good deal of sympathy for him in Romper."

"If the bartender had been any good," observed the cowboy thoughtfully, "he would have gone in and cracked that there Dutchman on the head with a bottle in the beginnin' of it and stopped all this here murderin'."

"Yes, a thousand things might have happened," said the Easterner, tartly.

The cowboy returned his pan of pork to the fire, but his philosophy continued. "It's funny, ain't it? If he hadn't said Johnnie was cheatin' he'd be alive this minute. He was an awful fool. Game played for fun, too. Not for money. I believe he was crazy."

"I feel sorry for that gambler," said the Easterner.

"Oh, so do I," said the cowboy. "He don't deserve none of it for killin' who he did."

"The Swede might not have been killed if everything had been square."

"Might not have been killed?" exclaimed the cowboy. "Everythin' square? Why, when he said that Johnnie was cheatin' and acted like such a jackass? And then in the saloon he fairly walked up to git hurt?" With these arguments the cowboy browbeat the Easterner and reduced him to rage.

"You're a fool!" cried the Easterner, viciously. "You're a bigger jackass than the Swede by a million majority. Now let me tell you one thing. Let me tell you something. Listen! Johnnie was cheating!"

"'Johnnie,'" said the cowboy, blankly. There was a minute of silence, and then he said, robustly, "Why, no. The game was only for fun."

"Fun or not," said the Easterner, "Johnnie was cheating. I saw him. I know it. I saw him. And I refused to stand up and be a man. I let the Swede fight it out alone. And you—you were simply puffing around the place and wanting to fight. And then old Scully himself! We are all in it! This poor gambler isn't even a noun. He is kind of an adverb. Every sin is the result of a collaboration. We, five of us, have collaborated in the murder of this Swede. Usually there are from a dozen to forty women really involved in every murder, but in this case it seems to be only five men—you, I, Johnnie, old Scully; and that fool of an unfortunate gambler came merely as a culmination, the apex of a human movement, and gets all the punishment."

The cowboy, injured and rebellious, cried out blindly into this fog of mysterious theory: "Well, I didn't do anythin', did I?"

Joseph Conrad

An Outpost of Progress

CHAPTER ONE

There were two white men in charge of the trading station. Kayerts, the chief, was short and fat; Carlier, the assistant, was tall, with a large head and a very broad trunk perched upon a long pair of thin legs. The third man on the staff was a Sierra Leone nigger, who maintained that his name was Henry Price. However, for some reason or other, the natives down the river had given him the name of Makola, and it stuck to him through all his wanderings about the country. He spoke English and French with a warbling accent, wrote a beautiful hand, understood book-keeping, and cherished in his innermost heart the worship of evil spirits. His wife was a negress from Loanda, very large and very noisy. Three children rolled about in sunshine before the door of his low, shed-like dwelling. Makola, taciturn and impenetrable, despised the two white men. He had charge of a small clay storehouse with a dried-grass roof, and pretended to keep a correct account of beads, cotton cloth, red kerchiefs, brass wire, and other trade goods it contained. Besides the

Joseph Conrad (1857-1924) was born to Polish parents living in the Russian Ukraine. Later, during over fifteen years of service on mostly British ships, Conrad learned the English language to such an extent that, when he decided to become a writer, it seemed only natural to him to write in English. He died a British subject, already famous in his lifetime for his short stories and novels. Many of Conrad's works, including *Heart of Darkness* and *Lord Jim*, deal explicitly with the experience of being a foreigner.

storehouse and Makola's hut, there was only one large building in the cleared ground of the station. It was built neatly of reeds, with a verandah on all the four sides. There were three rooms in it. The one in the middle was the living-room, and had two rough tables and a few stools in it. The other two were the bedrooms for the white men. Each had a bedstead and a mosquito net for all furniture. The plank floor was littered with the belongings of the white men; open half-empty boxes, torn wearing apparel, old boots; all the things dirty, and all the things broken, that accumulate mysteriously round untidy men. There was also another dwelling-place some distance away from the buildings. In it, under a tall cross much out of the perpendicular, slept the man who had seen the beginning of all this; who had planned and had watched the construction of this outpost of progress. He had been at home, an unsuccessful painter who, weary of pursuing fame on an empty stomach, had gone out there through high protections. He had been the first chief of that station. Makola had watched the energetic artist die of fever in the just finished house with his usual kind of "I told you so" indifference. Then, for a time, he dwelt alone with his family, his accounts books, and the Evil Spirit that rules the lands under the equator. He got on very well with his god. Perhaps he had propitiated him by a promise of more white men to play with, by and by. At any rate the director of the Great Trading Company, coming up in a steamer that resembled an enormous sardine box with a flat-roofed shed erected on it, found the station in good order, and Makola as usual quietly diligent. The director had the cross put up over the first agent's grave, and appointed Kayerts to the post. Carlier was told off as second in charge. The director was a man ruthless and efficient, who at times, but very imperceptibly, indulged in grim humour. He made a speech to Kayerts and Carlier, pointing out to them the promising aspect of their station. The nearest trading-post was about three hundred miles away. It was an exceptional opportunity for them to distinguish themselves and to earn percentages on the trade. This appointment was a favor done to beginners. Kayerts was moved almost to tears by his director's kindness. He would, he said, by doing his best, try to justify the flattering confidence, &c, &c. Kayerts had been in the Administration of the Telegraphs, and knew how to express himself correctly. Carlier, an ex-non-commissioned officer of cavalry in an army guaranteed from harm by several European Powers, was less impressed. If there were commissions to get, so much the better; and, trailing a sulky glance over the river, the forests, the impenetrable bush that seemed to cut off the station from the rest of the world, he muttered between his teeth, "We shall see, very soon."

Next day, some bales of cotton goods and a few cases of provisions having been thrown on shore, the sardine-box steamer went off, not to return for another six months. On the deck the Director touched his cap to the two agents, who stood on the bank waving their hats, and turning to an old servant of the Company on his passage to headquarters, said, "Look at those two imbeciles. They must be mad at home to send me such specimens. I told those fellows to plant a vegetable garden, build new storehouses and fences, and construct a landing-stage. I bet nothing will be done! They won't know how to begin. I always thought the station on this river useless, and they just fit the station!"

"They will form themselves there," said the old stager with a quiet smile.

"At any rate, I am rid of them for six months," retorted the Director.

The two men watched the steamer round the bend, then ascending arm in arm the slope of the bank, returned to the station. They had been in this vast and dark country only a very short time, and as yet always in the midst of other white men, under the eye and guidance of their superiors. And now, dull as they were to the subtle influences of surroundings, they felt themselves very much alone, when suddenly left unassisted to face the wilderness; a wilderness rendered more strange, more incomprehensible by the mysterious glimpses of the vigorous life it contained. They were two perfectly insignificant and incapable individuals, whose existence is only rendered possible through the high organization of civilized crowds. Few men realize that their life, the very essence of their character, their capabilities and their audacities, are only the expression of their belief in the safety of their surroundings. The courage, the composure, the confidence; the emotions and principles; every great and every insignificant thought belongs not to the individual but to the crowd: to the crowd that believes blindly in the irresistible force of its institutions and of its morals, in the power of its police and of its opinion. But the contact with pure unmitigated savagery, with primitive nature and primitive man, brings sudden and profound trouble into the heart. To the sentiment of being alone of one's kind, to the clear perception of the loneliness of one's thoughts, of one's sensations—to the negation of the habitual, which is safe, there is added the affirmation of the unusual, which is dangerous; a suggestion of things vague, uncontrollable, and repulsive, whose discomposing intrusion excites the imagination and tries the civilized nerves of the foolish and the wise alike.

Kayerts and Carlier walked arm in arm, drawing close to one another as children do in the dark; and they had the same, not altogether unpleasant, sense of danger which one half suspects to be imaginary. They chatted persistently in familiar tones. "Our station is prettily situated," said one. The other assented with enthusiasm, enlarging volubly on the beauties of the situation. Then they passed near the grave. "Poor devil!" said Kayerts. "He died of fever, didn't he?" muttered Carlier, stopping short. "Why," retorted Kayerts, with indignation, "I've been told that the fellow exposed himself recklessly to the sun. The climate here, everybody says, is not at all worse than at home, as long as you keep out of the sun. Do you hear that, Carlier? I am chief here, and my orders are that you should not expose yourself to the sun!" He assumed his superiority jocularly, but his meaning was serious. The idea that he would, perhaps, have to bury Carlier and remain alone, gave him an inward shiver. He felt suddenly that this Carlier was more precious to him here, in the center of Africa, than a brother could be anywhere else. Carlier, entering into the spirit of the thing, made a military salute and answered in a brisk tone, "Your orders shall be attended to, chief!" Then he burst out laughing, slapped Kayerts on the back and shouted, "We shall let life run easily here! Just sit still and gather in the ivory those savages will bring. This country has its good points, after all!" They both laughed loudly while Carlier thought: "That poor Kayerts; he is so fat and unhealthy. It would be awful if I had to bury him here. He is a man I respect." . . . Before they reached the verandah of their house they called one another "my dear fellow."

The first day they were very active, pottering about with hammers and nails and red calico, to put up curtains, make their house habitable and pretty; resolved to settle down comfortably to their new life. For them an impossible task. To grapple effectually with even purely material problems requires more serenity of mind and more lofty courage than people generally imagine. No two beings could have been more unfitted for such a struggle. Society, not from any tenderness, but because of its strange needs, had taken care of those two men, forbidding them all independent thought, all initiative, all departure from routine; and forbidding it under pain of death. They could only live on condition of being machines. And now, released from the fostering care of men with pens behind the ears, or of men with gold lace on the sleeves, they were like those lifelong prisoners who, liberated after many years, do not know what use to make of their freedom. They did not know what use to make of their faculties, being both, through want of practice, incapable of independent thought.

At the end of two months Kayerts often would say, "If it was not for my Melie, you wouldn't catch me here." Melie was his daughter. He had thrown up his post in the Administration of the Telegraphs, though he had been for seventeen years perfectly happy there, to earn a dowry for his girl. His wife was dead, and the child was being brought up by his sisters. He regretted the streets, the pavements, the cafes, his friends of many years; all the things he used to see, day after day; all the thoughts suggested by familiar things—the thoughts effortless, monotonous, and soothing of a Government clerk; he regretted all the gossip, the small enmities, the mild venom, and the little jokes of Government offices. "If I had had a decent brother-in-law," Carlier would remark, "a fellow with a heart, I would not be here." He had left the army and had made himself so obnoxious to his family by his laziness and impudence, that an exasperated brother-in-law had made superhuman efforts to procure him an appointment in the Company as a second-class agent. Having not a penny in the world he was compelled to accept this means of livelihood as soon as it became quite clear to him that there was nothing more to squeeze out of his relations. He, like Kayerts, regretted his old life. He regretted the clink of sabre and spurs on a fine afternoon, the barrack-room witticisms, the girls of garrison towns; but, besides, he had also a sense of grievance. He was evidently a much ill-used man. This made him moody, at times. But the two men got on well together in the fellowship of their stupidity and laziness. Together they did nothing, absolutely nothing, and enjoyed the sense of the idleness for which they were paid. And in time they came to feel something resembling affection for one another.

They lived like blind men in a large room, aware only of what came in contact with them (and of that only imperfectly), but unable to see the general aspect of things. The river, the forest, all the great land throbbing with life, were like a great emptiness. Even the brilliant sunshine disclosed nothing intelligible. Things appeared and disappeared before their eyes in an unconnected and aimless kind of way. The river seemed to come from nowhere and flow nowhither. It flowed through a void. Out of that void, at times, came canoes, and men with spears in their hands would suddenly crowd the yard of the station. They were naked, glossy black, ornamented with snowy shells and glistening brass wire, perfect of limb. They made an uncouth babbling noise when they spoke, moved in a stately manner, and sent quick wild glances out of their startled, never-resting eyes. Those warriors would squat in long rows, four or more deep, before the verandah, while their chiefs bargained for hours with Makola over an elephant tusk. Kayerts sat on his chair and looked down on the proceedings, understanding nothing. He stared at them with his round blue eyes, called out to Carlier, "Here, look! Look at that fellow there—and that other one, to the left. Did you ever see such a face? Oh, the funny brute!"

Carlier, smoking native tobacco in a short wooden pipe, would swagger up twirling his moustaches, and surveying the warriors with haughty indulgence, would say—

"Fine animals. Brought any bone? Yes? It's not any too soon. Look at the muscles of that fellow—third from the end. I wouldn't care to get a punch on the nose from him. Fine arms, but legs no good below the knee. Couldn't make cavalry men of them." And after glancing down complacently at his own shanks, he always concluded: "Pah! Don't they stink! You, Makola! Take that herd over to the fetish" (the storehouse was in every station called the fetish, perhaps because of the spirit of civilization it contained) "and give them up some of the rubbish you keep there. I'd rather see it full of bone than full of rags."

Kayerts approved.

"Yes, yes! Go and finish that palaver over there, Mr. Makola. I will come round when you are ready, to weigh the tusk. We must be careful." Then turning to his companion: "This is the tribe that lives down the river; they are rather aromatic. I remember, they had been once before here. D'ye hear that row? What a fellow has got to put up with in this dog of a country! My head is split."

Such profitable visits were rare. For days the two pioneers of trade and progress would look on their empty courtyard in the vibrating brilliance of vertical sunshine. Below the high bank, the silent river flowed on glittering and steady. On the sands in the middle of the stream, hippos and alligators sunned themselves side by side. And stretching away in all directions, surrounding the insignificant cleared spot of the trading post, immense forests, hiding fateful complications of fantastic life, lay in the eloquent silence of mute greatness. The two men understood nothing, cared for nothing but for the passage of days that separated them from the steamer's return. Their predecessor had left some torn books. They took up these wrecks of novels, and, as they had never read anything of the kind before, they were surprised and amused. Then during long days there were interminable and silly discussions about plots and personages. In the centre of Africa they made acquaintance of Richelieu and of D'Artagnan, of Hawk's Eye and of Father Goriot, and of many other people. All these imaginary personages became subjects for gossip as if they had been living friends. They discounted their virtues, suspected their motives, decried their successes; were scandalized at their duplicity or were doubtful about their courage. The accounts of crimes filled them with indignation, while tender or pathetic passages moved them deeply. Carlier cleared his throat and said in a soldierly voice, "What nonsense!" Kayerts, his round eyes suffused with tears, his fat cheeks quivering, rubbed his bald head, and declared, "This is a splendid book. I had no idea there were such clever fellows in the world." They also found some old copies of a home paper. That print discussed what it was pleased to call "Our Colonial Expansion" in high-flown language. It spoke much of the rights and duties of civilization, of the sacredness of the civilizing work, and extolled the merits of those who went about bringing light, and faith and commerce to the dark places of the earth. Carlier and Kayerts read, wondered, and began to think better of themselves. Carlier said one evening, waving his hand about, "In a hundred years, there will be perhaps a town here. Quays, and warehouses, and barracks, and—and—billiard rooms. Civilization, my boy, and virtue—and all. And then, chaps will read that two good fellows, Kayerts and Carlier, were the first civilized men to live in this very spot!" Kayerts nodded, "Yes, it is a consolation to think of that." They seemed to forget their dead predecessor; but, early one day, Carlier went out and replanted the cross firmly. "It used to make me squint whenever I walked that way," he explained to Kayerts over the morning coffee. "It made me squint, leaning over so much. So I just planted it upright. And solid, I promise you! I suspended myself with both hands to the cross-piece. Not a move. Oh, I did that properly."

At times Gobila came to see them. Gobila was the chief of the neighboring villages. He was a gray-headed savage, thin and black, with a white cloth round his loins and a mangy panther skin hanging over his back. He came up with long strides of his skeleton legs, swinging a staff as tall as himself, and, entering the common room of the station, would squat on his heels to the left of the door. There he sat, watching Kayerts, and now and then making a speech which the other did not understand. Kayerts, without interrupting his occupation, would from time to time say in a friendly manner: "How goes it, you old image?" and they would smile at one another. The two whites had a liking for that old and incomprehensible creature, and called him Father Gobila. Gobila's manner was paternal, and he seemed really to love all white men. They all appeared to him very young, indistinguishably alike (except for stature), and he knew that they were all brothers, and also immortal. The death of the artist, who was the first white man whom he knew intimately, did not disturb this belief, because he was firmly convinced that the white stranger had pretended to die and got himself buried for some mysterious purpose of his own, into which it was useless to inquire. Perhaps it was his way of going home to his own country? At any rate, these were his brothers, and he transferred his absurd affection to them. They returned it in a way. Carlier slapped him on the back, and recklessly struck off matches for his amusement. Kayerts was always ready to let him have a sniff at the ammonia bottle. In short, they behaved just like that other white creature that had hidden itself in a hole in the ground. Gobila considered them attentively. Perhaps they were the same being with the other—or one of them was. He couldn't decide—clear up that mystery; but he remained always very friendly. In consequence of that friendship the women of Gobila's village walked in single file through the reedy grass, bringing every morning to the station, fowls, and sweet potatoes, and palm wine, and sometimes a goat. The Company never provisions the stations fully, and the agents required those local supplies to live. They had them through the good-will of Gobila, and lived well. Now and then one of them had a bout of fever, and the other nursed him with gentle devotion. They did not think much of it. It left them weaker, and their appearance changed for the worse. Carlier was hollow-eyed and irritable. Kayerts showed a drawn, flabby face above the rotundity of his stomach, which gave him a weird aspect. But being constantly together, they did not notice the change that took place gradually in their appearance, and also in their dispositions.

Five months passed in that way.

Then, one morning, as Kayerts and Carlier, lounging in their chairs under the verandah, talked about the approaching visit of the steamer, a knot of armed men came out of the forest and advanced towards the station. They were strangers to that part of the country. They were tall, slight, draped classically from neck to heel in blue fringed cloths, and carried percussion muskets over their bare right shoulders. Makola showed signs of excitement, and ran out of the storehouse (where he spent all his days) to meet these visitors. They came into the courtyard and looked about them with steady, scornful glances. Their leader, a powerful and determined-looking negro with bloodshot eyes, stood in front of the verandah and made a long speech. He gesticulated much, and ceased very suddenly.

There was something in his intonation, in the sounds of the long sentences he used, that startled the two whites. It was like a reminiscence of something not exactly familiar, and yet resembling the speech of civilized men. It sounded like one of those impossible languages which sometimes we hear in our dreams.

"What lingo is that?" said the amazed Carlier. "In the first moment I fancied the fellow was going to speak French. Anyway, it is a different kind of gibberish to what we ever heard."

"Yes," replied Kayerts. "Hey, Makola, what does he say? Where do they come from? Who are they?"

But Makola, who seemed to be standing on hot bricks, answered hurriedly, "I don't know. They come from very far. Perhaps Mrs. Price will understand. They are perhaps bad men."

The leader, after waiting for a while, said something sharply to Makola, who shook his head. Then the man, after looking round, noticed Makola's hut and walked over there. The next moment Mrs. Makola was heard speaking with great volubility. The other strangers—they were six in all—strolled about with an air of ease, put their heads through the door of the storeroom, congregated round the grave, pointed understandingly at the cross, and generally made themselves at home.

"I don't like those chaps—and, I say, Kayerts, they must be from the coast; they've got firearms," observed the sagacious Carlier.

Kayerts also did not like those chaps. They both, for the first time, became aware that they lived in conditions where the unusual may be dangerous, and that there was no power on earth outside of themselves to stand between them and the unusual. They became uneasy, went in and loaded their revolvers. Kayerts said, "We must order Makola to tell them to go away before dark."

The strangers left in the afternoon, after eating a meal prepared for them by Mrs. Makola. The immense woman was excited, and talked much with the visitors. She rattled away shrilly, pointing here and there at the forests and at the river. Makola sat apart and watched. At times he got up and whispered to his wife. He accompanied the strangers across the ravine at the back of the station-ground, and returned slowly looking very thoughtful. When questioned by the white men he was very strange, seemed not to understand, seemed to have forgotten French—seemed to have forgotten how to speak altogether. Kayerts and Carlier agreed that the nigger had had too much palm wine.

There was some talk about keeping a watch in turn, but in the evening everything seemed so quiet and peaceful that they retired as usual. All night they were disturbed by a lot of drumming in the villages. A deep, rapid roll near by would be followed by another far off—then all ceased. Soon short appeals would rattle out here and there, then all mingle together, increase, become vigorous and sustained, would spread out over the forest, roll through the night, unbroken and ceaseless, near and far, as if the whole land had been one immense drum booming out steadily an appeal to heaven. And through the deep and tremendous noise sudden yells that resembled snatches of songs from a madhouse darted shrill and high in discordant jets of sound which seemed to rush far above the earth and drive all peace from under the stars.

Carlier and Kayerts slept badly. They both thought they had heard shots fired during the night—but they could not agree as to the direction. In the morning Makola was gone somewhere. He returned about noon with one of yesterday's strangers, and eluded all Kayerts' attempts to close with him: had become deaf apparently. Kayerts wondered. Carlier, who had been fishing off the bank, came back and remarked while he showed his catch, "The niggers seem to be in a deuce of a stir; I wonder what's up. I saw about fifteen canoes cross the river during the two hours I was there fishing." Kayerts, worried, said, "Isn't this Makola very queer to-day?" Carlier advised, "Keep all our meat together in case of some trouble."

CHAPTER TWO

There were ten station men who had been left by the Director. Those fellows, having engaged themselves to the Company for six months (without having any idea of a month in particular and only a very faint notion of time in general), had been serving the cause of progress for upwards of two years. Belonging to a tribe from a very distant part of the land of darkness and sorrow, they did not run away, naturally supposing that as wandering strangers they would be killed by the inhabitants of the country; in which they were right. They lived in straw huts on the slope of a ravine overgrown with reedy grass, just behind the station buildings. They were not happy, regretting the festive incantations, the sorceries, the human sacrifices of their own land; where they also had parents, brothers, sisters, admired chiefs, respected magicians, loved friends, and other ties supposed generally to be human. Besides, the rice rations served out by the Company did not agree with them, being a food unknown to their land, and to which they could not get used. Consequently they were unhealthy and miserable. Had they been of any other tribe they would have made up their minds to die—for nothing is easier to certain savages than suicide—and so have escaped from the puzzling difficulties of existence. But belonging, as they did, to a warlike tribe with filed teeth, they had more grit, and went on stupidly living through disease and sorrow. They did very little work, and had lost their splendid physique. Carlier and Kayerts doctored them assiduously without being able to bring them back into condition again. They were mustered every morning and told off to different tasks—grass-cutting, fence-building, tree-felling, &c., &c., which no power on earth could induce them to execute efficiently. The two whites had practically very little control over them.

In the afternoon Makola came over to the big house and found Kayerts watching three heavy columns of smoke rising above the forests. "What is that?" asked Kayerts. "Some villages burn," answered Makola, who seemed to have regained his wits. Then he said abruptly: "We have got very little ivory; bad six months' trading. Do you like get a little more ivory?"

"Yes," said Kayerts, eagerly. He thought of percentages which were low.

"Those men who came yesterday are traders from Loanda who have got more ivory than they can carry home. Shall I buy? I know their camp."

"Certainly," said Kayerts. "What are those traders?"

"Bad fellows," said Makola, indifferently. "They fight with people, and catch women and children. They are bad men and got guns. There is a great disturbance in the country. Do you want ivory?"

"Yes," said Kayerts. Makola said nothing for a while. Then: "Those workmen of ours are no good at all," he muttered, looking round. "Station in very bad order, sir. Director will growl. Better get a fine lot of ivory, then he say nothing."

"I can't help it; the men won't work," said Kayerts. "When will you get that ivory?

"Very soon," said Makola. "Perhaps to-night. You leave it to me, and keep indoors, sir. I think you had better give some palm wine to our men to make a dance this evening. Enjoy themselves. Work better to-morrow. There's plenty palm wine—gone a little sour."

Kayerts said "yes," and Makola, with his own hands carried big calabashes to the door of his hut. They stood there till the evening, and Mrs. Makola looked into every one. The men got them at sunset. When Kayerts and Carlier retired, a big bonfire was flaring before the men's huts. They could hear their shouts and drumming. Some men from Gobila's village had joined the station hands, and the entertainment was a great success.

In the middle of the night, Carlier waking suddenly, heard a man shout loudly; then a shot was fired. Only one. Carlier ran out and met Kayerts on the verandah. They were both startled. As they went across the yard to call Makola, they saw shadows moving in the night. One of them cried, "Don't shoot! It's me, Price." Then Makola appeared close to them. "Go back, go back, please," he urged, "you spoil all." "There are strange men about," said Carlier. "Never mind; I know," said Makola. Then he whispered, "All right. Bring ivory. Say nothing! I know my business." The two white men reluctantly went back to the house, but did not sleep. They heard footsteps, whispers, some groans. It seemed as if a lot of men came in, dumped heavy things on the ground, squabbled a long time, then went away. They lay on their hard beds and thought: "This Makola is invaluable." In the morning Carlier came out, very sleepy, and pulled at the cord of the big bell. The station hands mustered every morning to the sound of the bell. That morning nobody came. Kayerts turned out also, yawning. Across the yard they saw Makola come out of his hut, a tin basin of soapy water in his hand. Makola, a civilized nigger, was very neat in his person. He threw the soapsuds skillfully over a wretched little yellow cur he had, then turning his face to the agent's house, he shouted from the distance, "All the men gone last night!"

They heard him plainly, but in their surprise they both yelled out together: "What!" Then they stared at one another. "We are in a proper fix now," growled Carlier. "It's incredible!" muttered Kayerts. "I will go to the huts and see," said Carlier, striding off. Makola coming up found Kayerts standing alone.

"I can hardly believe it," said Kayerts, tearfully. "We took care of them as if they had been our children."

"They went with the coast people," said Makola after a moment of hesitation.

"What do I care with whom they went—the ungrateful brutes!" exclaimed the other. Then with sudden suspicion, and looking hard at Makola, he added: "What do you know about it?"

Makola moved his shoulders, looking down on the ground. "What do I know? I think only. Will you come and look at the ivory I've got there? It is a fine lot. You never saw such."

He moved towards the store. Kayerts followed him mechanically, thinking about the incredible desertion of the men. On the ground before the door of the fetish lay six splendid tusks.

"What did you give for it?" asked Kayerts, after surveying the lot with satisfaction.

"No regular trade," said Makola. "They brought the ivory and gave it to me. I told them to take what they most wanted in the station. It is a beautiful lot. No station can show such tusks. Those traders wanted carriers badly, and our men were no good here. No trade, no entry in books; all correct."

Kayerts nearly burst with indignation. "Why!" he shouted, "I believe you have sold our men for these tusks!" Makola stood impassive and silent. "I—I—will—I," stuttered Kayerts. "You fiend!" he yelled out.

"I did the best for you and the Company," said Makola, imperturbably. "Why you shout so much? Look at this tusk."

"I dismiss you! I will report you—I won't look at the tusk. I forbid you to touch them. I order you to throw them into the river. You—you!"

"You very red, Mr. Kayerts. If you are so irritable in the sun, you will get fever and die—like the first chief!" pronounced Makola impressively.

They stood still, contemplating one another with intense eyes, as if they had been looking with effort across immense distances. Kayerts shivered. Makola had meant no more than he said, but his words seemed to Kayerts full of ominous menace! He turned sharply and went away to the house. Makola retired into the bosom of his family; and the tusks, left lying before the store, looked very large and valuable in the sunshine.

Carlier came back on the verandah. "They're all gone, hey?" asked Kayerts from the far end of the common room in a muffled voice. "You did not find anybody?"

"Oh, yes," said Carlier, "I found one of Gobila's people lying dead before the huts—shot through the body. We heard that shot last night."

Kayerts came out quickly. He found his companion staring grimly over the yard at the tusks, away by the store. They both sat in silence for a while. Then Kayerts related his conversation with Makola. Carlier said nothing. At the midday meal they ate very little. They hardly exchanged a word that day. A great silence seemed to lie heavily over the station and press on their lips. Makola did not open the store; he spent the day playing with his children. He lay full-length on a mat outside his door, and the youngsters sat on his chest and clambered all over him. It was a touching picture. Mrs. Makola was busy cooking all day as usual. The white men made a somewhat better meal in the evening. Afterwards, Carlier smoking his pipe strolled over to the store; he stood for a long time over the tusks, touched one or two with his foot, even tried to lift the largest one by its small end. He came back to his chief, who had not stirred from the verandah, threw himself in the chair and said—

"I can see it! They were pounced upon while they slept heavily after drinking all that palm wine you've allowed Makola to give them. A put-up job! See? The worst is, some of Gobila's people were there, and got carried off too, no doubt. The least drunk woke up, and got shot for his sobriety. This is a funny country. What will you do now?"

"We can't touch it, of course," said Kayerts.

"Of course not," assented Carlier.

"Slavery is an awful thing," stammered out Kayerts in an unsteady voice.

"Frightful—the sufferings," grunted Carlier with conviction.

They believed their words. Everybody shows a respectful deference to certain sounds that he and his fellows can make. But about feelings people really know nothing. We talk with indignation or enthusiasm; we talk about oppression, cruelty, crime, devotion, self-sacrifice, virtue, and we know nothing real beyond the words. Nobody knows what suffering or sacrifice mean—except, perhaps, the victims of the mysterious purpose of these illusions.

Next morning they saw Makola very busy setting up in the yard the big scales used for weighing ivory. By and by Carlier said: "What's that filthy scoundrel up to?" and lounged out into the yard. Kayerts followed. They stood watching. Makola took no notice. When the balance was swung true, he tried to lift a tusk into the scale. It was too heavy. He looked up helplessly without a word, and for a minute they stood round that balance as mute and still as three statues. Suddenly Carlier said: "Catch hold of the other end, Makola—you beast!" and together they swung the tusk up. Kayerts trembled in every limb. He muttered, "I say, chief, I might just as well give him a lift with this lot into the store."

As they were going back to the house Kayerts observed with a sigh:

"It had to be done." And Carlier said: "It's deplorable, but, the men being Company's men the ivory is Company's ivory. We must look after it." "I will report to the Director, of course," said Kayerts. "Of course; let him decide," approved Carlier.

At midday they made a hearty meal. Kayerts sighed from time to time. Whenever they mentioned Makola's name they always added to it an opprobrious epithet. It eased their conscience. Makola gave himself a half-holiday, and bathed his children in the river. No one from Gobila's villages came near the station that day. No one came the next day, and the next, nor for a whole week. Gobila's people might have been dead and buried for any sign of life they gave. But they were only mourning for those they had lost by the witchcraft of white men, who had brought wicked people into their country. The wicked people were gone, but fear remained. Fear always remains. A man may destroy everything within himself, love and hate and belief, and even doubt; but as long as he clings to life he cannot destroy fear: the fear, subtle, indestructible, and terrible, that pervades his being; that tinges his thoughts; that lurks in his heart; that watches on his lips the struggle of his last breath. In his fear, the mild old Gobila offered extra human sacrifices to all the Evil Spirits that had taken possession of his white friends. His heart was heavy. Some warriors spoke about burning and killing, but the cautious old savage dissuaded them. Who could foresee the woe those mysterious creatures, if irritated, might bring? They should be left alone. Perhaps in time they would disappear into the earth as the first one had disappeared. His people must keep away from them, and hope for the best.

Kayerts and Carlier did not disappear, but remained above on this earth, that, somehow, they fancied had become bigger and very empty. It was not the absolute and dumb solitude of the post that impressed them so much as an inarticulate feeling that something from within them was gone, something that worked for their safety, and had kept the wilderness from interfering with their hearts. The images of home; the memory of people like them, of men that thought and felt as they used to think and feel, receded into distances made indistinct by the glare of unclouded sunshine. And out of the great silence of the surrounding wilderness, its very hopelessness and savagery seemed to approach them nearer, to draw them gently, to look upon them, to envelop them with a solicitude irresistible, familiar, and disgusting.

Days lengthened into weeks, then into months. Gobila's people drummed and yelled to every new moon, as of yore, but kept away from the station. Makola and Carlier tried once in a canoe to open communications, but were received with a shower of arrows, and had to fly back to the station for dear life. That attempt set the country up and down the river into an uproar that could be very distinctly heard for days. The steamer was late. At first they spoke of delay jauntily, then anxiously, then gloomily. The matter was becoming serious. Stores were running short. Carlier cast his lines off the bank, but the river was low, and the fish kept out in the stream. They dared not stroll far away from the station to shoot. Moreover, there was no game in the impenetrable forest. Once Carlier shot a hippo in the river. They had no boat to secure it, and it sank. When it floated up it drifted away, and Gobila's people secured the carcase. It was the occasion for a national holiday, but Carlier had a fit of rage over it and talked about the necessity of exterminating all the niggers before the country could be made habitable. Kayerts mooned about silently; spent hours looking at the portrait of his Melie. It represented a little girl with long bleached tresses and a rather sour face. His legs were much swollen, and he could hardly walk. Carlier, undermined by fever, could not swagger any more, but kept tottering about, still with a devil-may-care air, as became a man who remembered his crack regiment. He had become hoarse, sarcastic, and inclined to say unpleasant things. He called it "being frank with you." They had long ago reckoned their percentages on trade, including in them that last deal of "this infamous Makola." They had also concluded not to say anything about it. Kayerts hesitated at first—was afraid of the Director.

"He has seen worse things done on the quiet," maintained Carlier, with a hoarse laugh. "Trust him! He won't thank you if you blab. He is no better than you or me. Who will talk if we hold our tongues? There is nobody here."

That was the root of the trouble! There was nobody there; and being left there alone with their weakness, they became daily more like a pair of accomplices than like a couple of devoted friends. They had heard nothing from home for eight months. Every evening they said, "Tomorrow we shall see the steamer." But one of the Company's steamers had been wrecked, and the Director was busy with the other, relieving very distant and important stations on the main river. He thought that the useless station, and the useless men, could wait. Meantime Kayerts and Carlier lived on rice boiled without salt, and cursed the Company, all Africa, and the day they were born. One must have lived on such diet to discover what ghastly trouble the necessity of swallowing one's food may become. There was literally nothing else in the station but rice and coffee; they drank the coffee without sugar. The last fifteen lumps Kayerts had solemnly locked away in his box, together with a half-bottle of Cognac, "in case of sickness," he explained. Carlier approved. "When one is sick," he said, "any little extra like that is cheering."

They waited. Rank grass began to sprout over the court-yard. The bell never rang now. Days passed, silent, exasperating, and slow. When the two men spoke, they snarled; and their silences were bitter, as if tinged by the bitterness of their thoughts.

One day after a lunch of boiled rice, Carlier put down his cup untasted, and said: "Hang it all! Let's have a decent cup of coffee for once. Bring out that sugar, Kayerts!"

"For the sick," muttered Kayerts, without looking up.

"For the sick," mocked Carlier. "Bosh! . . . Well! I am sick."

"You are no more sick than I am, and I go without," said Kayerts in a peaceful tone.

"Come! out with that sugar, you stingy old slave-dealer."

Kayerts looked up quickly. Carlier was smiling with marked insolence. And suddenly it seemed to Kayerts that he had never seen that man before. Who was he? He knew nothing about him. What was he capable of? There was a surprising flash of violent emotion within him, as if in the presence of something undreamt-of, dangerous, and final. But he managed to pronounce with composure—

"That joke is in very bad taste. Don't repeat it."

"Joke!" said Carlier, hitching himself forward on his seat. "I am hungry—I am sick—I don't joke! I hate hypocrites. You are a hypocrite. You are a slave-dealer. I am a slave-dealer. There's nothing but slave-dealers in this cursed country. I mean to have sugar in my coffee today, anyhow!"

"I forbid you to speak to me in that way," said Kayerts with a fair show of resolution.

"You!—What?" shouted Carlier, jumping up.

Kayerts stood up also. "I am your chief," he began, trying to master the shakiness of his voice.

"What?" yelled the other. "Who's chief? There's no chief here. There's nothing here: there's nothing but you and I. Fetch the sugar—you pot-bellied ass."

"Hold your tongue. Go out of the room," screamed Kayerts. "I dismiss you—you scoundrel!"

Carlier swung a stool. All at once he looked dangerously in earnest. "You flabby, good-for-nothing civilian—take that!" he howled.

Kayerts dropped under the table, and the stool struck the grass inner wall of the room. Then, as Carlier was trying to upset the table, Kayerts in desperation made a blind rush, head low, like a cornered pig would do, and over-turning his friend, bolted along the verandah, and into his room. He locked the door, snatched his revolver, and stood panting. In less than a minute Carlier was kicking at the door furiously, howling, "If you don't bring out that sugar, I will shoot you at sight, like a dog. Now then—one—two—three. You won't? I will show you who's the master."

Kayerts thought the door would fall in, and scrambled through the square hole that served for a window in his room. There was then the whole breadth of the house between them. But the other was apparently not strong enough to break in the door, and Kayerts heard him running round. Then he also began to run laboriously on his swollen legs. He ran as quickly as he could, grasping the revolver, and unable yet to understand what was happening to him. He saw in succession Makola's house, the store, the river, the ravine, and the low bushes; and he saw all those things again as he ran for the second time round the house. Then again they flashed past him. That morning he could not have walked a yard without a groan.

And now he ran. He ran fast enough to keep out of sight of the other man.

Then as, weak and desperate, he thought, "Before I finish the next round I shall die," he heard the other man stumble heavily, then stop. He stopped also. He had the back and Carlier the front of the house, as before. He heard him drop into a chair cursing, and suddenly his own legs gave way, and he slid down into a sitting posture with his back to the wall. His mouth was as dry as a cinder, and his face was wet with perspiration—and tears. What was it all about? He thought it must be a horrible illusion; he thought he was dreaming; he thought he was going mad! After a while he collected his senses. What did they quarrel about? That sugar! How absurd! He would give it to him—didn't want it himself. And he began scrambling to his feet with a sudden feeling of security. But before he had fairly stood upright, a common-sense reflection occurred to him and drove him back into despair. He thought: "If I give way now to that brute of a soldier, he will begin this horror again tomorrow—and the day after—every day—and I will be lost! Lost! The steamer may not come for days—may never come." He shook so that he had to sit down on the floor again. He shivered forlornly. He felt he could not, would not move any more. He was completely distracted by the sudden perception that the position was without issue—that death and life had in a moment become equally difficult and terrible.

All at once he heard the other push his chair back; and he leaped to his feet with extreme facility. He listened and got confused. Must run again! Right or left? He heard footsteps. He darted to the left, grasping his revolver, and at the very same instant, as it seemed to him, they came into violent collision. Both shouted with surprise. A loud explosion took place between them; a roar of red fire, thick smoke; and Kayerts, deafened and blinded, rushed back thinking: "I am hit—it's all over." He expected the other to come round—to gloat over his agony. He caught hold of the upright of the room—"All over!" Then he heard a crashing fall on the other side of the house, as if somebody had tumbled headlong over a chair—then silence. Nothing more happened. He did not die. Only his shoulder felt as if it had been badly wrenched, and he had lost his revolver. He was disarmed and helpless! He waited for his fate. The other man made no sound. It was a strategem. He was stalking him now! Along what side? Perhaps he was taking aim this very minute.

After a few moments of an agony frightful and absurd, he decided to go and meet his doom. He was prepared for every surrender. He turned the corner, steadying himself with one hand on the wall; made a few paces, and nearly swooned. He had seen on the floor, protruding past the other corner, a pair of turned-up feet. A pair of white naked feet in red slippers. He felt deadly sick, and stood for a time in profound darkness. Then Makola appeared before him, saying quietly: "Come along, Mr. Kayerts. He is dead." He burst into tears of gratitude; a loud, sobbing fit of crying. After a time he found himself sitting in a chair and looking at Carlier, who lay stretched on his back. Makola was kneeling over the body.

"Is this your revolver?" asked Makola, getting up.

"Yes," said Kayerts; then he added very quickly, "He ran after me to shoot me—you saw!"

"Yes, I saw," said Makola. "There is only one revolver; where's his?"

"Don't know," whispered Kayerts in a voice that had become suddenly very faint.

"I will go and look for it," said the other, gently. He made the round along the verandah, while Kayerts sat still and looked at the corpse. Makola came back empty-handed, stood in deep thought, then stepped quietly into the dead man's room, and came out directly with a revolver, which he held up before Kayerts. Kayerts shut his eyes. Everything was going round. He found life more terrible and difficult than death. He had shot an unarmed man.

After meditating for a while, Makola said softly, pointing at the dead man who lay there with his right eye blown out—

"He died of fever." Kayerts looked at him with a stony stare. "Yes," repeated Makola, thoughtfully, stepping over the corpse, "I think he died of fever. Bury him to-morrow."

And he went away slowly to his expectant wife, leaving the two white men alone on the verandah.

Night came, and Kayerts sat unmoving on his chair. He sat quiet as if he had taken a dose of opium. The violence of the emotions he had passed through produced a feeling of exhausted serenity. He had plumbed in one short afternoon the depths of horror and despair, and now found repose in the conviction that life had no more secrets for him: neither had death! He sat by the corpse thinking; thinking very actively, thinking very new thoughts. He seemed to have broken loose from himself altogether. His old thoughts, convictions, likes and dislikes, things he respected and things he abhorred, appeared in their true light at last! Appeared contemptible and childish, false and ridiculous. He revelled in his new wisdom while he sat by the man he had killed. He argued with himself about all things under heaven with that kind of wrong-headed lucidity which may be observed in some lunatics. Incidentally he reflected that the fellow dead there had been a noxious beast anyway; that men died every day in thousands; perhaps in hundreds of thousands—who could tell?—and that in the number, that one death could not possibly make any difference; couldn't have any importance, at least to a thinking creature. He, Kayerts, was a thinking creature. He had been all his life, till that moment, a believer in a lot of nonsense like the rest of mankind—who are fools; but now he thought! He knew! He was at peace; he was familiar with the highest wisdom! Then he tried to imagine himself dead, and Carlier sitting in his chair watching him; and his attempt met with such unexpected success, that in a very few moments he became not at all sure who was dead and who was alive. This extraordinary achievement of his fancy startled him, however, and by a clever and timely effort of mind he saved himself just in time from becoming Carlier. His heart thumped, and he felt hot all over at the thought of that danger. Carlier! What a beastly thing! To compose his now disturbed nerves—and no wonder!—he tried to whistle a little. Then, suddenly, he fell asleep, or thought he had slept; but at any rate there was a fog, and somebody had whistled in the fog.

He stood up. The day had come, and a heavy mist had descended upon the land: the mist penetrating, enveloping, and silent; the morning mist of tropical lands; the mist that clings and kills; the mist white and deadly, immaculate and poisonous. He stood up, saw the body, and threw his arms above his head with a cry like that of a man who, waking from a trance, finds himself immured forever in a tomb. "Help! . . . My God!"

A shriek inhuman, vibrating and sudden, pierced like a sharp dart the white shroud of that land of sorrow. Three short, impatient screeches followed, and then, for a time, the fog-wreaths rolled on, undisturbed, through a formidable silence. Then many more shrieks, rapid and piercing, like the yells of some exasperated and ruthless creature, rent the air. Progress was calling to Kayerts from the river. Progress and civilization and all the virtues. Society was calling to its accomplished child to come, to be taken care of, to be instructed, to be judged, to be condemned; it called him to return to that rubbish heap from which he had wandered away, so that justice could be done.

Kayerts heard and understood. He stumbled out of the verandah, leaving the other man quite alone for the first time since they had been thrown there together. He groped his way through the fog, calling in his ignorance upon the invisible heaven to undo its work. Makola flitted by in the mist, shouting as he ran—

"Steamer! Steamer! They can't see. They whistle for the station. I go ring the bell. Go down to the landing, sir. I ring."

He disappeared. Kayerts stood still. He looked upwards; the fog rolled low over his head. He looked round like a man who has lost his way; and he saw a dark smudge, a cross-shaped stain, upon the shifting purity of the mist. As he began to stumble towards it, the station bell rang in a tumultuous peal its answer to the impatient clamor of the steamer.

The Managing Director of the Great Civilizing Company (since we know that civilization follows trade) landed first, and incontinently lost sight of the steamer. The fog down by the river was exceedingly dense; above, at the station, the bell rang unceasing and brazen.

The Director shouted loudly to the steamer:

"There is nobody down to meet us; there may be something wrong, though they are ringing. You had better come, too!"

And he began to toil up the steep bank. The captain and the engine-driver of the boat followed behind. As they scrambled up the fog thinned, and they could see their Director a good way ahead. Suddenly they saw him start forward, calling to them over his shoulder: —"Run! Run to the house! I've found one of them. Run, look for the other!"

He had found one of them! And even he, the man of varied and startling experience, was somewhat discomposed by the manner of this finding. He stood and fumbled in his pockets (for a knife) while he faced Kayerts, who was hanging by a leather strap from the cross. He had evidently climbed the grave, which was high and narrow, and after tying the end of the strap to the arm, had swung himself off. His toes were only a couple of inches above the ground; his arms hung stiffly down; he seemed to be standing rigidly at attention, but with one purple cheek playfully posed on the shoulder. And, irreverently, he was putting out a swollen tongue at his Managing Director.

Questions for Discussion

1. If both Pastor Dowe and Robert Aghion are "failed" missionaries, how is it that one can completely accept the host culture while the other completely rejects it? Is there a middle ground?

2. How well was Pastor Dowe prepared for what he finds at Tacaté; the Swede for what he finds in the American West; Kayerts and Carlier for what they find in Africa? How might they have been better prepared?

3. What is the specific cause of culture shock in each of the three stories in this section?

4. Pastor Dowe is the only one of the major characters in this section to survive his encounter with culture shock. What are likely to be the lingering effects of this experience on his personality? Will he be able to continue as a missionary?

5. What do Pastor Dowe's glasses and glasses' case represent in Bowles's story? Are there any other symbols in the story? What does Metzabok seem to stand for?

6. Do the cross-cultural settings of the three stories in this section affect the way in which the plot conflicts are resolved?

7. To what degree is culture shock responsible for the psychological breakdowns of the major characters in these three stories? Would the breakdowns have occurred otherwise?

8. What specific preconceptions of the major characters in these three stories contribute to their culture shock? Conversely, what preconceptions among their hosts exacerbate the situations?

9. All three of the stories in this section are written using third-person narration. How would the stories have been different if they had been told in the first person?

10. Judging from "The Blue Hotel" and "An Outpost of Progress," does the severity of culture shock depend on how different the host culture is from that of the sojourner? Is culture shock inevitable for all sojourners?

List of Additional Stories

Beerbohm, Max. "*The Feast* by J*s*ph C*nr*d." Joseph Conrad. *Heart of Darkness*. New York: W. W. Norton and Company, 1963. 159-61.

Bowles, Paul. "A Distant Episode." *Collected Stories 1939-1976*. Santa Barbara, CA: Black Sparrow, 1979. 39-50.

Conrad, Joseph. "The Heart of Darkness." *Stories and Tales of Joseph Conrad*. New York: Funk & Wagnalls, 1968. 272-361.

Gordimer, Nadine. "The African Magician." *Not for Publication*. New York: Viking, 1965. 129-46.

Jhabvala, Ruth Prawer. "The Aliens." *Like Birds, Like Fishes and Other Stories*. New York: W.W. Norton and Company, 1963. 84-106.

——————. "A Course of English Studies." *An Experience of India*. New York: W.W. Norton and Company, 1972. 106-36.

——————. "An Experience of India." *An Experience of India*. New York: W.W. Norton and Company, 1972. 188-220.

La Farge, Oliver. "The Creation of John Manderville." *The Door in the Wall*. Boston: Houghton Mifflin Co., 1964. 261-303.

Maugham, W. Somerset. "The Outstation." *The English Short Story in Transition 1880-1920*. Ed. Helmut E. Gerber. New York: Pegasus, 1967. 427-56.

Rakesh, Mohan. "Miss Pall." *Modern Hindi Short Stories*. Ed. and trans. Gordon C. Roadarmel. Berkeley, CA: University of California Press, 1972. 105-31.

Theroux, Paul. "White Lies." *World's End and Other Stories*. New York: Washington Square Press, 1980. 104-19.

Wells, H. G. "Pollock and the Porroh Man." *The English Short Story in Transition 1880-1920*. Ed. Helmut E. Gerber. New York: Pegasus, 1967. 380-94.

5. *Adaptation Phase*

Is it possible to adapt fully to another culture, to lose completely the feeling of being foreign? Perhaps not, at least not in an absolute sense. Yet, like a language spoken with faint traces of an accent, a non-native member of a culture may reduce his foreignness to such an extent that the faint traces of it that remain may pass unnoticed, or, if noticed, they may be regarded as cultural enhancements rather than as negative traits.

Adaptation may range from a comfortable sense of compatibility to an extreme feeling of over-identification. Most people who adapt experience the former, while very few undergo the extreme of the latter, when the host culture begins to seem like an extension or an elaboration of the individual's sense of self. Laurence of Arabia is a dramatic case of over-identification.

The characters in the stories of this section range from those who enjoy a comfortable compatibility with the host culture to those who go beyond compatibility to experience momentarily what Edward T. Hall has called "congruence" to those who have assimilated so well that they are able to epitomize aspects of the host culture in themselves.

The retired American couple in John Bovey's "The Overlap" represent the first in these kinds of adaptation. They have taken up residence in a small French village and have come to be accepted as full-fledged members of it. By the time they decide to return to their own country, they have become so thoroughly a part of the community that even the communist mayor expresses his sadness at their departure by saying that his friends will always remain, "*tout près de notre coeur.*"

In Oliver La Farge's "The Door in the Wall," the protagonist, a frustrated American anthropologist, is stymied in his efforts to gain acceptance into the rural Central American Indian society he is studying and decides to give up. But in the giving up, he frees himself suddenly from the limitations of his scientific, problem-solving thought processes. Through a series of what seems to him chance experiences, but which the Indians recognize as anything but chance, he has a flash of non-rational insight not only into the culture he has been studying, but into the nature of reality itself. This experience shatters the barrier which separated him both spiritually and intellectually from the people among whom he is living; he has found the "door in the wall" by which he can enter what for him will be a new realm of experience and understanding. What appeared primitive to the uninitiated Western mind turns out to be a view of life of great subtlety and sophistication.

It is possible that the protagonist in La Farge's story may even come to understand the Indian view better than the Indians themselves since he will now be in the position of both insider and outsider. This story suggests that it may only be the outsider, the foreigner, who has the necessary vantage point from which it is possible to fully appreciate the distinctive identity of a culture (cf. D.H. Lawrence's *Studies in Classic American Literature,* where Lawrence makes this same point). People who never find a way outside their own culture may, paradoxically, be barred from an appreciation of its essential nature.

In the next story of this section, "East and West" by Rudyard Kipling, we find a character, an Afghani, who epitomizes British culture to a degree impossible for the British themselves. Moreover, the Afghani in this story appears to have become thoroughly bi-cultural, i.e. able to slip out of one cultural self and into the other with no noticeable difficulty and without confusing the two. He would seem to be one of the earliest fictional representations of what Peter Adler has called "Multi-cultural Man" in his article "Beyond Cultural Identity" (*Topics in Culture Learning,* 1974: 23-40).

The last selection in this group, Jorge Luis Borges's "Story of the Warrior and the Captive," raises a number of important psychological questions about what it means to become totally assimilated into another culture. Borges suggests that leaving behind one's previous way of life to embrace another that is significantly different is tantamount to undergoing a religious conversion. And of course, as in religious or any other ideological conversion, there is a greater or lesser amount of emotion and psychological turmoil, depending upon the individual involved (compare "The Overlap" and "The Door in the Wall"). The motives and causes in individual cases may vary widely, but the underlying pattern of these experiences remains very much the same.

John Bovey

The Overlap

OUR HOUSE STANDS AT THE MIDPOINT of the long flight of steps that makes up the main street of Barjaux. From our terrace we look up to the Mairie, the church, with its hobnail steeple, and the fragments of fort which the villagers indulgently allow the Swiss occupants to call the chateau. Below us lie more houses, many of them crumbling shells with attics gaping at the sky, and then the path that winds down to the river. As in other mountain villages, the houses huddle together for defense against the blasts of the mistral, and the northern side of ours is tightly embraced by our neighbor's walls. The stones and mortar enclosing Mme. Cayrol are jointed imperceptibly into ours: no straight line divides us. Our southern frontier is more conventional: an open stretch of wire rather than a tangle of common masonry separates our garden from that of M. Gevaudan, our mayor.

Coming up the hill from the river in the late afternoon, Helen and I often pause (as our sixties rush past us, we pause more often on those interminable steps) until the western windows of our house catch fire above us in the sunset. The lower windows blaze up first, one after another, as if they were joined by fuses, like the chandeliers in a stage-set of Molière. The tiny dormer, which Cuquemelle, the albino carpenter,

---

John Bovey (b. 1913) served in the diplomatic corps for more than twenty-five years in Paris, Rotterdam, Casablanca, Oslo, The Hague, and Washington. His stories have been collected in *Desirable Aliens* (1980). He retired from the diplomatic service in 1972.

and Barnouin, the amorous mason, have installed in our attic, holds the light a few seconds longer than the others. As we resume our climb (Helen has kept thinner and more nimble than I), the watchdogs bay in relays, and the voices of late bathers float up to us, reverberating like bells from the surface of the river. The Mayor's dog Coca leaves her lair, which is half of a wine cask split down the middle, to sniff out the prospects for largesse from the wasteful Americans. Coca's chassis is dachshund, but other strains have given her long legs so that she seems to move on stilts. Sometimes Mayor Gevaudan himself, black curls flying, rushes past, clutching bundles of Communist leaflets in his arms. He singsongs, "*Bonsoir, 'sieur et 'dame,*" and runs to silence the scream of his telephone, which is Barjaux's chief link with the world of the valley. Now and then we hear murmuring from the Douarnez kitchen: Eulalie is pestling herbs for one of her potions. Her husband Amédée, red-eyed and tiny, buried in the folds of a cast-off jacket of mine, bumps his wheelbarrow, filled with weeds from our garden, down the steps, turning as he passes to whip off his cap. And as the twilight deepens, the peasants struggle up from the vineyards, and the shepherds from the moors with their goats, bells clanking, udders swinging.

Helen's hand brushes mine. Here in the hills, it is the hour of family reunion, of momentary idleness and unspoken affection. As we listen to voices from gardens and kitchens, we think of our daughter Eleanor, caught in the briers of New York. We hope for good news; about her health, her courses, her doctorate. Most of all we long for her to love and be loved, but we don't say much: only "Don't you wish she were here?"

In the beginning Helen had doubts about buying the house. She recognized that Barjaux, discovered by chance during a summer excursion, had become—especially for me—an incurable attachment. "But let's think it over." I knew what was passing before her inner eye: the long migration every June; the two of us climbing the eighty-seven steps, she darting ahead with groceries, while I came puffing after with bottles and books; the longer and longer intervals between walks on the moors; the fewer and fewer dips of gammer and gaffer in the river. A retired diplomat in Paris was one thing; a white-haired villager and wife holed up in the Cévennes, with an only daughter in New York, would be another. Eleanor would have to scrimp even more on the crumbs we could provide, while the conclusion of her thesis on Lamartine remained, like Zeno's tortoise, in that unbridgeable half-distance ahead. And Helen challenged me with the sequel: how could we imagine that our city mouse or her boyfriend Fred, who lived in the random universe of Jack Kerouac, would ever maintain a pied-à-terre inherited on the other side of the ocean?

"Anyway," she said, "boyfriends don't stay boyfriends forever. They're apt to fade away, unless"—her gray eyes brightened—"unless they can be turned into husbands."

"Let's face it," I said. "Fred is not a permanent factor. He's a wanderer: all those exits and alarms and excursions."

"Better Fred than the other lame ducks she's mothered. Or the political firebrands. And he hasn't done badly with his sculptures."

"Sculptures! Wire and string. They may go over big in the Broome Street lofts, but uptown—"

Helen bristled. "Who says they won't catch on uptown?"

"Don't get me wrong. I like Fred." (And it's true: I do—scruffy beard, granny glasses, adenoidish mouth and all.) "It's just that I don't see him as husband and father."

"How about just a father?"

"Good God!"

"Yes, good God. You see how old-fogey we are?"

"Either way we'd be on call, I guess."

"That's right. And if we have to help out two people instead of one, how do we swing the upkeep at Barjaux?"

But when the agent wrote us that she had another offer, Helen's misgivings shriveled in the blaze of my panic. We sent the down payment by return mail. And as we planned the restoration of the attic, wooing the elusive Cuquemelle and Barnouin with flattery and Pastis, I had secret visions of Eleanor installed under the new tiles. And alone. She could stow her nine-by-five cards in the workroom cupboard; she could rattle pots and pans with Helen (nothing can stale the variety of their cooking) and water the geraniums and gather the apricots. Her biting humor would surely spice up the bland diet of retirement. I could see her honey-colored hair swinging as she mounted the village steps in a loose-flowing summer dress. I could hear her high, clear voice pushing out French phrases for *Monsieur le Maire*, or for Mme. Cayrol and her grandson Raymond.

These *tableaux vivants* I did not share. Helen preferred to see Eleanor and Fred (or anyone) pinned to the mat of marriage; she dreamed of clusters of grandchildren to spoil.

Each of the three whitewashed rooms on our ground floor is supported by a separate cellar, hewn out of the hillside and vaulted in stone. Mme. Cayrol tells us that during the War of the Camisards, one of our predecessors kept Catholics hidden down there; for her, this man figures not as a *collabo* but as a hero. Marguerite Cayrol is one of the last Catholics in a village that was Protestant even under Richelieu.

"Today the chateau," she tells me, "is in the hands of heretics. And our mayor is a Communist."

"He's not what I'd call orthodox either."

"No, thank heaven he's not. *Un brave type*, M. Gevaudan: always out to help the village. But we keep you heretics buried at the other end of Barjaux, and we have the only cypresses in town." The sly, gap-toothed smile that our neighbor gives me is not that of a fanatic. "You must forgive our games. This is not Belfast, after all."

Except when grandsons come to visit, Mme. Cayrol is alone in the big house. M. Cayrol's name is inscribed on the plaque commemorating members of the Resistance who died at the stone bridge that crosses the River Cèze. Cayrol *fils* left the village before the war, when the silkworms disappeared and Parisians devoured the wine cooperatives. He runs a clothing store in Nîmes, but with little help from his boys.

Raymond, fresh-faced and husky as a soccer star, usually comes to his grandmother's from the university in Paris at midsummer. Except at mealtimes, Mme. Cayrol doesn't see much of him. He is on the river in his flatboat; by August his face and torso have turned caramel, and his ginger mustache, more luxuriant every year, is burned white. We often hear the whine of his motorbike as he rounds the hairpins of the road from the valley and erupts into the miniature square near the church, with a blue-jeaned girl on the pillion, clutching his flat midriff. Raymond has fascist leanings: he wears a *Jeune Nation* T-shirt. But in Barjaux, where politics is a sport, his affiliations are just a joke. So is his competition with the Mayor for the schoolmistress from Saint-Genest. Like Shakespeare's Dark Lady, Mlle. Claire is sallow, with wiry hair, but her big breasts make heads turn when she comes up the village steps.

Marguerite Cayrol reserves for Raymond the same masked tenderness that she gives to her flowers. She worries about his morals and disapproves of the schoolmistress. "Ah, Mademoiselle Claire," she says, weighting each syllable with irony, "What is a demoiselle doing on motorcycles? Or at meetings with men in that Mickey Bar? The Mayor's politics are his business. But the schoolmistress—what an example!"

Of the other grandson Mme. Cayrol rarely speaks. The Mayor tells us that Étienne suffers from *dépression nerveuse*: he has to spend more and more time at the asylum in Uzès. Sometimes his father brings him to the village: these are not happy days for his grandmother, who lives in dread of his wandering down to the river or waylaying girls on the paths across the moor. Now and then we hear raggedy-shouting from the kitchen on the other side of our wall. Or we glimpse Étienne through our neighbor's gate: he stands motionless under the umbrella of a fig tree, his black eyes flickering over the passers-by. The villagers take him fishing;

but the stigma of the loser is never erased from his long-chinned face.

This summer—our fifth in Barjaux—we wrestle, like Mme. Cayrol, with the complications of family reunion. One morning Helen overtakes her as she hobbles up to wait for the yellow truck of the postman. After the ritual exchange of "*ça va's*" my wife asks why Raymond has not arrived.

"Raymond, madame, is on maneuvers." Her jaw waggles. "In this republic of ours, everyone must do his service. Don't ask me for what."

"Perhaps he will come on leave?"

"Yes, in August. He may be allowed to stay on for the wine harvest. And for the hunting, of course, with M. Gevaudan. Grapes must wait for rabbits and partridges."

"And for the girls, I suppose."

"At Raymond's age it is hard to say which is of greater interest. And what about your family, madame?"

"Our daughter will come in August too. We've just had a letter."

Mme. Cayrol's face lights. "Ah, madame, what a pleasure for you both. As it will be for all of us, I am sure. Her first visit?" As if she didn't know! "But not her last, I hope."

"Let us hope."

Mme. Cayrol's bedroom is on the same level as ours: we hear her stirring on the other side of the wall. She moves slowly, slowly; often she groans or talks to herself. As she has no electric lights, she goes to bed early, and when the summer evening fades, we have to tiptoe in our bedroom.

All our windows open inward. Their little panes are framed in brown oak. The shutters have been stained to match, and no pair is like any other, so that to keep them from banging against the stones during the mistral, we have jury-rigged all manner of spikes and wedges on the walls. Viewed from outside, our windows make us feel proprietary; from inside, I tell Helen, they are magic easements: if they don't open on the foam of perilous seas, at least they admit us into a Van Eyck canvas: the blue-green of the Cèze as it winds through overarching gorges and forest at the bottom of the mountain.

Helen is less given to flights of fancy. She complains that our Renaissance perspective is bisected by the Mayor's television aerial, soaring shakily above his privy. Our British friends the Parkinsons, who live on the next mountain, advise us to take potshots at this landmark while M. Gevaudan is away at Party meetings. We snicker politely, but as outlanders we have no rights in the matter.

Like many communists of the Midi, M. Gevaudan is hospitable to all his subjects, including the two *Amérloques* (the local cell has not inoculated him), but he has little confidence in our durability. And he tunes in quickly to any condescension from city folk, whether or not they are Comrades. What would really make him happiest would be to turn the clock back half a century, to a point beyond his own memory. The villagers would return from the factories at Lyon and the atomic center at Pierrelatte; the summer folk—Swiss, Dutch, Parisian, American—would shutter their houses for good; the campers who litter the meadows with beer cans and scum the river with detergents would fold their tents forever. Prices of goat cheese and grapes would rise; M. Cayrol's sawmill would turn again. Coca would be taken out hunting every day, with a bit of poaching before the wine harvest. And he and his brother would have two children each.

Before Eleanor arrives, Helen and I make bets on her preferences. Helen predicts that she will go for M. Gevaudan, the romantic rebel, with his glossy beard and his long, harried stride that takes the village steps two at a time. I put my money on Raymond's ginger mustache and unthinking laughter. As it turns out, both of us are wrong.

Here in Barjaux the telephone never rings, except for the poor mayor; his kitchen has become a public telephone booth and a message center for troubled families and enraged summer folk, who expect him to needle delinquent masons and carpenters. When we call Paris from the mayor's, the circuits are filled with thready voices, undecipherable as phantoms, and we soon desist. No housecleaning zealots thump furniture over our heads. No cocktail parties and no television; once the dishes are done, we subside—or "bog," as Helen says—in our armchairs. Hers is Danish and supports the back scientifically; mine is fake Provençal, hideous but conducive to furtive dozing. Helen has learned not to twit me when the pages of the *Midi Libre* (which arrives in Barjaux a day late) tremble and droop in my hands.

Helen is reading Muriel Spark. She remains a metropolitan and secretly covets the Mayor's television. She misses her problem children too: the lame ducks of the Aid Society in Paris and the patients at the American Hospital. In Barjaux there are no study groups and no museums to befriend. The hours are less crowded than in the city, where chores take longer and bristle with confrontations and triumphs.

This summer I am reading Shakespeare, which I could never do in Paris or New York. Every night I take down the huge Rockwell Kent edition ("Doze with that one," Helen says, "and it will fall and kill you") from a niche in the stones, where scorpions (ours have a taste for ink and bindings) congregate in summer. I slog my way through *Henry VI* and whiz through *Henry IV* and *Othello* and *Troilus and Cressida*. The pentameters roll easily, with the river whispering down below, or the hooting of an owl to raise the hackles on my neck. The baying of watch-dogs and the shouts from the bowling ground fuse into the voices of Cyprus or Eastcheap, or the clashes of the Grecian camp. When I tear myself away from that swarming universe and go to stand on our terrace, the stars of Troilus's farewell burn above me. Or two cats, graymalkins out of *Macbeth*, stalk the garden: round and round, along the wall, across the terrace, through the shadows in M. Gevaudan's garden, and back to the wall. Suddenly they break off their patrol and leap into the gap where we keep our cement faun: with a whisk of their tails, they vanish like the weird sisters.

August, with its blunting heat, has come again; the pebbles of the river bottom are drying; the grapes are swelling in the vineyards. And Eleanor has arrived. She is alone, but she hasn't brought her nine-by-five cards. Her long hair has lost its sheen.

"You look tired, dear," Helen says. "And thin. You need rest."

Eleanor's face darkens, but it's her first night; she takes refuge in mockery. "Scribble, scribble: it's hard work, you know. Not like you two—Provençal song and sunburnt mirth. I'm an ink-stained drudge."

Eleanor stifles in the attic, which we have turned over to her with Chinese apologies. Even in a West End walk-up, one has a toilet of one's own and a rattly air conditioner, not a pitcher and slop jar. "I had no idea the house was designed for elves." And then she adds quickly, "But it's really very cute. Really."

Though she scorns to be explicit, we know that Eleanor is waiting to see whether her flight will shake things up with Fred. Like a Dharma bum, Fred has taken to the road, with two other sculptors and assorted girls from SoHo. He is heading for California, leaving Eleanor to stew over Lamartine in the N.Y.U. Library. But this time, Patient Griselda has pulled a fast one.

For Eleanor the high point of the day is not the afternoon descent to the swimming hole or the evening walks on the herb-perfumed moor. What she waits for is the shrill horn of the postman as he zig-zags up to Barjaux. Her hair swings bravely and her face lifts to the light as she climbs the steps to the daily conclave in the square. She greets the villagers more elegantly than we do, although alone with us she mimics their southern accents: "*Rieng pour toi dang le posta?*"

And alas, there is nothing. As she shuffles through the envelopes, separating personal mail from magazines and bills, her eyes cloud. We all go back down the steps in silence. Raymond, who has finally got his leave, stands by his motorbike, trying to look military; his "*Bonjour, mademoiselle"* gets only a curt nod. My toes curl for him: he isn't accustomed, as we are, to the Siberian exterior of Eleanor's warmth.

For all the rigors of military service, Raymond looks a bit white-faced. When the villagers discover that he deserts the bowling ground to visit Saint-Genest, they warn him against the girls of the town, drawing on images from local fauna and flora: "Watch out for the goats! Don't wear down the walnuts!" Raymond grins darkly at the exploits they attribute to him. But Mme. Cayrol has tempered his relish for Eleanor by telling him that he is confronting a *docteur-ès-lettres*. So our daughter is not invited to mount the motorbike. She affects to be greatly relieved.

"I'm not a cradle snatcher," she tells us. "I'm saving that for my desperate forties." She finds Raymond absurd, but I can see that he reminds her of Fred. "Always on the go-go-go. Keep whirling; land running. The merry-go-round makes me sick. How can you ever stop to sit and think?"

"You might try here," Helen says. "Plenty of time to sit." She looks sideways at me. "In Barjaux you can think standing up."

The other city slicker gives her a grimace of complicity. "It's not what you'd call a jumping town, is it? Except for the dogs maybe. And those damned scorpions."

"Scorpions don't jump," I remind her sharply. "They scuttle."

"Lucky for us! I got another one last night in the bookcase. With my slipper."

"Bravo! But be careful. Lay off the spiders: they're good luck. And the crickets, of course."

Helen snorts. "Spiders! Crickets! Why don't you team up with Eulalie Douarnez? You could get out some new potions." And then she adds, "I wonder what those scorpions are after anyway. Maybe they migrate for the same stupid reasons we do."

Eleanor gives her a smile that makes me shiver. "Not for love, that's for sure. They're smarter than we are."

A water shortage hits us: the river dwindles to a clay-colored trickle and the faucets hawk up air. M. Gevaudan takes heroic measures: through Party connections in Nîmes he arranges the visit of a cistern truck, and we all go on rations. "Emergency," he tells us, beaming across the fence. "And not a drop for the campers."

Eleanor says "Tut tut" and quotes Marxist scripture: "To each according to his need."

The Mayor smiles sourly, *"Ils m'emmerdent, les campeurs."*

His revolutionary charms don't turn Eleanor on: he is too strong for her and needs no protective net. But they like to sharpen their knives on each other. Eleanor leans against the fence; he looks up from his tomato plants, one eyebrow magisterially cocked, beard bristling like that of Raphael's Saint Peter, and launches into French politics. Giscard and Mitterand are pinned and dissected, and then Carter and even Brezhnev. The schoolmistress joins them, and sometimes Raymond wanders into the garden with his fishing rods. The presence of the Right eggs the others into conspiracy to shock him. Their talk grows hotter and wilder as the sun declines in the blushing sky: religion, nationalism, property, marriage—the exploded ruins of faith and empire fall in showers about their ears.

Finally M. Gevaudan adjourns the meeting to the Mickey Bar. "Rather fun," Eleanor tells us next day. "Everyone pickled and talking at once. Southerners are full of talk, and that's about it. Except for sex, of course."

The Mayor tells us solemnly that our daughter is very intelligent. He asks whether she is our sole heir.

I jump. Is this the cloven hoof of land hunger under the Marxist robe? But when I tell him that Eleanor's interests are urban, he dries up like the river. He is only thinking of the future of his subjects: what will become of our property?

With Mme. Cayrol, Eleanor gets off on the right foot by complimenting her on the *belles de nuit* that open into a riot of red and yellow in an old washtub near her gate.

"You speak our language well, mademoiselle."

"You are too indulgent, madame."

"Indulgent? Me?" She shoots me a look. "Ask your father. Or my grandson, to whom I give so many free lectures."

"Raymond listens very little to advice from women, I think."

I gape at this, but our neighbor holds her own. "Not even from a *docteur-es-lettres?*" She winks at me.

"Least of all, madame," Eleanor says cheerfully.

"But at his age, that's natural—as natural as bad advice from the old. And this month he is busy with the trout. Gamebirds and fish are always of interest, you know."

"Easier victims than we, madame."

"I wonder. Less of a nuisance anyway." Mme. Cayrol must be thinking of the schoolmistress.

"Well," says Eleanor, who must be thinking of Fred, "all sportsmen are a bit unfair, aren't they?"

Mme. Cayrol chortles, pressing gnarled fingers to her cheeks. "Ah, *pour cela,* mademoiselle. That's the least one can say."

After that the attachment between them is unbreakable.

The challenge of Eleanor's visit comes not from Raymond but from his brother. Released from the asylum, Étienne appears with his father in the last days of August. The villagers are putting in long hours in the vineyards, with watchful eyes on stray clouds, and the summer folk, incited by the waning arc of the sun, are polishing off social obligations.

"We must have a cocktail party," Helen says.

"Don't use that term around here."

But Helen has already drafted her decree. "We can ask the Mayor and his brother. The Parkinsons, of course. Maybe the Parisians who've opened the restaurant down by the bridge."

"What about our neighbors?"

Helen shakes her head. "Raymond and his father will be out on the moor with the shotguns, and Mme. Cayrol wouldn't leave the house in charge of Étienne. She never goes out anyway except on Bastille Day."

The Parkinsons arrive first from the other mountain, trailing a cloud of sons and daughters and grandchildren. The lilting British voices set off a paroxysm of yapping from Coca and her colleagues, and we watch anxiously as the picture hats come bobbing up the steps. The Mayor comes next, resplendent but uncomfortable in coat and tricolor tie.

The day is hot, and we bring Pastis and Scotch and what the younger Parkinsons call "small eats" out on the terrace in full view of passers-by. Suddenly we hear the creaking of Mme. Cayrol's gate. To our un-Christian consternation, Étienne ventures down the steps and into our garden; his black eyes burn with thirst for company. The Mayor and his brother look at each other, and then at Helen and me.

We call out to Étienne, and he climbs up to our terrace in a trance of diffidence. He is on parole from the asylum and can't drink, but Helen fetches him a coke. He holds it before his long-chinned face as if it were a chalice, and then goes to sit on the railing between Eleanor, whom he has recognized, and the Parkinson's youngest daughter Evelina, a sweet-faced girl with braids, who has just come back from a year of social work in Nigeria. Étienne begins to chatter as though he had downed several martinis. His French has specks of patois in it, like flour in gravy, and he rattles along to cover his stammer. The girls turn toward him, their behinds bulging over the stone ledge. They nod and sip and nod, interjecting syllables ("*Tiens!*" "*Dites donc!*") into the torrent of words, from which an occasional boulder of meaning—something about the *pétanque* matches or the wine harvest—rears up and then is submerged.

Presently we hear Mme. Cayrol piping shrilly, like Tristan's shepherd, from her garden. There is panic in her voice until Helen calls out, "We're all here, madame." She shuffles out in her bedroom slippers; when she sees Étienne, she presses a hand to her heart and gives a long sigh. She declines to join us but waits patiently outside her gate.

Etienne's pleasure has been cut off as if by the turn of a faucet. He shakes his head when we urge him to stay. Slowly he gets up from the railing, bows to the two girls and to Helen, and then his V-shaped mouth opens in an appalling giggle. When he has gone tit-tupping down our steps, I turn to the girls: "You both saved the day." Evelina's peaches-and-cream cheeks are suffused: "He was really rather sweet—like a Nigerian." Eleanor laughs: "You know, Dad, we understood nothing, not a single word." The Mayor, who has been experimenting politely with our Scotch, raises his glass to the girls.

After a minute, Evelina says shyly, "I say, was he perhaps a bit crackers?"

That night we hear footsteps in the attic, and then muffled weeping. Helen slips out from under the sheet and opens our bedroom door. When it gives out the usual high-pitched cry, the weeping stops. Helen stands poised, a billowy shape against the nightlight. But there is no sound, and she creeps back to bed, leaving the door open. "We absolutely must remember to oil that damned door," she says, as she has said every summer.

In the morning Eleanor, a little puffy around the eyes, announces briskly that she is off for Montpellier to look up friends from the Sorbonne, and then back to New York. "It's nice and peaceful here." She looks into the middle distance over my shoulder. "But you know how it is with me." She manages a smile. "Always on the prowl."

Helen and I babble in relays: we understand; next year more excitement; the Parkinson's secret swimming hole; concerts in the courtyard of the chateau; the centenary of Stevenson's travels.

Eleanor tries to refuse the check I press on her, but Helen makes her take it. Her eyes fill, she sniffles, and then goes next door to say goodbye to Mme. Cayrol and Raymond and Étienne. I escape down the village steps and back out the Renault.

Helen and I are driving back from the bus station in Saint-Genest when she breaks our silence to tell me that Eleanor is pregnant.

A few mornings later, when Helen has gone off to gather lavender, I hear the click of our gate, and Mme. Cayrol's gray head, with its bald spot, appears below the terrace wall.

I shout through the open window: "*Bonjour, madame!*" The visit has interrupted *The Winter's Tale*, but I am not really unhappy to leave Hermione and the woes of childbirth. "Come in, madame. Please."

The fingers that clutch at the railing are lumped with arthritis. In her other hand, Mme. Cayrol holds a tiny bottle. "*Voici,*" she says, panting. "They are *belles de nuit*. Try them in that shady patch under your wall." Inside the bottle are black seeds, pointed like cloves.

"You are too kind, madame. I'm sure you know how much we all admire yours."

On the terrace the wasps swarm around the sicky-sweet aperitifs to which Barjaux women are partial, so I persuade Mme. Cayrol to come into our "*living*." She admires the oak dining table, whose surface is pitted by two centuries in mountain kitchens, but I can see that her approval does not extend to the wispy-legged horses in the Dufy poster above the table. What really impresses her is our electric wiring: the stone walls being impenetrable, Hippolyte Barnouin simply fastened the gray cables with black staples to the vaults that top off the whitewashed walls.

"*Tiens!*" Mme. Cayrol peers upward. "It's like those striped arches in the basilica at Albi. Who did that for you?"

"Hippolyte Barnouin, madame."

"Very droll: I might have known. *Une fine mouche*, that Hippolyte."

"Yes, Hippolyte is very clever."

This sounds patronizing; Mme. Cayrol draws in a little. She tells me with dignity that clever artisans abound "in our villages." She powers herself cautiously into the functional chair, but refuses an offer of Pastis, finally consenting to try a 7-Up—"*pour vous faire plaisir, monsieur.*" She twitches her faded blue skirt around her knees; her brown eyes, flecked with cataract, gaze myopically at me. "*Eh bien, nos jeunes sont bien partis, n'est-ce pas?*" Her intonation has the meridional grace, strong on the final *e*'s. I am listening to a Roman matron, I feel: perhaps to the mother of absent Coriolanus.

"Yes, ours has left, madame. Your grandsons also?"

"Raymond went back to camp yesterday. And then he will return to Paris. After these visits he always seems so much farther away."

No need to tell her I understand: distances in scattered families mount with age in geometric progression. "You must miss him."

"Yes, monsieur, I miss him." She pauses for an instant. "I miss both my grandsons." She fidgets, looking for a new gambit. "We are close neighbors now, monsieur."

"Very. I hope we don't disturb you."

"On the contrary, monsieur. I am happier since you have come to Barjaux." She gives me a toothless smile and tells me that when Hippolyte installed our attic stairs, his drill went through the wall into her kitchen cupboard. "When I went to get supper, I found dust all over my dishes. And I could see light: it came from your windows."

"Hippolyte never told me a thing."

"He was embarrassed. But the next day he patched up the hole. In a way, I was sorry." She beams and twists her fingers together. "We are like that, you know: all tied up together. But that's as it should be, isn't it?"

"Of course."

She drains her 7-Up with a clicking noise and pulls herself to her feet. "I must water my flowers."

"We'll put in the *belles de nuit* this evening. Helen will appreciate your thinking of us."

"It is I who thank you, monsieur, and especially your dear daughter who has been so kind. But as she has left us—"

"Don't worry, madame. We'll tell her when we write."

"She gives great pleasure, your daughter, to everyone she talks with." Mme. Cayrol hobbles toward the door, turning shyly with her hand on the knob. "I only hope, monsieur, that God will send her greater happiness."

It is not the first time—nor the last, I am sure—that I am startled by Mme. Cayrol's perceptions.

The next day Helen and I stop at Mme. Cayrol's gate on our way up the hill with the garbage. She receives us in her garden, where she is taking the sun; she probably hesitates to ask the Americans, with their flush toilet and electric lights, into her house. So we stand there with our plastic bags—it makes an odd context for a call—and she hits us with the latest gossip.

"Mademoiselle Claire has announced her engagement."

"The schoolmistress?" Helen is astounded. "To M. Gevaudan, I suppose."

"Ah, no," says Mme. Cayrol with relish. "It's not the Mayor. It's our handsome mason."

"Hippolyte?"

"Ah, that Hippolyte! One can see he doesn't spend all his time on the rooftops. I told you he was a sly one."

"He has so many girls that we lost track. But so did the Mayor."

"I am told the bride is pregnant," Mme. Cayrol smiles wickedly; she must be relieved it isn't Raymond. "What a treat for her pupils! Let us hope that Eulalie Douarnez doesn't put a spell on her."

Helen laughs, but I wince. As the weeks pass with no word from New York, I find that an osmosis of village superstition has crept up on me. I keep running into Eulalie: she watches me from behind the grill of the ruin where she and Amédée nurse their poverty. When I greet her, she regales me with her exploits in a thick Languedoc accent: some gibberish about bringing back a faithless wife from Avignon.

"How did you manage that, madame?"

Her mouth puckers. "Relics, monsieur, from the bedroom. Hair, toenails, threads from the sheets. I pound them with basil and ewe's milk—but I mustn't tell you the amounts."

"Of course not," I say, as though I were a professional too.

"The faithful one spits in it and keeps it nearby. And the other one returns. Voila!"

I may smile at the notion of relics from Fred, but I find myself picking up pins and skipping even-numbered steps on the hill. I say nothing to Helen, but she is onto me. Like many people without superstitions, she has second sight for four-leaf clovers, which she hands over to me during our walks. "Maybe they will help with the thesis," she says.

Marxist schoolmarm as ever, Mlle. Claire persuades Hippolyte to do without the religious service. So we all gather at the Mairie, across from the ignored church, and M. Gevaudan, draped in his tricolor sash, drones his way sadly through the banalities of the Republic's wedding service. Then we drift down to his garden for a *vin d'honneur*. The Gevaudan brothers pour Pastis and take turns with the camera, while the women hand around curling sandwiches.

"No sacrament, no procession," Mme. Cayrol says. Usually she keeps her counsel, but today she is vehement. "Nothing, nothing. Just a convenience of administration."

"Everyone looks happy anyway," Helen says. She nods toward the pergola, where the bride, who has wound artificial orange blossoms into her stiff hair, beams up at the groom. Hippolyte's blue eyes shift uneasily as he watches old girlfriends, and drinking companions, but he straightens up when Cuquemelle, with his albino thatch trimmed to honor his colleague, proposes a toast.

Madame Cayrol sinks down on a shady bench. "Happiness, madame, is rather insipid at times—like that sparkling cider that goes flat before you can get it to your mouth. Grief is stronger stuff in the long run." She pulls her purple shawl around her. "Monsieur, it would be most kind of you to fetch me a glass of wine."

Later we learn from the Mayor that our neighbor has had a call from Nîmes that morning. Étienne has slashed his wrists. He botched it, and his father found him in time, but he has been sent back to the hospital in Uzès.

One evening in September, while Helen is chuckling over *The Prime of Miss Jean Brodie* and I am nodding behind the *Midi Libre*, we hear rapid footsteps on our terrace and then a rapping on the windowpane. It is the Mayor. He is panting a bit, and when I ask him in, he shakes his head and says hoarsely, "A call for you. New York, I think."

Helen jumps up, overturning a coffee cup. Mechanically she stoops to pick it up. We don't have to look at each other to tune in the same images. It's five weeks since Eleanor left us. We've kidded ourselves that silence is a better sign than the frequent letters that spell loneliness. But now we see the wheels of a bus, the stealthy climb of a rapist in the walk-up. Or we hear the hooting of an ambulance on Columbus Avenue.

We follow M. Gevaudan across his garden and into his kitchen, where the telephone receiver, abandoned on the oilcloth among the dishes, squawks in competition with the television. A hanging bulb, moved by the night breeze, casts our swaying shadows on the wall. The Mayor punches off the television and rousts Coca out of the armchair. Reluctantly she follows him on stilt legs to the porch, where he takes her like a child to be protected from the disasters of grown-ups. I pick up the phone with sweating fingers; Helen listens on the earpiece.

A thin voice cries, "Allo, allo!" then an electronic screech, and I hear Fred: "Where the hell are they anyway?"

"Fred!" I shout. "It's me. Where's Eleanor?"

"We've been trying to get you all afternoon."

"It's night here." (As though that made any difference.) "Is anything wrong? Is Eleanor all right?"

"She's fine. We have news for you." The syllables come burbling, as though from the depths of the sea. "Better for her to tell you herself, I guess."

Eleanor wastes no costly minutes: "We're getting married, Dad."

"Married!"

"That's right. In November."

"No kidding!" It's all I can find to say. "No kidding."

Eleanor's laugh is farther away than New York: a ghost cutting a caper. "Why would I kid you, Dad, on this solemn occasion?"

The blood returns to my cheeks. Helen grabs the phone, thrusting the earpiece into my hand. "Ellio, it's the best news ever." (*Ellio!* She hasn't called her that since she was in rompers.) "All our love to both of you." Helen levels off just on the edge of tears. "And is everything all right?"

"Just fine, Mom—worse luck! Wedding dress by Lane-Bryant, I guess." Their euphemisms bounce through the indifferent ionosphere. "But that's months away."

"We're dying to see you both."

"We don't plan to be married by M. Gevaudan." Eleanor's crust betrays just a crackle of anxiety. "We kind of wondered if you'd want to come all that way."

"Of course we're coming. What about Fred's parents?"

"We called you first." A pause. "Anyway, you remember there's only Fred's mother. In Chicago."

Helen raises an eyebrow at me. I push out of my mind the thought of our savings passbook. "Let me talk to Fred," Helen says.

"Hello, Mom." Fred brings it out queasily but without mockery. My heart warms: I see him in levis and a cutaway, his granny glasses misting over as he slices into the wedding cake.

We all blather on at the same time until Eleanor cuts in: "This is costing us bottles and bottles. Let's save it for drear November. Lots of love. To Mme. Cayrol too, and both the boys: Étienne especially."

Grandchildren: I shiver a little. Helen just says "Loads of love" and, as though handling an heirloom, puts the receiver on its cradle. A faint ding-ding, and we are back in the hush of Barjaux.

When he hears our news, the Mayor's eyes light as we have seen them do for other victories in Barjaux: a winning *pétanque* team, a house restored, better news of Étienne Cayrol, a sock in the Socialists' eye at elections. He takes down the Pastis, and the three of us sit silent, watching the milky clouds form in our glasses amid the ruins of his supper. Coca wags her tail and looks wistfully at the armchair.

When he clinks glasses with us, M. Gevaudan says, "I wish they could be here." His voice is filled with luminous sadness. Even assembled under the sign of love, each of us is alone, and no one more than the Mayor of our village.

As we climb back toward our lighted windows, I know that we have taken our first step on the road that leads away from Barjaux.

One night as I watch the autumn moon rising, orange and immense beyond the steeple, the log railing on our terrace crumbles under my arms and I barely escape pitching into the garden. When the first rains finally arrive, a tile comes loose from our roof, and the attic, empty now, begins to smell of mildew. Hippolyte and Cuquemelle are summoned to the rescue, but I feel uneasy: are these warnings to defectors?

The blue tents of the campers vanish, and one by one the summer folk close their shutters, but still we linger. M. Gevaudan tells us, with a wink, that if we last out October, he will proclaim us natives and reserve us a place on the village council.

The scorpions are in retreat too: one of them scurries for cover when I reach for the Shakespeare, then freezes on the whitewashed wall, venomous tail erect, as though immobility would make him invisible. I know that illusion: I am tempted to leave him as my hostage to borrowed time. But in the end I crack him sharply with my bedroom slipper. Helen gives a little cry. "It's not a cricket," I tell her.

Crickets and clovers—none of the auguries brings much luck to Marguerite Cayrol.

On a day of Indian summer, she goes to visit a friend across the river, who is known as the goat-lady because of her big herd of black-and-tans. The goat-lady's house is way off the main road, so that instead of taking the big bridge that bears her husband's name, Mme. Cayrol has to ford the river on stepping stones. Scorning offers of escort, she sets off, clutching a knobby cane and a bag of figs. We imagine her and the goat-lady sipping Bartissol and catching up on gossip: Hippolyte's marriage, followed by the succulent catalogue of his conquests; the wine harvest; M. Gevaudan's politics; the feud between the *garde-champêtre* and the nudist campers. We are sure that the Americans and their daughter are not exempted.

As we reconstruct the sequel, she starts back alone in the twilight, carrying a bag of goat cheeses. She has just reached the last stepping stone when her foot slips; she falls full length and smashes her hip. A goatherd, stumbling home from the Mickey Bar, finds her on the bank, staring up at the stars and hooting faintly, like an owl fallen from its nest. He goes back for the Mayor.

M. Gevaudan phones to Saint-Genest for an ambulance and mobilizes his brother and me and the carpenter, who rigs up a stretcher from an old door. With Cuquemelle's poll glinting in the moonlight like a beacon, we descend to the river. Gently the Gevaudan brothers roll Mme. Cayrol onto the door. She cries out once—"*Ah mon dieu, mon dieu!*"— and then subsides into faint moaning. Cuquemelle rescues the bag of cheeses. "She is not much of a load, *la Marguerite*," the Mayor says. But we go slowly, slowly up the village steps.

Near the church the blue light of the ambulance is whirling. An attendant, who looks about fifteen to me, slouches against the wall of the parvis, puffing on a cigar. The neighbors gather; Helen has come out with a shawl thrown over her bathrobe. She fishes the house keys from Mme. Cayrol's pocket and beckons to Claire Barnouin.

"Bring the crucifix," Mme Cayrol whispers. "It's at the head of the bed. And the bottle of *eau de mélisse*."

We all stand watching the light of the kerosene lamp flickering along from room to room behind the shutters. Later Helen tells me that the bedroom contains only a brass bed, a washstand, and a walnut armoire full of black dresses.

The attendant gives Mme. Cayrol a shot, and when the two women return, she is enjoying the first pleasure of morphine. She keeps repeating that her name is Marguerite. But no drug can dull the sudden pangs of dependence. "Don't go to so much trouble," she says to everyone and no one. "*Et appelez-moi Marguerite.*"

"No trouble, Madame Marguerite," M. Gevaudan tells her. After a quick whisper with the rest of us, he decides to stay in the village in case official help is needed. He deputizes Hippolyte as escort.

Mme. Cayrol stretches out a broomstick arm, groping for Helen's neck. "You've really done too much, and Monsieur too." She raises her head. "And don't forget to give my love to your daughter. Tell her its from your *drôle de voisine.*"

"Of course, Marguerite." Helen wipes her forehead, pecks her on the cheek. Then we slide her into the ambulance like a loaf into an oven. Hippolyte gives Mme. Claire a squeeze of the neck that translates, "Duty calls but keep the bed warm," and races down the steps to get his Deux-Chevaux. The ambulance trundles cautiously around the first hairpin and then picks up speed. Hippolyte's car comes darting after, side windows flapping. The firefly lights vanish in a rocky defile, only to reappear far below at the bridge. At the braying of the klaxon, we all draw together until this alien city noise has died away. The dogs prowl in circles around us. When a cloud floats black across the moon, the whisper of the river comes more clearly to us. The cloud moves on, and we break up and become just a lot of people going home.

At the end of the month, while we are crating up books and china, we hear the banging of shutters next door. It is Raymond, who has been sent to fetch some of his grandmother's effects. His mustachios have grown so long that he can curl them at the ends. He tells us that Mme. Cayrol is confined to a wheelchair in a rest home in Nîmes: she is not likely to climb the steps of Barjaux again. Her house, like ours, will be put up for sale. Raymond and his parents go to see her whenever they can, but not Étienne: no one knows whether he will ever leave the asylum.

We send our love and the last jar of the apricots from our tree. We conceal from Raymond that Amédée Douarnez, who can't tell flowers from pigweed, has ripped out all our *belles de nuit*. ("How could I help it," he says dismally, "if they won't come out until after dark?")

Raymond profits from his mission to join his hunting pals on the moor and in the *bal musette* at Saint-Genest. One night we hear giggles and faint cries through the stone wall, and the jingling of Mme. Cayrol's brass bedstead.

"Raymond has raided the valley."

"Men!" says Helen. "I've got a good mind to knock on the wall."

"'No sooner had, past reason hated.'"

"What?"

"Just talking to myself. The pleasures of old age."

The agent has found us a buyer: a spit-and-polish colonel from Metz, Protestant and a whiz at *pétanque*, with a taciturn wife in a bucket hat.

We couldn't have done better by the village. I swear M. Gevaudan to secrecy till we pass the word, but when people get ready to leave—whether it's a house or life itself—their wishes no longer matter. Once the deed is signed, our desertion is known all over the village. Now we grit our teeth for the farewells.

Fortunately the cold has speeded the diaspora of the other outlanders. The Mayor's brother and his wife and Cuquemelle drop in of their own accord. The Douarnezes do not appear; we shrink from intruding on their misery, and we don't want to hear Amédée apologize again for the flowers. Through the window I catch one glimpse of Eulalie shuffling down the steps, eyes fixed on the bowl in her hands, as though she were carrying the viaticum. I duck back before she sees me.

Raymond shouts *"Bon courage"* and roars off on his motorbike, with the rods of his faltboat slung over his shoulder, like arrows in a quiver. The shuttered windows of his grandmother's house remind me of closed eyes. The flowers dry into yellow and surrender their hold on the little parterre she had scooped out among the stones.

On our last Sunday, we go down to the Barnouins' house. Mme. Claire is peeling potatoes by the kitchen fire. When she gets up, we can see that her belly has begun to swell: the Marxist pedagogue looks a model of domesticity. Hippolyte is assembling cartridges in a scarlet harness that crisscrosses his chest. Regular meals are making him paunchy, and the faun's gleam has gone from his eye, snuffed out by the quieter comforts of the double bed.

We drink a glass of the new wine and talk of everything but departure: partridges, rabbits, the early frost, Mme. Cayrol. Hippolyte looks up from his gun, shaking his hair away from his eyes: "In America, will your house be of stone or of wood?"

"Neither," Helen tells him. "Concrete and steel. A building with hundreds of others in it."

"Tiens!" Hippolyte and Mme. Claire exchange pitying glances. And then it is time for the ritual sighs and good wishes for the journey and, on both sides, for the children.

As we climb the steps again, Mayor Gevaudan comes out on his porch, where the canopy of vines flutters crimson in the wind. Behind him we can see our windows blazing up in the sunset; this time the dormer holds the flame longer than usual, flashing toward the west minutes after the other panes have gone blank.

This is the hardest moment: at least it will be brief. M. Gevaudan takes my hand in both of his big ones (he is too shy to do this with Helen); his mouth opens, and nothing comes out. I wouldn't blame him if he said, "I knew you wouldn't stay the course."

But I have underestimated our mayor. His corkscrew beard trembles, and he brings out the words I know I shan't forget: "*Vous resterez tout près de notre coeur.*"

"Our heart." Helen looks at me; she has caught it too. And on that royal note, the foreign envoys take their departure.

Oliver La Farge

The Door in the Wall

DARTS OF AWAKENING BEGAN TO ENTER THE DREAM, the awareness that it was a dream, the sense of light beyond his eyelids, red, clashing with the clear light within his mind. It was a delightful dream and he did not want to let it go. Cayetano had somehow become a benevolent Pan, and the Dark Goddess was surely the most beautiful woman he had ever known and he loved her with a love entirely happy and pure, and besides, the answer to his months of fruitless seeking was in her hands, and already without words she was enabling him to understand the mystery of the axis.

Daylight, sound, and the natural completion of sleep were too much. Morning light coming directly through the high, unglazed east window was a bright bar passing above his cot, its shaft striking the whitewashed, adobe west wall to throw a softer reflection back into the big, bare room. Light spread into it also from the west window, and seeped in under the thatched eaves, which were carried on rafters that projected well beyond the walls.

Bert lay on his back, the dream still confusedly with him. He stared up at the inverted reservoir of darkness in the high pitch of the thatched roof, a sample of night permanently retained to join with each returning night and to give comfort to the family of bats that lived secretly up in the

Oliver La Farge (1901-1963), an anthropologist by profession, earned the Pulitzer Prize in 1929 for his first novel, *Laughing Boy*. Many of his short stories were first published in *The New Yorker* and *Esquire*.

roof tree; a thinly mysterious, temporary refuge from waking, from planning work, and an aid to the disentangling of dreams. Cayetano had been important in this one, and had at last revealed a benevolent, friendly self, which was obvious enough wish fulfillment, but the goddess, what did she stand for, whence did she come? It was she who had revealed to Bert the nature of the axis, which turned upon itself and became a circle, or rather a long oval, embracing all the Indian people of Rosario, and by means of which they became one and comprehensible. Waking further, he remembered the goddess in the Dresden Codex, the bare, young body and the bird of prey growing out her head, the cruel face. His goddess was all goodness. She was dressed, he realized, not as an Indian but in what he took to be the latest, North American high style. Did Freudians realize, he wondered, how clearly people often dream? This one was a simple compound of the ethnological quest that had so far proven vain, mixed with a somewhat sublimated sex, quite obvious after all this chaste time and with so many attractive, golden-brown women within reach.

He heard the axe chunk heavily into wood, the sound quite different from that of a machete striking, which could also be heard, but from a greater distance. Don Rafael's boy, next door. Listening to the heavy impacts and the long pauses between, he could visualize the long, perfectly straight helve, its distal end projecting more than a handsbreadth beyond the head, the whole raised to the full extent of straightened arms at each stroke and brought straight down, as though brute force alone must serve to split the wood.

He sat up on his cot, throwing off the light, bold-patterned, native blanket. Another day, another dollar. The Lip Woman would be here shortly and the horse must be fed. So forward, back and breast as either should be. Something accomplished, something done . . . The night had been heavy, stuffy. Everyone had told him that muggy weather came in March and April, to cool off again in May, but at two thousand meters and after the brisk, fresh months of the early dry season, he felt insulted. He leaned down, picked up his sneakers, shook them out carefully, and put them on. The earthen floor was bare and well swept, but bare earth in the tropics is never quite lifeless and you never set your unshod foot on it.

He stripped, poured cool water from the red clay jar into his basin and washed down, feeling better, brisker as he did so. Dressed, he went out to feed his horse. It was a good little animal that spent too much time in its shelter, eating cornstalks. As bored as I am, he thought. Ethnology is a slow process of gaining acceptance. And if you don't gain acceptance? You just go on and on being friendly with everyone, even the ones you'd like to haul off and kick in the butt, like Cayetano, the slippery cheat, you just go on and you hope. In May it will cool off and there will be a little rain, then in June the real rains come, *el invierno*, the winter. Depending on the extensibility of his money, and the deep need to be once more with his own kind, talk once more with an American girl, he would go out to teach Anthropology 4 at summer school. With nothing more to show than observations on material culture and technology containing nothing whatsoever new, and a command of the language called Raxti (or Rašti in proper, phonetic script) and more commonly referred to in Spanish as The Tongue?

He looked to the north and west, where the mountains rose, soft-edged ridge behind ridge, green going into blue, knowing the fragrance of the great evergreens up there in the cold country. They said there was quite a ruin at Yumbalán. It might be a good idea to go up there, get away from here for a while, a day or two on horseback, a week of good, clean, impersonal archeological scouting. You don't have to be a diplomat to clear bush and make a map, you just see a job and go to it.

He had built a fire in the three-stone, Indian fireplace (one of the great advantages of a dirt-floored, thatched building was that you could have a fire inside it) and put the coffee water on to boil by the time the Lip Woman tapped gently at his open door. Her name, actually, was Malín Palín, but that was not how he thought of her. She was between old and young, small-boned and slender, always neat—as most of the Indian women were—and afflicted by a pair of buck upper incisors that, through the years, had battered her lower lip into a state of acute tenderness and swelling. Bert knew better than to set up shop as a doctor in a tropical village; one would wind up doing nothing but tend the sick, but she was related to Cayetano in some complex way—always Cayetano, wherever he turned—and the very oddity and simplicity of her affliction prevented refusal.

The Lip Woman spoke no Spanish at all. She greeted him in The Tongue, "*Ah in-tat.*" Almost no other Indian save Cayetano would use that language with him. He answered, "*Ah in-nan.*"

She stepped inside the doorway and far enough to one side to be out of sight of anyone passing along the road, and stood in the penumbra like a docile child, her hands clasped against her sash with a package in them wrapped in green leaves. In the tribal style her hair was done in two braids, which were wrapped in multicolored, bright bands of local weave, then made into a crown around her head. The effect was gay and some-what royal, above the worn face and the striped blouse faded to dimness by sun and washing. The sash at her waist was new and fresh; below it hung the narrow, calf-length skirt, blue, green, and white with fine touches of yellow. As he squeezed ointment onto a bit of cotton wool, Bert thought that these women aged remarkably well. From the habit of carrying loads on their heads they stood beautifully erect and walked with an interesting, gliding walk. They seemed to spread hardly at all as they grew older, and their wrists and ankles stayed neat. He dabbed ointment on the woman's lip. More than two months of this treatment had worked visible improvement. Less of the Ubangi effect.

She said, "Thank you," and held out the green package. "There was no egg today. Here is a banana."

He took it and thanked her.

At the door she turned to say, "We have seen each other."

"We have seen each other, then."

That was the *despedida*, the goodbye. It was an automatic, set form, but each time he heard it he had to record that it was a lie. Not with any of them had there been mutual seeing, the meeting of two human beings, but only good manners and the formality of smiling, and, on his part the unending, gentle search for the aperture that they, gently and expertly, kept hidden. He was as near to a real personal relationship with the Lip Woman as he was with anyone in the community. He could have had another tube of that excellent ointment shipped to him within a fortnight and have given her one with which to treat herself, as he would do when it was time for him to leave, but he counted on that morning ritual. They never said more than they had said today, yet it was a moment of simple, human contact that meant more to him than he realized.

He set about getting breakfast. His other meals he ate at Doña Candelaria's, but breakfast he cooked for himself, preferring something approaching his home style. The Lip Woman had brought him a *plátano*, a cooking banana, which, sliced and fried, made an excellent tropical replacement for bacon. As he cooked and ate, a solid North American breakfast with two fried eggs and yet exotic to the extent of the fried banana and the shortbread lightly flavored with anise, his mind mechanically went over the day's routine. Out of order, he thought first that Cayetano was due for a session with him in midafternoon. If he did not fail to turn up, as sometimes happened. I am getting a Cayetano complex, he thought. It was the man's curious charm, his elusiveness, and the stubborn feeling that he, Bert, would have suffered an intolerable defeat if he left here without having discovered what his informant really was, sorcerer, soothsayer, healer, or priest of the old religion, or—the thought laden with anticlimax and ridiculousness—just another Indian, a little better educated, a little smarter, than most.

He had hired the man to teach him Raxti and guide him in observing the open, permissible things, such as the crafts of weaving and pottery-making, the manner of building a house, the farmer's cycle and the crops, and to arrange for his supply of firewood and feed for the horse. The ethnologist, working with a rustic innocent, had the advantage of all the decades of study of ancient and modern Maya culture, the survivals in Guatemala and in Chiapas that have been so well described, Bishop Landa's remarkable account of Yucatan in the sixteenth century and all the other early sources. So when you looked at a field you casually referred to the "holy corn," in talking of planting you mentioned prayer, in discussing the structure of houses you referred to the four directions, and as you worked on your vocabulary you asked how one said "year bearer," or "days without name," or "watcher of the soul." According to the rules, the naive Indian would be so astonished that a stranger from a far land should know enough to speak of such things that he would answer unguardedly. Thus the door was open and the scholar's foot was in it, and you went on from there. But Cayetano, sober, was merely blank, and Cayetano, tipsy, assumed an amused, flirtatious, wily expression that made you want to shove his teeth down his neck. And Bert was sure that it was this same Cayetano who had made it impossible for him to get into any real talk with any other Indians.

As a normal part of linguistic work, you collect texts. You ask for stories, tales, and if you don't get anything but thoroughly dull personal experiences, you suggest as though it were but a random fancy that your informant tell you about the beginning of the world, before the sun rose, how the mounds at Chuultún, Holy Stones, the ruin at the edge of the village, were built. All Bert got for his pains were simplified Bible stories, and as to Chuultún, the same "Who knows?" that had been Cayetano's refrain when the two of them went there. You could see where they had burned the incense, where the thick smoke of the fat pine had blackened the stones and where the resin had run down, spots of beeswax from a type of candle that had been millennially old when the Spanish first landed, and that nobody in the village admitted to ever having heard of. Cayetano knew nothing about any of it, not a thing. Oh no, not he.

The Ladinos, who were amazingly ignorant about the Indians whom they exploited and among whom they lived out their lives, all thought Cayetano had some esoteric position but no one was sure just what. Don Pedro, the *alcalde*, said he was a *zahorín*, Don Rafael that he was a *brujo*, Don Angel, the telegraph operator, that he was a *chimán*, and Doña Candelaria that he was a *curandero*. Try to pin them down, and about all you got was that the other Indians held him in respect, addressing him as *Cham—Cham Caitano*—and he was some sort of witch. Perhaps in fact there was no hidden hierarchy here and the man was nothing special. Perhaps. But the Catholic priest thought he was, which was why he objected to Bert's using him as an informant. And then, the very fact that he often turned up slightly drunk but under control and never got really drunk strongly argued some form of Mayan priesthood.

Some of this Bert reviewed in his thoughts, concluding, well, I'll have another session with him and it'll probably be the same old nothing. In the meantime, more of the same old stuff, they're due to thatch Juan Manuel's house today, the market, lunch at Doña Candelaria's, and so on, and on. Lunch would probably be cold minced mutton chopped up with mint again, since they'd had hot mutton last night. It was an agreeable dish, the first forty-five times. Late this afternoon, he might be able to get in a ride. Change of scene—he knew all the scenes. I chose ethnology because it was live, a game of human contacts. I should have been an archeologist straight out, and be busy now at some nice, acquiescent, productive ruin.

He took pencil and notebook. It was better to leave the camera behind. For some reason, they didn't mind his sketching, in fact, they were amused to see what he produced, but the camera, with its single, intense eye, made them extremely uneasy. It was common to hear the Indians speak of people looking, or even thinking too much about someone, and from their tone of voice he gathered that such looking and thinking had evil power. The camera, he thought, was a machine for intensified looking, while a drawing was a neat and clever trick. The same verb, *ts'ibli*, served for drawing and writing, which took one back to the ancient Mayas with their fine arts and their hieroglyphs. *Ts'ibli* was permissible, as it was not, for instance, with many Indians of his own Southwest, and when, as he sometimes did for pleasure, he worked up a sketch into a crude water color, those who saw it were entranced. To the equipment in the handy, *ixtle*-fiber pouch he slung from his shoulder, he added a sketchbook and a couple of HB pencils.

At his doorway he was stopped by two half-grown boys. In this warm weather they had shed the black wool tunics he had come to regard as a fixed part of the native costume, retaining the pajama-like, white cotton garments with the fine lines of red and blue decoration on the fronts of their shirts. That decoration, laboriously woven in by the women, was hidden during most of the year, to be revealed in this brief period when wool was uncomfortable.

They raised their hats and greeted him in Spanish, the Indian Spanish, lilting, monotonously musical in its rise and fall, high-pitched, with a limited vocabulary and the phrasing often directly translated from The Tongue.

"Good day, señor. Forgive the trouble, señor. Big your heart, señor, that you let us look into your gun that loads from behind." Strangers to him, they did not call him Don Alberto.

To people who had little acquaintance with anything but muzzle-loaders, the brilliance of his shotgun barrel when you broke the gun and held it to the light was a first-class marvel, the fame of which had spread wide. He was in no hurry, and anyhow, it is part of the ethnological game always to be obliging. He got out the gun, a single barrelled 16-gauge, broke it, demonstrated. They looked, were duly impressed, thanked him at courteous length, and departed. Of such things were his days composed. He looked up. The meek, musical, almost whining approach, the effect of almost servile friendliness, like the farewell, "We have seen each other," were deeply false and close to taunting. What would boys that age know? Not much, probably, but whatever they did know they would keep masked from him, from the Ladinos, from the priest.

He looked towards the church, whose hexagonal, buttressed apse rose blank and high a hundred feet west of his door, solid, with the old, conquering, Spanish solidarity that carried an echo of the strength of Rome, the domes, the arched bridges, the towns laid out in the rectangular plan of the *castra*, the last flicker of the tradition of the Caesars carried here, to Central America. Draw a line west from its altar for half a mile and it took you to the center of Chuultún. The Maya Caesars had their staying power, too, and they had chosen for their temple the spot with the better view, looking across the valley to the distant volcano, Tsacuinic, looming on the horizon, too regular a triangle to be quite credible in nature.

It was the projected line that had generated the idea of the axis in his dream, but he could see no source or logic in the mystery of the oval. Somewhere along the common line of the two hostile antiquities there was a division. On this side of it lay what was known to all, on the other, what belonged to the Indians only. This division existed within the people themselves. Why was the line so uncrossable in this particular village? The Indians came to mass with moderate regularity, made a great and traditional thing of the major feasts, dug out of their penury the gifts of food, fuel, and services that maintained the churchly establishment. They were distinctly more devout than the Ladino men, even though they liked to pray in front of the church and then, inside, to the dark figure of the "Old Virgin" in the corner rather than to the altar, upsetting the unfortunate German who had been dropped here to take care of their souls. In their devoutness was a paradox. An axis is nothing but the name for a spatial relationship. There was the altar in the church of Nuestra Señora del Rosario and an altar, or several altars, at Chuultún. Was there any connection between them, and if so, what? There, he thought, in a nutshell are my goal and my frustration. If I knew that, I'd have a center on which to build an ethnography. Nuts.

He turned west, wondering whether it was the young and earnest German priest, living in this village that had for centuries been a mission, visited only a few times a year, that had caused the Indians to clam up especially tightly. Or was his own technique just not good?

On this part of the central street, close to the plaza, the way was wide and straight, its reddish dirt unrutted, since wheeled vehicles could not travel the long, twisting, climbing trail, the *camino real*, that led to Rosario. On either side stood the houses of the Ladinos, twelve in all, including the vacant one he had rented, rectangular, precise, well whitewashed, brightened by brilliant reds and blue on doors and shutters. One other, like his own, had a thatched roof; the rest showed the red-brown of tile. They stood close to the roadside, several of them extending high, white walls to embrace a larger, outdoor area. They gave definition and an almost urban trimness to their stretch of street.

Doors in several houses opened onto tiny shops in which a dozen or less kinds of articles might be offered for sale, nails, priced by the dozen for little ones, so much apiece for the biggest, tallow and paraffin candles, *aguardiente* or the more highly prized, pale yellow liquor, San Lázaro (it would revive a corpse, the inevitable saying went), an empty Cinzano bottle, which was accepted all through these parts as a standard measure for liquids, with its cork carefully attached by a string, brown salt from Ixtepec, a bolt of cloth, links of highly spiced sausages. The title of a book came to his mind, as it had done heaven knew how often in the past three months, "Penny Capitalism." The Indian women in the market place were penny merchants, as were the Ladinas in their houses. Two networks of minuscule trade wove through the village and reached beyond to other plazas, other markets, coffee and grain from Rosario for woolen goods from San Miguel, salt from Ixtepec, and wheat flour from the cold country. He had enough material to do a nice chapter on trade and economy. There were clear distinctions between what Ladinos and Indians dealt in and how they offered their wares—except for Antón Luch, whose house, tile-roofed and long, was the last on the right in the little urban parade and who maintained the only real store in Rosario.

Antón was Indian, although obviously of mixed blood. Rumor gave him a Swiss father. To his emporium, Bert thought, I must now wend my way or run out of cigarettes. Giving Scylla a wide berth, I tack towards Charybdis. The thought, like the thought of penny capitalism, had been amusing the first time and had grown stale and inescapable. When one depends upon one's self for one's amusement, how dull one becomes, how repetitious. The mind insists on bringing up over and again the thought of which it has grown weary. He was protected from any danger from Charybdis by the unyielding chastity of Antón's daughters, or at least, by the fantastic price set upon them, and as for Scylla, it was no temptation.

Scylla was a small house on the same side of the street as his own, the domain of La Concha. La Concha, not Doña Concha, when the Ladino men spoke of her among themselves, was said to be a widow. Over the rough counter of her little shop she sold, among other things, liquor by the drink without benefit of license. In the back of the house, it was well known, she sold her favors when anyone turned up who would purchase them. Actually, no one had flatly told him that, but it was there by inference, in often repeated jokes, in a tone of voice, an occasional snicker. If she had ever had charms, they were long gone; from the standpoint of Bert's less than thirty years, she was old. She served the drinks in little shot glasses, badly in need of washing. One visit to her tavern was sufficient for him, and she herself, he thought, was well enough symbolized by the glasses. No, not a temptation. His Scylla and Charybdis did not amount to much; he could hardly claim that his strolls down Ladino Row were fraught with danger. He crossed to the other side of the street before he reached La Concha's house, mechanically, thus avoiding the chance of having to exchange greetings with her. It seemed silly, but her over-friendly manner gave him the creeps.

He turned into Antón's store. The older sister was on duty behind the long counter. She had waited past her time; you could see that a few years ago she had been a beauty, but now the hooked, Maya nose had begun to dominate her face and her cheeks had lost roundness and smoothness. Her mouth had bitterness in its curve and all her expression was underlain by resignation.

She said, "*Buenos días, don Alberto,*" excused herself, and ducked quickly out the back door of the shop.

Bert understood. Antón, whose optimism he considered pathological, must have given orders as soon as he settled in Rosario that the *norteamericano*, or the *gringo*, or whatever he called Bert (to many Indians he was a German, *un alemán*, the generic for tall, fair-skinned people, just as *turco* embraced the whole Levant, including Armenians), the distinguished foreigner, the scientist, was to be waited on by the younger daughter, she whose charms were at the perfection of their bloom.

The girl came out promptly, modest, eyes downcast. Her costume was the same as the Lip Woman's, except that it was made entirely of silk. Her blouse, sash, and skirt glowed, her hair wrappings were brilliant against her black hair. Her skin was golden, with a warming, red flush in her cheeks. Her upper eyelids had an exotic, Oriental curve that gave length and the effect of hidden knowledge to her liquid, brown eyes. Her

face was a charming oval, her nose fine-nostrilled, not yet noticeably
large, her lips attractively bowed. Her figure was slender and, Bert was
sure, elegant. Age, he estimated, allowing that tropical women mature
early, about sixteen.

She had only two packs of Bon Ton cigarettes left, she said, taking
them out of the one glass case, where they were displayed as a sign of the
quality of the emporium. Bert was the only person thereabouts who
would spend the equivalent of twenty-five cents U.S., half a day's pay for
a good workman, on a pack of smokes. This was a betrayal of secret
wealth, of vast riches concealed behind the simplicity of his overt way of
living that, he knew, caused some talk and the raising of prices when he
was a buyer. The mules from Sacabil had been delayed, she explained, by
a landslide on the road near Uyalá. Her Spanish was more correct, more
neatly expressed, than Cayetano's, as good, in fact, as any local Ladino's,
although it kept a trace of the Indian lilt. Antón's children had been to
school, even, shockingly, to the Protestant mission school at Sacabil, but
when the older girl came home and appeared on the street dressed like a
Ladina, nay more, with her hair done up on top of her head, city style, the
Ladina women had fallen upon her, torn loose her hair, ripped her dress,
and set her and her sister once and for all in their place.

The classic definition of a Ladino is a person whose mother tongue is
Spanish and who behaves as such. The last, faint echo of a memory of the
Caesars, the legions, the builders of arches, was long gone and the memory of Spain had become a dim tradition that called for touchy pride and
forbade men to do manual labor, but there was a distinction to be maintained at almost any price. Antón Luch had made it known that to the
Ladino who would lawfully marry one of his daughters he would give the
fabulous dowry of two thousand *pesos de oro*, a little more than a
thousand dollars U.S. Back of that inducement lay the advantages of
alliance with his varied trade, his mule trains, his acres of farming land,
the many interests of a man with more drive than any two others in the
region; yet no one as yet had come forward to ask for either daughter.
Only by such a marriage could the women shed the bright, becoming
tribal costume for the ill-shaped clothing of a Ladina, only thus could
Antón have the pleasure of knowing that his grandchildren would be
Ladinos. Under no circumstances would he consider a marriage with an
Indian. Often idle, lazy, not too honest, yet a real pride stood up in the
Ladinos and the older of Antón's daughters had passed her prime; her
hopes, whether they were the same as her father's or what they were, were
ended and now the second one was coming ripe and due in time to wither
on the vine. Every Ladino buck for leagues around, every passing, enter-
prising traveller, had had a try at getting one or other to his bed, but their

virtue was irrefragable and matrimony was the one thing never offered. There was an irrationality to this refusal, for it was obvious enough that most Ladinos were part Indian and plenty of crossing over had happened, not only when the *conquistadores* married Aztec and Quiché and Raxti princesses, yet now the lines were drawn and Antón's daughters could not cross them.

He said, no, he did not want anything else. She asked if he needed San Lázaro; he said not for now, he had a sufficiency. He would have been inclined to buy out the store, if thereby he could have got her to look him directly in the eye, have broken through to communication, to knowledge of the person, the thoughts, wishes, and all too probably despairs behind that lovely, guarded face.

Cayetano came in. He greeted the house in Spanish, then addressed Bert by name. Bert answered, the girl did not. Cayetano wore a shoddy blue suit, the decorated, native shirt showing under the open jacket, the standard, local, smallish palm-leaf hat, and sandals. He was slim, neat, grey-haired. A straggly beard on his chin, below his hooked nose, did give him a certain goatlike look, and even while the ethnologist spoke to him he remembered that in his dream this man had somehow been connected with Pan.

Cayetano said, "I was looking for you, señor. A little business has come up, so that I cannot come to your house at three today, so if it suits you, I shall come at five."

Like most Indians, he dealt exactly in hours of the day, although he seldom saw a clock of any kind.

It did not really suit, for five was the period Bert liked to have to himself, to enjoy a drink in preparation for the evening meal, but business is business. "Very well, at five, then."

The girl put the cigarette packs on the counter. He laid down the coins, avoiding any chance contact of hands. Her smooth, firm forearms ran into delicate hands the skin of which had not yet been ravaged by the endless grinding, the handling of lime, the biting, homemade soap, that were inseparable from women's work.

He said, "*Con permiso,*" as though she were not Indian, told Cayetano "*Hasta la vista,*" and left.

Antón's Spanish name, Antonio Pérez, was painted large across his store. Antón was rich, Antón was powerful, and apparently, being a man, he could dress as he pleased, even to shoes, but no Ladino would call him "*don,*" none, so far, would marry one of his daughters. Bert imagined the kind of man who might do so, one off the very bottom of the pack, and what the girl's life would be like thereafter, her husband never forgetting that in fact she was Indian, the grudging acceptance and more or less

veiled venom of the Ladina women, the many kinds of ready cruelty in a
society in which at best a woman was a drudge except, perhaps, for the
brief period of her beauty. More likely the younger girl would wither as
her sister was already well along in doing, in a land where spinsterhood
was almost unthinkable. His bowels were wrung with more than compas-
sion while for a moment he indulged wild fantasy.

Scylla and Charybdis after all, he thought, disgust on one side of the
street, pity on the other—pity, and desire. He should have bought a roll of
cornhusk cigarettes while he was in the store, to hand out to Indians, but
he was not going back there now. He could pick some up at the market.
Now he headed for where the house was being built.

From here on, along the *camino real*, Indian houses were distributed
haphazard. They did not front on the road, but stood more or less back
from it, each in its own yard, some with the definition of a fence or line of
cactus, some with no boundary mark. Fruit and alligator-pear trees
shaded the grounds, here and there were gardens or small plantings of
corn, and there were many flowering bushes. The road was narrow or
wide as chance willed, bending to one side or the other, an irregular
thoroughfare of earth laced with paths worked by the feet of men, horses,
mules, dogs, and pigs.

The building of a house was the work of a convivial group of men,
calling to each other, often laughing. The framework was complete and
the thatch was going onto the hip roof. They would have the thatching
done before the day was over, so tomorrow—the fourth day, the inevitable, Indian four—they would tie on the walls of horizontal rods and
plaster them with mud. Then there would be drinks, music, and feasting.
There would also be prayer. What prayer? Led by whom? Not by Padre
Greiz, that was sure. Cayetano told him only, "They pray, they pray to
God, is all," closing him out.

There was nothing here that had not been fully described long since.
All he needed to do was to be sure that there was no variation of interest,
nothing, for instance, as archeologically significant as a building with
rounded ends. Some of the men greeted him in Spanish, not in The
Tongue. He sketched the wrapping by which the juncture of a rafter, a
plate, and an up-right was bound into a secure joint with *liana*. A couple
of men, bundles of thatch on their shoulders, stopped to look, admiring
the correct reproduction, pleased, he thought, at this display of interest in
their work, then they went on. He had not been totally ignored, yet after a
few minutes he began to have once more an odd feeling of uncertainty
that in fact he was present.

He went on, to the market, which in this village was not held at the
plaza, but where the east-west *camino real* was intersected by the north-

south one. It was an informal market, the vendors scattered along the north-south road, sitting in the sun or in shade, as if they were on a picnic, an effect helped by the fact that no houses stood close to the crossroads. To the south, the municipality had put up two long sheds, which were probably essential during the rainy season. Now they were used only when someone had meat to sell, the carcasses being hung in the shade on hooks built in for that purpose. That got the meat away from the rest of the market, a godsend, for even fresh killed meat gives out a slight but oppressive odor in warm weather and the sight of the massed flies is depressing. More important, to Bert's mind, at the crossroads itself, in the northwest quadrant there was a large ceiba, its bole well over six feet in diameter, its wide-sheltering leaves richly greened and neatly pat-terned, and opposite it a wooden cross twice as tall as a man, set in a square, solid base of roughly squared large stones. As every Maya scholar knows, the ceiba was to the ancients a tree of many sacred values. On the top of the cross's base and on the ground in front of it were miniature stone fireplaces, well smoked, like the ones at Chuultún, and there were always fresh flowers at the foot of the cross itself. The Maya cross—Bert could almost recite a long bibliography about it, from sixteenth century Spanish missionaries on up to within the last decade, some contending that it was pre-Columbian and Christian only by coincidence, some con-tending the opposite. Perhaps the axis continued to this point. There was something that bound the Indian community together, and until you uncovered that, all you had were observations, pieces, individuals, and never the whole.

The older, permanent, local market women had their places under the ceiba. They formed a sort of club. Along the road were younger vendors of less status and people from other villages, only a few today as it was not Rosario's market day. The woman from whom he usually bought his eggs was there, so he went to her. Far from refrigeration, one bought one's foods in small quantities, to be consumed fresh; in this case, two eggs at a time. They had long ago established a set price, so the transaction was not interesting to either of them, but she brightened and they had a brief, agreeable interlude of haggling when he also purchased one of the packages of a dozen cornhusk cigarettes, tied together with another strip of cornhusk, that she displayed on her napkin. Like most Indian women, she spoke very poor Spanish, but they dealt in that lan-guage. He had given up trying to get them to use Raxti; it was part of the refusal, the rebuff. Here at the market, their domain, one felt, the women were pleasant enough. Passing them on the street, unlike the men, they simply did not speak, although they never failed to greet other Indians. The men had to deal with Ladinos and had developed a formula to suit;

the women wished only to avoid them and the avoidance extended firmly to visiting foreigners, however kindly intentioned.

He looked over the vendors along the road, to see if there was anything worth noting. His interest really quickened when he saw a little bundle of long, slender, black beeswax candles near one woman's knee. Very seldom had he seen anything to do with the old ritual exposed for sale. He had wondered if that might not be because of the priest's presence. As he turned towards the woman, she quietly drew a striped napkin over the candles and over herself the inevitable, infuriating, perfect armor of incomprehension. In Guatemala, ethnologists such as Chesnes and Van Cleve had bought materials for ceremonial offerings without difficulty, but not Bert Whittaker in Rosario. Still, he had added a tiny item to his knowledge. He had several times bought honey from that woman, so her household presumably kept bees. This helped confirm, what he thought most likely, that the candles were made locally. To find them on sale in the market meant that some demand existed for them, and since they were never used for light, or in the church, then he was correct in concluding that they were burned in Mayan rituals. Not much had been added to what he already knew, but it was an item, making, you might say, a day not totally lost.

He turned back towards his house, hearing behind him the sound of soft, casual talk and a woman's mild laugh. Isolated, he thought, how isolated can you get? You hear of the loneliness to be experienced in big cities, but it could not be more acute than here in Rosario, a face-to-face community with a total population for the whole *municipio*, the village itself and all outlying settlements, of not over four thousand.

Don Gregorio joined him, on his way to the *cabildo*. It was Don Gregorio's turn that year to be municipal treasurer, a carefully rotated office vital to the Ladino economy. Not as tall nor as fair as Bert, he was, nonetheless, taller and fairer than Latin Americans are popularly supposed to be. Strong genes of the half-Gothic conquerors, Bert had wondered, or a passing traveller of northern stock a few generations back? The former, as like as not. It was his opinion, from his impression of the present-day product, and allowing for the Indian admixture, that these highlands must have been occupied by men from the north of Spain, the fair-skinned, blue-eyed, addicted warriors of Castille, Leon, and Aragon.

They exchanged the inescapable courtesies. "Don Alberto, good morning, at your service." "Good morning, Don Gregorio, at your orders." These they followed with chitchat. In his relations with the Ladinos, who counted him as essentially of their group, Bert had reached their chronic condition. There was simply nothing new to be said. The main difference on that score between himself and these natives was that they had lived all their lives in a state of boredom, relieved from time to time by the most minor incidents, by courtship, adultery when practicable, and by occasional drinking bouts, and they took their condition for granted, accepting it passively, whereas he was painfully aware of the monotony of his routine.

Don Gregorio said, "There's the priest's boy at your door. You will be invited to lunch and then asked for money. Did you know that at the end of the last rains, a leak showed itself in the church roof?"

"No. If there is a leak, I shall be glad to make the little contribution I can."

"We shall appreciate it. With your permission."

"It is yours."

The Ladino left him, and he turned towards his house.

The boy was in his mid-teens, one of the few Indians who attended the little school, primarily for young Ladinos, where Don Tomás presided with more interest than Bert would have expected over the drone of study and the uncertain voices of recitation. He wore the usual palm-leaf hat, a clean blue shirt, tieless and buttoned at the neck, dark trousers, and sandals. He doffed his hat to Bert and they exchanged the Spanish greetings, then, as Don Gregorio had forecast, he gave him the priest's invitation to lunch. Bert accepted and asked the boy to tell Doña Candelaria that he would not be eating at her place.

He decided to honor the occasion by wearing a white shirt and tie, if only as a way of showing that, in the cause of correctness, he could confine his throat just as Padre Greiz did with his collar. The slight difference would be that by noon the priest's collar would not be quite clean. This thought, momentary in his mind, was an expression of a lack of sympathy between the two men. In general, North Americans and North Europeans feel a common unity as against the run of Central Americans. They share the knowledge of a world in which things are done so differently, so exactly, that it would be impossible to convey the way of doing or the concepts behind it to an ordinary Ladino. They expect to find in each other common grounds of education, and they hope for a language to use together other than Spanish. Given two such men, young, of about the same age, the expectation of companionship becomes even stronger.

Padre Greiz, escaped in his late teens from East Germany, spoke his native tongue, competent Spanish with a heavy accent, and knew Latin. Bert could read German as a professional necessity, slowly, dictionary in hand. He was not capable of even a simple conversation in it, and had decided it was wiser to profess no command of the language at all. Their medium of communication, then, was Spanish. The priest, unlike many of his fellow-countrymen, had no interests outside his own work, no curiosity about The Tongue, no sympathy with anthropology, which sought to study in detail and thus preserve what he wished, quite simply, to destroy. He was a plodding, earnest, unhappy young man, theologically trained and yet uneducated. Between the two men there existed the empty form of a relationship, that reminded Bert of when, during his military service, he had for a time been associated with a man who had been in his class for several years in grade school. There was a theoretical bond that in fact did not exist, on account of which they liked each other less than they would have had they come together in the special world of the Army as strangers.

Well, he thought, tying his tie, so the roof leaks and the rains will come in June. He guessed the expedition's funds could be tapped for ten dollars. Yes, a voucher for that much would pass. Ten dollars would buy a lot of work hereabouts. If need be, he could kick in a little of his own money. An instructor's pay is small, but while he was in the field, he had nothing but those extravagant cigarettes, the inexpensive local liquor, and his laundry to spend it on. He took bills from the locked, tin box he kept under some clothing in one of his pack boxes.

The priest's lodging was small. It consisted of little more than a moderate-sized living room, off which at one end there was a mere cell of a bedroom, off the other, a small room or large closet with a window in it not over a foot square, which everyone spoke of as the *oficina*. What business had once been transacted through that wicket Bert had no idea. Padre Greiz stored the grain there.

The establishment was tile roofed and stone floored. It had one good-sized, glass window on the south side, the glass imported by Greiz, its bringing a miracle of transportation on the backs of men chosen in public conclave for their sobriety and sure-footedness. The other windows had only shutters. There was no provision whatever for heat, which was typical. At this altitude, the rooms would be a penance of cold and damp throughout the rainy season. Somehow, in crossing the ocean and fighting their way up from the hot, coastal lowlands, the Spanish had lost the memory of their fine, medieval fireplaces. At all altitudes one built for unbroken hot weather. Then, at the rear one erected an Indian house, dirt-floored, stick-walled, thatch-roofed, where the cooking fire could burn. To this humble and necessary annex the ladies and gentlemen (or his reverence, the priest) retreated during waking hours in cold weather, to extend hands over the coals, or sit squatting on low stools, Indian fashion, and getting in the way of the cook. The alternative was to sit in one's *sala*, correctly (as when receiving a stranger or an enemy), in overcoat and muffler, and take nips of liquor at intervals.

Bert stopped at the front door to be invited in. He and Padre Greiz exchanged the Spanish greetings. As between a North American and a German, the set courtesies sounded more than perfunctory. Speaking Spanish is something of a game; one with a feeling for the language enjoys both its capacity for sharply pointed, direct meaning and the sonorousness that makes trifles sound epic. The formalities are inherent in the language; one cannot stop with the equivalent of "Hello" or "Grüss Gott," but must complete the little ritual. In addressing one native to the language this seems natural and proper, and one can, on occasion, enjoy the fine-pointed, Spanish trick of conveying hostility through the very perfection of one's politenesses. With the German, Bert found the exchange almost disagreeable. If they had liked each other better, perhaps they could have amused themselves parodying it, but their relationship was not warm enough, and the German had little humor. He urged his guest to sit and insisted on his taking the comfortable chair with the cowhide seat and back.

Here in his house, the priest wore the robe of his order, in which it was unlawful, in that republic, for him to appear in the street. Had he done so, the Ladinos would have turned him in. They did not admit to being anti-clerical, but they did not relish having a vicar in residence. Don Gregorio, with whom Bert had a more definite friendship than with any of the others, had frankly told him that it was more convenient to have the priest at a little distance. He said that the priest's presence distracted the women from their work and gave them too many ideas. The Ladinos expressed devotion, and left almost all of the worship to women, children, and Indians.

The monastic costume was fitting in that plain room and gave it a slightly romantic quality. The whitewashed walls had become uneven and out of true with the passage of time. Their rugged bareness was broken by a few articles of furniture, mostly heavy. There were the new table, by the glass window, a big, old one in the middle of the room, laid now for the meal with a plaid native cloth that gave a note of brightness, an old chest, one old and one new armoir, the old piece massive and deeply carved in a way that was a primitive reflection, another distant memory, of medieval Spain.

There was a crucifix on one wall, hand carved of wood, elaborated, highly varnished, suggestive of cuckoo clocks. A definitely bad chromo of the Scared Heart and a good print of a German landscape by a modern painter of whom Bert had never heard were the only outright decorations. What books the priest owned were kept in one of the armoirs; Bert thought he would have displayed them.

Against one wall a shelf hung by ropes from the crude, pole ceiling.

On it stood half a dozen bottles, in each of which something different, a fruit, a citrus peel, was steeping in liquor. That, too, seemed appropriate to the monastic life. Experimenting with liquor was about the only hobby the padre had. Bert noticed that he had finally thrown out the bottle that contained his most disastrous failure, an attempt to obtain the effect of Chartreuse by soaking pine needles in San Lázaro.

His host stood by the shelf. "An aperitive? 'A little wine for thy stomach's sake?'" The quotation was so inevitable it was painful. "Here—this is the best, with the lime. It has a freshness that is pleasant in this hot weather. So," (the word was así, but it had the true ring of the German so) "we make good appetite."

Bert disliked the effect of drinks at noon, he foresaw heavy, hot-weather sleepiness, but he could not refuse the wine glass filled and handed to him. Glass was Padre Greiz's luxury, he thought, tumblers, wine glasses, salt cellars, and the famous window.

The priest said, "Salud," raising his glass.

"Salud." Their eyes met, blue to blue, and Bert felt a twinge of shame at his lack of sympathy for this man whose life must be so dreary.

A fresh aroma of lime rose from the drink. And on top of the loneliness and monotony, did he scourge himself in the privacy of his cell, as one heard they did? Bert sipped.

The priest looked pleased. "I concocted it as an aperitive; just enough honey to counteract the bitterness of the lime peel. If I can get some vermouth brought in, it might be interesting to mix it, like one of your American cocktails."

Bert thought of a blend, room temperature, with sweet Cinzano, and said nothing.

The priest studied the liquid in his glass. It was clear, its natural, faintly yellow tinge shaded slightly towards green by the lime. The maid came in to set a water jar on the table. She was an elderly widow, dressed in the tribal costume. She, too, Bert had gathered, was connected in some way with Cayetano, who seemed to be a sort of spider web woven through the community. Was it mere chance that the two aliens, each charged with a potential danger to ancient ways, were visited and served by Cayetano's kin—or the man himself? It was a niece of Cayetano's who swept Bert's house twice a week, assorted relatives or connections who brought firewood and fodder. Cayetano was a web, or had a web, or all the Indian community was united by a web, strong, invisible. The web and the axis. He glanced at the woman. She was a trained servant and had an unusual command of Spanish for a woman.

Greiz turned his glass. "That Cayetano of yours—I have heard a new story about him. It seems that he really is a brujo. He had a quarrel with

Don Rafael one time, just after Rafael had received a shipment of six bottles of San Lázaro. Cayetano cast a spell on them, and the liquor turned blue. It is one of those stories that one must not believe, yet one can hardly dismiss. Rafael called in witnesses. They tasted the liquor. It was all right, only it was blue."

Bert had become alert. Van Cleve had reported almost the identical incident at Jacaltenango in Guatemala. The point had been that it was a perfectly harmless form of magic, performed, not by a *brujo*, a sorcerer, but by an Indian of priestly status whom the Ladino had mocked.

"Don Rafael told you this?"

"His wife told me first, then he confirmed it. I imagine a number of the others will confirm it. It is a sin to believe such things, but one must make allowance for them." He twirled his glass again. "These men here— they volunteer nothing. I've been here a year, and half of them have not yet been to confession. On Fiesta and Easter they kneel in the back of the church. They might as well be Protestants, like you. As for the women, they confess whenever they have a chance, for lack of occupation, and use piety to pass the time."

The maid had left the room.

"And the Indians?" Bert asked.

"They support the church, and at heart they are heretics. Christians? The situation here calls for an interdict, only the people would not even notice it."

The best thing seemed to be to keep quiet and take another sip of the lime drink.

The priest went on, letting out frustration. "It's the centavos the Indians find, the food they bring, their service, that make it possible for me to be here. I think that, contrary to the Ladinos, they like having a priest in the village. What have you gathered?"

"I think they do." He said it solely to cause pleasure.

"So they drop in to hear mass when they feel like it, on a Sunday or a weekday morning, and they pray at all hours. Have you noticed how they pray outside the church, the way they do?"

"Yes, they face four ways."

"And you know that's heathen. As an ethnologist, you must know."

The maid brought in the soup, self-effacing, not looking at either of them. Bert was conscious of her, and of the boy seated the other side of the doorway, in the kitchen. At that moment he felt honestly sorry for the priest.

"They're just as bad inside," he went on, between mouthfuls of soup and little, slurping noises. "They all but ignore the altar, turn around and firmly pray facing west, west, my God, and then over into the corner to adore the 'Old Virgin,' that crude, wooden statue you took such care photographing. As for the *patrona*, she'd might as well not exist."

Bert said, "You must remember that the old one was *la patrona*, and quite famous, until some one brought in the present one about fifty years ago." He refrained from any comment on relative artistic quality. "It is natural that the Indians should continue to revere the original."

Something important about the old image teased at the back of his mind, but he had no chance to call it up now.

The priest said, "Hmm. They retain everything old. You visit Chuultún frequently?"

"Not frequently. Any time I go there, a man or two just happens to come strolling along from one of the nearby fields, with a machete in the crook of his elbow. I'd like to map it, but I think better not."

"Yes. There is an account in Schulz of the disappearance of two Ladinos at the end of the last century, probably killed for prying there."

Bert was surprised. Schulz's *Żur Ethnographie des Nördlichen Mittelamerika*, though rather out of date, was still a standard work. He did not know the priest had read anything in that field. "Yes, I remember."

"The Ladinos flatly will not back me up if I try to do anything about those altars out there. They are cowards."

"Also, they remember the uprising at Santa Catalina."

"No doubt. I am not afraid to die, but there is no service to God in dying pointlessly, and all I could achieve would be that perhaps a few of these poor, deluded people would be taken and hanged."

Talk stopped while he devoted himself sturdily to eating. For a time, remarks were occasional and unimportant. When the meal ended, the priest offered another liqueur, which Bert refused. He said a second grace, then accepted with appreciation one of the ethnologist's expensive cigarettes.

"I want to ask you for a little help," he said.

Here comes the bite, Bert thought.

"I can do nothing about Chuultún, but at least I can control my own church. I must get rid of that Old Virgin. She is not really Christian. The carving is crude, the features are Indian, and the face and hands are dark brown. It was not an accident that they were left unpainted. I cannot imagine what the authorities were thinking of when they let her be installed."

The woman servant was standing just beyond the doorway, beside her the youth, still seated, back to them. Bert waited, saying nothing. For a moment or two, in fact, he could not have spoken, for suddenly he realized that the dark goddess of his dream had been a blend of that image and Antón's younger daughter. The girl and the image had the same shape of eyes.

"As an ethnologist," Greiz went on, "you know to what lengths the Indians went—and still go—to get objects of their ancient cult into the Christian temples. Well." His voice became businesslike. "You said that figure was an antiquity. Find me a buyer; you can do it easily, and then I can get a really handsome representation of Our Lady to replace her, or something else. There is a store in Olintlán that offers very fine work, mostly Italian. With your help, this much I can do."

Bert hesitated before answering. He felt really sorry for this priest, he was shocked by the proposal, and he foresaw disagreeableness.

"I regret greatly, Padre," he said, "I fear it cannot be done, and I have to confess that I am in part the cause of that. You have seen my letter of authorization and instruction from *Educación Pública*, and you may remember that I am required to report any antiquity of quality that should be listed in the National Treasure."

The priest did not speak, but his way of looking at Bert changed, hardened, and his lips pressed together.

"You see," Bert said, wanting to explain, wanting to make it clear that he had not acted of his own choice, "that statue is described by Tomás Gage, who passed through Rosario about 1630. It was carved in the late sixteenth century by a famous *santero* in Olintlán, some of whose works are still in the cathedral there. All of his work has that rather stiff, primitive quality. As far back as Gage's time it was an object of special veneration. So I reported it and sent in a photo, and I have an informal letter of acknowledgment. I understand that the *cabildo* has also been notified. You should have received a notice, too, since the church and the image are in your charge. I suppose they'd send it to the archbishop, and so on down, and that might take time."

There was a silence of some seconds, then the priest's expression brightened.

"But then, *amigo*, should the image not be removed to Olintlán and deposited in the National Museum?"

"The policy is to keep objects of the National Treasure *in situ* where possible, and seeing how well this one has been cared for, and knowing the local reverence for it, I'm afraid I recommended that it remain in your church."

"I see." The priest stared at the smoked-down remnant of his cigarette and pressed it out in a small earthenware dish. The silence hung.

Bert rose. "I give you thanks for a very excellent lunch."

"You are welcome."

The ethnologist hesitated, then said awkwardly, "Don Gregorio tells me that you need funds for repairing the church roof before the rains start. May I make a small contribution?"

"That your *idol* may be well covered?" The whole force of it was there, in the voice and the few words.

"Forgive me. By your leave."

"It is yours. *Buen Provecho.*"

"*Igualmente. Hasta la vista.*"

He was grateful to be out of the house. He walked towards his own with energetic strides, feeling that he had done an important thing, not only for the charming, archaic figure in the church but for the goddess of his dream, who was once more vivid in memory. She was taller than either the Luch girl or the Old Virgin, and her dress, of bright Oriental material, now he knew was taken from the very smart one that pretty girl—what was her name?—had worn at a dance in the Christmas vacation. The voice, now, it belonged to the actress the University Dramat had had as a guest of honor and with whom he had talked for perhaps two minutes. Of what extraordinary leaps and creations is the mind capable in the freedom of sleep!

He entered his house and sat down. He had carefully not told the priest that the famous *santero* he had mentioned was, also according to Gage, Gonzalo Martínez Choy, descended from Raxti nobility, that he had had trouble with the Inquisition, and that a little before Gage's time there had been talk of destroying all his work because of just what Greiz saw in this example.

The exhilaration died away. The meal had been too heavy for a sultry day, the drink had left him flat, he felt heavy and sticky. Cayetano was not coming until five. What to do now?

You'd might as well face it, what you've done has been to get through a morning, as you've gotten through so many mornings, so many days. Killing time. Now, how do you get through the afternoon? Why not write to the University and say straight out that this expedition is a failure, that the thing may be here but you can't get to it, and you are coming home? And there is no goddess and never has been, make up your mind to that.

Well, this was the siesta hour. He lay down. Before long, lying still became a torment. He sat up, thinking of the long patience and the curious accidents that had opened the way for other ethnologists among the highland Maya. But there was no sign of anything breaking for him, and how long is simple patience supposed to last? Hell, he decided, I'll saddle up and take a dip in the blue pool.

The pool was in the tall forest, about a league up the mountains, a slight widening in the narrow, swift Río Raxjá with a ledge of rock below it forming a natural, partial dam with a small area of quiet water above it. Springing out of limestone a few miles further up the mountain, the stream was strikingly cerulean, its water briskly cool. The people of Rosario did not bathe in it, preferring the broader, slower, tepid Conapjá on the edge of the village. The pool was Bert's own discovery, made through idly following a dim trail. So far as he knew, no one else ever came near there. At this place he had a happy sense of true solitude, of being unreachable, entirely unwatched. His tethered horse sought blades of grass along the bank while he subjected himself to the delightful shock of entering the water, rolled in the stream, clung to a rock and felt the rush of the main current against his body, climbed out, dried himself, and smoked at great leisure. Coming or going, uphill or down, it was a slow, scrambling ride between there and the village, harder on the horse than on himself. By the time he got back, he would have lost this freshness, but he knew how to enjoy the moment while he had it.

He let the horse pick its way back, his mind between thinking and not thinking, vaguely considering new devices that might take him through the wall of secrecy, then meditating fancifully and driftingly on the dark goddess, the Old Virgin, and the axis. They came out of the big trees, passed along steep slopes patched with fields, rounded a shoulder of mountain into the full heat of the afternoon sun. They reached level ground, approaching the cool green of the coffee plantation. The horse stirred itself into a jog trot, knowing that it was near its stable and feed with easy going between.

Rounding a corner of the *cabildo*, they entered the plaza, a rough, rectangular field, with another big ceiba— another possible point on the axis—at the west end opposite the church. There was a commotion on the plaza, many men and boys moving to and fro about a medium-sized, bay horse that maneuvered in a circle, its head high, its heels threatening. About three yards of rope trailed from its hackamore. No one was really trying to get hold of the rope.

Bert recognized Don Rafael's best horse, a fast and rather mean animal. There was no sign of its owner or his son. Then he found himself beside Doña Clara, Don Rafael's wife.

She said, "Don Alberto, can't you catch him? You rode him once; he must know you a little. These people are all afraid. There is not a man among them."

The sensible answer is no, but you can't make it. Why not? A Kiplingesque, silly feeling of a standard to maintain in a foreign land? Or just a private feeling about yourself that is inherent in your culture? Annoyed and feeling a bit silly, he dismounted and asked the first handy Indian to hold his horse.

He moved slowly towards the bay. It inched away and its ears went back on its head. Someone on the other side spread arms wide and the bay hesitated. Bert leaped, grabbed the rope, and tried to brace himself. The horse swirled away, scattering people, and Bert went flat on the ground, knowing with relief that in a few seconds it would be all right for him to let go, his demonstration of whatever he was demonstrating having been made. Then a pair of dark hands seized the rope just above his own and Cayetano said in Spanish, "Hang on, Don Alberto." Bert turned over, got his feet under him. Don Gregorio and Don Tomás suddenly emerged from the crowd and joined them. When the horse lunged again, they were able to hold. After that it was possible for Doña Clara to work her hand up the rope to the hackamore, speak to the horse, touch its nose, be recognized. The *mozo* whose daily chore it was to feed the bay joined her. After a little quieting, the horse could be led off, Doña Clara thanking Bert duly before they went.

There was talk, liveliness, vivacity among the people on the plaza. Something has happened, an incident, almost an event, and that was a boon from God. Don Gregorio congratulated Bert on his seizing of the rope, said frankly that he had always been afraid of the animal, went on to discuss its good qualities, for all Ladino men are horse lovers, then allotted a word of praise to Cayetano. Don Tomás also had his say, then the two of them took their departures with the usual ceremony.

Cayetano said, "It is almost five, señor. Shall we go to your house?"

As they walked together, Bert leading his mount, he said, "I was surprised when you came to help me. I didn't think you would put yourself into an affair of Don Rafael's."

"You are the sort of man who would have hung on until he had been dragged and hurt."

Now, what do you say to that? They put up the horse together. Then they went indoors and sat by the table. The bottle of San Lázaro stood on one of the pack boxes lined up against the back wall. (Bert's furnishings were even more Spartan than Padre Greiz's.) His watch showed ten to five, and he felt ripe for a drink.

After a moment of hesitation he said, "*Un trago, Cayetano?*"

"Why not?"

Bert put the bottle on the table and poured Cayetano a shot in an earthenware *copita*, knowing that Indians are not accustomed to mixed or watered drinks. His own he diluted, with cool water from the porous, clay jar, in an enamel cup. The Indian drank, giving thanks in The Tongue and raising his hat a couple of inches above his head as he took the liquor down. Bert had himself a hearty, comforting swig.

Encouraged by that, feeling somehow nearer to Cayetano than he ever had before, he decided to try a new feeler. Putting the words together slowly in Raxti, he said, "They say that you know how to turn liquor blue. Perhaps there is something you know."

He was pretty sure that "something you know" in this language, as in some related ones, was a euphemism or disguise for having magical or ceremonial knowledge.

Cayetano's eyes half closed, almost sleepily, and he half smiled. There, suddenly, was the benevolent, wise goat, the Pan figure, of the dream. "Perhaps I know a little something. They say that you bathe in Blue River. Have you not heard that that is dangerous, *Cham* Berto?"

Bert started, hearing the Indian title of respect, much stronger than *don*, with a quite new, and, he supposed, Indian version of his name.

Cayetano went on. "That river, it is a seizer. It seizes the souls of people unless they say a prayer when they cross it. No one bathes in it."

It is hopeless, Bert thought, to expect to make a move of any kind without its being known. He took another sip from his cup. "Perhaps there is a little something I know."

Cayetano said, "So says my heart."

Without by your leave, he refilled his jigger and drained it, lifting his hat as before and saying "Through God." Then he produced a cornhusk cigarette and asked for a match. He lit the cigarette, mumbled some words over it, then took a long puff.

Still speaking in The Tongue, he said, "The priest wanted to sell the Lady Mother Virgin, but you stopped him, so I am told. I think you should know about that Lady Virgin, then you can begin to understand our people." For Virgin he used the Spanish word, *virgen*, but the titles he gave her were Indian. "It is all right for you to know this, for I know that there is something you know and that your heart is clear."

He took yet another drink. Bert was experiencing something like goose pimples of excitement. Some degree of drunkenness, he knew, was quite commonly a requirement before a Mayan priest or whatever you would call him could do his stuff.

"I shall tell you this story now. You just listen to it. It is hard to tell you things when I have to keep stopping to let you write, and it troubles my heart to talk to that machine with the ribbon spinning in it. I shall tell you this without stopping, and tomorrow morning I can come here and break it into pieces for your writing, or tell it into that machine—but I am not sure about that, for this is delicate." As he talked, he inserted words or phrases in Spanish occasionally, to clarify his meaning to the white man.

"In the ancient time, before the sun rose, the Lady Our Mother was here then."

Before the sun rose—that was old Mayan, you got it in the Popol

Vuh and Annals of the Cakchiquels, and Landa had recorded it for Yuacatán.

"Her heart fought" (that meant that she was frightened) "for her children, that the people with four eyes were coming to steal them. At night they came into the houses like bats and stole them. A safe place to put her village was what she was looking for as she went about, her heart hurting.

"Then the Lord Tsakwinik came to her." Cayetano gestured towards the west, where Tsacuinic's blue triangle cut the sky.

It was getting better and better, and it did not stop. The myth established the lord or spirit of the volcano as protector of a mother goddess. The goddess founded her village at this place and had what was to become the ruin of Chuultún built. In the name of the goddess, gentle and loving, very much the one of his dream, Bert thought, the people paid their tribute of offerings to the protecting god. Back of all this, cloudy, not apparently much of a factor in this particular myth, was Christ, walking about forming the earth and causing the sun to rise. After the sun rose the people could not recognize the four directions. The sunlight, also, drove back the people with four eyes, two in the front of their heads and two in the back. They had had the advantage in the long twilight; in the brightness of the sun, they were blinded. The Lady Our Mother Virgin (Bert, listening, was still thinking of her as his goddess) then told her children where the church was to be built. When it was built, she established herself on the altar, after she had planted the two ceiba trees. She left it said how the ritual should move, from the point of sunrise to the point of sunset, and the offerings to the Lord Tsakwinik.

With that, it was clear, the myth proper ended. Cayetano had another drink and Bert fixed one for himself. Cayetano lit a cigarette and talked on, narrating historical facts. Ladino priests had come and set up other images in the church, but not until when Cayetano was an infant did one come who made himself so strong that he could put the Lady Our Mother to one side and set up a Ladina Virgin at the altar. With soldiers in the village he did this. Putting the Mother aside made no difference. The prayer still ran from the east to her, then to Chuultún, from where one also prayed eastwards to her and westwards to the volcano. On the completion of Thirteen Men—that is, the two hundred and sixty days after the entry of the Year Bearer, when the same lord with the same number occurred again—certain reverend men, *Cham Winikop*, arrived at the crater of Tsacuinic to burn incense and offer turkeys.

After a pause, Cayetano said, "There it is, Cham Berto. What says your heart?"

"My heart says that it is a good story, a strong story." The room was getting dark. Making time to think, he set out and lit a pair of candles. "So here you know the Year Bearer and the count of the days and numbers?"

Truly, Cayetano looked like an amused old goat. "It is getting late, and I must see to the corn my sons are bringing in. I shall be here in the morning. If you are to learn these things correctly, we must not hurry." He stood up. "Thank you for the drinks." He touched the bottle lightly. He passed around the table, and into the blue, deep dusk of the doorway. "We have seen each other."

"We have seen each other, then."

Indeed they had seen each other; for once the words were true. He felt as if he were breathing once more after long stifling. There was the thought of success, the hope that isolation might be ended, the excitement of the information itself. Almost enough to make you start believing in dreams, but when you thought about it, you could see how all you had done was to synthesize innumerable small observations and mix them with the double symbolism, of sexual desire and of his quest, of his composite goddess.

He looked at his watch. Time to start for Doña Candelaria's shortly, but this occasion called for a little extra celebration. He poured a moderate drink into his cup, then he set down bottle and cup and stared. The liquor had turned blue. His scalp crawled, then he laughed aloud. It was, in this case, a gesture of friendship, an assurance. He tasted the stuff. No change. A really nifty trick, he thought, I hope I can get him to show me how he does it. He finished the drink, neat, lit a cigarette, then rose, slightly tipsy and very happy, to go to dinner.

Rudyard Kipling

East and West

ONCE UPON A TIME, WHEN THE HIMALAYAS were but callow crestlings, the Aravalis formed a chain of islands running north and south across the ocean that then buried India. "And where the city roars hath been/The stillness of the central sea." Up to this point my record of an unsentimental journey from Ajmir to elsewhere had progressed beautifully; but my friend Sinbad the traveller entered, and with him a mountain of luggage. He was not exactly a blood relation, or even connected by race; being a Peshwari Yusufzai, and a *Kazi* to boot. Still he came from the Punjab, and was therefore welcome. "It is hot" said Sinbad removing the dust-coat that fettered his massive torso:—"Bring me soda-water, O peon!" The peon was a Panjabi Mahommedan, and had forgotten the soda-water. "Pig!" quoth my friend Sinbad, and slapped him on the head twice. "Very good" said the peon, and walked away. My friend Sinbad and I fell atalking.

But here let me describe him—this Afghan who dressed like an Englishman, and travelled after the English fashion, and used soap and shoe-horns and corkscrews and nail-scissors, an English of the finest water. They lie who say that the Afghans are not the Tribes that went astray. My friend Sinbad had the head of a Rabbi, such as men put in paintings—brown, olive color, marked like the face of a cliff set in black

---

Sometimes associated with British colonialism in India, the poet, short-story writer, and novelist *Rudyard Kipling* (1865-1936) is, in actuality, often quite sympathetic to non-British points of view.

hair firm as wire. It was a grand head on its bull neck, and our tongue suited it not; God having made it for Pushto; or a more gutteral speech if such a one exist.

"He is a pig" said my friend Sinbad. "All native servants are pigs. Is this not so?" The head was the head of Essau indeed, but the sentiments seemed foreign to it. "They are all pigs" said I; and my friend Sinbad settled himself cross-legged on the seat and was silent—sunk in impenetrable reserve. There is but one Interpretress who speaks all the tongues of the East, and appeals to all hearts; and her name is Tobacco. My friend smoked. Further, he smoked from my cigar-case. The East and the West confronted each other on opposite sides of a first class carriage. The East yawned.

(Under the shadow of the Edwardes' Gate in Peshawar, lives an old shop-keeper. It was he who told me many many lies, but one truth. "All *Kazees* will talk if you let them alone. Most Afghans not." I let my friend Sinbad alone, and smiled. My friend Sinbad talked.)

We had acquaintances in common. It was the first stepping stone. We knew many officials. This was the second. We had met each other before. Careful cross-verification of dates showed this to be true. This was the third.

Sinbad fenced in his speech. Was preposterously virtuous; unnaturally advanced; inordinately civilized. I was no servant of the Government. Held no post of authority or responsibility; and loose views on many things. Sinbad fenced no longer. We descended from generalities into particulars and affairs political.

"Who will be our next Lieutenant-Governor?" asked Sinbad. "God knows!" said I. "We shall see." "It may be Mr. Cordery or Sir Lepel Griffin" quoth he. "They are high in favor with the Viceroy. And what do you think?" said I. "They are strong men" said Sinbad; and he rubbed his knees softly. "Either will be good." "And our present Lieutenant-Governor" said I "What do you think of him?" My friend blew the smoke through his nostrils and replied. "He is a hard man to natives. He will not listen to them when they come to talk. You know this also, do you not?" "I have never gone to talk to him. It may be as you say, I have heard so." My friend looked distressed. It was possible that I had lied. I hastened to reassure him. He smoked more easily. "And what do you think of Sir Alfred Lyall?" asked I. "Have you had dealings with him?" My friend Sinbad slapped his thigh:—"Yes! Ah! He is a jewel of a man. He will hear you always." "Tell me something I want to know" said I. "With you people, is it not true that you prefer a man who will listen, when you come to *mulaqat Karo* him, even though he gives you no redress, to a man who will not hear you, even though he *does* do something for you?" "Say it again" said my friend. I repeated the clumsy sentence, and Sinbad thought. A *chinkara* grazing among the tussocks without in the sunshine bounded away from the train, and had nearly reached the horizon before he answered. "By Jove!" said he, "I believe you are right. We are a queer people!" It is strange to hear an Afghan say "By Jove!" and "queer," but my friend Sinbad was very English. He had annexed Britannia—shield, trident and lion—as he had another side to him—the reverse of the coin stamped with the Queen's Head. So English was he, that I could discuss many things without—visibly at least—wounding his feelings. "But you also are a queer people" said he. "Why do you try to make us like you." It was the reverse of the Queen's Head—the protest against the soap and the nail scissors; the trowsers that chafed, and the coatsleeves that cut. "We are all mad, we English, from our birth up," said I. "It is our custom." My friend Sinbad laughed and the windows rattled:—"That is a joke; but there is much truth in it. But I tell you that you are doing a little good. Not much, you understand, but still a little." "As how?" said I. "I will explain. When I was a child, I began to study the English language. That was in Peshawar thirty years ago. All my friends and relations said that I should become an infidel, a *kafir*, and were very angry. Nowadays one hears nothing of that sort of prejudice. One can be a good Mahommedan and speak English tolerably well at one and the same time. You have done this much good anyhow." "And in other ways is the English Government of any use?" I was prepared for what would follow. My friend Sinbad spoke at great length on the peace and the law and the order of the land, and stopped short. "And then?" "Well, I will tell you the truth. In many ways you are a good Government, but in many ways you are great—you are, yes, you are awful fools." (He took a fresh cheroot and began again). "You have two fools of parties in your country. Is it not so. Every five years one party does one thing, and the next five years the other party comes and undoes it. How can you make *pukka bundabusts* with the Ameer, with Russia or with anybody else? Who is to believe you? It is not the country's fault, of course! It is the fault of a party—your great fools of parties. I tell you that you are just as bad as the Hindus and Mahommedans at Mohurrum time; only with you it is always Mohurrum. You are one country; why do you not be sensible and have one party?" I was not prepared to explain the whole British Constitution with all its sacred rules and ordinances off hand. I took refuge in blue clouds of smoke and bowed my head. My friend Sinbad then returned to the charge. "When you have only one party" (Shades of Chamberlain and Churchill and the holy two millions of electors!) "and that party lasts for ever, there will be no Government on earth like yours. As it is, you are in many ways great fools." Perhaps my friend Sinbad's deep bass voice added force to the statement which was old enough in all conscience, but novel from the odd twist he gave it.

His eye caught by the flutter of a lady's dress on the platform. "Who is that?" asked Sinbad. "An Englishwoman travelling alone from one end of India to the other." "Yes! Yes! I know that but—Ah! I see what you mean. You mean that we cannot do that. No; it is true enough. By Jove! I tell you that a native lady would cry like a baby all the way from Calcutta to Peshawar. She would not know what 'ticket' meant. You could not leave her alone without help for a minute. She would die of fright!" "And do you consider that an advantage?" said I. "Most certainly not. You are entirely in the right there. Quite so. That is where we make our mistake. One of these days it will be set right, but not now or a hundred years hence." (My friend Sinbad slapped his thigh more vigorously than ever.) "And how will it be set right?" "One of these days both Hindus and Mahommedans will see that it is safer to let out their women than to keep them in *purdah*. Outside there are hundreds of thousands of eyes, and a woman cannot go wrong if she would. Inside the *purdah* (My friend Sinbad checked himself and played with his watch chain) things are sometimes different." "It is a great pity" he continued reflectively "that we never educate our wives." (I thought he was playing for the gallery; and sucked the end of my cheroot in silence. But he was not): "I tell you that a married woman who is intelligent is a great help. She can talk to a man about his work and his ambitions after he is out of office, and that is a great help. I have met men—of this country you know—who have married English wives, and they have told me so. Our women are great fools. They are pretty, of course; but that is all. It would be pleasant to find one that can talk." My friend Sinbad looked pensive; his mind wandering along some well worn *pugdandi* of thought.

Presently his eye brightened, and he shook himself:— "By Jove! I was a great devil in my youth. A great devil, by Jove!" He threw back his head and laughed aloud—not with the laughter of civilization, but the laughter that betrayed his origin—mirth, savage and boisterous that had nothing in common with gold watch-guard, English clothes, patent trunks or first-class tickets. I confess I liked him the better for it. He was of his own people again. Thereafter spoke and laughed hugely over queer tales of crooked intrigue, in which midnight assassination on housetops, stealthy prowls through narrow blind gullies, feud, lust, and blood were picturesquely intermingled. And the lamps that they put into the roof near Jaipur, for it was growing dusk, jangled and rattled as he laughed. Yes, my friend Sinbad was better in this fashion. I forgave him the shoehorns, and the trunks, and the corkscrews, and button hooks with which he had encrusted himself. "Come!" he concluded. "You are the first Englishman I have spoken to like this. God made us all men, and you talk to me as a man to a man. By Jove, you shall eat with me! It is a poor meal but we will eat together after the fashion of my country." And after the fashion of his country did my friend Sinbad and I eat. He rose and washed his hands from the wrist. I followed suit; and watched while he got the meal ready on the seat of the carriage. "Look you, I can eat with knives and forks like you can, but when I am alone I eat like my people. One can be as English as the English and yet remain very much a native. Is it not so?" And with one or two of his stories still ringing in my brain I answered that indeed it was very much indeed so. Sinbad was wrong in saying that his was a poor meal. It was the richest that I have ever eaten—a compound of mutton, cabbage, potatoes, butter and condiment.

Whether the novelty of the meal predisposed me in its favor, or whether I was genuinely hungry I cannot tell, but it seemed a most excellent dish. Terribly unwholesome and indigestible, but savory and appetizing. My friend Sinbad helped me to the daintiest bits on a piece of bread, but my clumsy western fingers made an unmitigated failure of the business. Whereupon he placed a *chapatti*, plate-wise, at my disposal and the meal went merrily forward. At its conclusion we rose and washed our hands, and paid mutual compliments of the most constrained kind; forgetting that just before we had been talking as "a man to a man." Presently, however, over the after-dinner smoke, conversation drifted into free and unfettered channels. We spoke of travelling allowances, and the yearly growing stinginess of the Government. "It is a rich Government" quoth my friend Sinbad "Rich as a *bunnia*, and twice as mean." He quoted instances of reduced expenditure to prove this, and branched off on to a discourse on the comparative morality of nations. "What I say is this; and this I do not say to all Englishmen. God made us different—you and I, and your fathers and my fathers. For one thing we have not the same notions of honesty and of speaking the truth. That is not our fault, because we are made so; and in a land where most men are liars, it is the same just as if most men were truth tellers. And look now what you do? You come and judge us by your own standard of morality—that morality which is the outcome of your climate and your education and your traditions. You are, of course, too hard on us. And again I tell you that you are great fools in this matter. Who are we to have your morals, or you to have ours? You know that in three generations a pure-bred Englishman dies out in this country. I have seen that as well as read it in books. And yet you think that we are to be judged by your morals. It is a mistake." My friend Sinbad quoted the case of a native official who, not so long ago, had been judged by our standard of morality and found sadly wanting as an instance in point. "You say he was a blackguard, is it not so?" asked my friend Sinbad. "It is said that he was a blackguard" I replied suavely. "Well by Jove! he was a blackguard from your own point of view. A big blackguard. But he was what you call a "strong" man, and he did much good work for our Government." (My friend Sinbad was English once more, and had reannexed Britain), "Much good work; and work that no one but a strong man could have done. If we had let him alone, he would have done much more. Not with clean hands perhaps, but still better than anyone else." The Gospel of Expediency always delighted me, and moreover I had had a sneaking affection for that "big blackguard"—a respect born of his magnificent vitality: his astuteness and most British coolness under trying circumstances. My friend Sinbad and I agreed cordially on this point. God made us—East and West—widely different. We could not adopt each other's clothes or customs. Why insist upon uniformity in morals? My friend came out with a quotation from a French author to clinch the matter—accent and delivery both faultless. Not only had he annexed Britain then—this extraordinary jumble of conflicting nationalities,—but the Republic as well. There were French novels in his portmanteaux. Thereafter we spoke French for a season; till the kaleidoscopic *Kazee* took refuge in Persian and Arabic, and we returned together to the safe intelligibility of English. An hour passed in the discussion of domestic trivialities—light converse on horses, the women of all India, the wines of all Europe, and the depravity of native servants. Lastly we touched on the why and the wherefore of a recent judicial appointment in the Punjab. "It was not wise" quoth my friend Sinbad "neither Hindus nor Mahommedans were pleased; and the Commission were very angry. One of the *burra Sahibs* in the Punjab told me that he did not think the appointment should be in the gift of a Provincial Government. I think so too. The Supreme Government should nominate. I tell you it was not a good thing." The train rattled into that Zag-a-Zig in the desert—Bandakui—and our roads were divided.

"You change here?" said my friend Sinbad. "I am sorry. You have talked with me and smoked with me and eaten with me like a man. Shall I say as a compliment that you are almost worthy to be an Afghan?" "And you Sinbad to be an Englishman but"—"Ah, yes, my friend. It is true. But God has made us different for always. Is it not so?" And as I dug up the sleepy *Khansamah* for a cup of abominations called tea, me thought that Sinbad had stumbled upon a great truth.

Literally and metaphorically we were standing upon different platforms; and parallel straight lines, as every one does not know, are lines in the same plane which being continued to all eternity will never meet.

Jorge Luis Borges

Story of the Warrior and the Captive

ON PAGE 278 OF HIS BOOK *La poesia* (Bari, 1942), Croce, abbreviating a Latin text of the historian Peter the Deacon, narrates the destiny and cites the epitaph of Droctulft; both these move me singularly; later I understood why. Droctulft was a Lombard warrior who, during the seige of Ravenna, left his companions and died defending the city he had previously attacked. The Ravennese gave him burial in a temple and composed an epitaph in which they manifested their gratitude (*contempsit caros, dum nos amat ille, parentes*) and observed the peculiar contrast evident between the barbarian's fierce countenance and his simplicity and goodness:

> *Terribilis visu facies, sed mente benignus,*
> *Longaque robusto pectore barbara fuit!*[1]

Such is the story of the destiny of Droctulft, a barbarian who died defending Rome, or such is the fragment of his story Peter the Deacon was able to salvage. I do not even know in what period it took place: whether toward the middle of the sixth century, when the Longobardi desolated the plains of Italy, or in the eighth, before the surrender of Ravenna. Let us imagine (this is not a historical work) the former.

[1]Also Gibbon (*Decline and Fall*, XLV) transcribes these verses.

Jorge Luis Borges (1899-1986) acquired an international reputation as a writer, largely through his unique mastery of the short story form. However, in the Spanish-speaking world, he also has a reputation as an excellent poet. Almost all of his stories have been translated into English.

Let us imagine Droctulft *sub specie aeternitatis*, not the individual Droctulft, who no doubt was unique and unfathomable (all individuals are), but the generic type formed from him and many others by tradition, which is the effect of oblivion and of memory. Through an obscure geography of forests and marshes, the wars brought him to Italy from the banks of the Danube and the Elbe, and perhaps he did not know he was going south and perhaps he did not know he was fighting against the name of Rome. Perhaps he professed the Arrianist faith, which holds that the Son's glory is a reflection of the Holy Father's, but it is more congruous to imagine him a worshiper of the Earth, of Hertha, whose covered idol went from hut to hut in a cow-drawn cart, or of the gods of war and thunder, which were crude wooden figures wrapped in homespun clothing and hung with coins and bracelets. He came from the inextricable forests of the boar and the bison; he was light-skinned, spirited, innocent, cruel, loyal to his captain and his tribe, but not to the universe. The wars bring him to Ravenna and there he sees something he has never seen before, or has not seen fully. He sees the day and the cypresses and the marble. He sees a whole whose multiplicity is not that of disorder; he sees a city, an organism composed of statues, temples, gardens, rooms, amphitheaters, vases, columns, regular and open spaces. None of these fabrications (I know) impresses him as beautiful; he is touched by them as we now would be by a complex mechanism whose purpose we could not fathom but in whose design an immortal intelligence might be divined. Perhaps it is enough for him to see a single arch, with an incomprehensible inscription in eternal Roman letters. Suddenly he is blinded and renewed by this revelation, the City. He knows that in it he will be a dog, or a child, and that he will not even begin to understand it, but he also knows that it is worth more than his gods and his sworn faith and all the marshes of Germany. Droctulft abandons his own and fights for Ravenna. He dies and on his grave they inscribe these words which he would not have understood:

> *Contempsit caros, dum nos amat ille, parentes,*
> *Hanc patriam reputans esse, Ravenna, suam.*

He was not a traitor (traitors seldom inspire pious epitaphs); he was a man enlightened, a convert. Within a few generations, the Longobardi who had condemned this turncoat proceeded just as he had; they became Italians, Lombards, and perhaps one of their blood—Aldiger—could have engendered those who engendered the Alighieri . . . Many conjectures may be applied to Droctulft's act; mine is the most economical; if it is not true as fact it will be so as symbol.

When I read the story of this warrior in Croce's book, it moved me in an unusual way and I had the impression of having recovered, in a different form, something that had been my own. Fleetingly I thought of the Mongolian horsemen who tried to make of China an infinite pasture ground and then grew old in the cities they had longed to destroy; this was not the memory I sought. At last I found it: it was a tale I had once heard from my English grandmother, who is now dead.

In 1872, my grandfather Borges was commander of the northern and western frontiers of Buenos Aires and the southern frontier of Santa Fe. His headquarters was in Junín; beyond that, four or five leagues distant from each other, the chain of outposts; beyond that, what was then termed the *pampa* and also the "hinterland." Once—half out of wonder, half out of sarcasm—my grandmother commented upon her fate as a lone Englishwoman exiled to that far corner of the earth; people told her that she was not the only one there and, months later, pointed out to her an Indian girl who was slowly crossing the plaza. She wore two brightly colored blankets and went barefoot; her hair was blond. A soldier told her another Englishwoman wanted to speak to her. The girl agreed; she entered the headquarters without fear but not without suspicion. In her copper-colored face, which was daubed in ferocious colors, her eyes were of that reluctant blue the English call gray. Her body was lithe, like a deer's; her hands, strong and bony. She came from the desert, from the hinterland, and everything seemed too small for her: doors, walls, furniture.

Perhaps the two women felt for an instant as sisters; they were far from their beloved island and in an incredible country. My grandmother uttered some kind of question; the other woman replied with difficulty, searching for words and repeating them, as if astonished by their ancient flavor. For some fifteen years she had not spoken her native language and it was not easy for her to recover it. She said that she was from Yorkshire, that her parents had emigrated to Buenos Aires, that she had lost them in an Indian raid, that she had been carried off by the Indians and was now the wife of a chieftain, to whom she had already given two sons, and that he was very brave. All this she said in a rustic English, interwoven with Araucanian or Pampan, and behind her story one could glimpse a savage life: the horsehide shelters, the fires made of dry manure, the feasts of scorched meat or raw entrails, the stealthy departures at dawn, the attacks on corrals, the yelling and the pillaging, the wars, the sweeping charges on the haciendas by naked horsemen, the polygamy, the stench and the superstition. An Englishwoman had lowered herself to this barbarism. Moved by pity and shock, my grandmother urged her not to return. She swore to protect her, to retrieve her children. The woman answered that she was happy and returned that night to the desert.

Francisco Borges was to die a short time later, in the revolution of seventy-four; perhaps then my grandmother was able to perceive in this other woman, also held captive and transformed by the implacable continent, a monstrous mirror of her own destiny. . .

Every year, the blond Indian woman used to come to the country stores at Junín or at Fort Lavalle to obtain trinkets or makings for maté; she did not appear after the conversation with my grandmother. However, they saw each other once again. My grandmother had gone hunting one day; on a ranch, near the sheep dip, a man was slaughtering one of the animals. As if in a dream, the Indian woman passed by on horseback. She threw herself to the ground and drank the warm blood. I do not know whether she did it because she could no longer act any other way, or as a challenge and a sign.

A thousand three hundred years and the ocean lie between the destiny of the captive and the destiny of Droctulft. Both these, now, are equally irrecoverable. The figure of the barbarian who embraced the cause of Ravenna, the figure of the European woman who chose the wasteland, may seem antagonistic. And yet, both were swept away by a secret impulse, an impulse more profound than reason, and both heeded this impulse, which they would not have known how to justify. Perhaps the stories I have related are one single story. The obverse and the reverse of this coin are, for God, the same.

For Ulrike von Kuhlmann
Translated from the Spanish by James E. Irby

Questions for Discussion

1. "The Overlap" is the only story in this collection in which the protagonists are "old," i.e. of retirement age. The general belief among those who study cultural adaptation is that the younger a person is, the easier the adaptation process is likely to be. The age of the couple in "The Overlap," however, does not seem to pose an obstacle to adaptation; in fact, it may even provide them with certain advantages not available to younger persons in a similar situation. How can this be explained? What kinds of problems would an elderly American have, if any, in adapting to a culture in which the elderly are revered? What kinds of problems do you think the elderly of other cultures have in adapting to American culture, which is so emphatically youth-oriented?

2. What is the overlap in "The Overlap"?

3. Anthropologists are trained to discover what makes other cultures tick. However, it often happens that when they go into the field, their inquiries into the workings of another culture open up windows and

doors onto the nature of their own personalities and their own cultures. Do you think that it is possible to become close to another culture without gaining significant insights into oneself and one's own culture? Explain how this might happen.

4. What distinguishes the main characters in the stories of this section from those in the stories of the Shock Phase? What do these differences explain about the nature of the culture shock experience?

5. Easy adaptation to another culture would seem to be a rare occurrence, yet some people are obviously more adaptable than others. What kind of person would seem to be the most adaptable? The least? To what extent would the characteristics of the host culture determine what kind of person would be the most adaptable?

6. Sinbad, in Rudyard Kipling's "East and West," appears to have mastered European, especially British, culture to a fault. What do you think might have been the greatest obstacle to his adaptation?

7. We see how well Sinbad seems to be able to interact with an Englishman on the Englishman's terms. How well do you think he gets along with his own countrymen? Which culture do you think Sinbad is now most at home in?

8. To what extent does adaptation to another culture involve the psychological abandonment of one's own native culture? Can anyone ever abandon his own culture completely? Do you think that it is possible to adapt fully to another culture without understanding it very well?

9. Jorge Luis Borges' "The Story of the Warrior and the Captive" illuminates how cultural adaptation may extend into the deepest psychological recesses of the human personality. Do you think that a person is aware of many of the steps in his own adaptation? Which ones is he most likely to be aware of? Which is he least likely to notice? Would an extremely self-conscious person be a good adaptor? Why or why not?

10. Jane Bennet has argued that culture shock is not essentially different from the kinds of shock that people undergo as a matter of course during a long and eventful life. Do you agree with Bennet's contention? Crises can arise at every stage of life: adolescence, divorce, the death of someone close, war, natural disaster, etc. Which of these of "noncultural" kinds of experiences would seem to be similar in their effects to culture shock?

List of Additional Stories

Blackwood, Algernon. "The Valley of the Beasts." *An Anthology of Famous British Stories.* Ed. Bennet Cerf and Henry C. Moriarty. New York: The Modern Library, 1952. 644-60.

Camus, Albert. "The Renegade." *Exile and the Kingdom*. Trans. Justin O'Brien. New York: Vintage, 1957. 34-61.

Chekhov, Anton Pavlovich. "Priznatel'nyj nemec." ["The Grateful German"] *Polnoe sobranie sočinenij i pisem v tridcati tomax. Sočinenij.* ["Complete Collected Works and Letters in Thirty Volumes. Works"] Vol. 2. Moscow: Nauka, 1975. 252-53.

Gallegos, Rómulo. "Los emigrantes." *Obras completas.* Vol. 1. Madrid: Aguilar, 1959. 1333-53.

Greene, Graham. "Cheap in August." *Collected Stories.* New York: Viking, 1973. 79-109.

Mansfield, Katherine. "The Baron." *The Short Stories of Katherine Mansfield.* New York: Alfred A. Knopf, 1980. 41-44.

Santos, Bienvenido N. "Scent of Apples." *Modern Philippine Short Stories.* Ed. Leonard Casper. Albuquerque: U. of New Mexico Press, 1962. 90-99.

Stevenson, Robert Louis. "The Beach of Falesá." *The English Short Story in Transition 1880-1920.* Ed. Helmut E. Gerber. New York: Pegasus, 1967. 240-302.

Wells, H. G. "The Country of the Blind." *An Anthology of Famous British Stories.* Ed. Bennet Cerf and Henry C. Moriarty. New York: The Modern Library, 1952. 548-68.

6. Re-Entry Phase

RETURNING TO ONE'S NATIVE COUNTRY after a long and successful sojourn in another culture can lead to unexpected problems. As was pointed out in the General Introduction, those who adjust most thoroughly to life in the host culture often have the greatest difficulty upon their return. When immersed in the life of another culture, one tends to forget that time is also passing at home. Moreover, upon returning, one finds that people at home have little more than a passing interest in the experiences of a person who has been away. For people in the home culture, those experiences are remote in both space and time and are of little relevance to life here and now.

After an initial period of excitement and elation at being home again, the returned foreigner, like Marco Polo, may experience surprise, then disappointment and dejection at not being able to communicate to others the experience he has undergone while away. Not only has time marched on during his absence, leaving him somewhat out of step, but when people expect him to be much the person he was before he left, he may feel that a significant part of himself is being ignored and that he is unwanted. As a result, he may find himself rejecting his native culture in return.

The stories in this final section treat various facets of the Re-entry Phase of the experience of being foreign. "Yard Sale" by Paul Theroux reveals how obnoxious the returned foreigner's tendency to put on public display his other-cultural experiences can appear to those who stayed at home. Such displays often carry with them a not-so-subtle implication of cultural superiority.

271

A more extended and detailed depiction of re-entry is rendered by George Moore in "Homesickness," a story that ends with the returned sojourner rejecting his homeland and departing from it once again. While at first life at home seems far superior to the life he has been leading in America, it is not long before it begins to pall and to restrict the sense of ease and freedom in human relations which he had acquired in New York City.

Finally, in the shortest piece in this anthology, "The Captive," Jorge Luis Borges invites us to consider the profound gap that separates any two cultures, especially as it appears in the person who has thoroughly adjusted to a culture other than the one in which he was born and raised. Merely recognizing the gap, the story suggests, is a deeply moving personal experience, one that few of us appreciate fully.

A sojourn in another culture can open one's eyes not only to other ways of life but also to aspects of one's own culture and of one's innermost self that could not otherwise have been made visible. This is particularly apparent when one returns home after a lengthy sojourn, for it is then that one is in the best possible position to test George Macdonald's assertion that

> Home is the only place where you can go out and in. There are places you can go into, and places you can go out of, but the one place, if you do but find it, where you may go out and in both, is home.*

The mark of the successful sojourner is not that he has finally come to appreciate fully the true meaning of home, or that he may have relinquished one home for another more suited to him, but that he has found two places "where he can go out and in."

*Cited in W.H. Auden. *A Certain World: A Commonplace Book*. New York: The Viking Press, 1970. 184.

Paul Theroux

Yard Sale

As THINGS TURNED OUT, FLOYD HAD NO CHOICE but to spend the summer with me in East Sandwich. To return home to find his parents divorced was awkward; but to learn that they had already held their yard sale was distinctly shaming. I had been there and seen my sister's ghastly jollity as she disposed of her old Hoover and shower curtains and the chair she had abandoned caning; Floyd senior, with a kind of hostile generosity, turned the whole affair into a potlatch ceremony by bestowing his power tools on his next-door neighbor and clowning among his junk with the word "freebie." "Aunt Freddy can have my life jacket," he crowed. "I'm not your aunt," I said, but I thanked him for it and sent it via the local church to Bangladesh, where I hoped it would arrive before the monsoon hit Chittagong. After the yard sale, they made themselves scarce—Floyd senior to his Boston apartment and his flight attendant, my sister to the verge of a nervous breakdown in Cuttyhunk. I was glad to be deputized to look after little Floyd, and I knew how relieved he would be, after two years in the Peace Corps in Western Samoa, to have some home cooking and the sympathetic ear of his favorite aunt. He, too, would be burdened and looking for buyers.

At Hyannis Airport, I expected a waif, an orphan of sorts, with a battered suitcase and a heavy heart. But Floyd was all smiles as he peered

The American short-story writer and novelist *Paul Theroux* (b. 1941) travels extensively and frequently uses foreign settings in his work. *The Mosquito Coast*, his most recent novel, was published in 1982.

273

out of the fuselage, and when the steps were lowered and he was on them, the little plane actually rocked to and fro: Floyd had gained seventy-five pounds. A Henry Moore moppet of raw certainty, he was dark, with hair like varnished kapok and teeth gleaming like Chiclets. He wore an enormous shirt printed with bloated poppies, and the skirtlike sarong that Margaret Mead tells us is called a *lava-lava*. On his feet were single-thong flip-flops, which, when he kicked them off—as he did in the car, to sit cross-legged on the bucket seat—showed his toes to be growing in separate directions.

"Wuppertal," he said, or words to that effect. There was about him a powerful aroma of coconut oil and a rankness of dead leaves and old blossoms.

"Greetings," I said.

"That's what I just said."

"And welcome home."

"It doesn't seem like home anymore."

We passed the colonial-style (rough-hewn logs, split-rail fence, mullion windows) Puritan Funeral Home, Kopper Krafts, the pizza joints, and it occurred to me that this part of Route 132 had changed out of all recognition. I thought: Poor kid.

The foreknowledge that I would be led disloyally into loose talk about his father's flight attendant kept me silent about his parents' divorce. I asked him about Samoa; I was sure he was aching to be quizzed. This brought from him a snore of approval and a native word. I mentioned his sandals.

He said, "My mother never wears sandals. She's always barefoot!"

I determined upon delicacy. "It's been a hard year."

"She says the craziest things sometimes."

"Nerves."

Here was the Hyannis Drive-In Movie. I was going to point out to him that he while he had been away, they had started holding drive-in church services on Sunday mornings—an odd contrast to Burt Reynolds in the evenings, the sacred and the profane in the same amphitheater. But Floyd was talking about his father.

"He's amazing, and what a sailor! I've known him to go out in a force-nine gale. He's completely reckless."

Aren't the young downright? I thought. I did not say anything about the life jacket his old man had given me; I was sure he had done it out of malice, knowing full well that what I really coveted was the dry pinewood sink lost in the potlatch.

"Floyd," I said, with a shrill note of urgency in my voice—I was frantic to drag him off the topic I knew would lead him to his parents' fractured marriage—"what about Samoa?"

"Sah-moa," he said, moving his mouth like a chorister as he corrected my pronunciation. So we have an emphatic stammer on the first syllable, do we? I can take any amount of well-intentioned pedantry, but I draw the line at condescension from someone I have laboriously diapered. It was so difficult for me to mimic this unsayable word that I countered with "And yet, I wonder how many of them would get Haverhill right?"

Floyd did not move from his Buddha posture. "Actually, he's wicked right-wing, and very moralistic about things. I mean, deep down. He hates change of any kind."

"You're speaking of—?"

"My father."

Your psychiatrists say grief is a great occasion for rationalizing. Still, the Floyd senior I knew was indiscernible through this coat of whitewash. He was the fiery engine of change. Though my sentence was fully framed, I didn't say to his distracted son, That is a side of your father I have not been privileged to observe.

"Mother's different."

"How so?"

"Confident. Full of beans. Lots of savvy."

And beside herself in Cuttyhunk. Perhaps we do invent the friends and even the parents we require and yet I was not quite prepared for what Floyd said next.

"My sister's pretty incredible, too. I've always thought of myself as kind of athletic, but she can climb trees twice as fast as me."

This was desperate: he had no sister. Floyd was an only child. I had an overwhelming desire to slap his face, as the hero does in B movies to bring the flannel-mouthed fool to his senses.

But he had become effusive. "My sister . . . my brother . . . my grandmother"—inventing a fictitious family to make up for the one that had collapsed in his absence.

I said, "Floyd dear, you're going to think your old auntie is horribly literal-minded, but I don't recognize your family from anything you've said. Oh, sure, I suppose your father *is* conservative—the roué is so often a puritan underneath it all. And vice versa. Joseph Smith? The Mormon prophet? What was it, fifty wives? 'When I see a pretty girl, I have to pray,' he said. His prayers were answered! But listen, your mother's had a dreadful time. And, um, you don't actually have any brothers or sisters. Relax. I know we're under a little strain, and absolutely bursting with Samoa, but—"

"In Samoa," he said, mocking me with the half sneeze of its correct pronunciation, "it's the custom to join a local family. You live with them. You're one of them."

"Much as one would join the Elks around here?"

"It's wicked complicated."

"More Masonic—is that it?"

"More Samoan. You get absorbed kind of. They prefer it that way. And they're very easygoing. I mean there's no word for bastard in Samoan."

"With so little traffic on the roads, there's probably no need for it. Sorry. I see your point. But isn't that taking the extended family a bit far? What about your parents?"

"He thatches roofs and she keeps chickens."

"Edith and Floyd senior?"

"Oh, them" was all he said.

"But you've come home!"

"I don't know. Maybe I just want to find my feet."

Was it his turn of phrase? I dropped my eyes and saw a spider clinging to his ankle. I said, "Floyd, don't move—there's a creature on your foot."

He pinched it lovingly. "It's only a tattoo."

That seemed worse than a live spider, which had the merit of being able to dance away. I told him this, adding, "Am I being fastidious?"

"No, ethnocentric," he said. "My mother has a mango on her knee."

"Not a banjo? When I saw him wince, I said, "Forgive me, Floyd. Do go on—I want to hear everything."

"There's too much to tell."

"I know the feeling."

"I wouldn't mind a hamburger," he said suddenly. "I'm starving."

Instead of telling him I had cassoulet waiting for him in East Sandwich, I slowed down. It is the fat, not the thin, who are always famished; and he had not had a hamburger in two years. But the sight of fast food woke a memory in him. As he watched the disc of meat slide down a chute to be bunned, gift-wrapped, and clamped into a small Styrofoam valise, he treated me to a meticulous description of the method of cooking in Samoa. First, stones were heated, he said, then the hot stones buried in a hole. The uncooked food was wrapped in leaves and placed on the stones. More hot stones were piled on top. Before he got to the part where the food, stones, and leaves were disinterred, I said, "I understand that's called labor intensive, but it doesn't sound terribly effective."

He gave me an odd look and excused himself, taking his little valise of salad to the drinking fountain to wash it.

"We always wash our food before we eat."

I said, "Raccoons do that!"

It was meant as encouragement, but I could see I was not doing at all well.

Back at the house, Floyd dug a present out of his bag. You sat on it, this fiber mat. "One of your miracle fibers?" I said. "Tell me more!" But he fell silent. He demurred when I mentioned tennis, and at my suggestion of an afternoon of recreational shopping he grunted. He said, "We normally sleep in the afternoon." Again I was a bit startled by the plural pronoun and glanced around, half expecting to see another dusky islander. But no—Floyd's was the brotherly folk "we" of the native, affirming the cultural freemasonry of all Polynesia. And it had clearly got into his bones. He had acquired an almost catlike capacity for slumber. He lay for hours in the lawn hammock, swinging like a side of beef, and at sundown entered the house yawning and complaining of the cold. It was my turn to laugh: the thermometer on the deck showed eighty-one degrees.

"I'll bet you wish you were at Trader Vic's," I said over the cassoulet, trying to avert my ethnocentric gaze as Floyd nibbled the beans he seized with his fingers. He turned my Provençal cuisine into a sort of astronaut's pellet meal.

He belched hugely, and guessing that this was a ritual rumble of Samoan gratitude, I thanked him.

"Ironic, isn't it?" I said. "You seem to have managed marvelously out there in the Pacific, taking life pretty much as you found it. And I can't help thinking of Robert Louis Stevenson, who went to Samoa with his sofas, his tartans, his ottoman, and every bagpipe and ormolu clock from Edinburgh in his luggage."

"How do you know that?" he asked.

"Vassar," I said. "There wasn't any need for Stevenson to join a Samoan family. Besides his wife and his stepson, there were his step-daughter and her husband. His wife was a divorcée, but she was from California, which explains everything. Oh, he brought his aged mother out, too. She never stopped starching her bonnets, so they say."

"Tusitala," said Floyd.

"Come again?"

"That was his title. 'Teller of tales.' He read his stories to the Samoans."

"I'd love to know what they made of 'Weir of Hermiston.'" It was clear from Floyd's expression that he had never heard of the novel.

He said gamely, "I didn't finish it."

"That's not surprising—neither did Stevenson. Do much reading, Floyd?"

"Not a lot. We don't have electricity, and reading by candlelight is really tough."

"'Hermiston' was written by candlelight. In Samoa, it would be an act of the greatest homage to the author to read it that way."

"I figured it was pointless to read about Samoa if you live there."

"All the more reason to read it, since it's set in eighteenth-century Scotland."

"And he was a *palagi*."

"Don't be obscure, Floyd."

"A white man."

Only in the sense that Pushkin was an octoroon and Othello a soul brother, I thought, but I resisted challenging Floyd. Indeed, his saturation in the culture had made him indifferent to the bizarre. I discovered this when I drew him out. What was the food like after it was shoveled from beneath the hot stones? On Floyd's report it was uninspired: roots, leaves, and meat, sweated together in this subterranean sauna. What kind of meat? Oh, all kinds; and with the greatest casualness he let it drop that just a week before, he had eaten a flying fox.

"On the wing?" I asked.

"They're actually bats," he said. "But they call them—"

"Do you mean to tell me that you have eaten a bat?"

"You act as if it's an endangered species," he said.

"I should think Samoans are if that's part of their diet."

"They're not bad. But they cook them whole, so they always have a strange expression on their faces when they're served."

"Doesn't surprise me a bit. Turn up their noses, do they?"

"Sort of. You can see all their teeth. I mean, the bats'."

"What a stitch!"

He smiled. "You think that's interesting?"

"Floyd, it's matchless."

Encouraged, he said, "Get this—we use fish as fertilizer. Fish!"

"That's predictable enough," I said, unimpressed. "Not far from where you are now, simple folk put fresh fish on their vegetable gardens as fertilizer. Misguided? Maybe. Wasteful? Who knows? Such was the nature of subsistence farming on the Cape three hundred years ago. One thing, though—they knew how to preach a sermon. Your agriculturalist is so often a God-fearing man."

This cued Floyd into an excursion on Samoan Christianity, which sounded to me thoroughly homespun and basic, full of good-natured hypocrisy that took the place of tolerance.

I said, "That would make them—what? Unitarians?"

Floyd belched again. I thanked him. He wiped his fingers on this shirtfront and said it was time for bed. He was not used to electric light: the glare was making him belch. "Besides, we always go to bed at nine."

The hammering some minutes later was Floyd rigging up the hammock in the spare room, where there was a perfectly serviceable double bed.

"We never do," I called.

Floyd looked so dejected at breakfast, toying with his scrambled egg and sausage, that I asked him if it had gone cold. He shrugged. Everything was hunky-dory, he said in Samoan, and then translated it.

"What do you normally have for breakfast?"

"Taro."

"Is it frightfully good for you?"

"It's a root," he said.

"Imagine finding your roots in Samoa!" Seeing him darken, I added, "Carry on, Floyd. I find it all fascinating. You're my window on the world."

But Floyd shut his mouth and lapsed into silence. Later in the morning, seeing him sitting cross-legged in the parlor, I was put in mind of one of those big lugubrious animals that look so homesick behind the bars of American zoos. I knew I had to get him out of the house.

It was a mistake to take him to the supermarket, but this is hindsight; I had no way of anticipating his new fear of traffic, his horror of crowds, or the chilblains he claimed he got from air conditioning. The acres of packaged foods depressed him, and his reaction to the fresh-fruit department was extraordinary.

"One fifty-nine!" he jeered. "In Samoa, you can get a dozen bananas for a penny. And look at that," he said, handling a whiskery coconut. "They want a buck for it!"

"They're not exactly in season here on the Cape, Floyd."

"I wouldn't pay a dollar for one of those."

"I had no intention of doing so."

"They're dangerous, coconuts," he mused. "They drop on your head. People have been known to be killed by them."

"Not in Barnstable County," I said, which was a pity, because I felt like aiming one at his head and calling it an act of God.

He hunched over a pyramid of oranges, examining them with distaste and saying that you could buy the whole lot for a quarter in a village market he knew somewhere in remote Savai'i. A tray of mangoes, each fruit the rich color of old meerschaum, had Floyd gasping with contempt: the label stuck to their skins said they were two dollars apiece, and he had never paid more than a nickel for one.

"These cost two cents," he said, bruising a grapefruit with his thumb, "and they literally give these away," he went on, flinging a pineapple back onto its pile. But his disbelief was nothing compared to the disbelief of shoppers, who gawped at his *lava-lava*. Yet his indignation at the prices won these people over, and amid the crashing of carts I heard the odd shout of "Right on!"

Eventually I hauled him away, and past the canned lychees ("They grow on trees in China, Floyd!") I became competitive. "What about split peas?" I said, leading him down the aisles. "Scallops? Indian pudding? Dreft? Clorox? What do you pay for dog biscuits? Look, be reasonable. What you gain on mangoes, you lose on maple syrup!"

We left empty-handed. Driving back, I noticed that Floyd became even gloomier. Perhaps he realized that it was going to be a long summer. I certainly did.

"Anything wrong, Floyd?"

He groaned. He put his head in his hands. "Aunt Freddy, I think I've got culture shock."

"Isn't that something you get at the other end? I mean, when the phones don't work in Nigeria or you find ants in the marmalade or the grass hut leaks?"

"Our huts never leak."

"Of course not," I said. "And look, this is only a *palagi* talking, but I have the unmistakable feeling that you would be much happier among your own family, Floyd."

We both knew which family. Mercifully, he was gone the next day, leaving nothing behind but the faint aroma of coconut oil in the hammock. He never asked where I got the price of the Hyannis-Apia airfare. He accepted it with a sort of extortionate Third Worlder's wink, saying, "That's very Samoan of you, Aunt Freddy." But I'll get it back. Fortunately, there are ways of raising money at short notice around here.

George Moore

Home Sickness

HE TOLD THE DOCTOR HE WAS DUE in the barroom at eight o'clock in the morning; the barroom was in a slum in the Bowery; and he had only been able to keep himself in health by getting up at five o'clock and going for long walks in the Central Park.

"A sea voyage is what you want," said the doctor. "Why not go to Ireland for two or three months? You will come back a new man."

"I'd like to see Ireland again."

And he began to wonder how the people at home were getting on. The doctor was right. He thanked him, and three weeks after he landed in Cork.

As he sat in the railway carriage he recalled his native village, built among the rocks of the large headland stretching out into the winding lake. He could see the houses and the streets, and the fields of the tenants, and the Georgian mansion and the owners of it; he and they had been boys together before he went to America. He remembered the villagers going every morning to the big house to work in the stables, in the garden, in the fields—mowing, reaping, digging, and Michael Malia building a wall; it was all as clear as if it were yesterday, yet he had been thirteen years in America; and when the train stopped at the station the first thing he did was to look round for any changes that might have come into it. It

---

George Moore (1852-1933) endeavored first to become a painter then later turned to fiction, in which he established a reputation as one of the best writers of his generation. His most highly regarded works are a novel, *The Lake* (1905), and a three-volume autobiography, *Hail and Farewell* (1911-1914).

was the same blue limestone station as it was thirteen years ago, with the same five long miles between it and Duncannon. He had once walked these miles gaily, in little over an hour, carrying a heavy bundle on a stick, but he did not feel strong enough for the walk today, though the evening tempted him to try it. A car was waiting at the station, and the boy, discerning from his accent and his dress that Bryden had come from America, plied him with questions, which Bryden answered rapidly, for he wanted to hear who were still living in the village, and if there was a house in which he could get a clean lodging. The best house in the village, he was told, was Mike Scully's, who had been away in a situation for many years, as a coachman in the King's County, but had come back and built a fine house with a concrete floor. The boy could recommend the loft, he had slept in it himself, and Mike would be glad to take in a lodger, he had no doubt. Bryden remembered that Mike had been in a situation at the big house. He had intended to be a jockey, but had suddenly shot up into a fine tall man, and had become a coachman instead; and Bryden tried to recall his face, but could only remember a straight nose and a somewhat dusky complexion.

So Mike had come back from King's County, and had built himself a house, had married—there were children for sure running about; while he, Bryden, had gone to America, but he had come back; perhaps he, too, would build a house in Duncannon, and—his reverie was suddenly interrupted by the carman.

"There's Mike Scully," he said, pointing with his whip, and Bryden saw a tall, finely built, middle-aged man coming through the gates, who looked astonished when he was accosted, for he had forgotten Bryden even more completely than Bryden had forgotten him; and many aunts and uncles were mentioned before he began to understand.

"You've grown into a fine man, James," he said, looking at Bryden's great width of chest. "But you're thin in the cheeks, and you're very sallow in the cheeks, too."

"I haven't been very well lately—that is one of the reasons I've come back; but I want to see you all again."

"And thousand welcome you are."

Bryden paid the carman, and wished him Godspeed. They divided the luggage, Mike carrying the bag and Bryden the bundle, and they walked round the lake, for the townland was at the back of the domain; and while walking he remembered the woods thick and well forested; now they were wind worn, the drains were choked, and the bridge leading across the lake inlet was falling away. Their way led between long fields where herds of cattle were grazing, the road was broken—Bryden wondered how the villagers drove their carts over it, and Mike told him that the landlord could not keep it in repair, and he would not allow it to be kept in repair out of the rates, for then it would be a public road, and he did not think there should be a public road through his property.

At the end of many fields they came to the village, and it looked a desolate place, even on this fine evening, and Bryden remarked that the country did not seem to be as much lived in as it used to be. It was at once strange and familiar to see the chickens in the kitchen; and, wishing to reknit himself to the old customs, he begged of Mrs. Scully not to drive them out, saying they reminded him of old times.

"And why wouldn't they?" Mike answered, "he being one of ourselves bred and born in Duncannon, and his father before him."

"Now, is it truth ye are telling me?" and she gave him her hand, after wiping it on her apron, saying he was heartily welcome, only she was afraid he wouldn't care to sleep in a loft.

"Why wouldn't I sleep in a loft, a dry loft! You're thinking a good deal of America over here," he said, "but I reckon it isn't all you think it. Here you work when you like and you sit down when you like; but when you've had a touch of bloodpoisoning as I had, and when you have seen young people walking with a stick, you think that there is something to be said for old Ireland."

"You'll take a sup of milk, won't you? You must be dry," said Mrs. Scully.

And when he had drunk the milk Mike asked him if he would like to go inside or if he would like to go for a walk.

"Maybe resting you'd like to be."

And they went into the cabin and started to talk about the wages a man could get in America, and the long hours of work.

And after Bryden had told Mike everything about America that he thought of interest, he asked Mike about Ireland. But Mike did not seem to be able to tell him much. They were all very poor—poorer, perhaps, than when he left them.

"I don't think anyone except myself has a five-pound note to his name."

Bryden hoped he felt sufficiently sorry for Mike. But after all Mike's life and prospects mattered little to him. He had come back in search of health, and he felt better already; the milk had done him good, and the bacon and the cabbage in the pot sent forth a savory odor. The Scullys were very kind, they pressed him to make a good meal; a few weeks of country air and food, they said, would give him back the health he had lost in the Bowery; and when Bryden said he was longing for a smoke, Mike said there was no better sign than that. During his long illness he had never wanted to smoke, and he was a confirmed smoker.

It was comfortable to sit by the mild peat fire watching the smoke of their pipes drifting up the chimney, and all Bryden wanted was to be left alone; he did not want to hear anyone's misfortunes, but about nine o'clock a number of villagers came in, and Bryden remembered one or two of them—he used to know them very well when he was a boy; their talk was as depressing as their appearance, and he could feel no interest whatever in them. He was not moved when he heard that Higgins the stonemason was dead; he was not affected when he heard that Mary Kelly, who used to go to do the laundry at the Big House, had married; he was only interested when he heard she had gone to America. No, he had not met her there; America is a big place. Then one of the peasants asked him if he remembered Patsy Carabine, who used to do the gardening at the Big House. Yes, he remembered Patsy well. He had not been able to do any work on account of his arm; his house had fallen in; he had given up his holding and gone into the poorhouse. All this was very sad, and to avoid hearing any further unpleasantness, Bryden began to tell them about America. And they sat round listening to him; but all the talking was on his side; he wearied of it; and looking round the group he recognized a ragged hunchback with grey hair; twenty years ago he was a young hunchback and, turning to him, Bryden asked him if he were doing well with his five acres.

"Ah, not much. This has been a poor season. The potatoes failed; they were watery—there is no diet in them."

These peasants were all agreed that they could make nothing out of their farms. Their regret was that they had not gone to America when they were young; and after striving to take an interest in the fact that O'Connor had lost a mare and a foal worth forty pounds, Bryden began to wish himself back in the slum. And when they left the house he wondered if every evening would be like the present one. Mike piled fresh sods on the fire, and he hoped it would show enough light in the loft for Bryden to undress himself by.

The cackling of some geese in the street kept him awake, and he seemed to realize suddenly how lonely the country was, and he foresaw mile after mile of scanty fields stretching all round the lake with one little town in the far corner. A dog howled in the distance, and the fields and the boreens between him and the dog appeared as in a crystal. He could hear Michael breathing by his wife's side in the kitchen, and he could barely resist the impulse to run out of the house, and he might have yielded to it, but he wasn't sure that he mightn't awaken Mike as he came down the ladder. His terror increased, and he drew the blanket over his head. He fell asleep and awoke and fell asleep again, and lying on his back he dreamed of the men he had seen sitting round the fireside that evening, like specters they seemed to him in his dream. He seemed to have been asleep only a few minutes when he heard Mike calling him. He had come halfway up the ladder, and was telling him that breakfast was ready.

"What kind of a breakfast will he give me?" Bryden asked himself as he pulled on his clothes. There were tea and hot griddle cakes for breakfast, and there were fresh eggs; there was sunlight in the kitchen, and he liked to hear Mike tell of the work he was going to be at in the farm—one of about fifteen acres, at least ten of it was grass; he grew an acre of potatoes, and some corn, and some turnips for his sheep. He had a nice bit of meadow, and he took down his scythe, and as he put the whetstone in his belt Bryden noticed a second scythe, and he asked Mike if he should go down with him and help him to finish the field.

"It's a long time since you've done any mowing, and it's heavier work than you think for. You'd better go for a walk by the lake." Seeing that Bryden looked a little disappointed he added, "if you like you can come up in the afternoon and help me to turn the grass over." Bryden said he would, and the morning passed pleasantly by the lakeshore—a delicious breeze rested in the trees, and the reeds were talking together, and the ducks were talking in the reeds; a cloud blotted out the sunlight, and the cloud passed and the sun shone, and the reed cast its shadow again in the still water; there was a lapping always about the shingle; the magic of returning health was sufficient distraction for the convalescent; he lay with his eyes fixed upon the castles, dreaming of the men that had manned the battlements; whenever a peasant driving a cart or an ass or an old woman with a bundle of sticks on her back went by, Bryden kept them in chat, and he soon knew the village by heart. One day the landlord from the Georgian mansion set on the pleasant green hill came along, his retriever at his heels, and stopped surprised at finding somebody whom he didn't know on his property. "What, James Bryden!" he said. And the story was told again how ill health had overtaken him at last, and he had come home to Duncannon to recover. The two walked as far as the pinewood, talking of the county, what it had been, the ruin it was slipping into, and as they parted Bryden asked for the loan of a boat.

"Of course, of course!" the landlord answered, and Bryden rowed about the islands every morning; and resting upon his oars looked at the old castles, remembering the prehistoric raiders that the landlord had told him about. He came across the stones to which the lake dwellers had tied their boats, and these signs of ancient Ireland were pleasing to Bryden in his present mood.

As well as the great lake there was a smaller lake in the bog where the villagers cut their turf. This lake was famous for its pike, and the landlord allowed Bryden to fish there, and one evening when he was looking for a frog with which to bait his line he met Margaret Dirken driving home the cows for the milking. Margaret was the herdsman's daughter, and lived in a cottage near the Big House; but she came up to the village whenever there was a dance, and Bryden had found himself opposite to her in the reels. But until this evening he had had little opportunity of speaking to her, and he was glad to speak to someone, for the evening was lonely, and they stood talking together.

"You're getting your health again," she said, "and will be leaving us soon."

"I'm in no hurry."

"You're grand people over there; I hear a man is paid four dollars a day for his work."

"And how much," said James, "has he to pay for his food and for his clothes?"

Her cheeks were bright and her teeth small, white, and beautifully even; and a woman's soul looked at Bryden out of her soft Irish eyes. He was troubled and turned aside, and catching sight of a frog looking at him out of a tuft of grass, he said:

"I have been looking for a frog to put upon my pike line."

The frog jumped right and left, and nearly escaped in some bushes, but he caught it and returned with it in his hand.

"It is just the kind of frog a pike will like," he said. "Look at its great white belly and its bright yellow back."

And without more ado he pushed the wire to which the hook was fastened through the frog's fresh body, and dragging it through the mouth he passed the hooks through the hind legs and tied the line to the end of the wire.

"I think," said Margaret, "I must be looking after my cows; it's time I got them home."

"Won't you come down to the lake while I set my line?"

She thought for a moment and said:

"No, I'll see you from here."

He went down to the reedy tarn, and at his approach several snipe got up, and they flew above his head uttering sharp cries. His fishing rod was a long hazel stick, and he threw the frog as far as he could in the lake. In doing this he roused some wild ducks; a mallard and two ducks got up, and they flew towards the larger lake in a line with an old castle; and they had not disappeared from view when Bryden came towards her, and he and she drove the cows home together that evening.

They had not met very often when she said: "James, you had better not come here so often calling to me."

"Don't you wish me to come?"

"Yes, I wish you to come well enough, but keeping company isn't the custom of the country, and I don't want to be talked about."

"Are you afraid the priest would speak against us from the altar?"

"He has spoken against keeping company, but it is not so much what the priest says, for there is no harm in talking."

"But if you're going to be married there is no harm in walking out together."

"Well, not so much, but marriages are made differently in these parts; there isn't much courting here."

And next day it was known in the village that James was going to marry Margaret Dirken.

His desire to excel the boys in dancing had caused a stir of gaiety in the parish, and for some time past there had been dancing in every house where there was a floor fit to dance upon; and if the cottager had no money to pay for a barrel of beer, James Bryden, who had money, sent him a barrel, so that Margaret might get her dance. She told him that they sometimes crossed over into another parish where the priest was not so averse to dancing, and James wondered. And next morning at Mass he wondered at their simple fervor. Some of them held their hands above their head as they prayed, and all this was very new and very old to James Bryden. But the obedience of these people to their priest surprised him. When he was a lad they had not been so obedient, or he had forgotten their obedience; and he listened in mixed anger and wonderment to the priest, who was scolding his parishioners, speaking to them by name, saying that he had heard there was dancing going on in their homes. Worse than that, he said he had seen boys and girls loitering about the road, and the talk that went on was of one kind—love. He said that newspapers containing love stories were finding their way into the people's houses, stories about love, in which there was nothing elevating or ennobling. The people listened, accepting the priest's opinion without question. And their pathetic submission was the submission of a primitive people clinging to religious authority, and Bryden contrasted the weakness and incompetence of the people about him with the modern restlessness and cold energy of the people he left behind him.

One evening, as they were dancing, a knock came to the door, and the piper stopped playing, and the dancers whispered:

"Someone has told on us; it is the priest."

And the awestricken villagers crowded round the cottage fire, afraid to open the door. But the priest said that if they didn't open the door he would put his shoulder to it and force it open. Bryden went towards the door, saying he would allow no one to threaten him, priest or no priest, but Margaret caught his arm and told him that if he said anything to the priest, the priest would speak against them from the altar, and they would be shunned by the neighbors.

"I've heard of your goings-on," he said—"of your beer drinking and dancing. I'll not have it in my parish. If you want that sort of thing you had better go to America."

"If that is intended for me, sir, I'll go back tomorrow. Margaret can follow."

"It isn't the dancing, it's the drinking I'm opposed to," said the priest, turning to Bryden.

"Well, no one has drunk too much, sir," said Bryden.

"But you'll sit here drinking all night," and the priest's eyes went to the corner where the women had gathered, and Bryden felt that the priest looked on the women as more dangerous than the porter. "It's after midnight," he said, taking out his watch.

By Bryden's watch it was only half past eleven, and while they were arguing about the time, Mrs. Scully offered Bryden's umbrella to the priest, for in his hurry to stop the dancing the priest had gone out without his; and, as if to show Bryden that he bore him no ill will, the priest accepted the loan of the umbrella, for he was thinking of the big marriage fee that Bryden would pay him.

"I shall be badly off for the umbrella tomorrow," Bryden said, as soon as the priest was out of the house. He was going with his father-in-law to the fair. His father-in-law was learning him how to buy and sell cattle. The country was mending, and a man might become rich in Ireland if he only had a little capital. Margaret had an uncle on the other side of the lake who would give twenty pounds, and her father would give another twenty pounds. Bryden had saved two hundred pounds. Never in the village of Duncannon had a young couple begun life with so much prospect of success, and some time after Christmas was spoken of as the best time for the marriage; James Bryden said that he would not be able to get his money out of America before the spring. The delay seemed to vex him, and he seemed anxious to be married, until one day he received a letter from America, from a man who had served in the bar with him. This friend wrote to ask Bryden if he were coming back. The letter was no more than a passing wish to see Bryden again. Yet Bryden stood looking at it, and everyone wondered what could be in the letter. It seemed momentous, and they hardly believed him when he said it was from a friend who wanted to know if his health were better. He tried to forget the letter, and he looked at the worn fields, divided by walls of loose stones, and a great longing came upon him.

The smell of the Bowery slum had come across the Atlantic, and had found him out in his western headland; and one night he awoke from a dream in which he was hurling some drunken customer through the open doors into the darkness. He had seen his friend in his white duck jacket throwing drink from glass to glass amid the din of voices and strange accents; he had heard the clang of money as it was swept into the till, and his sense sickened for the barroom. But how should he tell Margaret Dirken that he could not marry her? She had built her life upon this marriage. He could not tell her that he would not marry her . . . yet he must go. He felt as if he were being hunted; the thought that he must tell Margaret that he could not marry her hunted him day after day as a weasel hunts a rabbit. Again and again he went to meet her with the intention of telling her that he did not love her, that their lives were not for one another, that it had all been a mistake soon enough. But Margaret, as if she guessed what he was about to speak of, threw her arms about him and begged him to say he loved her, and that they would be married at once. He agreed that he loved her, and that they would be married at once. But he had not left her many minutes before the feeling came upon him that he could not marry her—that he must go away. The smell of the barroom hunted him down. Was it for the sake of the money that he might make there that he wished to go back? No, it was not the money. What then? His eyes fell on the bleak country, on the little fields divided by bleak walls; he remembered the pathetic ignorance of the people, and it was these things that he could not endure. It was the priest who came to forbid the dancing. Yes, it was the priest. As he stood looking at the line of the hills the barroom seemed by him. He heard the politicians, and the excitement of politics was in his blood again. He must go away from this place—he must get back to the barroom. Looking up, he saw the scanty orchard, and he hated the spare road that led to the village, and he hated the little hill at the top of which the village began, and he hated more than all other places the house where he was to live with Margaret Dirken—if he married her. He could see it from where he stood—by the edge of the lake, with twenty acres of pasture land about it, for the landlord had given up part of his demesne land to them.

He caught sight of Margaret, and he called her to come through the stile.

"I have just had a letter from America."

"About the money?"

"Yes, about the money. But I shall have to go over there."

He stood looking at her, wondering what to say; and she guessed that he would tell her that he must go to America before they were married.

"Do you mean, James, you will have to go at once?"

"Yes," he said, "at once. But I shall come back in time to be married in August. It will only mean delaying our marriage a month."

They walked on a little way talking, and every step he took James felt that he was a step nearer the Bowery slum. And when they came to the gate Bryden said:

"I must walk on or I shall miss the train."

"But," she said, "you are not going now—you are not going today?"

"Yes," he said, "I am coming back."

"If you are coming back, James, why don't you let me go with you?"

"You couldn't walk fast enough. We should miss the train."

"One moment, James. Don't make me suffer; tell me the truth. You are not coming back. Your clothes—where shall I send them?"

He hurried away, hoping he would come back. He tried to think that he liked the country he was leaving, that it would be better to have a farmhouse and live there with Margaret Dirken than to serve drinks behind a counter in the Bowery. He did not think he was telling her a lie when he said he was coming back. Her offer to forward his clothes touched his heart, and at the end of the road he stood and asked himself if he should go back to her. He would miss the train if he waited another minute, and he ran on. And he would have missed the train if he had not met a car. Once he was on the car he felt himself safe—the country was already behind him. The train and the boat at Cork were mere formulae; he was already in America.

And when the tall skyscraper stuck up beyond the harbor he felt the thrill of home that he had not found in his native village and wondered how it was that the smell of the bar seemed more natural than the smell of fields, and the roar of crowds more welcome than the silence of the lake's edge. He entered into negotiations for the purchase of the barroom. He took a wife, she bore him sons and daughters, the barroom prospered, property came and went; he grew old, his wife died, he retired from business, and reached the age when a man begins to feel there are not many years in front of him, and that all he has had to do in life has been done. His children married, lonesomeness began to creep about him in the evening, and when he looked into the firelight, a vague tender reverie floated up, and Margaret's soft eyes and name vivified the dusk. His wife and children passed out of mind, and it seemed to him that a memory was the only real thing he possessed, and the desire to see Margaret again grew intense. But she was an old woman, she had married, maybe she was dead. Well, he would like to be buried in the village where he was born.

There is an unchanging, silent life within every man that none knows but himself, and his unchanging silent life was his memory of Margaret Dirken. The barroom was forgotten and all that concerned it, and the things he saw most clearly were the green hillside, and the bog lake and the rushes about it, and the greater lake in the distance, and behind it the blue line of wandering hills.

Jorge Luis Borges

The Captive

THIS STORY IS TOLD out in one of the old frontier towns—either Junín or Tapalquén. A boy was missing after an Indian raid; it was said that the marauders had carried him away. The boy's parents searched for him without any luck; years later, a soldier just back from Indian territory told them about a blue-eyed savage who may have been their son. At long last they traced him (the circumstances of the search have not come down to us and I dare not invent what I don't know) and they thought they recognized him. The man, marked by the wilderness and by primitive life, no longer understood the words of the language he spoke in childhood, but he let himself be led, uncurious and willing, to his old house. There he stopped—maybe because the others stopped. He stared at the door as though not understanding what it was. All of a sudden, ducking his head, he let out a cry, cut through the entranceway and the two long patios on the run, and burst into the kitchen. Without a second's pause, he buried his arm in the soot-blackened oven chimney and drew out the small knife with the horn handle that he had hidden there as a boy. His eyes lit up with joy and his parents wept because they had found their lost child.

Maybe other memories followed upon this one, but the Indian could not live indoors and one day he left to go back to his open spaces. I would like to know what he felt in that first bewildering moment in which past and present merged; I would like to know whether in that dizzying instant the lost son was born again and died, or whether he managed to recognize, as a child or a dog might, his people and his home.

Translated from the Spanish by Norman Thomas di Giovanni

291

Questions for Discussion

1. Of the major characters of the three stories in this section, which has been most successful, which the least, at re-adapting to his own culture? Why?

2. Do any of the characters in the stories of the previous sections show greater promise of successful re-adaptation to their native culture than the characters of the stories in this section? What might explain their greater success?

3. Returning home involves not simply a return in space but also a change in time. Is the sense of movement in time that the person returning has, one of going forward into the future, back into the past, or both? How does this experience of time apply to the three major characters of the stories in this section?

4. Would an experience of severe culture shock make it easier for the sojourner to re-adapt to his own culture? Conversely, would a person who had been very successful as a sojourner find it very easy to readapt?

5. Is it possible for a person to arrive at a state where he feels at home in neither culture? What recourse does such a person have? Do you think that Floyd, in "Yard Sale," might become such a person? What about the Irishman in "Homecoming" and the white woman living with the Indians in "The Captive"?

6. What kinds of adjustments must people of the home culture make for returned sojourners? Compare the reception given Floyd by Aunt Freddie with that given to the Irishman by his friends in his native village.

7. Other considerations aside, how would the length of the sojourn affect a person's ability to re-adapt to his own culture?

8. Are some cultures easier to re-adjust to than others? Compare, for example, the re-adaptation of a person from a highly traditional non-technological culture with that of a person from a modern Western European culture? What effects might other factors, such as size, ethnic homogeneity, historical continuity, and geographical location have upon a person's re-adaptation?

9. Would a person's initial reason for leaving his own culture have an effect on his ability to re-adapt? Explain why or why not?

10. Would a spouse and family acquired in the other culture complicate or facilitate re-adaptation to the home culture? Would successful adaptation to another culture enable a person to be more successful in marriage in his own culture?

List of Additional Stories

Ahmad, Shahnon. "Caught in the Middle." *Short Story International* 5.25 (1981): 71-80.

Akutagawa, Ryunosuke. "The Handkerchief." *Exotic Japanese Stories. The Beautiful and the Grotesque. 16 Unusual Tales and Unforgettable Images.* Trans. Takashi Kojima and John McCittie. New York: Liveright Publishing Corporation, 1964. 140-51.

Baldwin, James. "This Morning, This Evening, So Soon." *Stories in Black and White.* Ed. Eva H. Kissin. Philadelphia: J. B. Lippincott Company, 1970. 254-304.

Barthelme, Donald. "Thailand." *Sixty Stories.* New York: G. P. Putnam's Sons, 1981. 433-36.

Cheever, John. "Woman without a Country." *The Stories of John Cheever.* New York: Alfred A. Knopf, 1978. 423-28.

La Farge, Oliver. "The Real Thing." *The Door in the Wall.* Boston: Houghton Mifflin, 1965. 189-240.

Farzan, Massud. "The Plane Reservation." *New Writing from the Middle East.* Eds. Leo Hamalian and John D. Yohannan. New York: New American Library, 1978. 327-33.

Haylock, John. "Photographs." *Short Story International* 7.40 (1983): 21-39.

Hemingway, Ernest. "Cross Country Snow." *In Our Times.* New York: Scribner's, 1925. 137-148.

Hesse, Hermann. "Homecoming." *Stories of Five Decades.* Ed. Theodore Ziolkowski. Trans. Ralph Mannheim. New York: Farrar, Straus and Giroux, 193. 158-93.

Ik, Kim Yong. "From Here You Can See the Moon." *Short Story International* 6.31 (1982): 73-82.

Jhabvala, Ruth Prawer. "The Award." *Like Birds, Like Fishes, and Other Stories.* New York: W. W. Norton and Company, 1963. 45-59.

Sharat Chandra, G. S. "Bhat's Return." *Missouri Short Fiction: 23 Stories.* Kansas City, MO: BKMK Press, 1985. 1-8.

Theroux, Paul. "The English Adventure." *World's End and Other Stories.* New York: Washington Square Press, 1980. 74-82.